Delilah,
My Woman

Delilah, My Woman

M. F. Sullivan

Text:
M. F. Sullivan

Cover Design:
Nuno Moreira (hbk)
Rafael Andres (pbk, ebk)

Typesetting:
Jennifer Cant

Web:
www.delilahmywoman.com

Email:
inquiries@mfsullivan.com

Typeface:
Minion Pro

Printed in the United States of America

Second Edition

ISBN: 978-0-9965395-0-0 (hbk)
ISBN: 978-0-9965395-2-4 (pbk)
ISBN: 978-0-9965395-4-8 (ebk)

"Human life is but a series of footnotes to a vast obscure unfinished masterpiece."

—Vladimir Nabokov, Lolita

Act One

Chapter

1

As Susan discovered me in Martin's place off the highway that September afternoon, I was absorbed in drawing practice. That was sixteen years before I loved Delilah, and twenty-two before all three of us died. I don't remember the sound of the store's bell, but her first words still singe my heart:

"When are you going to start doing that for a living?"

The molasses-thick voice shattered my trance. As I flipped the butcher paper before me, I looked up and saw first those eyes, glittering emeralds in a porcelain mask. Then, the unsmile of *Mona Lisa* on lips like supple petals, and the carmine hair, and the column of her neck, and the, and the, and—she had asked me something.

"Someday," I said (or sputtered) as I pulled myself together, having forgotten in my work who and where I was, emerging in this new world with this dream alive before me, appalled to be a mere seventeen years old in her presence. "Can I help you?"

"You could let me see some of your work." Smiling, lilting, she lifted her eyebrows, then rolled her eyes toward the case. "Or, if that's too much to ask, six two-inch slices of veal shank, please. I'm making ossobuco. Have you had it?"

"Not yet, but I've heard good things." A shiver raced through my bones. I hopped to it, washing my hands and pulling on the plastic gloves which barely covered my palms. I looked as foolish as I felt and covered it by asking, "Throwing a dinner party?"

"No, no, I don't know many people. I just spoil myself now and again, and buy in bulk."

Beneath her silk blouse, her breasts swelled with every breath. I cleared my throat. "Here I guessed people were beating down your door."

"Only colleagues, sycophants and enemies. Friends are hard to come by, especially when one is new."

1

That explained it. I laughed as I cut the veal. "You didn't seem like you're from here. Where'd you leave?"

"New York."

"Why would anybody move from New York to Ohio?"

"Ohio isn't bad. It's the kind of quiet I like."

"I don't know. I need more to stay alive than slowly emptying farmland."

The woman tilted her head, her stare into and through me sparking wild fantasies about what she might think of me. "I suppose a boy so talented would be too ambitious for a state like this."

"Don't butter me up before you see my work."

"So let me see more, then."

I glanced at her, then at my papers. They were rough self-portraits, as was most of my work from the butcher shop. After wiping my hands, I pushed the pages across the counter, feverish as my fingers slid within her reach. Imagine having a woman like this. She was twice my age if the hairlines accenting her features were any indication, but this added to her charm. Just think of all she could teach a boy like me. "You must be special. I never show my work to anybody but a teacher."

"I could be a teacher." She bent over the counter, her mane surging before her breasts to swing like the jade necklace hanging between them. I wrapped her order, one eye upon the green pendulum until she said, "Wonderful. You have a talent for the human figure, and your blocking—though I suppose it's called 'composition' with visual artists—is stunning."

"I'd love to show you more if you'll be this good for my ego."

"I can be cruel when necessary."

"I hope so. Praise without criticism is nothing."

My words lit a spark in her eye. She looked over the last page, a profile angle I'd struggled with throughout the day. As she glanced between the two of us, she placed a forefinger in the center of the page. "Your nose isn't so snubbed, more aquiline. I think it's your perspective that needs adjusting. That aside, it's a fine afternoon's work. I want to see what you manage when you're inspired. What do I owe you?"

The figure I gave her seemed low, but her arched brow was worth it. "Half-off. Welcome to the state, but my condolences for being here."

Her smirk drove a furrow into her cheek, and I followed the dart of her eyes to the closed door behind me. "Don't you have a supervisor?"

"Martin's asleep. I think he does it because he can't stand his wife, and she's the real owner, but she doesn't come by much. He trusts me." Her continuous stare of bland amusement got a grin out of me, and I ducked my head to count her change. "It's all right, the drawing keeps me out of trouble."

"Well don't blame me if you get into it. I asked for no such thing."

As I passed the bills to her, she gripped my hand. "My name is Susan Sinclair."

"Richard Vasko."

The smile she wore was the sort favored by prowling cats. "Well, Richard, you should let me cook you ossobuco sometime."

My throat dried in response to the invitation of this new species—so unlike the girls I took as tonic for small-town boredom. "Whenever you want to see me, I'll come by."

"I'm having a work party on Friday. It's going to be tedious, but I'd love to see you there. Bring the sketchbook I know you have."

"Where? When?"

Susan reached forward, slim fingers stretching as if to stroke my face. I froze while she slid the forgotten pencil from behind my ear, the curve of her wrist carved by Canova's chisel and smelling of frankincense and rose. "It starts at seven. Do drugs bother you?"

"Not in the least."

"I didn't think so." She tucked the package under her arm, and I saw one edge of her glowing smile as she turned away. "I'll see you on Friday, Richard."

There were one, two, three, four, five, six steps between her and the entrance, her snakeskin heels tapping each upon my heart until she was through the door. I could already feel the down of her flesh but had not the faintest idea how I might manage to touch it.

Once she vanished from the shop, the only evidence I had of her existence was the cursive upon my portrait: her address, her number, and her name. Susan Sinclair. It slithered from my tongue as she had from the door, the sibilant sound crawling down my spine.

Was this a prank? I stepped outside to see who might be waiting to laugh, but found the parking lot empty. The incredulity of it all stretched the final hours of my shift beyond reason; yet when it was over, I dawdled as if the apparition might make a second visit, the same day, the same place. Friday was four days away, longer than the highways beneath our slate sky, and I was bound to spend each one of them asking the same question: why would such a woman invite me to her house? Maybe she wanted to push drugs. It was the simplest explanation for my confused and flattered ego, though not the most pleasant, because I didn't want drugs as much as I wanted her. Still, better to be realistic than disappointed.

At home, I showered and dressed in silence. My mother wouldn't be home until nine or later, so now seemed as good a time as any to see friends and clear my head. Ever since my arrest for burglary (an egregious miscategorization to be elaborated upon in due time, as I was not there to steal anything but perhaps an apple from the kitchen), she had kept keen note of whom I was with and for how long. This did not stop me from defying her, but merely having to account for myself grated me. She thought she was protecting a troubled boy from himself. She did not know what kind of person I was. I kept that from her, and much else. Even my work she saw only on the sporadic occasions when she dared visit my room. She knew me to be territorial, and was herself appalled by the state in which I lived. The bed had not been made since she determined that asking me to do so was out of the question, though she did endure the war-zone of sketches and socks for as long as it took to change the sheets each week. She was not above snooping during these excursions, so contraband was camouflaged amid books and light sockets and folders of drawings. Even then our relationship was built upon lies.

Upon reflection, Evangeline is the closest I have to a regret. Her death was civilian casualty, as it were. She never did anything cruel to me—on the contrary, she was permissive unless I was out of hand. This was good, because I hated being a child. Given the option, I would have skipped the entire thing and become conscious for the first time there, in Martin's shop off the highway, as Susan spoke to me. Even as a small boy, nothing seemed to excite me. I was eager to get out, to do what adults do, to have all their privilege and rights and powers. I was no monster when I was young, though like most children, I had my share of behavioral issues. I was as likely to lie about what I had for lunch as I was about whoever broke that noxious purple vase, for instance; but I have always been fond of animals, and would never hurt one. I must also profess a certain fondness for fire between the ages of eight and fourteen, though that love mellowed into an affection for fireworks as I came into adulthood. And, being the sort of boy who could one moment "act like a little adult," as cooing friends of my mother put it, then turn and torment his small peers when outside supervision, I developed an early aptitude for duplicity. But until I got bored of school somewhere around seventh grade, I was a straight-A student, and after, a blossoming artist.

Why am I telling you this? What are you? I can sense you on the edges of my perception, but have no perception, and find no edge to what I perceive. This is no afterlife, or supernatural event. This is eternity, yet no different than waking. I remember my death and experience it, remember these things yet experience them now, too, as do you, through me. What are you—checking my baggage, as it were? Judging me? Are you God? What are you?

Whatever you are, do you really think I sounded any worse than other children? Not at all. I never would have killed anyone if not for Susan.

Not to say I wouldn't have been cunning.

My desperation for the keys of adulthood did take me in a certain direction, and that is one of perversion. As a boy of ten wandering the library unsupervised, I stumbled upon a book: *The Sexual Criminal*. Long-since had I become acquainted with sexuality through an uncle's stash of magazines and my mother's repulsive collection of cracked-spine romance novels. As such, it was never any mystery what men and women did together, or what separated adults from children. The idea, and the very word, fascinated me as it would any boy my age, but I could never shake the feeling that there must have been something more secret. More intimate.

The book I discovered in that empty corner of the library held the answer in black-and-white photographs. Naked bodies, gouged and gashed, strangled and splayed. I turned each musty page with reverence, my hands quivering. Then, I saw Her. A girl, a few years older than I was, face-down upon the sofa, frozen by death as she pulled herself upon the cushions, gown bunched around her pale thighs. One could not see her face, only a mass of hair black above her lily neck, and so her age became ambiguous.

At the footsteps of my mother, I tore the soft cover from the book and jammed it into my backpack. Evangeline, relieved to find me, failed to notice my trembling hands or flushed face or opened backpack. Once home, I squirreled the treasure away, afraid to look, as if she might sense the heat of my perverse pleasure and come looking to snuff its flame. It sat behind the books of my childhood, and every night, I thought about it with a rabbit's heart. But more than the book, I thought about Her. That girl. And when I could brave the book, I admired her. Not just her, but the text about her. Strangled and beaten to death. Raped. I hardly knew what rape was— but I knew about sex, and knew about crime, and as I absorbed this crime's lurid details along with the details of many others in that catalog of violence, I puzzled it together rather quickly. While the photographs were riveting, the text was better: long and detailed explorations of criminal psyches written decades before I was born and well beyond my reading level, advanced as it was for my age. I slogged through it once, twice, a thousand times over the years, moonlight or flashlight illuminating the stories of death for my young eyes. No doubt it informed the library I cultivated later in life: a collection of books about serial killers, psychopathy, deviant psychology, and as much perverse literature as I could swallow—though that last one may have been Susan's special touch.

When I was very young, my creative urge had been the sort which gave itself to games of fancy. As I aged, though, the use of my imagination exploded into more than just art, as imaginary friends blossomed into an imaginary existence. I entertained vivid fantasies beginning around twelve. The star of these fantasies was always the same: a young woman, black-haired, with warm, white flesh and eyes that knew tragedy. The Girl. I could utilize her in any way. Sometimes, inspired by the book, I would be a criminal, but more often my proclivities were justified by status as a king or clergy or monster. Somehow, the Girl would fall into my clutches, a lamb in the maw

5

of a wolf. And while at first I only dreamed of sex, her origins inspired my fantasies to greater heights. What had haunted me about the book's photos, and about the Girl, was the look they offered behind the curtain of sex. Christians and Sex Ed and soap operas watched by my mother portrayed sex as the most complete form of intimacy, and all the while, I chuckled with my Girl over how silly they were. There was something beyond that, and that something was a secret. There were naked bodies beneath clothes, but there was a better kind of nakedness, of red blood and pink entrails. Could you really say you knew anyone until you knew what was inside of them?

So while other boys dreamt of the real girl next door, I amused myself with The Girl of my imagination. Soon my Woman, she was my companion through the years, entertaining me in class and inspiring me to paint. She had a mind of her own, a mind within my mind, and I valued her as I might an abused lover. But now with Susan in my mind I could not think of my Woman, and with my outlet lost I felt like a withdrawing addict. Knowing it would be some time before my mother returned from work, I dressed and made my way to Gavin's house.

Most friendships become fragments lost in the lake of the mind. While I can name names and outline in a few sentences the broad brush-strokes of my relationship with figures of the past, I am hard-pressed to reminisce with concrete detail. When my few friends are feeling nostalgic, I am the one found smiling and nodding to avoid the need for actual contribution, because drugs and drink have wiped my memories clean. Little of value has been lost, however, as most visits with Gavin and Mark involved sitting around their basement, smoking weed, and playing videogames on their Sega Genesis. Earlier in our friendship we had spent more time out of doors, typically at night, but after my arrest, our time together was restricted by my mother's watchful eye. Substance abuse was not out of the question, so long as we did not leave the house. So, like most nights, I found myself with my feet on a battered coffee table, passing the bong between my comrades. We did not discuss Susan. I did not want their advice. I did not want anyone to know she existed, as if their knowledge of her might weaken the strength of her enchantment. We did not talk about anything. We laughed, coughed our way through our games, invited over Jerry and his beers, and I don't recall the walk home, or even leaving: just a blur of faces, ending in my mother's soft Virginian scowl, tightened as she stared from her seat in the corner of the couch.

"Where were you?"

"Gavin's."

"You're drunk."

"So are you half the nights. I just need to lie down."

"You know you shouldn't waste your time with that boy."

"It's all right. Mark and Jerry were there, too."

With her mouth stretched, frog-like, Evangeline crossed her arms. "And what did you boys do, then? Aside from drink."

"Talked. Played Genesis. Honest truth, ma, we didn't do anything illegal."

"Did you smoke?"

My eye-roll was the cornerstone of most expressions used when dealing with her. "Yes, Mom. I know they're bad."

"And illegal. You can't smoke before you're eighteen."

"I don't think the cops are so hard up they're going to bust down the door for nicotine consumption by a minor."

"That doesn't mean you should smoke. You're poisoning yourself. Why do you feel the need to do this, Richard? You come home every night smelling like alcohol and cigarettes."

But she couldn't smell the weed, and that was all that mattered. I walked over to kiss her head. "Look, ma, we had some fun. I'll sleep it off. Are you saying you never got drunk with your friends?"

"I never broke into houses."

"Jesus." My hand dragged down my face. "It all comes back to that."

"What else am I supposed to think you're doing?"

"Sitting in a friend's basement, playing videogames."

Evangeline unleashed the type of heavy sigh that meant she was tired of hearing me hammer my point. "Go to bed, Richard. I'm tired. Why do you keep me up like this?"

"Nobody's asking you to stay up," I shouted from the stairs, which she hated because the neighbors might hear, although they were surely used to it by then. "It'd be nice to come back to a quiet house sometime."

In my room, I locked the door and found the book. I admired a few favorite pictures one by one before pausing on the standby. The Woman. As I settled back I felt her rest upon my chest with the pressure of a succubus. Ethereal kisses planted themselves on my mouth and cheeks.

But my apparition vanished when the name of the day emerged through the fog of my unconscious: Susan. My hand settled on my chest. I considered the sway of her hips as she exited Martin's shop. The image blinded me, and I draped myself in the covers as if to fend off a terrible force that might come crawling from the dark to snatch me up. But nothing arrived, and the next morning I was drained by my hangover, and felt no closer to seeing her again.

Chapter

2

I have nothing worthwhile to mention about the following week, because each day was tedious as I waited for Friday. People came in and out of the shop. I fought with my mother, probably. Look—really, I don't remember that week at all. I don't think I lived it. I was too busy thinking about Friday, muttering lines to myself in the mirror, doing push-ups, and many other things which fluttered back to me now and then in later years and never failed to induce an agonized cringe.

When the party stood on the horizon at last, I sat in my room and thumbed through the last year's sketchbook. Among the studies of friends and *in utero* half-concepts, I saw every flaw. What would she think? Already, I was humiliated, and couldn't bring myself to draw while I waited. For the first time in five years I tidied my room without being badgered, because something needed to fill the time. When I saw the floor, it would be time to go, and I'd make it there with the party in full swing. But leaving the house after nine was a hard sell, and my jailer frowned even before my request for furlough.

"Whose house will you be visiting?"

"Gavin and Mark's. I'll be a few hours."

"So late?"

"Mark works after school, and Gavin was helping their dad around the house today. Besides, it's Friday."

"You look awfully nice." With a single sniff and one eye narrower than the other, she asked, "Are you wearing cologne?"

"It's body wash."

The antique lamp harshened her face with the shadows of a Hollywood interrogation. "Should I let you out after the other night?"

I jammed my feet into my shoes. "I'll be fine. I'm a man, and you're treating me like I can't take care of myself."

"Seventeen isn't close to a real adult."

"Why don't you trust me?"

She spread her hands with a scoff which I hated. "Can you blame me?"

"It was a phase."

"Purple hair is a phase. Burglary is a problem." Every word over-enunciated and exaggerated, 'purple' forcing her to make a face like a chimp I'd seen on a field trip to the Columbus Zoo. I hated that more than the scoff.

"It wasn't burglary. I didn't steal."

"Then why were you there?"

The sketchbook pages fluttered with my exasperated wave. She wouldn't understand if I explained it to her. We communicated in different languages. I spoke Latin and heard nothing but "Bar-bar-bar."

Evangeline stared from hollow eyes, until, with a sigh, she concealed herself behind her VC Andrews-style dime store novel. "Try to be home before the sun comes up."

To linger was to remain subject to her mercurial decision-making. I kissed her cheek, then darted to the freedom of my car. There, I lit a joint, then pushed the secondhand Lincoln down the street while the old man-transmission protested all shifts, up or down. The sound was warm, and I was warm, and my sketchbook sizzled in the passenger's seat. It was forty-five minutes from the town of Marion to Susan's house, and once on the 23 south, my molecules vibrated with the fresh air. Emptiness afforded a meditation the town couldn't, and, as I followed those great ribbons of ink between blonde farmland, my hands could negotiate the wheel and windows and radio with automation, leaving my mind free to grapple with Susan, and all the possibilities it had ascribed to her in four days. Absence made her tower in my psyche; naivety kept me from questioning my luck too closely.

Youth was my weakness. Though bright, I was an idiot in any room without other teenagers. I was convinced I knew better than the world what people wanted, needed. They were beneath me. It would be years before I learned I couldn't understand them the way most do—grasp them on an intellectual level, perhaps. But the roots of most actions escaped me with the coy intrigue of a book title on the tip of the tongue. It would be years before I recognized the missing element was missing to begin with, and decades before Delilah sparked my longing for it.

Beside a highway littered with abandoned barns and unkempt homes, there loomed a Victorian mansion under renovation, its exterior painted fresh pistachio. Light poured from the windows to reveal rooms animate with people whose cars enclosed the property in a vehicular moat. More guests idled on the porch. Based on area, I supposed she lived in comfort, but had not anticipated this.

The porch light illuminated smiling obstacles for me to dodge as I returned greetings with nods. Within, the foyer thrummed with activity:

a living room overflowing with dancers; a gaggle of twentysomethings chattering against one wall; a man with a guitar trying to earn their attention, or anyone else's. An Aryan poster-girl wandered from the kitchen with a party cup in her unsteady fist, then noticed my sketchbook when she bumped into me.

"You're an artist?"

"I paint."

"There haven't been enough of us tonight. Everybody is theater or music. What year are you?"

Her shirt read 'CCAD'—Columbus College of Art and Design. I humored her. "Sophomore."

"Me, too! I can't believe I haven't seen you around. Is this your first year here?"

"I transferred my credits from Chicago."

Her eyes widened. "Why come here?"

"It was expensive, and I've heard Columbus is just as good. Buddies from Ohio said good things about the arts here. Actors, huh?"

"Yeah, I guess Susan is an actress. Did she model for your class, too?"

"She wanted to see my work."

A streak of envy blushed the girl's spray-tan face. "Oh. She introduced me to someone who sells good molly."

"Well, I don't know. Maybe that's all she wants. Seen her around?"

"She's dancing, I think." The girl pointed to the packed living room, the source of grunge which drowned the lone guitarist. No doubt the music was meant to appeal to the guests, because with the sea of bodies removed, the house possessed distinction. In the wrong hands it might have felt a little Addams Family, but gleaming marble floors and radiant lighting upon beryl walls imbued it with vigor.

As I observed, the music made a psychedelic transformation: a Jefferson Airplane song I still shudder to hear, the only Jefferson Airplane song that seems to play in my presence, the very song which would be responsible for a bad acid trip several years later, around '93 or '94. My attention snapped to the throng. With little beyond a wave to the girl, I wedged my way through the dancers.

Yes, here. I felt her feet as they tapped upon the floor. So it was that I found her, hips and legs turning in a ballerina's pirouette polluted by the sinuous writhing of belly dance. Her mane blossomed like burgundy smoke while she spun, stopped, undulated once to send ripples through her golden dress, then smiled bright enough to reflect the lights. She smiled as she danced—for herself—but this did not deter a handful of boys from ogling without looking her straight on.

I did, though. As I stared into her, something wrenched apart inside me, and

I recognized then the chasm in myself. Her dancing marked uncharted territory: all this ocean inside, demanding I fill its snarling maw with Susan. I had read so much and done so little outside the boundaries of imagination. Perhaps she might teach me.

Before I reached for her, seconds before, the bridge came, and grace overcame her face; her eyes opened, then fell into me. They smiled, molded by lines to match the ones around her mouth.

"Richard! I gave up hope."

She bounded upon me, hands on my shoulders so her lips might sear my cheek.

"I brought you my sketchbook." The words felt rehearsed because they were all I could remember to say.

"So I see." Hands on mine, hands that blistered my flesh, she swept us through the parting crowd and made me think of Moses. "Show me! You must show me now."

Her words had the density of butterscotch. Being then an aspiring alcoholic, I recognized the control she kept over them and laughed at her, at myself, at the whole mad dream upon whose cusp I swayed. "You're drunk."

"You're not? We must remedy that." She tugged me into stride, and I smelled rosy femininity in the aura of her hair.

"I thought you didn't know many people."

"I don't." She released me to better dance to the kitchen with the fading music. "I can't imagine you know many people, either. What would you like to drink?"

I admired the bar, picked-over, but no less a bounty of liquor. "Anything?"

"I won't tell."

"A screwdriver."

"Screwdrivers are for breakfast, darling. How about a vodka tonic?"

"Whatever you want."

"That's a dangerous thing to say. You can't imagine what I want." While I shivered, she set to work. "Do you drink often?"

"Sometimes. Booze is harder to get than anything illegal."

"The troubles of regulation. Don't worry, you'll make it. We all do."

"You never know. I could be hit by a bus tomorrow."

Tittering, Susan pushed a cup into my hands. "I can't wait to see what's in that book of yours. We're out of limes, but you won't know the difference."

The first mouthful made me shiver a second time, now under the pressure of her heavy hand. I pictured her rousing from bed at noon, having luxuriated a few dreamy hours in nothing but black lingerie. Observe: the goddess pours herself a Bloody Mary of ambrosia to awaken, drinks red drink with ruby mouth. "Fantastic."

"Good. Upstairs, we must go where I can focus."

And focus she did, ignoring the guests who greeted her with joy or dared lay a friendly paw upon her. She missed not a beat in our conversation. "What do you do if you don't drink?"

"Smoke weed, pop pills. The usual. It's relaxing to work while I'm stoned."

"Do you draw every day?"

"Always. And if I'm not doing it, I'm thinking about it."

"Admirable dedication." She unlocked one of many shut doors with a key I had not noticed her produce, pausing only to hustle me inside and close it behind us.

Her bedroom was a jungle of culture. Upon phthalo-green walls hung framed prints: Sargent, Magritte, Goya. The four-poster bed in the center of the display was made to a set director's specification, with comforter moss and copper beneath pillows so plush the very clouds envied. Her cherry vanity, her tarot cards, her copy of Bataille's *Eroticism*, her volume of paintings by Waterhouse. And suffused in it all was her scent, like flowers damp in the morning. With an optimistic thrill, I felt myself having her in this room. "Your house is incredible."

"You haven't seen its dustiest corners yet." Smirking, she slid from her silver kitten heels and dropped into the carved oak chair at the roll-top desk. As she propped her feet, she said, "It's a work in progress. I've only been in it three or four months. Come here, let me see you."

"There's not much to see."

"*Son of Man* isn't on my wall because Magritte was humble. Let me see." As she accepted the battered tome, she smiled. "Have a look around. If I get to see you so compromised, it's only fair."

At the sound of her leafing through my soul, I drained half my cup. I memorized the authors on her shelves and resolved to refresh my relationship with what names I knew, then noted those I didn't so I could look them up the next day. I wanted to inspire in her the same enchantment she wove in me. Educated discussion about names like DH Lawrence and Céline could facilitate that. It was hard to impress this woman if her quality of life was an indication, but if she was half as intelligent as she appeared to be, she did not set a high bar for the behavior of a teenager. This was to my favor, because with even a little effort, I could get far ahead.

"Who is this?"

I confronted Susan's muggy smile and the page she held for me, a study of Evangeline reading. "My mother."

"Is that so?" She smiled, and I imagined a hint of venom glistening at the corner of her mouth. "She is lovely, in an aged way. But you must get your looks from your father."

"I wouldn't know. He died when I was a kid."

She lowered the book to regard me through eyes which still smiled. "Didn't she keep any pictures of him?"

"None that I know of. I think it's too painful for her. I don't know what I'm missing, so I can't miss it."

"Well: I don't think you're missing much, if you ask me. No father is God. Just a human man, flawed like everybody else."

"Plus, I was able to get away with more because I had one pair of eyes watching me instead of two."

We laughed together, and I dared journey to her side to see what she did, page for page. All her focus poured into my work. She was silent as she glossed over Mark, paused at Gavin. As she lingered over my grandmother, she smiled.

"You have a knack for the form. Real talent. These people are dead on this page but with a few years' hard work, maybe decades, you'll reach sublimity. You're already well on your way."

My face burned. "You say that to all the boys you bring home."

"I'm not in the custom of bringing boys home. Are you in the custom of accepting the invitations of older women?"

"Speaking in percentages, we're at one hundred. But I can't say I've had opportunities."

She giggled, tracing the cheek of a self-portrait from March. "Now this is beautiful. This has something the others don't. A spark." Susan flipped between the rendering of myself and those of my friends and family. "You portray yourself with a breath of life. Know thyself."

"What do you think I can do to give my other figures that kind of life?"

"I'm an actor and musician, dear, not a painter. You'll have to work out the details on your own, but it would be my pleasure to guide you near them." Admittance of ignorance highlighted her wisdom. My hand settled flush to the back of her throne as she continued, "For instance, the trouble isn't with your art. It must be the way you're looking at these people."

As she flipped the page, I asked, "How long have you been in music?"

"Not as long as I've been acting."

"I'd love to see you on a stage."

Her divine head tilted to let me see her smile. "Would you like me to dance for you?"

The words remained unformed in my mouth, but effort allowed a nod. Still smiling, she set aside my book and rose, writhing along to The Rolling Stones, reverberating through the floorboards. Her hands explored her hair, her breasts, stomach, hips with the tempo of the song. She smoldered, the heat of her lapping my flesh. Self-control began to fade in the influence of my body, snarling with want of her. I stepped close as she turned her clockwork hips away, my body pressed to her back. My hand traced the path blazed by her own, and my head tilted over hers, and her mouth tasted like vodka and coffee liquor and a soft tongue that writhed with her body until she froze, struggled, played hard-to-get and then relented at last to the supplications of my mouth. What rose for an instant as a caw of disagreement melted into a velvet moan. She allowed me to push her back against the desk, and as she did, she felt through my jeans to incite me. My kisses blanketed her cheek, her ear.

"There are caveats to having me at your age. There are things you do not know, and may never."

The curve of her neck was soft beneath my teeth. "I'll tell you whatever you want, anyway."

"Even if I never tell you anything in return?"

"Whatever you want."

Her chuckle trembled down my spine. "Don't worry. If you're good, I'll tell you plenty. It's important to be candid in a friendship. And don't you think we'll make good friends?"

I leaned up to let my nose brush hers. "Why would you want to be my friend?"

"I see my distant self in you." Now she turned away to thumb through my pages, past a deified Black Dahlia idea that was only ever half-formed, past Odysseus in Circe's arms, past an ethereal portrait of my Woman, whose features only came together behind closed eyes. "You have so much potential. Have you applied for schools, at least?"

"You sound like my mother."

"Mothers do know best, they say. Do it, Richard, please. You do want to paint, don't you?"

"I need to. If I'm not making art I have no reason to live."

"What do you want to achieve with your work?"

"Significance. To exist after my death, alive in art and history books."

"But even that significance won't be permanent. Someday this planet will be nothing and we will all be lost to infinity."

I stared at my sketchbook, one hand still against the curve of Susan's waist. "I think about that a lot."

"Does it frighten you?"

"No. It just makes me question the point of it all."

"The point, Richard, is in the pleasure of living."

That time, she kissed me, and punctuated it with a yawn as she pulled her mouth away. "This ecstasy is wearing off, but you must come again."

"Yes, please."

"Have dinner with me in a week, next Sunday. Let me spoil you."

I nodded all the way down the stairs, Susan leading me, Susan breaking up the party, Susan kissing the corner of my mouth as we paused in the foyer,

Susan making me forget I had forgotten my sketchbook until I was through my front door, Susan deafening me to my mother, Susan blinding me to my Woman, Susan keeping me up all night because I could think of nothing but seeing her alone next Sunday.

Chapter

3

The morning after the party, I sprang to work on my application to CCAD. Though procured before my early graduation, it had not been blemished with so much as my name. Now seemed as good a time as any. Whether I was doing it for myself or for Susan, though, was a question I dusted into my brain's distant recesses, usually reserved for nightmares and trauma. Of course I was doing this for myself. This was my work, my future. This had nothing to do with impressing my soon-to-be mistress.

Still in pajama pants, I reclined at my desk to read the listed requirements. I needed not just a portfolio, but references. Though I began providing the paper application's requested details, the inanity of the categories (name, sex, age, driver's license, pilot's license, maternal great-aunt's maiden name) faltered my resolve. There were more urgent priorities than this. Sighing, I left the comfort of my room. My mother's was closed, and had been since I returned home. I migrated to our dining nook and the dust-coated IBM upon which she had once written letters to the friends she once had. One at a time, the clattering keys' discordant tones combined into symphonic sentences which barely varied between letters. Two were addressed to the art teachers who had nurtured my talent for three breezy years; the third, I intended for an English teacher whom I had charmed into turning a half-blind eye to my frequent, unexplained absences. When I learned of her early retirement upon calling the after-hours line for her address, I selected instead a favored history teacher. This was the change I was affecting when, at ten, my mother shuffled downstairs in pursuit of the coffee whose scent saturated the house. As her clouded eyes focused on me, she smiled.

"What are you doing up before noon? Don't you know it's Saturday?"

"I'm getting references. Applications aren't due until February, but I don't want to do it last minute." I stayed focused on the typewriter but she just kept asking questions.

"I didn't think you were applying to schools this year."

"I've been thinking about it for a while."

"Are you going to apply to Ohio State, too?"

"Painting is my life. Why study something else?"

"Aren't you worried about getting a job after school?"

I shrugged. Getting a job was the last thing I wanted to consider.

"It might be good for you to work out a long-term plan, honey. You don't want to be like me, jumping from job to job because you don't have any training. You want to be successful."

"You've got a good life. You've got a roof over your head, me for a son ..."

She smiled with a grandmother's weariness, not a mother's. "Yes, and I have you as a son. I know I haven't always been the greatest mother, Richard, but I've done the best I could. I hope you'll appreciate that someday."

"I do now. Say, how's Chet?"

One guaranteed method of shifting conversation from her self-pity was to ask instead about her boyfriends, but the brevity of her relationships meant even this ground was perilous. For now, she lit up at mention of his grade school name, so for the next few months, at least, I would have a conversational escape route. "He's so much fun. We played euchre with Bettie and Gilbert last night. Oh, Chet made the most delicious sangria."

"Sounds like a fun guy."

As she continued to speak, I grew deaf. I had not met one of my mother's boyfriends since I was seven years old. Bruce had taken a healthy interest in my behavior issues and was the sort of man to volley around idioms like, "straighten up and fly right," or, "this is the last straw." I reciprocated his desire for improving my behavior with a pair of scissors and the clothes he had once brought over when intending to stay the weekend. Duly punished, I watched him slink home from my window, and a week later, my mother wept in her dark bedroom. Things had been easy since, and the distance had allowed me to be supportive of figments rather than take instant dislike to the overgrown frat boys she so admired. That any mother of mine could chase such a human bewildered me, but so did her opinions on religion and politics. We were different as Raphael and Picasso, but she labored under the delusion that we were, beneath our differences, more or less the same.

As I finished the third letter, I became aware she watched me. I glanced over, and she grinned from the kitchen. "What's going on with you?"

"Nothing."

"Look at you, Mister Energetic, you've written three letters. You cleaned your room last night, even!"

"You know I hate it when you snoop in there."

She waved away my comment. "If I didn't know any better, I'd almost think you're in love."

The word sent a rush of images through my brain: Susan dancing, laughing, sighing against my jaw. My face burned. "I'm not."

"Then why are you blushing?"

"Because that's a ridiculous question." I snatched the letters and their envelopes from the table as I beat my retreat upstairs. "You're being crazy."

"There's no shame in love!"

Shut in my room again, I intended to photograph my work with Evangeline's '88 Kodak, left from her aborted interest in photography. The matter of which pieces to select, though, presented a challenge. My closet overflowed with canvases, painted and repainted when we didn't have money or space for new ones. Then, I was still a child, and my work was still childish in theme and form. Susan had complimented my talent, not my skill. As I sorted through India ink illustrations of hazy dreams and grim interpretations of fables, I agreed with her. My work was good for someone of my age and limited background, but it was unhewn. Talent was a poor substitute for training, and though my mother wanted me to go to school for something practical (dentistry or computers were her favorite suggestions), I craved to hone my passion.

My mother said it herself: I didn't want to end up like her, satisfied with a life fleeting as a ripple across a pond. Inside me was a need to paint, deeper than any urge for food or drugs or sex. My life bowed to art, first and only.

After consideration, I selected seven pieces which had, at the time of their creation, felt like flowers pushing through dirt. Years later I do not remember what they were, or care to. Anything I produced before 2003 was significant only as it served my development. I have no patience for insignificance.

After a shower, I took the photos for development, and, lured by the pleasant, almost-autumn weather, explored the stores downtown. The area was in terrible condition then and has only grown worse since I left. But just then it was pleasant to meander down the street, hot with the hope of a chance encounter.

What if I bumped into Susan around town? Sure, she lived well outside of it, but she had to shop somewhere. Not that there was much shopping to be done: we were lucky to have the bookstore I wandered to. I reconsidered the authors I had seen in her bedroom last night. Figures like Bataille and Foucault I knew only in passing, because their names were steeped in sex. They went a long way to speaking of her tastes, as did volumes of de Sade. The air around her exuded debauchery.

After much searching and good luck, I stumbled upon a copy of *Venus in Furs* on a dusty back bookshelf. Now this was just the thing! Not a good book, but a good symbol. To find this book in a town so relentlessly Christian was a sign.

At home, I stowed the gift and again pored over the application. All was straightforward until it requested a paragraph ('Your Personal Statement') along with a blurb explaining I was to write about my ambitions. Any meditation on the subject produced Susan, a non-answer. Though smitten, I wasn't fool enough to dream a future in her. But, if she fulfilled her promise, she might help me find one in myself. She had to, because when I chased her from my psyche along with my weakened Woman, I found I had nothing at all. Wasn't it enough to want to paint? Why couldn't I have been born into a society where I was not obliged to work for food or shelter, and could while away my days playing in oils and charcoals? What use, goals or money, or even significance, when it all could end tomorrow?

Stuck, I set the application aside and rose to do the only thing I knew to do: I painted.

Chapter

4

The night Susan consummated our friendship, her home was warm with the aroma of sizzling veal. Her olive gown shimmered as she kissed my cheek, then ushered me into the foyer. Through a slit down the side flashed the muscles of her dancer's thighs, which, like the rest of her legs, extended beyond reason. Beneath the fabric, they seemed disembodied; the trunkless limbs of a crime scene. I trembled as I imagined how and where they might end.

Knowledge that I was being seduced alleviated for my ego any lingering doubts about what she wanted. I smoothed my hair as I caught my reflection in the dining room window. Was it such a mystery, what made me worth the effort?

As she indicated I should sit at the head of her table, I drew the book from my sports coat. "I brought you a gift."

"*Venus in Furs*." Susan accepted it with a grin that narrowed her eyes. "How wonderful."

"I didn't see it on your shelves, but I saw de Sade, so I thought you might like it. It seems like you."

"Have you read it?"

I nodded. "I visited the library a few days in a row last summer to finish it."

"Thoughts?"

"I wasn't impressed. But I wasn't impressed by de Sade, either."

"Do you know why you weren't impressed by this one?" When I shook my head, she whispered in my ear, her voice an octave that rattled my marrow. "Because Wanda was a weak woman. But I am not."

Then, she was gone. Goosebumps crawled along me while I sank into my seat. She took the book into the kitchen and transformed it into two wheat-colored plates arranged with veal shank, couscous, a side of wilted spinach with roasted garlic. She alighted upon the chair to my right, where her legs unfurled to slither against mine.

As she poured two glasses of burgundy wine, I said, "I don't see why these old books are popular now that they've broken their ground. They're unreadable, even if they do manage to sometimes be a little sexy."

The thrill of making her laugh was a cousin of sexuality, at least. "Perverts aren't in it for the lyrical prose, darling."

"Maybe they should be. Then there'd be more of them."

"You say that as if you aren't one yourself."

"Me? I'm pure as the driven snow." I batted my eyelashes while she looked at the ceiling to hide her grin.

"Your work says otherwise. If anything, your deviance is advanced for a boy your age."

"Most people wouldn't sound so delighted by it."

"Why hide that I am? Go on, try your supper."

I did, and the young flesh melted in my mouth. Its chef watched with an expression of feline contentment until I said, "Incredible."

"I'm glad you have such good taste."

"Of course I do. I'm here, after all."

"Try not to lay it on too thick, or you'll sound more like a poet than a painter."

"Is there any real difference?"

"I suppose not. There's quite a bit of poetry in your sketchbook; and melancholy. If Baudelaire were a painter. On one page I see a luscious portrait of a young lady, and the next, a corpse with flowers springing from her eyes and mouth. Was that an intentional before-and-after?"

"It was a study on beauty. My mother thought it was morbid."

"I think it's sublime." The word purred from her as she spread the fingers of one propped hand. "People who use words like 'morbid' do so because they are terrified that their lives may end; they do not embrace the end as a reason to enjoy life, but instead see it as punishment."

For a flash I perceived the Woman tiptoeing around my consciousness, inspiring me to say, "I think that death is something people apply subjective ugliness to, but it's nature. It can be ugly, or beautiful."

"Have you ever faced a significant death? Since you can remember, I mean."

I shook my head. "I've had a grandparent and a cousin die, but they didn't mean anything."

"I suppose the shadow cast by your father's death would be long enough."

"Have you ever lost somebody?"

With a swirl of her glass, Susan reclined in her seat. "If I am to tell you the things you want to know about me, you must promise me something." As I leaned forward, she said, "You must never tell anyone the truth about our relationship."

Lying was an easy thing to ask of me, but this was direct enough to give me pause. "Isn't a request like that supposed to be a red flag?"

Ah, her even smile just then. I imagine that, as a girl, Susan stood at the mirror for hours to devise her perfect set of smiles. This one would grow to be both my most and least favorite—and from the correct angles, it bore no resemblance to a smile at all. "I'd say you've ignored most red flags so far. Why entertain this one?"

"Because it's entertaining." I worked on the couscous to match her pace. "That's a very candid request."

"We understand each other, and you're a bright boy. I wouldn't insult your intelligence by lying to your face, or veiling threats. I just want to make sure we speak the same language."

"So, tell me why I should lie about you."

"Because I asked you to." Now it was she who batted her lashes, and though I laughed, there truly was unspeakable charm in it. "No? Not good enough? Well, then, consider my legal well-being. You, my spring blossom, are a tender seventeen summers, and woe unto those of us who might pluck you."

I finished my wine in a single swallow which sizzled down my esophagus, then set aside the glass only to have her refill it. As I grasped my bearings, I said, "I can't imagine what kind of fit my mother would have if she found out."

"So you see? Better that our friendship's foundation should be upon white lies. Why build a house on uneven ground when a bit of work will smooth it out?"

"If you were a man, you'd sound like a sex predator."

"Well, legally speaking, I am one. Or will be, at any rate." Forearm poised upon the table, Susan cocked her head to regard me with eyes of smoldering forest. "There is so much inside of you that I'd love to pull out. It makes the risk worthwhile."

The combination of her visceral choice of words and her body language sparked something primeval in me. I stood, my chair screeching, my mouth hungry for hers, my hands furious for her flesh—

"Ah-ah." She did not move, still posed with a cobra's contemplation. "Not yet. You haven't finished your dinner. I can't give you dessert."

I froze.

"Sit down, pull in your chair."

I sat down and pulled in my chair. She leaned forward.

"You must give your mother a hard time. Do you know why that is?"

"Why?"

"Because she doesn't know how to control you. But I do, Richard." With that sly smile still in place, she pushed aside her half-filled plate, full or bored

22

of it or more interested in me. "I can only imagine the hell-beast you were as a little boy."

"Have you ever had children?"

A stillness became her face. Her posture straightened as she veiled her lips with her wine glass. "I've never been a mother. This was an intentional decision, you understand, but once in awhile I pine for what never could have been."

"There's too many people in the world, anyway."

"Not enough. In a sea of human faces, I count but a handful of people. The trouble is those who shouldn't have children, because they seem most liable to have litters."

I chuckled into my glass. "My mother is one of those. I'm just glad she stopped at one."

"Surely she isn't so bad. After all, she's raised you." As if this were an achievement!

"It's not that she's bad. It's that she can't accept that I am my own human being."

"Of course she can't. She's your mother. It's no surprise that she has trouble letting go."

"She feels less like a mother. More like a pal half the time and a patient the other half."

"Is she ill?"

"Depressed." I glanced at my reflection, split by the tongs of an antique silver fork which, for all I knew, was the age of the house. "Which reminds me—what am I supposed to tell her when she figures out I'm not visiting friends?"

Her eyes consulted a corner on the right side of her overflowing mind. "Tell her you've met a girl your age. What's her name?"

The Woman danced past the dining room, all dark hair and milk flesh. "I don't know."

"Think of one."

I shut my eyes, plucked the dark and pulled away, "Dolores."

"Dolly. How sweet. You've met a girl named Dolly, and she lives outside of town with her mother, Augusta. Me."

I laughed. "Are you just now making this up?"

"What is lying but improv, darling? Besides, there are seeds of truth. My middle name is Augusta."

"Regal."

Smiling, Susan wiped her fingertips upon a burgundy napkin. "At any rate, if she asks what you're up to, tell her you're helping Dolly's mommy restore her rickety old house."

"You know, I get the feeling you're untrustworthy."

"And I'm positive you are. Can I leave you alone with my silverware, or are you seducing a rich young widow to rob her of prized possessions?"

Though she giggled, I was stung. So she'd gone so far as to read the notes I'd scribbled here and there through the sketchbook, smatters of journal amid artwork. I should have expected that, but wasn't prepared for her to bring it up. Certainly not so lightly. Humor fled my face. "I was arrested for burglary, but that doesn't mean I was there to steal."

Sobering, she placed her hand on my forearm. "I'm only teasing you." As I topped off my wine glass with my free arm, she asked, "What were you doing there, if not stealing?"

I stared down at the shank, the bit of bone gray-white in the center. This was something I'd told no one, police or friends or family. It was due to their inherent inability to understand. Susan, though, might manage it. You might, too, if you, whatever you are, feel that light of empathy the way Delilah did. But just then, at that dining room table, I did not think Susan would understand because she was empathetic. I thought she would understand because I was starting to get the sense she might be like me. I had friends, sure, and family, but I didn't connect with any of them. Sometimes, I was convinced I was the only one in the world who felt that way, so alone in a room full of people—but Susan knew just what that was like. Maybe she was right about them, then—people, non-people. I met her gaze, which she used to probe the depths of my brain as I said:

"When I was fourteen, I met the Patrokolis brothers, Mark and Gavin. They moved from Boston that year, and we started hanging out at lunch, then after school, then we were spending weekends together. I even went to church with them—I haven't been to Mass with my mother since I was eight. But all that was because they were criminals. They burglarized houses and sold drugs, so I had a great opportunity to learn something exciting. But when we did our first house together I didn't want to steal anything. I just wanted to look. It was like stumbling across a fox den."

As I wiped my mouth on a napkin nicer than the clothes in my closet, Susan did the same. Then she folded her hands just as I realized I had folded mine.

"It was thrilling. A man's house is his life. It was breaking into somebody's life. And when they were asleep upstairs, I'd look at them. I wouldn't do anything to them, not even touch them. Just look. That was how I got caught."

"You must have felt powerful, watching them sleep." Her fingertips drifted across her lips. "I imagine it would be easier to tell the police you were there to steal a VCR."

"Yes, of course—but there's more than that. It's like ... " I grasped for an analogy.

"Being close to them," she suggested.

"Exactly." And that one little word I myself had uttered was the one which shocked me, because it symbolized the ease of our connection. She smiled into me, then rose to collect our dishes. The air trembled in her wake. Somewhere, water ran. I pushed away from the table and found her rinsing plates in a kitchen of gleaming appliances fit for a cooking show. Her back, turned to me, was left bare by her dress. I approached her with the caution given a wild animal. My hands settled on her waist, though they itched to trace the slope of her spine. Instead, I kissed the nape of her neck, inhaling frankincense as I murmured, "You never answered my question."

"Didn't I?"

"Have you ever lost someone close to you?"

She faced me. "I've lost more people than I've kept. I can relate to you, Richard. My mother died just after I was born, and my father passed away when I was seven."

I allowed her to step past so I might follow her to her sitting room, with its books and fire and a radio playing Nina Simone, whose bourbon voice imbued the velvet of the chaise lounge in which Susan reclined. "I was married once, and I lost him, too, although his death was considerably happier than the others."

"What happened to him?"

"He died doing what he loved: putting up Christmas lights. Sit down, sweetheart."

As I obeyed, one hand dared rest upon her ankle. "My father was in a car accident. What happened to your parents?"

"Mother suffered from psychosis after I was born, so I'm told. Father found her with her head in the oven upon coming home from work one Tuesday."

"Jesus." I tried not to look as fascinated as I was. "What happened to your father?"

Smiling, Susan shifted her feet into my lap. "Do you really want to know what happened to my daddy, Richard?" The words curdled from her lips so sneeringly they told me all I needed to know, yet I wanted more.

"Absolutely."

"Well, since you told me about your burglary, and I understand you, I'm sure that you'll understand me. But promise again: you may do as you please, have what and whom you please, but keep our secrets, whatever you do."

"Whom could I tell?"

"Your mother, your friends."

"You don't think I'm a snitch, do you?"

"No, I think you're a braggart."

I laughed, my fingers tracing the sides of her feet in search of a buckle. "You've got me. I promise I'll keep your secrets, if you'll keep mine."

25

"Always." Susan blazed into me while I loosened one set of golden straps, then another, slipping both shoes from her pale feet. At last, she said, "My father died because I killed him."

My hands cruised over one smooth shin to rest upon her knee. "Did he have it coming?"

"He was a mean, lazy booze-hound who beat me because he didn't know how else to handle me. Now, I admit to having sticky fingers, but that doesn't give a father license to bully his little girl."

I bent my head to kiss her ankle. "Did you get away with it?"

"Of course. I sprinkled rat poison in his whiskey, and the neighbors who knew he was beating his seven-year-old daughter told the police it must have been a suicide, because who could bear such guilt? My uncle testified the same, and took me in once the matter was cleared up."

I pushed my fingertips beyond the hem of her dress, creeping beneath the tide to stretch toward the deeper trench. She licked her lips, her head cocked. "Does that excite you, Dick?"

"You excite me." I hadn't been called 'Dick' by anyone but my extended family for years, but it sounded beautiful from her. "Everything you do is erotic."

"It's an affliction. Come up here."

I crawled the length of her body, my hands bracing against a hip, a rib, a breast. These, my lips grazed as my head lifted to hers. The flush in her face was definite as mine, and not the fault of the wine.

"You have such stony eyes for a boy your age. Like glaciers." She placed her hand on my cheek, her thumb upon my left temple, though her touch burned also in my right. "You don't smile with them very often, and when you do it's more as if you're narrowing them."

"I don't think about it."

"You should. It'll help you pass."

"Pass?"

"As human. You're like me, Richard. I see it in you. Feel it on the surface of your skin." As she slipped free the top button of my shirt, her knuckle brushed the bobbing apple of my throat. "You're afraid to show yourself to me because you think nobody can understand you. You've been conditioned to believe the way you are is evil and wrong, even if you don't care it is. But what you fail to recognize is that we are the same species. We are not black sheep, my boy, but wolves in their clothing."

And she smiled again, that sickle grin haunted by narrowed eyes and the vibrations of pure evil. My jaws clamped upon hers and she made as if to suck my soul straight through my mouth. Reality dissolved into a phantasmagoria of limbs plastered across my still-trembling memory. All that was years ago, but I still pick out the moment, that first moment I drowned in the sea of her. The entire universe laser-focused on one point, this point, me, us, the pleasure so intense that it overwhelmed my senses. I felt the pressure of a raging ocean tight around my skull while the thrashing serpent beneath me, above me, around me, dragged me ever deeper into the void's awful pitch. But a man's skull is only built for so much pressure, and when it burst, the death was great and the peace, immeasurable.

Susan was by no means my first sexual encounter, but she was the first actual person I was with, and the only one until Delilah. The figments before and between them never provided any thrill, or what little they did was quick to die. Sex was a dull endeavor after a certain point, even as a young man, because the secret intimacy in my treasured book of black-and-white was what I wanted, and what I knew I couldn't have. But something in these two women, first Susan, then Delilah, nourished me. They, like the book, each seemed to herald greater intimacies—of the mind and of the soul. Each needed only stir just so in the middle of sleep for me to be driven mad with craving for their bodies and the minds within them. And because Susan arrived first, when I was so young, I had never dreamed of anything so fulfilling, at least not with anyone but my nebulous Woman.

After, we reclined in her bed, having made our journey upstairs pending brief recovery. It was good to be in her room again. I felt victorious. (A foolish boy, I tell you!) Her fingers traced up my stomach. "I have a gift for you, too, you know."

I sat up, and she rose to slide a silver robe over her shoulders. A whimper escaped me. "Seems more like you're taking something away."

With a twinkle of amusement in her eye, she said, "A little imagination is healthy. Believe me, darling, I'm the furthest thing from self-conscious there is, but a lady must maintain some mystery."

"Must she?"

"Oh, yes." Susan turned her grin upon my sketchbook, still on the desk, a package of watercolor pencils resting there. She pressed them both into my hands with a kiss on my cheek before arranging beside me, one arm draped behind her head, her merciful robe drooping open to reveal the edge of one nipple, still rosy with excitement. "For you. Why don't you try them out?"

Gleeful, I selected the first pencil I put my hands on and set about rendering her sculpted torso, every muscle tight beneath her pale skin, hidden by her half-opened robe. Though she watched me while I worked, neither of us spoke until I offered, "I'm starting my CCAD application."

"Are you!"

"Sent letters for my references yesterday. I hope they liked me as much as I think they did. The essay is giving me trouble, though."

"Worried about your writing?"

"Worried that I don't have any plans. They want to know my goals. What goals? I just want to paint. I don't have anything in mind for the future. Who knows where or who I'll be in a year, let alone five?"

"Goals are meaningless in the end. 'Man makes plans and God laughs,' they say."

"So what am I supposed to do?"

Her eyes turned ceiling-ward, Susan pursed her lips. "When I was your age, I was at a loss for direction. I was a struggling actress with no money and a job singing in a bar if my table-waiting services weren't required. So, do you know what I did?"

"What?"

"I looked toward my mother. I looked up her old friends, colleagues. I got to know her as I never could have otherwise. And I learned from the mistakes she made, like settling down with someone for the sake of settling down; having a child. Once she was an opera singer. A soprano, poised for greatness. But instead she died on the kitchen floor to the sound of a screaming infant. And I am not the type of woman to lose my life in her kitchen, Richard."

"How would you like to lose your life?"

She chuckled. "I can't imagine. It's not so much that I'd like to, as that it's an inevitability. But, if I must choose some way, I suppose it would be to die at the hands of someone I loved. Perhaps when old and infirmed, I'll have my pool-boy over-medicate me."

We laughed together, but her words seared my very blood. What would it feel like to squeeze that throat? What colors would she turn? Like watching the spectrum unfold before my eyes. I imagined running my fingers across her stomach lining, down her lungs. No doubt they were made for an anatomy model. What texture were her organs? Like velvet, I was sure. Her corpse would be beatific. Susan was too beautiful to have an ugly death.

"If you do look into your father, though, Richard," she said, apropos of nothing as I finished her nose, "don't ask your mother. Family members and lovers never know the same person that friends do. If your mother is so torn up about it she won't keep a photograph, she won't be keen to talk about him."

Chapter

5

My father's grave was in Pickerington, the town where I was born. It was small, idyllic in the most generic sense of the word, and solidly Midwestern, still with brick streets here and there. My father would have been young when he was in that accident. One can only get so far in thirty years. Where would he have been buried with more time? The grounds of the cemetery were well manicured, at least, and green even with autumn lurking.

After a night of fitful sleep following my dinner with Susan, I left for the cemetery as soon as my mother's car pulled out. Now that I was there, the office was still closed, and I sat in the car wondering why I'd even come. I had spent the night before with the most amazing woman I'd never known to dream of, and here I was, sitting in a cemetery parking lot as if I expected to find my father's high school yearbook inscribed on his headstone.

Still, I supposed it was necessary closure. When I was very small I was not entirely convinced my father was dead at all. The concept did not resonate with me for some time; but when it did, it didn't resonate with force, because I had no idea what kind of man he was. For all I knew, my father had been a saint, or a criminal. My mother had said more than once that he was a doctor, maybe hoping to nudge me into the field, but if he was anything like the fruit of his loins, he could not be all good.

At eight o'clock, the mortuary opened, and I was through the doors seconds later. The receptionist, a Golden Girl in a black pantsuit, looked up from an array of folders. Before her, I cleared my throat.

"I'm looking for my father's grave."

She retrieved a pad and pen, her expression of corporate sympathy. "What's your father's name?"

"Julius Vasko. V-A-S-K-O."

While she hustled off, I lowered into one of the peppermint armchairs scattered through the lobby. A gas fireplace was empty against the west wall, the light provided by gray morning sunshine seeping through the building's glass facade. A chapel across the lobby lay open so I might cast a voyeuristic eye upon a mortician wheeling a casket up the aisle.

The process of funerals seemed strange, but perhaps that was because the two I had attended had not been for close relatives. They, like the concept of their deaths, were abstractions at the times they left my life. I needed no public consolation or sympathy. Evangeline had not understood that, and, at my grandmother's funeral, placed her hand upon my shoulder and assured me it was fine to cry. She didn't realize I had no tears to shed.

Would I have wept at my father's funeral, I wondered? Perhaps that death would have fazed me. My life was branded by death beginning with the accident which killed him. Susan's was, too. What mark did that give us? Was that the mark we saw in each other?

"Excuse me, sir. Do you know what year he passed?" The woman was standing in the doorway to her office, hands folded.

"1974 or 1975."

She was gone three minutes before she returned with, "Do you happen to know the section he's in?"

"I'm sorry."

Fifteen minutes elapsed before she returned, looking bedraggled. Her brow knitted as she approached. "Is there any other spelling? Another name?"

"You couldn't find him?"

"There's no record of a Julius Vasko, or any Vasko, being buried here. Is it possible you have the wrong cemetery?"

"This was where my mother said he was buried."

She spread her hands, thin lips open to grasp for words which wouldn't contradict my mother, yet still admit defeat. "I'm sorry, sir. It just doesn't seem he's here."

"You're sure you've checked everything?"

"We have a directory full of names and their graves. There's no one by that name there, no one in the deed ledger. He isn't here."

My gaze trailed toward the generic mountain landscape on the wall. "Sorry to waste your time."

"Good luck."

In the car, I stared the building down while my thumb massaged the wheel. The cemetery glittered damp from sprinklers, the air nipping with the first hints of October. I started the car and pushed it through the gates, through the town, through the highway for fifty minutes. I did not drive home.

My memory was not failing me. Evangeline had pointed it out multiple times when we passed through Pickerington for one reason or another. How could she be mistaken? She wasn't that stupid a woman. But if she wasn't stupid, she was lying. Why? Nothing made sense. I could hardly drive and certainly couldn't drive home. There was only one person I could talk to about this.

By nine I was knocking at the oak door. When Susan appeared, it was something out of my fantasies, her body wrapped in a silk kimono and her hair in a wild bun in the back of her head. I couldn't appreciate any of it, even her smile, and returned her greeting by gasping, "He's not at the cemetery."

"Who?"

"My father. He's not in the cemetery. May I use your phone?"

"Oh, Richard. Certainly."

The telephone was rotary, chosen for form over function. I rolled my eyes at her while she tittered, then swept me to the kitchen with its conventional wall-mount. There I left a message for Martin in as husky a voice as I could manage, adding a cough at the end. When I was finished, Susan patted a chair in the dining nook. "Sit down. What happened, now?"

I explained the details, her fingertips perched against her chin as she listened. When finished, she suggested, "Perhaps they couldn't find him."

"They checked everything."

"Surely you don't think your mother is mistaken about where your father is buried?"

"I don't know what I think."

Drumming her fingers upon her mug of coffee, she leaned forward. "Have you considered the possibility that your father is not dead?"

Clouds were rolling in, heavy but for a few streaks of flat sky. They seemed mere inches above the tree line an acre back. "Why would she hide that from me?"

"People lie for many reasons. The truth might hurt."

"How could the truth hurt more than the lie?"

"Well, he's not present in your life, is he?" Susan looked out the window with me. "You don't know why that is. It's easy to assume he was a runaway father, but perhaps there was more to it than that. Perhaps he was an unpleasant man, and your mother wanted to protect you. Or perhaps she wanted you to herself."

"That doesn't seem fair. It makes me look stupid. I'm sure my whole family knows the truth, too." Pin-pricks of anger ran down my scalp. I could have flipped the table. Instead, I bolted from my seat to pace the kitchen. "I can't believe she would lie like that."

"You're quick to vilify her."

"She vilifies herself."

Susan crossed her legs, the fabric of the kimono falling away from one pale thigh. "What will you do if he is alive?"

"I don't know where to look, but I have to find him somehow."

"What do you know about him?"

"That he's dead." I laughed and shook my head. "I know nothing about the man. Who knows what else she's been lying about?"

"Why not consider each fact true until proven false? You know his name."

"I know he's a doctor."

"Of what?"

"She never said. Just a doctor. And he must have worked in Ohio."

"So we start there. Let's look in the phone book, consult the medical board. The record of licensed doctors is public, I believe."

I nodded. "That seems like a good place to start. But is it that easy to find someone?"

"If you really want to find him, you will. But, Dick, what happens if you find your father and discover he didn't want to be found?"

My tongue curled in my mouth. The notion was one I had tried not to entertain, but here she thrust it beneath my nose. "Then he shouldn't have knocked up my mother. He should have made her abort me. If he didn't want me, then I was a mistake, and he should own up to me."

Susan snatched my forearm as I passed, shocking me as she yanked me close. "You were not a mistake," she said, grave. Her free hand caressed my face. "You are exactly the person who should be here, alive, with me. Everything in this world exists with purpose."

"What purpose? Goals are meaningless, remember."

"They are. The purpose is life itself."

"A work of art with no theme is weak art."

"Art and meaning are subjective."

My teeth ground behind my lips. Susan's thumb brushed my nose. "I'll help you find your father, darling, however I can."

"Will you come to the medical board with me? I don't know where to go, or even how to ask for what I want."

"Of course. But you know what I think you should do right now? Go home, pick up a brush, and paint."

I nodded. "When can we go?"

"I'll look them up, and if we can't do it over the phone, then we'll set a date."

"All right." With a deep breath, I grabbed her hand. "Thank you, Susan."

She kissed my knuckles. "We make a good team. Besides, this is all quite scandalous. I admit a certain amount of curiosity."

I chuckled humorlessly. "I know what you mean. If it wasn't me this was happening to, I'd be fascinated."

The drive home was long, and as I passed Waldo, it started to rain. Slick roadway sang beneath the tires. Was it raining on my father, too? Was he even alive, or was I just looking for excuses to hate my mother?

I couldn't jump to conclusions. Susan's thrill in the face of a mystery echoed my own, but it was buried in anger and confusion. I grasped for an explanation. Perhaps there was a misunderstanding, but I recalled at least three distinct occasions in which Evangeline and I had driven past Pickerington, and she had uttered some variation of the phrase, "That's where your father is buried."

By the time my key was in the front door, the grass was soggy. The apartment was quiet. She wouldn't be home for another six or seven hours. Even so, I locked my bedroom door. I selected my last fresh canvas and placed it upon my easel. Then I sat down on my bed, rolled a joint, and made a day of it. Music that was more sonic experience than song filled the room and kept my rhythm as I worked. Cronus disemboweling Uranus, I still recall. It was crude, and ill-directed, because no matter what frustration I poured into it, all my angry thoughts traced themselves back to their source: my mother. Evangeline was the one who kept him from me, for better or for worse, and that kind of deceit was beyond forgiveness.

When she returned at five, she had the audacity to knock on my door. "Sweetheart? Why aren't you at work?"

"I'm not feeling well. I stayed home. I'm working."

"You should be in bed if you feel sick." She tried the locked door, sighed as its handle bounced back. "I hate it when you do this."

"I'd like it if you left me alone." The struggle for calm was immense. I wanted to scream and accuse, but instead stayed where I was, brush frozen in my hand, synthetic hairs grinding into the oil on my pallet. "I don't want to see anyone right now."

"What's wrong? Are you okay?"

"No. I don't want to talk about it. Leave me alone."

"Oh, Richard. Is it this girl you've been seeing?"

"No, she's incredible." With that slip, I scowled. "It's none of your business what it is, but it isn't her."

"I'm worried."

"You'll live. Let me paint."

She fell quiet, then murmured something. I sighed. "What? I can't hear you."

"I love you," she repeated.

I turned my stereo up and poured my attention into the canvas. Her bedroom door slammed. No doubt she wept behind it. I stared down the wall as if trying to transmit hatred through its molecules. Her presence on the other side distracted me as I worked, and too soon I lost focus on the piece, which I painted over white.

I sat on my bed to sketch something new on butcher paper, a shiver of inspiration down my spine. There was a better work to be had. Something better suited to the situation. Orestes strangling Clytemnestra. I could have Susan pose for me. She'd be a graceful model.

It felt right to compose, right to imagine. The lines flowed from the tip of my pencil and into rough shapes which, even lacking in detail, prickled the crown of my skull. When something felt this right to create, it was quality.

I didn't know my own mother, or my own father. Even my own life, the basis for the person I was, seemed somehow artificial. But in the middle of it all, I had something I knew to be true, and that was Susan. She was true in that I couldn't trust her. She showed me what she was, helped me see what I was, and untrustworthiness begot understanding to strengthen our bond. If anyone could help me weather this storm, it was her.

Chapter

6

The medical board possessed a sterility which the mortuary had lacked, its surfaces being either reflective or white as substitute for real upkeep. The twentysomething female employees were cross-eyed with boredom by our request at first, but upon noting Susan's Prada shoes, and her shimmering necklace, and the way she carried herself, the girls agreed to help us determine whether or not her sister's doctor was truly licensed to practice. Susan was concerned that this man might simply be feeding her sister pills and enabling her addiction, you see. She wasn't even sure what kind of doctor he was, as her sister had only described their meetings in the vaguest terms. In the end, yes, they would indeed be so kind as to let us know, and get back to us within fourteen business days.

In her Mustang, I sulked and smoked with the temple of my forehead against the window. In return for her help with the medical board, I had agreed to accompany her shopping in Columbus, so on top of a fourteen-day wait I faced a day-long trial. Susan cooed at a red light, lifting one hand from the leather wheel to pinch my cheek. "Why so glum?"

"What if they don't find him?"

"Then we'll look elsewhere. Relax."

"What if by the time I find him, he really is dead?"

"If he's alive now, don't you suppose the odds favor him staying alive until you find him?" She lowered the mirror to smooth an out-of-line brow hair, then straightened her autumn leaf fascinator. "I can relate to wanting to find someone. It's been years since I've seen my uncle. I'm starting to think he's hiding from me, though I know a good private detective to call if that really seems to be the case. Maybe we can call him for your father, if the medical board doesn't pan out."

I dodged that possibility and asked instead, "Why would your uncle hide from you?"

"Oh, I don't know, Richard. I think most people find me troublesome for extended periods of time. My uncle did."

"What happened?"

"From what I understand, he loved his sister quite a lot. And I looked just like her, my mother, so he loved me quite a lot, too. He loved me so much that, when I was twelve, he began to show me in secret. It carried on four years."

"Jesus."

"Any discomfort was a footnote, darling. I was quite confused at first, but when he started loading me up with gifts, I realized the rules. A fortysomething man with a twelve-year-old girl in his checkbook." Susan shook her giggling head, as most women might when describing youthful antics, like graffiti, or shoplifting. A new spark lit her eye. "I had immense power over him. But he was never unkind, even when I was at my cruelest. He tried so hard not to hurt me. What he did filled him with grave sadness, the way dying drug addicts can't stop. In a way, he was my first love. I haven't seen him in years."

In an insane swell of emotion, I was jealous. Of course, I was angry he had hurt her, but my disdain for this stranger was borne from blackened envy at the thought that someone else had known her as I had. "Did the secret get out?"

"No, I got fed up. I realized I couldn't let things go on if I was to have true control, so at sixteen I ran to New York. Incidentally, I stopped in Columbus for a time on the way."

"Is that why you came to Ohio now?"

"I suppose so."

I touched her knee. "Thank you for telling me that."

"I've never told anybody. But you deserve to know it."

"Why?" I shook my head as I reclined my seat to prepare for our cruise through the country. "What are you getting out of this relationship, Susan? I don't understand. Power, I guess. You like that. But what else?"

"Isn't power enough?"

"You could have power over any seventeen-year-old."

"Do you find it so difficult to believe I relate to you? That I enjoy the idea of taking care of you? That I am fond of you?"

My ears prickled as I stared out the window. "I'm fond of you, too. You just seem too good to be true."

"Well, I am." Susan narrowed her eyes as she gazed ahead. "At some point, we must pay a price for having everything we love, even if that price is simple as a missed opportunity. Our price remains to be seen. But I'm not concerned by price tags. Are you?"

"They're all I see when I go into a store."

36

"You're in trouble, then, because I'm afraid the prices here are kept behind the counter."

With a grin, I nuzzled her shoulder. It was impossibly soft, warm, and instantly soothing in a way nothing else had ever been. The words leaped out of me all at once: "Would you model for me?"

"I would be honored. What's the subject?"

"Orestes slaying Clytemnestra."

"Shouldn't your mother pose for that?"

"No. I need you."

"Of course I will." That smirk. I remember it, still. "I can't wait to see it."

I smiled, and said nothing as we continued our drive into Columbus. By the time we caught sight of the few skyscrapers, my father was forgotten and I was perked by Susan's spirit. The city helped, because it was not a big city, or a good city, but Columbus was far better than my hometown, simply in that it was not my hometown. Not even shopping could dampen its effect.

We pulled into a parking spot next to a line of boutique stores. I stepped from the car and admired the curve of her neck as she fed the meter. Then she led me to the corner, a shop with glass windows displaying easels and stools. I all but dove inside.

"This is amazing!" The place was filled with plenty to buy and a mere one other customer.

"I'm glad you like it. I noticed it on the way back from my acting workshop last week and it made me think of you."

"You should have warned me about this place. I would have brought more cash."

"Nonsense. I wouldn't have brought you if I didn't intend to treat you. Get whatsoever your little heart desires."

My eyes swept the cluttered shelves. "My heart desires a lot."

"You don't think money is an object, do you?"

As I kissed her, she sighed into my mouth, murmuring, "Sweet boy." Almost an hour later, the total bill was in the thousands. Susan paid it smilingly, half in cash and the rest in check because she had underestimated my appetite for supplies and had not brought enough to cover the expenses. I was dazed as the clerk helped us pack the car with Utrecht paints in oil, watercolor, and gouache; new brushes, new canvases; turpentine, rags, two easels of different types, palette knives, and several palettes, including the one I would keep until my death, by then stained with not just my mother's blood; charcoal, ink, pencils and pens; paper, glaze, mat board, and things I'm sure I'm leaving out. My smile was larger than my face. Once Susan tipped the clerk twenty dollars and we were again alone in the car, I laughed like a boy on the verge of mania.

This woman had just spent over a thousand dollars on me. Me. For my art. I had more supplies than I knew what to do with, in a wider selection than provided by my old high school. Shell-shocked, I barely remembered to thank her, and when I did, it was profuse.

Her head tipped back from her laughter. "It's my pleasure."

"I don't think all this is going to fit in my room. I'm shocked it fits in the car."

"It's for your studio, darling."

"We don't have one."

"You and your mother don't, but we do," she said, wiggling her finger between the two of us. "Won't you love that? You may see me anytime and work in peace and quiet, with your mother far out of your mind. And this way, you'll always have a willing model."

At the house, we spent twenty minutes hauling everything up the narrow stairs and arranging it in one of the spare bedrooms, which Susan had furnished with an adjustable desk, a few stools, a couch, and a chair. Through two small windows poured columns of sunlight which picked out the dust as it danced in the air with balletic grace. When all was arranged, I kissed her upon the couch, and when she was splayed beneath me, we broke the studio in. After, she reclined to watch me collect charcoal, paper, and a drawing board.

"Where the hell do you get this money, Susan? I don't mean to pry, but it's shocking you spend so much on me. You've only known me a few weeks."

"I'm fond of making investments. It's a habit I learned from my husband." Smiling, Susan sat up to arrange her hair. "He was a successful stock-broker for most of his life, and when he died, he left the brunt of his fortune to me. Though he was a generous man, so the amount he donated to charity before I touched my parcel was somewhat grotesque." Her nose wrinkled, mouth skewing into an amalgamation of pout and scowl.

"Are you sure you didn't nudge his ladder a little?"

"That's what his family suggested, and while I confess I had more than one homicidal ideation involving him, I was not responsible for his demise. The footprints in the snow that day proved it. He managed it all himself."

"Didn't his family get anything?"

"Oh, no. He had written them out of his will. They never spoke to him much in the final years. I think he knew I never loved him, but I endured him all the same, and strove to make his last years pleasant. That was more than his family ever did." As she spoke, I perched upon my stool, and her eyes flickered over me. "Shall I be your Clytemnestra now, my Orestes?"

"Please."

She snuffed her cigarette, eyes low until she stretched, when they lifted to the top of my head. "How shall I pose?"

"Like you're being strangled."

The smile she struggled to hide was a sly one. "Would you like to help me get into character?" Her eyes boring into mine, she lifted her neck and arched her back. "Come, my lost son. Betray your mother."

The board and charcoals almost dropped to the floor as I shot from my seat. I stepped forward, lowered my hands to her warm neck. It was pale as a Parthenon column, defined by equine muscles melting into gentle clavicles. I pecked her drooping lips, and squeezed. Her pulse beat against my fingers as her tightened windpipe jumped. She stared up at me, her brow furrowing, then lifting, her eyes hooded and beautiful mouth agape. Her face underwent superb metamorphosis: it was the first time I saw it in real life—that change, from apple to violet to grape. Aroused all over again, I imagined crushing her windpipe until she stopped moving for good in spite of her being far better alive than dead. With two hands, my own two hands, I could control anything: even Susan.

I came back to myself with new clarity of vision for my piece, and the realization that I needed to release her. As I did, she gasped, moaned, her eyes opening and curling to match her leer.

"I think I have it, now."

"Good." I leaned her back across the arm of the couch with her upper back and shoulders bowed. I draped a cloth around her breast and arm, then dragged a stool close and began with that throat, bared with pornographic sublimity.

Chapter

7

What had left my mind while enveloped in my new studio was the issue of a two- to three-week wait without guarantee of satisfaction. Being impatient and entitled a boy as I was, this was unacceptable. Already prone to boredom, I sensed the uncertainty ahead as animals fear, and reacted by radiating sullen resentment toward friend and coworker alike. Most had grown accustomed to my moods, and, so long as I functioned, attributed my sulking to the usual melodrama of teenage manufacture. I had no need to lie to anyone but Evangeline, and the distance kept by others gave me time to brood about my paternity.

Susan was my solace. She would deliver the verdict once her phone rang. If only I lived with her, I might find out directly. I might not have to waste time behind a butcher's counter, each customer more decrepit and impossible to please than the last.

How long might this go on, this labor? To be sure, the job was temporary, as are all things, but what would come after? A convenience store? An office? Any work done every day for no more than a paycheck reeked of slavery. Within me burned the fear of losing myself to a mundane career and becoming the means to a company's end. From where I was, I could see no way out.

Evenings at home were not much better, for while Susan had invited me to visit her as the mood struck, I hesitated to spend time out, lest I stoked my mother's suspicions. Already, she was nosing where she needn't. A handful of days after Susan and I put in our request, Evangeline joined me on the couch where I lay staring at the phone. I'd avoided her through conflicting schedules and strategic absences, but now we were here, and her hand was on my ankle until I shifted away.

"Not feeling much better, honey?"

"Worse."

She plucked a few specks of lint from my jeans. "Are you sure it's not that girl? You're looking at the phone an awful lot."

"I'm waiting for her to call, she's not bothering me."

"Where did you meet her?"

"Work."

"What's her name?"

The Woman was warm, as if I hadn't neglected her for weeks. "Dolly. Dolores, but her mom calls her 'Dolly'.

My mother smiled. "That's a beautiful name. Do you know what it means? 'Sorrows'."

"It suits her, then." I grinned a little, and realized now was the opportunity I'd craved; to tell the world about Susan. I sat up as I said, "She's beautiful, and intelligent." As I spoke, my image of Susan dissolved into that of the Woman. "And she's kind. Gentle. But, yeah, sort of sad. And she thinks I'm talented."

"That's because you are. I just wish you'd paint something nice for once."

It had been a fine conversation while it lasted. "She's also supportive of my work."

"I'm supportive, honey. I want you to be happy, that's all. You surround yourself with so much ugliness."

"You say this all the time. I'm not unhappy because my work is challenging. I have other reasons to be unhappy."

"Like what?"

I crossed my arms. "Try being fatherless."

Evangeline wilted a few inches. "I wish you could have your father, too."

"Well, to quote grandma, 'Wish in one hand and shit in the other.'"

Though she hated that word and I saw her face tighten for an instant, it soon melted back into grief. "Sometimes I'm ashamed of the way I've handled things."

"Good. You should be." I rose and, in a habit no doubt picked up from Evangeline herself, began snatching clutter as though intending to teach her a lesson by aggressively re-shelving books. "Why won't you just tell me about him? You never talk about him."

"You don't understand. I have a good reason."

"Well, why can't you tell me where he's buried?"

The blood drained from her face, as it had when she saw me the first time after my arrest or when I broke my leg in second grade. "What are you talking about?"

"I went to the cemetery. They couldn't find his grave, or his name. He's not there."

"That's just bad bookkeeping."

"Then why don't you take me to see him?"

Her lips tightened. "I haven't been there since the funeral. I don't remember where he was buried."

41

"Convenient that you should forget where your own husband is. I'm going to work."

"Why does every conversation we have turn out this way?" The squeak in her voice meant she was close to tears.

"Because you're a liar."

Safe in my room, with an orchestra of new pencils brought from Susan's and creamy new paper, I could draw nothing. Perhaps it was that place, its earth salted by Evangeline's selfishness. I had also not touched the CCAD essay since first confronting it.

Who was he? What had he (or, more likely, she) done to deserve this? The shadow of a dead stranger blotted out my work. I needed air.

After turning out the lights, I looked through the window and considered my mental map of the neighborhood. One house about half a mile away had been the source of idle amusement before Susan. Although I had not broken in (and had not originally intended to), I did watch. I saw the mother and college-age daughter in the mall together and, stricken by their Mediterranean features, followed them home. I had been at it for three weeks when Susan arrived, when I forgot they existed. Now I recalled, and after one in the morning, wide awake, I dressed head to toe in black and crept from my room.

Through the back door, in the patch of dirt beside our enclosed patio, I uncovered my tools. My record would show five days in detention and community service for too many weeks, but I had only lost one torsion wrench. Nobody knew I had many more. As a boy, lock-picking had been a hobby sparked by a library book and fostered by a mischievous uncle who thought it an amusing and harmless talent. It found application years later, many times over, and though Evangeline knew I had the kit, she was neither able to prove nor locate it because I had loaned it to the Patrokolis brothers the week of my arrest.

With the right wrench and pick for the lock, I set out on foot and only donned the ski mask and gloves when I was halfway there. The trees were balding orange-brown, now, and the wind nipped. The streets were empty of even a cruiser, but still, I restricted my path to back yards for the final block. The family's single security light was located stage right, just before the gate to their yard. Why have more than one, after all? Such a safe neighborhood. Never a need to so much as update their locks around these parts.

The door gave way to a kitchen which looked and smelled like the seventies, right down to the floor-to-ceiling wood paneling in lieu of wallpaper. I took a deep breath of it, of these strangers, of years' worth of tears and joys and love and plenty more I couldn't know. My body vibrated with the high of adrenaline. I dragged a gloved fingertip across the surface of the kitchen island and checked the fridge to find it full. Having helped myself to a generous portion of pumpkin pie, I ate as I moved through the living room. Upon the mantel stood photos of a brown-haired father beside a strong-featured daughter and her proud Italian mother who looked somehow purer, having aged into her features and confidence. I wondered how Susan might look in ten, twenty years.

Beside the vomit-colored sofa towered their collection of inoffensive VHS tapes: Disney cartoons, war films, home movies. I unplugged the television and hid the remote behind a middle school photo of the daughter. In the study, I discovered their names: the DiSilvas. Bert and Lena and Tracy. Upstairs, I found that Lena and her husband did not shut their bedroom door, since they were the only people in their safe little house. I moved through the dark, each step measured, each foot placing the kind of slow pressure one uses to nudge a car just a mile faster. Then, I was beside Lena, who slept with her lips just parted, her lids fluttering. Her brow half-furrowed as my moonlight shadow fell upon her, and I feared she might awaken, but she only turned her head as though to send me back to bed. There, I collected the gossamer dreams of her breath and used them to fuel my own. I did not imagine my Woman there as I once had. Now, I thought only of sleeping Susan.

I watched as Mrs. DiSilva shifted in her sleep for ten beautiful minutes, then left the peace of their room because each second I stayed I tempted fate just a bit more. On my way out, I started the coffee pot for them. I admit I did steal Mrs. DiSilva's pale orchids, arranged in a shrieking orange vase. The next day, at her speck in the desolate countryside, Susan dropped the vase into the garbage and rehoused the flowers into one of flaring jade.

"Exquisite, Dick. But wherever did you find that appalling bit of ceramic?"

"It's a hand-me-down."

"Handed down willingly, was it?"

I was already fighting a grin. With anybody else I could hold a poker face, but Susan absorbed my burglary as childhood mischief. "I wouldn't say it was unwilling, either."

Her fingers traced the white petals. "It would be hypocritical to click my tongue. When I was a girl I'd steal whatever I put my hands on. The trick is to do as you please, so long as you don't get caught. I have a present for you, too, by the by."

Upstairs, she turned on her bedroom light to reveal countless bags from chic boutiques found nowhere near Marion. As though discussing the weather, Susan reclined on her bed while saying, "Take off your clothes, let's see what fits you."

"This looks more like a trap than a gift." I eyed both my benefactor and her offerings with the kind of weariness that could only be exhibited by a seventeen-year-old used to wearing a collection of rock band t-shirts (color options: black, charcoal, navy).

She propped her grinning cheek upon her fist. "Are you afraid jaws might close any minute?"

"No, I'm afraid I'm going to be stuck trying on clothes forever."

"It will be quick."

"I've heard that one before. Shopping with my aunt and grandmother taught me many valuable lessons about trust."

"Did they also teach you it's much more efficient when you spend less time complaining, and more time trying on clothes?"

Smirking, I slipped off my t-shirt and jeans, not failing to notice the flare in Susan's nostrils, or the expansion of her pupils from cold pinpoints to new moons. "Don't you think my mother is going to notice all this?"

"These are for when you stay with me. Start with the slacks."

I pulled them around my hips and spread my hands. Susan coaxed me over with a fingertip, which I obeyed, shuffling to demonstrate my unwillingness. She turned me left and right, ran her hands over my legs and up my thigh to check the seam of the crotch. When she got there, she chuckled, her eyes flicking towards mine. "Rather snug, aren't they?"

"They'll fit better soon." I cleared my throat, looked down at myself, then at my reflection in the mirror. "I like them."

"Excellent. You are, after all, a young man. You'd ought to begin dressing like one."

Somehow I had forgotten this was supposed to be an ordeal. I grinned like a fool as I bent to try the burgundy shirt she'd lain out. While I straightened, Susan tilted her head as if admiring a work in a gallery. "I have superb taste."

"Flatterer."

She observed me in silence for a time while I went through several pairs of jeans, a champagne shirt, a leather jacket, and then a sweater. As I straightened the collar of the black shirt beneath, she rose.

"What will you do when you find him, Dick?"

"I don't know." The reflection of her arms slipped around the reflection of my waist and I felt their touch only after I saw it. "What will you do when you find your uncle? Leave me for him?"

"Of course not. I'll only leave you when you chase me away, and we'll both know when it's time for that."

"Why would I do a stupid thing like that?"

One hand traced across the backs of my shoulders as she swept to unpack the bags, satisfied her money had not been wasted. "You know, I've thought about killing my uncle when I find him, but that seems so easy, and of such unnecessary risk. Blackmail is more sensible."

"Yeah?"

"Of course. After all, Dick, a man's reputation is the crux of his life. It is his friends, family, power. And, though illegal, hebephilia is not an illness the way pedophilia is, but incest is an aberration in the eyes of society."

"Isn't it to you?"

"Of course. But when a behavior so abhorrent becomes self-aware, its repellant nature fuels its eroticism. The same can be said of all sexual deviations. A happy necrophiliac is not one consumed by guilt after each encounter, but instead one who celebrates the wrongness of his actions. Why, I might call incest the purest form of love, assuming both parties are engaging the behavior consensually. Otherwise, it's a power game. My uncle started it as a power game—gave me power over him as penance—but we might have been so much happier, and healthier, if he had accepted his desires."

Did she realize how the things she said might be received by someone normal? Was she saying them because she knew they would intrigue me? I checked the time and slid the sweater over my head, then collected my t-shirt. Someday I'd be able to stay and revel in her placid madness, but for now I was bound by the clock. "I always feel like I should tell you I'm sorry a thing like that happened to you, but it never seems to bother you."

"Not at all. I was a different person, then. Someday I'll be another person. Someday, so will you. All pebbles in the stream, my heart, don't pay them much mind until the boat begins to sink."

I nodded. I felt good. I took one of my new shirts with me for the next day. At home, I discovered with joy it was still suffused with her scent, and I used it as a pajama shirt, instead.

Chapter

8

A week later, after six in the evening, the phone rang one and a half times before I burst from my room to snatch it from its cradle.

"There is no record of a Doctor Julius Vasko in the state of Ohio, period."

I sat on the top stair. "What are you talking about?"

Susan heaved a sigh. "I mean they called, darling. The answer is no."

"Didn't they say they had a lot of records to check? What happened to fourteen days? It's been ten."

"'Vasko' is not a common surname, is it? Not much confusion to be had. And I may have called them back to nip at their heels a bit. I like speedy customer service."

My smirk was forced. "Yes, it's good I didn't have time to get my hopes up."

"So pessimistic. Don't you make a hobby of invading the lives of strangers? Why not invade your mother's life. She relinquished the right to privacy when she started lying."

"We've lived together for seventeen years. You think I've never gone through her stuff?"

She chuckled. "Naturally, but you were never looking for something like this, were you? For all you know, in your past snooping you came upon something of use, but because you weren't looking for it, you didn't see it."

"Maybe you're right." I consulted the hall clock as I rose. "I have to get to work. She'll be home soon."

"Do not get caught, Richard. Don't leave or take evidence. We don't need her turning this around on you."

"Don't worry about it. I love you."

The words slipped out. I gaped in their wake and hung up the phone as she began to speak. I couldn't bear to hear what she said next, because it would have been a lie.

Yes, as I searched my mother's room for evidence of him, of anything resembling him, I thought of Susan's words the week before. She was so certain a time would come when I would cast her off, and it was not a woman being insecure. On the contrary, she had seemed most self-assured. What was it that was so wrong in her? What might I come to see?

Under the bed was an old cigar box of photos. I did find one with a brown-haired man, but Evangeline was a blonde who dyed her hair brunette, and my black hair had to come from somewhere. Nothing in the box was labeled with my last name, and none of the men pictured resembled me, so I replaced it as I found it.

In the closet, though, I knew there were shoeboxes of papers. At first I found old tax forms, receipts, expired coupons. But after three or four such boxes, I found one full of letters. I flipped through them, many from student loans or telephone companies, and halfway through the stack it blurred from business to pleasure; mostly letters from friends who had drifted away because all her energy had gone to handling her son. A few sappy notes from lost suitors.

And there, near the bottom of the stack, I found it still sealed: an envelope with a sticker for the return address. From the Office of Doctor Julius Vasko. The postmark was from '85. I would have been ten years old. The urge to open it burned through me, but Susan was right. My mother was not a stupid woman, and if she discovered I had been going through her correspondence, she would have pitched a fit and used it as an excuse to restrict me further, even though I was only doing as was my right. I was a complete victim. The address was more important than anything he had to say to my mother, at any rate.

Chicago, Illinois. So this was why the medical board had come back with nothing. Orange Grove. I memorized the address as I heard the front door creak. I scrambled to cram back everything as I had found it, the letter included, then struggled to escape the closet before she found me there.

"Richard? Richard?"

I had no time to close it properly. As I left, the closet door cracked. I darted to the hall. She was on the stairs just as I shut her door behind me, then jerked open the linen closet next to it. Her head emerged from the stairwell, crowned by a knitted brow. "What are you doing?"

"I'm getting some towels."

"I heard a door."

"It was stuck." Towel tucked under my arm, I slammed the closet to emphasize my point. Orange Grove Road, Chicago, Illinois. Looking my mother in the face was too difficult because it made me want to push her down the stairs.

"What do you need towels for? I just put up fresh ones."

47

There was no time to formulate or censor thoughts. I opened my mouth, and it happened. "I don't want to live with you right now."

That idiot, gaping expression of ignorant disbelief—I hated it more than I hated her. "What are you talking about?"

"You're a liar. I would like some space away from you, because every second I am around you I'm angry and disgusted. Hypocrite."

Evangeline's face disfigured with wrinkles of grief. "But where will you go?"

"Dolores and her mother invited me to stay with them."

She was already sobbing—deep, quaking gasps of air that resonated through her chest. "You can't leave! You're just seventeen, you're still a boy. My beautiful, blue-eyed baby boy. I love you, Richard. I'm sorry I've had to lie to you, but—"

"You haven't had to do anything." I moved past her, into my room, and shut the door behind me. I packed a bag with books and little else, because Susan had bought everything from boxers to pajamas. My library and the CCAD application were my only possessions of value. It was heavy as a dead body, that bag, and I slung it over my shoulder with a grunt as I left my room to find Evangeline hysterical with the understanding that I meant every word I said.

"Please, Richard, don't leave me. I'm your mother. I love you."

"You don't love me enough to tell me the truth."

"I'm trying to protect you."

"We both know the only one you're protecting here is yourself."

Stricken, she lowered her head and turned away. I did the same, taking the stairs two at a time and snatching my shoes on the way, unwilling to tarry as long as they took to tie. Orange Grove Road, Chicago, Illinois. My mother was Roanoke, Virginia, born and raised. She told me she'd moved with my father, who had interned in Virginia but craved to return to Ohio. What was this man doing a place like Illinois?

At Susan's house, that beacon in the middle of the country, I found a key taped to the front door. I let myself in to find Miles Davis simmering through the house. In the foyer I dropped my bag, then followed the sound to the kitchen, where she sang along over a pot of stew. I kissed the nape of a neck left naked by the bun of her hair.

"I brought my books," I said.

"So you're moving in? Wonderful. A little sooner than expected. I thought you might just want to talk after today, but relocation? Did it go that badly?"

"I have proof of him, or Evangeline does, at any rate. He's alive."

She paused in the middle of chopping carrots, but didn't turn. "What have you found?"

"A letter. I didn't open it—she still hasn't opened it, and she got it seven years ago. But he's real. Julius Vasko on Orange Grove Road in Chicago, Illinois."

She spun on her heel to grasp my hands, her eyes bright. "Oh, Richard, this couldn't be more perfect. I have some friends in Chicago who have been nagging me to celebrate Christmas with them for years. Perhaps we ought to take them up on it. Gives us a bit of time to find him, too."

The follies of youth! I celebrated this happy accident by kissing her. "Thank you for this. For everything. I couldn't have found anything if it wasn't for you. I wouldn't know there was anything to find."

Susan smiled, her hand resting on my cheek. "My pleasure. We are the same, my dear, so in helping you, I've helped myself. Dinner won't be ready for another hour or two. Put away your books and paint a little. I'll get you when it's ready."

I kissed her again. The bag was a challenge to haul up the spiral stairs, but it calmed me to see my library on the shelves of my studio. All other things, though, were not as smooth. My inability to remain permanently at Susan's house before the very moment I found the key on her door had hampered my progress on Clytemnestra's death. The figure of Orestes was likewise a challenge as I had only myself for a model, and once my books were away I stood in the mirror, trying again and again to communicate the perfect perspective, the right angles, to make it all seem organic. Some fudging allowed me to produce a passable mannequin, but once I filled in details, I was again displeased. In an attempt to distance myself from the figure I had snuffed its spark. Nor was Clytemnestra quite alive, her resemblance to Susan being a suggestion. A quiet feeling of helplessness settled in my chest. It was possible—likely, even—that my skill was not yet up to the level the work demanded.

She found me asleep on the couch two hours later, sketchbook splayed upon my chest, and after putting away the stew, Susan slipped under my arm to sleep alongside me.

Chapter

9

The month and a half with Susan comes to me now with the gauze of a dream, because that was how it seemed when I lived it. I was prince in a kingdom whose only other inhabitant was its ice sculpture queen. She came and went as she pleased and took no issue with my doing the same: though, supplied as I was with food, drugs, paint and sex, I had no reason to leave the house. I left only for my job, the drive tiring and each day a waste of what could have been. I didn't want to get into trouble; I only wanted to be home, to spend my time with Susan. My intuition suggested our affair would be an abbreviated one, and my heart responded by slamming at the cell doors of my ribs and screaming her name.

On the third work-day after moving in—a half-day, mercifully—I returned home to have her usher me right back out the door after a shower and change of clothes. A few hours later we stood in the Cleveland Museum of Art.

"You know, when I was here in 1976, they had *Madame X*, fresh from the Met. She moved me."

"How old were you?"

"Seventeen."

I laughed. "Cradle-robber. I was one."

"Yes, but now you're seventeen. We were all one, once." Smiling, Susan ruffled my hair and led the way, spoon from a three-dollar scoop of fruity ice cream occasionally drifting into her mouth. "When I saw *Madame X*, I realized she was exactly what I wanted to be. She was beckoning me to New York with her. So, I went."

"You don't stay in one place often, do you?"

"Not if I can help it." Noting the distress betrayed by my twitching lip, she caressed my cheek. "I never leave forever, as much as people often wish I would."

"No, but it makes me want to spend all the time we can together. I can't do that when I'm wasting my time at work."

"So quit."

Just like that. The words were so freeing I didn't understand them, as if they were not even foreign words, so much as meaningless noise. I asked her to repeat herself.

"I said: so quit. There's no reason for you to work when we're together. Besides, I hate to hear men complain about their jobs."

I grabbed her, and her mouth tasted like raspberry sorbet. The yoke was lifted from my shoulders with two words. They had been given to me as a gift and with them came freedom. If I had posited the idea to Evangeline, she would have launched into an hour-long tirade about responsibility, and the need to regain her trust after 'something like that,' and how I should have considered myself lucky I was even able to find a job; but Susan seemed to believe it was my choice to work. And, I realized, it was.

I turned in my two-week notice the next day. Martin was six feet of margarine and took the note in his pudgy hand while I explained, "I just don't think I can focus on work that isn't mine right now. Or ever, but especially right now."

"Your drawing," he confirmed, nodding at the note, scratching an upper lip which once sported a mustache, portrayed in old photos on his dusty pine desk in the cluttered back office. "Going to school? You should work until you go, save some money."

"I will. I'm working for Mrs. Sinclair."

"That's the family you're living with, the Sinclairs?"

"Yeah. Mrs. Sinclair is—'kind' isn't it, but she cares, and doesn't judge. I feel like I could tell her anything."

Martin arched a brow. "Everybody could use a little judgment, you ask me."

"You sleep in your chair two hours a day."

The gray old man scoffed, dropped the letter on a stack of tool order forms, and said, "Your mother's been calling, by the way. I didn't want to get into it. But she's been checking in to see if you're at work. Should I be worried about you?"

"I'm doing better than ever," I said as I filled out my starting time and got to work. After the day was done, I did not go into town to see the Patrokolis brothers, against whom Susan had passingly warned me more than once. I did not call my mother, or think about her. For the first time in my life, I felt free.

I came to understand that the luxuries Susan afforded me carried the price of a high standard. She expected me to spend much time painting, and I was happy to oblige. When not painting, she urged me to read, pushing philosophical tomes from Aristotle to Zarathustra, fine literature, and the vast collection of plays which made up the majority of her library. I was so busy I hardly thought about my father, or the trouble I was having with the essay, and she broached neither subject. In the mornings, she cooked breakfast (the only meal she cooked once we lived together). Afterwards, she did yoga in the sunshine, a line of cocaine, and, after a shower, went off to her acting class. Sometimes she came home straight after; sometimes she did not return until four or five, with shopping bags, or drugs, or no excuse for her absence besides a smile. In the evenings, she taught me to dance, and at night, she taught me how to please a woman. And, true to her warning, she was not always kind. But her unkindness was not needless; barbed words from Susan were well-aimed knives of criticism that sank deep into the weaknesses for which they were meant. Once, in an effort to break out of my slump with the death of Clytemnestra and try something experimental, I took a stab at a cubist portrait. In slithered Susan to straighten. With an armful of sketches, she paused behind me. Then, after a moment, her hand rested on my shoulder.

"Stop doing that."

I scoffed. "That's it? No commentary? No suggestions for composition or form?"

"Not for that."

My ears rang. "Is it that bad?"

"That's not a Vasko, that's a Picasso pretender trying to break the rules before he's ready to, and in a manner that's already been done. Stop now before you're in too deep."

Arm lifting away from the canvas in more shock than agreement, I turned to stare at her. She pecked my cheek.

"There's a good boy."

Bristling, I took the canvas from its easel. "I hate it when you call me that."

"You know I only mean it with affection, Dick. But, very well. I bend to your preference."

"Thank you."

"Consider adjusting your tone in the future." Smiling in the crocodile way that didn't touch her hooded eyes, Susan tapped the tip of my nose. "I detest being snapped at."

Suddenly, I found myself looking at her toenails, fresh-painted in steel polish. "I'm sorry."

"Fibber. But I forgive you all the same. After all, with the size of our egos, an accurate critique can hit a nerve. That nerve is there so you know a valid critique from an invalid one. I've learned to nurture it, and my work is stronger for it."

And that was it. Nothing near my fights with Evangeline. There was no escalation after the confrontation. By the next day, I agreed with her, glad she'd kept me from wasting my energy. The following Sunday, it had slipped

my mind entirely, and we were back to where we were every Sunday afternoon since my moving in: the living room, across the walnut coffee table
from each other as she shuffled her softened deck of tarot cards. It was her
custom every Sunday, I found, and each week as she consulted her cards in
complete silence, I watched her, enraptured by the echoing air, the stillness
of her body. She was always so still, right from the moment she arranged
them to the moment she swept them back into the deck. She never offered,
and I never asked. But that Sunday, she smiled up at me. "Why don't we do
one for you this time?"

If anyone in that world of mine had mystical powers, it was Susan. As I
tell you this story, you experience it, and I experience it in telling it to you,
as if I am really living all this again—is that all there ever was, me telling
this? Is that how all of this came to be? Even now I do not know, but I do
know that Susan knew. Whatever mystery there was to the universe, Susan
saw through it, read its secrets constructed in the patterns of cards and stars
and the beauty of an arrangement of icicles hanging from the overgrown
oak tree in the back of the house. Maybe she only seemed to know when she
was young, but by the time she returned to destroy all I had built with
Delilah, she had most certainly come to understand.

"Will I find my father?" I asked at last.

Susan lowered her eyes to the cards, correcting, "What can you do to find
your father?"

"What can I do to find my father, and what will happen if I do?"

At her behest, I cut the cards in three, then restacked them and drew from
her ensuing fan. She stopped me at twelve, though the twelfth practically fell
out of the deck, as I recall—along with half the others, but she only took the
top card. My selections, and the one chosen for me, were arranged in a cross
and a row, which she then flipped one at a time. After a few moments of
silent study, Susan laughed. Not at me, or the cards, it seemed. Rather, it was
if at a private joke.

"I'm glad. What good things are in store for you, my dear!"

"Are you sure?" It didn't look promising. There in the center of it was The
Tower, the problem crossing me, she would later explain, and the black
background of the picture—and the people falling to their deaths from it
amid a thunderstorm—did not harken a bright future. Nor did the Hanged
Man beside it. How funny: I never could have recalled these details in life.
Now I do just fine!

"In the big picture. Though falling from a tower is seldom a pleasant
experience, Dick."

"I never would have guessed." I stared down at the cards and frowned,
less rattled and more trying to read into it what she did. "What is it saying,
though?"

"You are facing a serious change. Something that will transform you."

She directed my attention to the row, more comforting than the cross. "Now you are this." A young man holding a gold coin—the Page of Pentacles, I think. "And soon you will be this." A Knight of something. The creative suit—wands, that's right. "Our page here is a bright, creative boy, much like you. Bury yourself in the creative process, enjoy the act of painting, and try to focus on that. Good news is coming and will be the root of the change, I'm almost sure. You will meet someone generous, and sympathetic. He will aid you." I leaned forward as she spoke, looking amid the Chariot, and cards of wands and cups. "That is, assuming you cope with the change he brings. It will be swift. Perhaps, even violent. When the world changes so, you must change with it, and when illusions fade away you must adjust to reality. And you must always remember that what has been built can and will be destroyed, eventually, even if that destruction is in a hospital bed at the age of eighty. But if you study your artistic masters, and take joy in the process of creating your work, you will integrate the change and become like the knight—fearless, avant-garde, self-confident."

I pointed at the card with a nude woman bending over a pool of water into which she poured more from her clay pot, one of the many cards facing me, and to her reading, reversed. "Who is she," I asked. "You?"

She smiled. "She is the illusion. Your arrogance. She is your fear. You fear I am an illusion, and I will be shattered, and I suppose you are right."

"I'd love you if you were a serial killer," I blurted, and she tilted back her head to cackle.

"My sweetheart. I'll hold you to that if I ever need help hiding a body." She tapped my nose, then lunged forward and kissed me, her tongue plunging deep into my mouth. I kept trying to push closer to her, lean closer, until I slipped from the couch and onto my knees. She laughed as I rearranged myself on the floor across from her with very little dignity.

"I don't think you're as bad as you think you are. A little twisted, maybe, but ... "

"I'm much worse than I think I am." Her smile just then belonged more to a woman under a Bodhi Tree than a chandelier. "But not so bad, really. We cannot do a thing we were not made to do. Otherwise, we wouldn't be us."

The message came far sooner than expected; and, though I had forgotten all about the reading by the time of its arrival, now with this chance to see each moment lined up within me or you or us, I find her portent eerie. Of course even that may have been done with intention, but I watched her shuffle those cards, and cut them myself, and cannot account for those significant ones so arranged, nor the events which followed shortly thereafter.

On December 12th, snow blasting the house with white fog, our telephone rang. Susan picked up from the kitchen, and as I entered, I heard her say, "That's wonderful news, I'm so relieved. I was hoping the doctor could work with my son again. I'll call his new office immediately. We're moving back in less than a month and I'm sure he's quite busy."

As she dropped the phone into place, she handed me a slip of paper. I trembled as I read it, copper excitement flavoring my mouth.

"Yes, Doctor Vasko is a licensed psychiatrist in Chicago, but he isn't on Orange Grove anymore. He moved offices last year; this is the new address."

I threw my arms around her neck and kissed her cheek, her mouth. She laughed and held me. After that, Clytemnestra began to come easily; but the more I worked on Orestes, the less pleased I was with him. The figure was malformed in some way when I held it to the mirror, lacking spark and drive. But my spirit was too high to be bogged down by my creative woes. The irony is that I believe she did all she could to keep me happy and better me as a person, and in many regards, she was successful. But I doubt her intentions were to make me into the man I am today. Instead she wanted to groom an heir, and it was going well for both of us until I met my father.

Our appointment was two days before Christmas. I sped most of the way to Chicago until she insisted she drive, because crossing state lines with a minor (with drugs in the glove compartment, no less) would be "problematic, were we pulled over." While she drove, I took advantage of her skirt to distract her, and had her worked into such a frenzy that in the hotel room, the first thing she did was mark her aching territory. I was just as relieved, and after a shower together, we slept early and woke late. My appointment was shoehorned into the end of the day before the doctor's two-week long vacation, because Mrs. Sinclair was concerned with her son's well-being around the holidays and needed him to see the doctor whose abilities had been lauded to her. Six-thirty in the evening.

At lunch, she told me, "Avoid expectations, good or bad. Whatever happens, happens."

I nodded, but it was a hollow gesture. Expectations were impossible to avoid. He was marked as a compassionate man by agreeing to pencil in a troubled boy two days before Christmas while his family examined the area for properties. Was that the person he really was, or would he change when he recognized me?

The evergreen carpet in his waiting room smelled like a recent cleaning. His receptionist checked us in with Susan providing information while I, the troubled son, fell into a chair with a breath deep to the bottom of my lungs. The young woman was understanding, and Susan kissed my forehead as I took my seat. "I know you want to do this alone. I'll read in the car."

I nodded, heard her go, but did not watch her. I watched, instead, his burgundy office door. My pulse thudded in my fingers. More than once, Susan had expounded upon the benefits of meditation. Though the concept seemed boring and pointless to me, I found myself practicing it then. I counted no more than five breaths without thinking of Evangeline, thinking of Julius, thinking of myself, and beginning again.

Six was on the tip of my brain when the door opened. I jolted upright. First came a sunken housewife with a hollow face, who looked around the room as if expecting her husband to emerge from the plastic houseplant in the corner. The doctor was just behind her.

We focused on one another at the same time, and though he guided his patient out and shook her hand, he looked back at me again, then again, his eyes the same steel, his hair the same black, but with gray around his temples. Even his bone structure resonated with mine, the strong cheekbones and nose contributing a look of hawkish intellect. He had the aura of a man in his fifties who still felt forty: thick, not fat; tall posture (just taller than mine); hands which had never labored.

As the front door closed after the woman, Julius turned to me. "You must be Mr Sinclair."

I nodded. I could not speak. I stood, shook his hand (huge, or perhaps it was my imagination, because when next we met I swore it was mine that engulfed his), and followed him into the office. Behind the closed door, we stared each other down, each man's brain groping for a place to begin. Neither of us wanted to speak until my tongue loosened itself. "My name is Richard Julius Vasko."

Julius took a sharp breath upon what was no doubt confirmation more than revelation. He nodded, continued to nod as he sat in his chair. His eyes narrowed as he examined my face; I remained standing in a strange office full of dusty DSMs. Leaning back in his seat, he rested his thumb against his mouth in consideration.

"I've wondered about you," he said after a low breath. "For seventeen years. My only son."

I jammed my hands into my pockets. "I've wondered about you, too. But only since recently. Mom told me you were dead."

Julius, though stung, nodded. "That was probably easiest. I sent her a letter once, but she never wrote me back. I wouldn't either, if I were her. Is she married?"

"No."

"Why don't you sit down, son?"

Although the epithet was no doubt used liberally with any boy under the age of twenty, I was glad to hear it. I lowered into the couch as he said, "I'm sorry that I'm not a part of your life, Richard. I won't try to shift the blame because everything is my fault. The circumstances made it impossible for us to be a family."

The golden band around his ring finger shone dully in the light. "Did you have an affair?"

"Yes." He frowned not at the ring, but at his desk. "I was afraid and selfish. I told myself everything I did was because I loved your mother, but in the end I was just cruel. When she left, I realized what a fool I'd been, but it was too late. It took me years to track you down."

"Why did she just sit back and let this happen? She could have at least gotten financial assistance from you."

"How much do you know about your mother and I, Richard?"

"She refuses to talk about you. All I've ever known is that you were a doctor, and she only thought to mention that when I was ten."

His lips turned white as they pressed together. "She has every right to decide what to tell you, but it might be gracious of her to settle your mind. Especially now that you've met me in person." Pausing, Julius offered a small, crooked grin. "You look so much like your mother."

"I don't think I look anything like the woman."

Julius' brows knit in what seemed to be sympathy. "Are you in school?"

I shook my head. "I graduated early, but I'm applying to Columbus College of Art and Design."

"You're an artist?"

"I hope so."

His laughter revealed luminescent teeth. "Well, I'm sure you are. The Vaskos are a creative bunch. Singers, actors. My daughter Vera writes her heart out."

I straightened. "I have a half-sister?"

"Two. Ada is thirty-three, and Vera is thirty."

I memorized the names, feeling the age gap more than I heard it, while Julius rose to show me the silver-framed photos on his desk. The first was of three little girls at a tea party, two of them grinning boldly at the camera while the third looked over her bare shoulder at the Bichon Frisé to whom she fed table scraps. In the second photograph, years later, two young women with dark hair and bright blue eyes reclined grinning on the beach, their faces highlighted with feminine vitality. My sisters were truly beautiful, though theirs were softer features than mine or my father's. They must have taken after their mother.

"That's their cousin in the older one," he explained, absently. "My sister's daughter."

"I have another aunt, too?"

"Yes." He cleared his throat while replacing the photographs. After regarding them, he looked at me, his lips twitching with grief. "I've made a lot of terrible choices in my life. Sometimes, you try to be a good person, and it backfires on you and everyone you love. Sometimes you feel like there's nothing right with you. But I'm so glad you came here to meet me, Richard. It makes me feel like maybe I have the opportunity to—not make it right, but lessen the impact of all that I did. To get to know you. There's so much I want to tell you, so much I know you came here to discover—but it's truly your mother's business to do that."

My teeth ground together. "She refuses to tell me anything."

"It's your right to know. Tell her that. Tell her it would show you she respects you. Tell her, even though I'm in no position to make this request, that I asked her to do it."

I nodded, frustrated and longing for the safety of Susan. I rose. "I think I should go. I don't know what to do with myself."

A chuckle emanated from his chest. "I know what you mean. I'm overwhelmed. But I want you to come again. I want to get to know my son."

Then he hugged me. I didn't know how to react and patted him on the back, the scent of him somehow familiar. Smiling, he walked me into the Chicago cold. I got into the car with Susan, who stared beyond me as I settled in. When I looked up, Julius was frozen in the doorway, either overwhelmed by my leaving or by the beauty of my companion.

She tilted her head, the ghost of a smile on her mouth as she admired him. "Yes, I was right. You look just like your father."

"Can we go home soon? Ohio, I mean. I'm not really in the mood for a Christmas party."

"Of course. We leave tomorrow afternoon," she declared, starting the car. "I've never cared much for this city, anyway."

Chapter

10

It is easy to recognize the building blocks of tragedy through the lens of hindsight, but in the moment I saw no further than my nose. I knew now that I could travel in only one direction for what I sought, and that was back the way I came. I had not seen my mother in almost two months, but when we returned from our trip at nine the next evening, the first thing I did was announce to Susan that I was going out. "So soon, so late?"

"I have to talk to my mother."

Marble stoicism became her face. I wonder what went through her mind as she nodded, "I imagine you would."

I kissed her, then drove, and the journey to my old home seemed longer than the one to Chicago. I would give her one chance to tell the truth: if she didn't take it, I would get the answer from the letter. I was not prepared. I did not know what I should have been preparing for, but I remember thinking how the clouds looked suffocating; a black darker than the sky whose starlight they snuffed.

By ten, I was knocking on Evangeline's door, but the lights were out and there was no response. As I let myself in, her shrill call cut down the stairs. My name.

"Yes, mother," I said, cramming my keys into my pocket lest she try to hide them. "I'm here."

Though she ran down to embrace me, I stood like a sculpture. She recoiled with a frown until I said, "I met my father."

Her eyes and mouth widened as if she'd been slapped. "What did he say?"

"That I deserved to hear the truth, and hear it from you."

The speed with which her eyes produced tears unnerves me even now. "You'll hate me."

"I already do, because you think I'm a child you can keep in the dark. You'd better tell the truth, because I will find out if you don't, and I will never forgive you."

Her tears were silent, at least. She sat on the bottom step as though to consult the shoes piled by the door. Every second my skin grew tighter, until, fed up with her silence, I mounted the stair to climb past her. As my left foot reached for the next, I managed to catch through her hiccups the sentence: "You're adopted."

Adrenaline overcame my heart, my stammering heart on the verge of true revelation. I did not turn, but I did pause. "What did you say?"

"I knew a man," she continued, as if it was fine to continue conversing when the earth had stopped spinning, "I thought I loved him. I thought he loved me. We got married, but we found out I couldn't have children. So we decided to adopt. And oh, Richard, I fell in love the instant I saw you. You were three months old. My beautiful little boy, your name fit you so well I couldn't bear to change it—and, when Geoffrey left me a year or so later, I was glad I didn't, because it meant I wouldn't have to explain the truth to you. You would just be my son. Mine, like you were never anybody else's. I love you so much." She whispered the words, her shoulders jerking. "Does it matter if I didn't give birth to you? I've loved you all the same. I've loved you whether you were good or bad or sick or well. I've loved you enough that you never went without, even if it meant I did. Does it matter where you came from?"

Did it? I breathed in and out. Did it matter? In and out. It did matter. Of course it mattered. It mattered because horror cast its shadow across my trembling back. My stomach tightened into the very bottom of my throat. Julius Vasko was my father. What, then, of my mother?

I took the stairs two at a time and used the hand rail to propel myself over the final three. Far away, Evangeline called my name. Sound waves moved as though deadened by liquid while I slammed open the closet door and jerked the light alive. Boxes of bills flew as I pursued the gray box of letters and found it as I had left it. She was behind me while I tore through her correspondence and found, with slamming pulse, the letter from Julius. My hands shook so violently that I dropped the envelope while opening it, and when I picked it up, a scrap of paper wafted to my feet. Hyper-focused on the letter, I little more than half-noticed it.

Dear Ms. Evangeline McDonnell,

I'd like to preemptively apologize for disrupting your life with this letter. It comes only out of love for your son, because he is also mine. I do not expect the two of us to ever meet. Nor should we. I have a family of my own to consider, unfair as it is to Richard, and sorry as I am of it.

I do not know anything about you, or him, or how much you have told him. Whether or not you do is up to you. If you have, I would be overjoyed to meet him, or at least you might consider giving him the enclosed photograph of his mother. It is many years old, taken before we knew she was pregnant. I have not seen her since she was carrying him, and deserve to have lost them both. I was a sick man, wrong, and I hurt her deeply. I do not deserve to have a part in his life. Perhaps she should remain uninvolved as well, but a boy still deserves to know what his mother looks like.

Feel free to ignore me. As pleased as I would be to hear that Richard is doing well, you owe me no favors, and perhaps a white lie is friendlier than the truth of his heritage. Thank you for taking the time to read my letter, though, Evangeline. I pray every day that the two of you are happy, and healthy, and that someday I might have the chance to meet Richard and make amends for what my cruelty inflicted upon him.

Yours,
Julius Vasko

My teeth chattered. The picture. I retrieved the fallen scrap and focused first on emerald eyes against porcelain, laughing from the past at the punchline of a seventeen-year-long joke. With time, the teenage girl constructed herself around the eyes: first the hawkish Vasko nose, then mahogany hair, then proud jaw open in girlish guffaw. I swayed against the door jamb. The back of the photograph read: *Susie Vasko, 1974.*

The world melted away until I was floating in space. A photograph fell from a stranger's numb hand. My flesh peeled from me and a lifetime of confusions were set straight by this one explanation; a terrible chain of epiphanies, this truth that dried my mouth and constricted my skin against my bones and made Evangeline's hand scorch me when it rested upon my shoulder.

Neither of us anticipated I might react as I did, but the price of truth was blood, and Evangeline was a scapegoat, because if she'd told me the truth when I was a boy or anytime between then and the day my mother walked into the butcher's shop, I would have been fine. But it was her fault; Evangeline's fault that I was fucking my own mother, that I was the child of a vile union, that I was in love with real, flesh-and-blood, sensuous Susan while for my whole life this pretender before me had never understood me because I was never hers to understand, and now she'd finally managed to ruin me.

All this, I shouted at Evangeline while strangling her to death. I was too angry to enjoy it, or observe it. Reality was a flash of white heat, and then she was dead on the floor with my hands around her neck. She did not deserve to die on that floor. Susan did. Still, the death beneath me was release. It brought me back to my body, made me aware again of solid space around me. I remembered I was human. I rolled off of her and took a deep, wracking breath, then crawled downstairs to light a cigarette.

61

So this was how it happened. The idea of murder didn't trouble me. The idea of jail time didn't bother me either, when I got right down to it. I was troubled because I hadn't been present to take part in it. A life could be snuffed out and feel like the aftermath of a party one was too drunk to recall. Death had always been close to me, but now it became real in a moment when nothing else was. My entire life, history, being, came into question as I lit one cigarette with another. My questions took priority over the corpse upstairs.

My mother. My real mother. There was no way she couldn't have known. This was done with purpose from the start. She knew what she would do to me the second she walked into the store. But this one transformative truth answered many other questions, like the one which had ping-ponged through my skull since the beginning: Why me?

Breath by breath, I collected myself. There was so much certainty now. Before, I had been an animal. But Susan awoke me, and I found myself naked in my garden and surrounded by lesser beings. It finally made sense—the way I had always been. I took after my mother, after all. And, as I considered the ceiling, I realized this was true in more ways than one.

What would happen now? If this was discovered, I would go to jail. But it was a crime of passion. Wrath, pure and simple. The courts might not see that, but I knew one person who would.

I folded up the letter, slipped it and the photo into my back pocket, and dialed Susan. As she picked up, I said, "Something happened. I need your help."

"Give me your address, and directions."

I recited, the words automatic, because the gravity of her voice paralyzed me. After, she said, "Do not touch anything. Open the door for no one but me."

The line went dead. I sat down and thought about the first time, at the party, when I kissed her and felt that one shimmer of hesitation, mere seconds before cumulative hours of reciprocation. I counted my breaths. I did not think about the thing upstairs which was once Evangeline, nor about jail, nor the way I was floating on an ocean with legs exhausted by the work of treading water. I did not think about my mother.

What did cross my mind, though, was a question. A question that you, my friend, may have asked already, and the very same I posit to you now: Had I known it all along?

When the knock came, a sliver of me prayed it was the police. No; there she stood, a peephole between us, her arms crossed and her hair in a tight bun high upon the back of her head. I counted to five and let her in, and she looked me up and down as she shut the door behind her with one gloved fingertip. Her lips were stretched to the grim width of a mortician's, those piercing eyes seeing everything that had happened while she was not there to supervise. I felt small beneath them. She waved a hand as she ordered, "Show me."

Silent, I led her up to Evangeline's old bedroom. She approached the body, each step of her heeled boots muffled but no less sharp. For a time, she stared, until at last, she asked, "What happened?"

"I got angry, and the next thing I knew, she was dead."

"What were you fighting about?"

"We weren't. Not really."

"Then what happened?"

I stepped towards her. She remained still, noble, cruel. "I was adopted," I said.

She blinked, long and slow, her hooded lids hiding and unveiling seawater eyes.

"Why did you give me up?"

"Because one day, I caught myself pressing a pillow to your wailing face."

To hear her say it wracked my frame. I sat upon the edge of the bed, my hands folded between splayed legs. "Why?"

"I could never be a mother, Dick. Not to a child. But perhaps I could to a man."

I struggled to breathe, my shoulders lifting with the effort. "You seduced me."

"You wanted me. And you are a very attractive young man, Richard. I know only one way to interact with attractive men who want me. Blame Julius, if you like."

My hand moved over my mouth, down my jaw and neck. "I wouldn't have. If I had known, I wouldn't have."

"Bullshit." My gaze snapped to Susan, who shed her gloves. She never looked away, penetrating me as she said, "If you had known, you would have wanted me that much more."

She strode towards me and bent to my level, her face hovering near mine. "Tell me it doesn't make you want me right now, in this bed. Your mother's bed."

I breathed. She didn't. I lunged for her mouth to steal the air trapped in her lungs, and we tore from each other buttons and zippers and fabric. I felt between her legs, her home, church, inviting and mine, or once mine, or I might pretend it was mine. My mother straddled my lap and a few minutes later the explosion that resounded between us was sublime as it was deafening. Yes, I reveled in it. In her, this, our self-aware depravity. And you look upon my acts with disgust, my observer, but I tell you that you cannot know without having been me. Your revulsion comes because a voice in the back of you understands me. Because she has seduced you, too, you understand my attachment to Susan: mother or not.

"I wish you would have told me," I said as we dressed.

"What difference would it make? We still found Julius, either way."

"Maybe Evangeline wouldn't be dead."

"Are you remorseful?"

"What happens if I'm caught?"

"Just do as your mother tells you, my darling, and you won't be."

Chapter
11

Two and a half hours later, Susan was using Evangeline's license to purchase a Greyhound ticket to Richmond while I stared at a corpse in the disused guest bathroom of Susan's house, in which she had bothered hanging neither towels nor shower curtain. It dawned then that she had not brought a single guest over since my moving in, and that, between last leaving Martin's place, and arriving in Chicago to meet Julius, in all that time I hadn't lain eyes on a human being who wasn't her, unless it was Norma Desmond in *Sunset Boulevard* or Travis Bickle in *Taxi Driver*.

"I will get off in West Virginia and be back," she told me as she crammed her luggage full of clothes, make-up, photographs, anything a sentimental woman on the lam might take. "I may be some hours, perhaps a day or more, because," as she tarried by the mirror to tuck a few stray hairs into the black beanie I'd fetched, "I have to take her car to the station, then taxi back to someplace around here, then find my car—goodness knows if I even will, dark as it is, you really are a trying child at times, my darling—and then, I must drive it back to the house."

I let most of what she said glide through me. "What am I supposed to do in the meantime?"

"You're the butcher, Dick. Can't you figure it out?"

"Yeah, and then? The ground is rock solid, it's almost January."

She pinched my cheek, then resumed zipping the bag. "Haven't you been in the cellar? There's quite a lot of room down there, and it's not all finished. Warmer than outside, even if only a little. Put her in the ground there for now, and we'll move her after the spring thaw."

So there I was: boning knife, hammer, ill-suited hacksaw, each object discovered in the pantry or found abandoned in the cellar by the previous owner. It was not so different from butchering a hog with poor tools, but my muscles were already sore from the effort required to haul the bundle of carpet and death to and from the car, an issue with which Susan assisted only disdainfully. The matter of getting the blood out was my first challenge, however. Animals are slaughtered hanging upside down so the heart flushes out the blood with its final, panicked beats. But this heart had been at rest a few hours already, and the blood was sitting stagnant; if this process was going to be palatable it would be necessary to remove it. I slit the femoral and radial arteries, then brought the heart back to beating with CPR. A few beats in, blood belched against the porcelain. The shade which lapped the white canvas of the tub provoked me to gasp at the beauty. All I had ever read in that book of dreams came back to me, along with the Woman, whose spectral arms rested around my shoulders to assure me that I may have been changed, but I was not abandoned. Art had not abandoned me.

My skull aflame, I snatched two buckets from the gardening shed. I positioned Evangeline half-hanging over one porcelain edge, her hands in one bucket with the second jammed beneath cellulite thighs in the tub. As I pumped the heart, life swelled from her veins. Something came of every death, as it cast away the old to make room for life. Most fed worms, but some, perhaps, could be part of something greater; something that echoed through the universe and grasped me as its transmitter.

My neck was stiff by the time the veins were as empty as they would get. I transferred all the blood into one bucket, which I stored in the cellar freezer. Upstairs, I put on the most powerful and abrasive music I knew—a band named for a beautiful, hateful bird—then set back to work. And work it was! Dismembering a human's corpse was a greater challenge than a hog's, but the principles carried over. The knife became a chisel and the hammer's edge a mallet to first dislocate, then crush an exposed shoulder socket. The smell made me vomit more than once that first time, because this was different from animal death; it was something every human was made to react to. Still, on I labored, and by five-thirty in the morning what was once Evangeline had transformed into a toothless head, two arms with no fingertips, two legs, and a torso.

There was no time or frame of mind for a break. The cellar was crowded by the possessions of its old owner, furniture filling the three rooms like set pieces abandoned by a new director. In the back, I pushed aside a vanity and another dresser, and began to dig a grave. I had been awake twenty hours, which seemed longer than my lifespan to that point, and so much shorter at once, as if this time and space was removed from the perception of reality to produce its own endless instant of labor.

I did not stop until I was a solid three feet down. By then it was noon, and I had deposited the parts in the cellar freezer, because I realized now how much work it was, digging an arm's length-hole to a depth of six feet. Only at the halfway point did I rest, and then only for a few moments, my cheek pressed against the chilled brick wall. Round two was much shorter, only another hour and a half before I decided four feet was fine. Bodies were buried at six to surpass the frost line, so while the cellar was cold, there seemed little risk of a frost-and-thaw cycle to exhume the pieces prematurely. Besides, come spring, I would be doing all of this again. The ground was not entirely frozen, but it was a cold basement, and the dig was more challenging than anticipated. Excuses, excuses. Reasons for laziness. What a fool I was. But every artist is a primitive once; a toddler drooling upon the crayon clenched in his fist. And, in all artists, there are elements of luck and tenacity which drive development.

Head, then torso, then limbs, I dumped the remains of something which was once Evangeline into the hole. Each was self-contained in a saran wrap encasement with bleach sloshing beneath the plastic. (At seventeen I did not realize quicklime was a far more useful agent; nor did I have time to obtain it.) When, after three more hours of work and many breaks for cigarettes, the hole was filled and disguised to my liking, I pushed the vanity back into place, then the dresser.

My ascension to the main house seemed eternal. Upstairs, I washed and bleached the bathtub, the floor. I was on my hands and knees until my joints ached. I showered when it was all done, the water warm, and I stepped out confident, alive. Through the fog, I met the shadowed eyes of my reflection and found he was a new man. Always, he had been a Vasko: but now he understood just what that meant.

After a certain point, the momentum of exhaustion takes on an energy of its own, and sleep loses purpose. At the desk in my studio, I selected a pen, flipped to the essay page of my application, and wrote:

Art is real. Life ends. Relationships. But the voice of art is real, and speaks forever the same truths. I want to produce artwork that shocks, and arouses. Something that presents challenges to echo in the hearts of those who look upon it. Through my work, I will carve out my voice, and use it to thrive for eternity.

Then, I went to bed, and found none other than my mother. I crawled into her arms, and she awoke from her doze to say, "It is annoying and difficult to be Evangeline for six hours. I cannot imagine enduring it for a lifetime."

We slept entangled, and fifteen hours later awoke the same. We did not speak, though we kissed. I breathed her warm neck, and she kissed my forehead, and after a few moments of lingering there, we went about our days.

That afternoon, as Susan occupied herself with a monologue, I retrieved the frozen bucket and shut myself in the studio. I saw the painting, now, Orestes and Clytemnestra. Now its reverberations were significant, bright in my heart. The unprocessed blood would dry dark copper, I knew, but at the time I had neither knowledge nor means to process it into true paint. It was fine enough for me. I did what I could, first my pencil, then my brush flowing with grace. The painting revealed itself from a primordial source, and I worked for twelve hours with gouache paint and then the blood, sometimes mixing the two, then slept on my couch when exhaustion reclaimed me. Susan did not disturb me, and it was the same for seven days in which I left the studio only to eat or relieve myself. She understood my need for solitude and did not speak when our paths crossed. I was grateful.

The detectives came as I was finishing the painting, as Clytemnestra was wracked by death throes. I heard the knock on the front door. From my doorway, I heard Susan answer, her voice echoing through the foyer. "Good afternoon, gentlemen. Can I help you find someplace?"

"We're actually looking for someone, Mrs ..."

"Ms. Vasko. Well, Sinclair, but I am in the process of fixing that."

"Divorce?"

"Widow, I'm afraid."

"Sorry for your loss," consoled a second male voice, more tenor than baritone.

"It was one of the worst days of my life. What can I do for you fellows?"

"My name is Detective Jameson, this is my partner, Detective Rizk. Does a Richard Vasko stay here?"

"I should hope so. He is my son, after all."

Their pause was cutting as a gunshot. Detective Jameson was poised to do most of the talking, and ended the silence by asking, "You are his mother?"

"Of course."

"The information we have states that Evangeline McDonnell is his mother."

"Ah." As Susan spoke, a sorrowful note touched her voice. Even I was almost convinced. "I am afraid that, when I had Richard, I was unprepared to be a mother. I placed him up for adoption, but when I began to regret it, I sought him out. And it was a good thing I did."

"Yeah?"

"Oh, yes. Evangeline was appalling. Negligent, I might say. She left him so often to his own devices while pursuing lovers, the poor boy. When I found him he was so lonely. Struggling for attention, acting out. We got to know each other and decided the best course of action was for him to be where he belongs."

"We heard he was staying with a girlfriend." Rizk, now. I imagined a short, bald, Arab man, and was soon to find out I was right.

"Detective," cooed Susan, "if you loved your mother but still couldn't get along with her, would you really want to tell her that you preferred another mother to her?"

"I suppose not."

"Why don't you two come in from the cold? Though, I would like to make it clear that if you do not have a warrant, you do not have my permission to open or search anything."

"No, ma'am, we're not here with a warrant. We were just hoping to ask Richard a few questions."

"Regarding?"

"Regarding his ... adopted mother's disappearance. Is he at home?"

"My God, how terrible. Would you follow me? I believe he's working upstairs."

At those words, I shut my studio door and stowed away the bucket, stained as it was. Then I resumed my work, the canvas facing away from the door. The knock came seconds later. The door opened and behind it stood Susan, and behind Susan stood a pair of men, one tall with blond hair and hard Slavic features despite his Irish name, and the other, yes, a balding Arab. They both peered at me as I stepped from behind the canvas. "Sweetheart," said Susan, "these men are detectives. I'm sorry to say something may have happened to Evangeline."

"We don't know that yet," said the blond. "We're just trying to get a clear picture of what's going on."

"What's happened?" I furrowed my brow while Susan ushered the men in, observing me with stony approval.

Wetting his lips, Jameson delicately began. "Son, when was the last time you spoke to Evangeline?"

"She called me a week ago—um, Christmas Eve, actually. I went over that night and we had a talk, but it wasn't very productive. I was just too tired to deal with her, I went home after maybe an hour."

"What did you talk about?"

My expression tightened, my focus shifting to the window. "She called to tell me she was leaving, since I didn't need her anymore."

The detectives exchanged glances. "Did she say where she was going?"

"Ah, Richmond, I think. I asked her why not, you know, Roanoke, because that's where our—her relatives live. She said she wanted to be alone."

"Wouldn't she tell her boyfriend, or put in notice at her job?"

"I don't know how many times my mother quit a job without giving notice. She's an irrational victim of her irrational whims. I don't know what she was thinking. Maybe it's a cry for attention. Whatever it is, it's the kind of thing I'm sick of. I hope she's happy, but I can't have a relationship with her right now."

Detective Rizk inclined his chin. "Chet told us it wasn't great to begin with. What made you move out?"

"When I found out she was lying to me about my adoption. It took Susan introducing herself for Evangeline to tell me the truth. She was too selfish to do it before."

Every word emerged while I stared one detective or the other in the eyes. Most of it was true, after all. They shared a nod, then focused again on me.

Rizk again. "I'm sure Evangeline is all right. We just need to pursue every possibility."

"Sure. Will you follow up with me if you confirm anything?"

"You bet," said Jameson. "We appreciate your cooperation, Richard. What are you working on over there?"

"It's a surprise for mom." I nodded to Susan, whose feline smile was a ghost upon her lips as she watched my performance from the wall. "I'd offer to show you, but it's not done."

With a congenial smile, the blond lifted his hands. "Hey, I understand. Can't bother an artist at work." And then he turned a gracious, hungry smile upon Susan, and I imagined putting my paintbrush through his eye. But, soon enough, she had led them from my sight, and as the car pulled away I felt a surge of victorious relief. Another knock came soon, and as Susan took my invitation, she chuckled. "That was very good, Dick. You're a natural."

"It hardly felt like lying at all." We shared a grin. Then, setting down my brush, I asked, "Would you like to see it?"

Her expression brightened. "It's finished?"

"As it'll ever be."

She shut her eyes, and I turned the easel to face her. Hands on her shoulders, I guided her just before the painting. As I released, she opened her eyes, and gasped in a manner close to a sigh of bliss.

"Oh, Dick."

Clytemnestra's expression resembled an orgasm, eyes rolled back beneath drooping lids while her parted mouth searched for air. The figure bore complete likeness to Susan, though I do not doubt what my subconscious caught of Evangeline's demise was represented, for her purpling face mixed its own color upon my palette, just as the face of Orestes built itself when I stopped denying that the character I painted was a facet of his artist. The columns of his arms emerged from beneath his mother's delicate jaw, led to powerful shoulders below an expression whose clenched teeth summoned at once his intense loathing and deep pleasure.

"This is so very intimate."

My hand rested upon the base of her neck, fingertips twitching beneath her sweater to drink the warmth of her flesh. She took my free hand. After a moment of silent examination, she said, "Isn't it funny. Her hair has the color of dried blood."

"Seven or eight washes of it."

She did not even turn to look at me. Instead, she nodded—slow and even bobs of her head. "The composition is so dynamic, the figures so alive. Darling, this is sublime. May I keep it?"

"It's yours."

Only now did she turn her smile upon me. "I'll cherish it. Wouldn't you like a drink? We haven't spoken in some time."

"I haven't felt like speaking."

"And now?"

My gaze stayed level with hers, somehow. "I could use a drink if I'm going to."

Susan led the way to her room, and though she turned her back I knew she watched my every move through the reflection of her vanity. "How do you feel?"

"Good. I don't think they'll be back. There's so much meth in town that Marion cops have plenty to deal with as it is."

"I don't think they will either, once they do a bit more research." She pressed my first drink in a week into my hand. "I have thought about a great many things this week, Dick."

"So have I."

"I am concerned that, if I stay, we both risk premature death. Now, whether that death be private murder or public execution is a different matter, but we are intelligent enough to know where this will end." Though her words were solemn, there was a twinkle of humor in her eye, as if she were playing a game. "Do you know why that is?"

"No."

"Because we are this much in love, my darling." She took a pull of her drink and so did I. As she lowered the glass, she said, "What a petty word it seems when I say it—'Love'. People use it for everything. When I was your age, an apartment complex I lived in sent fliers to the tenants on Valentine's Day: 'We love our residents.' What does that even mean? It's a concept so important, but people use it so often it means nothing. It cannot begin to contain the way I feel about you. You told me you loved me once—do you, still? Is that the word you would choose?"

"No." I nursed my vodka tonic and licked my lips free of the bitter taste. The more I thought about it, the less I had to say. "I don't think there's a word I could choose, now. Nothing works."

"It doesn't, does it? You know, the reason I came back to you was to have more to extort Julius with, but instead I found this. You. You may resemble your father, but you are your mother's son."

Her throat hypnotized me by its constriction. I drank instead of kissing it, because I had no way of knowing what was acting and what was real. The booze was real.

"I am sad to say all of this to you, darling, but I do not think we are ready for each other. This is too much for us. Neither of us have lived enough yet." My glass was empty, now. "I don't care. I want you."

"I know, darling. You're too young to care. You want to challenge death, tiptoe into it like a child playing in a stream. That's fine. Natural. But we both have too much to live for yet. It would be true tragedy were the world to lose us early."

Brain hot and cold at once, I examined the ridges of the glass. "So you're leaving me again."

"I must, for your sake and mine—for the same reason I left the first time. But self-preservation is not my only reason. I care too much to see you throw everything away."

"How can you do this?"

"Asked the murderer. I won't be gone forever, Dick. It may seem a long time—it may be a long time—but I will be back. And we will both have grown, then, and will understand what it means for the two of us to be together."

As I shot from my seat, every drop of blood rocketed into my skull. Dizzy, I fell back on the edge of the bed, and the sound of Susan's glass being set aside echoed that of my own when it dropped to the floor. "What did you give me?"

"Something to ensure you wouldn't do anything rash." Those fingers combed my hair as their owner blurred in and out of focus. Was that glint in her fuzzy eye a trick of my drugged mind? "It hurts me to do this, though you might not believe it. I'll miss you." Her mouth strained.

"Where are you going?" The words were malformed, and perhaps it was the drugs, but my own eyes brimmed. "You can't leave me. Don't leave me."

The last time I would hear my mother's voice for twenty-two years was as she cooed, "I'm not, not forever. We'll see each other again. Just sleep for now, my darling. You won't even know I'm gone."

And for seven hours or so, she was right.

Chapter

12

Consciousness unveiled a half-empty closet, a missing car, and Clytemnestra absconded along with her model. After wandering the skeleton in which I found myself enclosed, unsure whether I was awake or asleep, I returned to the dead temple of a dead goddess and discovered upon the nightstand a letter to which fresh panic had blinded me:

My Darling Richard,
Beware. Compassion brings sentimentality. I am moved to see you sleep, as it will be the last time for a longer time than I can say. My return will be by no means swift, and while you await me I anticipate you will nurse resentment as much as passion. And I will nurse the warmth that wracks me as I watch you breathe, and congratulate myself for giving you up instead of putting you down.
There is money enough on the kitchen counter for two or three substantial grocery trips. Spend it on drugs at your own peril. Send me your acceptance letter when it arrives. In the post-script, I have included a PO Box at which you may also contact me should you face a true emergency (e.g., the sustained interest of certain detectives, hospitalization for cancer stage III or later, emergence of schizophrenia). I will retain ownership of the house, but you are responsible for its upkeep.
Do not doubt my return. Death could not keep me from you, even if it came. Someday I will arrive again, and you may have all but forgotten me (as though you ever could), but I will come all the same with the force of Heaven's bull. And I cannot wait to see what man I find awaiting me.
Your Loving Mother,
Susan Augusta Vasko née Sinclair

The address was in New York. I lowered the letter. From my studio, I retrieved the bucket that once contained Evangeline's blood but now held a foul jelly. I cleaned it out, returned it to its home. I did not look at the stack of bills on the counter. Instead I selected the whiskey with the highest alcohol content and sat in a silent living room that smelled like her. All of her favorite books were gone from the sitting room. It was too depressing there. Outside, a storm blazed, as if Nature was discouraging the idea of hunting her down. The living room was cold, and I was cold, and the whiskey was warm and the television was loud.

Over the next two weeks I did not paint, or draw. Instead I constructed something of a nest for myself upon the couch where I slept and drank, littered with blankets and the few VHS films Susan bothered to own (cheerful fare like Lynch's *Eraserhead*, for instance), along with some books she had left behind. Bottles were always in easy reach, and it became my mission to dry the house once I blew through the drugs she'd left behind, mostly weed and cocaine, but also half a bottle of Valium, which was nice. Properly drunk and stoned, I'd wander into the woods behind the house, crunching through snow and over roots in hardly more than an overcoat and pajamas, half-hoping I'd freeze to death, not at all sure what I wandered for. The forest was an intricate skeleton, barren of even animals. My feet sank an inch or more each step, my pants often catching on barbs and sticks I failed to notice until too late. One afternoon, I discovered the crest of a rocky bank, the stream half-frozen and all mud. When I reached it, I started crying for some reason, and couldn't remember why I'd even thought to leave the house, and returned to my den to huddle amid my bottles.

What was I going to do now? I'd have to get a job, eventually. Live like a real person. What kind of miserable idea was that? How would I have time to paint? The idea was so revolting—here I was with all the time in the world, and already I couldn't create.

As she said: the sting indicated truth. Knowing myself as I do now, I would have killed her if she had stayed, and I was already lucky enough to get away with one murder. But would I have been wholly to blame had I killed her before she left? You're gifted with empathy, aren't you? Are you using it?

Back then, I didn't believe I'd have killed her. I just wanted to have her. All I wanted was Susan, my mother, and she had turned away from me. So I stayed drunk as long as I could until Detective Jameson knocked on the door.

All perpetrators of criminal and civil misdeeds know too well the sobering effect an unexpected knock can have on a man. As it was two o'clock and I had been awake a mere hour, I had not made much progress toward drunkenness; so when I opened the door to find the detective peering from behind his Sunday-afternoon smile, I was in quick control of my faculties.

"Richard, good to see you again. Is your mother home? I didn't see her car."

"She's running some errands in Columbus. I hate going shopping. Did you need to see her?"

He disguised his disappointment rather well, all told. "I'm here for you, anyways. May I come in?"

I stepped aside, my body between him and the nest of blankets and bottles hidden, blessedly, by the angle of the couch in the living room. What would Susan do? "Can I make you coffee?"

"It's all right, I won't be here long. I just wanted to let you know that we're closing the investigation."

My posture snapped straighter. "You found her?"

"We have sufficient evidence to conclude Evangeline is alive, we just don't know where. A woman of her description was seen taking a Greyhound to Richmond, Virginia on Christmas Morning." He shook his head. "What a day to pick."

"I'm just glad to hear she was seen." The exhalation of relief was genuine, though misappropriated. "You had me worried, Detective."

He smiled. "If you want to track her down, I'd suggest a private detective. As much as I'd like to help, we have enough to do without worrying about a woman who doesn't want to be found. Besides, you have your birth mom."

As I nodded, he put his hand on my shoulder. The touch of a human being was razorblades raking under my skin. "You'll be fine. Oh, and I have something for you." From his pocket, he withdrew a trio of letters, each opened, each addressed to me in familiar handwriting. "Sorry we had to open them, but my boss insisted we get a warrant to investigate you. But all we found were some glowing recommendations, and that burglary charge." He tilted the letters away from me. "Keeping out of trouble?"

I extended my hand. "I'm thinking these days it was a cry for attention, just as much as Evangeline's."

He nodded, then handed over the letters. "Good kid. Your mom taking care of the guardianship issue?"

"We're in the middle of it now."

"The red tape." He grinned. "All right, well, stay safe. Don't let me see you around too much, you understand?"

"I understand."

I watched him go, and my lungs expanded free and deep into my body. Standing in the hall, I read each letter in turn; each, as the detective said, glowing. They reminded me that I still had some direction. The Woman stirred in the back of my mind, then, and unfurled herself across my imagination as if to prod me into action.

For the first time since Susan vanished, I braved her bedroom to change into fresh clothes, and left the house. Treacherous snow was little challenge and it felt good to be in town, to see people living and breathing, cars driving, streetlights changing. In the library I made duplicates of my recommendation letters and filled out an additional application, this time to the Chicago Art

Institute. Three days later I had them all turned in, and five weeks later I had acceptances and moderate scholarships to both. I chose Chicago, told myself I was doing so for the name and not for its proximity to anyone I might know, and resentfully mailed my acceptance to the PO Box.

In April, there arrived a check with five zeroes. For a time I fantasized about traveling abroad with it, but my schooling was of no small import, and a path felt good. Freedom would come with better work. Pride, with time. I tried to assure myself that I was doing all of this for me, but even then, I did not wholly believe it.

A summer passed. I worked little, ate little, and left the house only to move Evangeline's body in the dead of night, the stench vile for even the moments I hauled the pieces from basement to back yard. At the end of August, ready to end my solitude, I packed my car with supplies, my books and some clothes, and left for Chicago.

As a boy, my antagonistic attitude towards my peers led to swift and justified ostracization. Now, far from home, I grasped my opportunity to forge a new identity. Susan's lessons in acting did not go to waste. I used my imagination, observed those around me, and pretended very well that I was a pleasant, outgoing young man just like a thousand other pleasant, outgoing men. Had you been my fellow student, or even if we had crossed paths on the street, you might have admired the way I laughed with my friends, or observed with approval my return of a clumsy stranger's unmolested wallet. All of this was a caricature of the people around me. Inside festered the same poison as always, which manifested in my fantasies, my work, and my relationship with Julius.

It was October of 1993 when I next sat in his office. Though he smiled, and greeted me with warm embrace, he was swift to retreat behind his desk as if sensing that my perception of him had altered since our first meeting. "I'm glad you're here. I hadn't heard anything, I was starting to get worried."

"I haven't been talking to anybody."

"Is that why you came to me?"

I managed a grin. "I'd think that, as both a psychiatrist and my father, you're qualified to offer advice."

"To other people, maybe. But this is such an unusual circumstance. I'm afraid you might not think my advice carries much weight."

"Your being a rapist doesn't impact your ability to give objective advice to others. It just means that advice needs to be taken with a grain of salt."

Julius bowed his head over the pen he fondled. "I suppose that's the least that could be said of me. Have you heard from your birth mother recently?"

"No."

"Should I be sorry to hear that?"

"Probably not."

He nodded, gaze fixed on his calendar. I stole weary glances into the silver-framed past, as a lucky dog licked crumbs of cake from my mother's tawny fingertips, her half-sisters, half-cousins oblivious to the saccharine scene. When I managed to look away, I blurted, "I'm going to school here. Studying art."

"Are you? Good."

"It feels strange." I considered how liberating it had been to have all the time and encouragement to do as I pleased. Though enforced projects could occasionally engage me on a level my own works could not, more often they were pulled from me as bothersome teeth. I had neither time nor energy to work as I pleased, and did not know how I would please if I did. I squinted. "All that I'm doing now feels empty. I'm just doing it because it's all I think I can do."

"Sometimes we have to pick a direction and start walking. Life never has prearranged plans for us. The best option is to find the scent of what you want, and follow it until you discover what it really is."

"What do you want, Julius?"

"To be a good person." This was not a rehearsed statement, but a question to which he had an eager and spirited answer.

"Do you think you are?"

He exhaled, long and slow. "I've made mistakes."

"I'll say."

His gaze flickered toward me, then back to the wiggling pen. "Sometimes, after a day here, I wonder if there's such a thing as a good person. Everybody's terrible to somebody else."

"I used to think Evangeline was terrible. Then, I met Susan."

"I used to think I was a good person before I knew her. She turned me into an animal."

"You can't blame her for being victimized, especially not since she was a little girl."

Face drawn, Julius looked over his shoulder, to the window. "I don't deny I scarred her. I did. But you have to understand that your mother is something else. I don't say what I say to poison you against her, but because you deserve to know the whole truth."

"She poisoned me, herself."

"Her father, Richard Harrison—she named you after him. He used to be a good man, but when Augusta died, he couldn't handle it because he knew he would never have anything like her again. He drank, and he took it out on Susie. Because she was in a violent home, she exhibited violent behaviors. Aggression, killing animals. Killing people, or, at least, killing one person and plotting to kill others."

Julius rocked back in his chair, away from the desk and toward the window. "I demonize her in an attempt to self-justify. She was a lost little girl, but sometimes I feel she could have been born a princess and become Jezebel."

It was like hearing a story from my true crime books; better because I'd lived it. "Why did you do what you did?"

"I loved Augusta." His eyes were wet, and he inhaled sharply, smiling. "She was my fraternal twin. It didn't matter. She loved me, and I loved her. Your grandmother was a wonderful woman. I've never met a person so warm, and kind. But when we couldn't be together, she married a laborer to spite our family."

"And she killed herself."

"Yes." He regarded the space somewhere past his knees, hands folded against his ribs. "We couldn't be together, and after she gave birth to Susan, she felt very alone. I tried to take care of Susie whenever I could after that." His hand rested upon the left side of his face. "She was a ray of sunshine, that girl. Whenever she came over she'd tell me she wished she could stay with us forever. That she wished I was her daddy."

"Were you?"

"There are certain possibilities I don't enjoy entertaining."

I laughed, because that was all I knew to do, and sat up to examine the bookshelves on the opposite side of the room from Julius. "Has anybody ever told you that you're a coward?"

"Your mother said that when I saw her in February."

My face spiked with heat. I whipped around, one hand upon the shelf behind me. "How was she when you saw her?"

"Worried about her?"

My fingers curled into fists as I leaned against the bookshelves. "That's not the word. Interested, maybe."

"What did she do?"

I grinned, glancing to the door. "Doctor-patient confidentiality, right?"

"I'd hope you'd trust me because I'm your father."

"But as far as the rest of the world is concerned, I'm your patient."

"Yes."

"I just like a firm understanding of my rights."

And so I told him everything, even about Evangeline. I told him because he had to sit there and listen. The expressions on his face trailed from sympathy, to horror, to grief. He wept into his hands as I finished, and his pain was satisfying.

"I'm so sorry, Richard. I'm sorry she put you through all that. I'm so sorry about Evangeline."

"It was a shame." I meant it, in a way. At least if I had Evangeline I'd have a soft place to fall.

"It was more than a shame, it was a tragedy." He looked up, his eyes narrowing at me, faintly. "But I suppose I can't ask Susan's child to feel too broken up about something like that."

"I suppose not. But don't forget, I'm your child, too. And she might be. My God." Now, I laughed. "You're my father, my great-uncle, and potentially my grandfather. More of a family stump, isn't it?"

"I'm glad you find it funny."

"How else am I supposed to find it?" The humor fell from my face. "My whole life has changed."

"It doesn't have to. Your parents don't make you who you are."

"No, but your reactions to your experiences do. People operate in patterns. Families operate in patterns."

"Look." He faced me full-on, now, his hands spread. "Just because you are your mother's son, does not mean you have to be your mother's son. You don't have to be my son. Do you know how lucky you are to be raised outside of the Vasko family?"

"Very lucky, considering how good Susan is in bed."

Julius' expression was one I had difficulty reading, some bizarre amalgamation of disgust and jealousy, and, perhaps, disgust at his own jealousy. "You're starting to concern me."

"Well, you're my therapist. I'm supposed to be honest with you, aren't I?"

"Is that all I am?"

"So far. And so far my psychiatrist is just as damaged as me." I looked around. "Can I smoke in here?"

"By the window," he said in grudging tone as he scooted back to his desk. While I withdrew the pack, he said, "You shouldn't, you know."

"I shouldn't do a lot of things. Do you know why you're just my psychiatrist, Julius?"

"Why?"

"Because I can't very well expect to meet my family, can I?"

He shrank an inch while I shoved the window open. "That's a lot to ask, Richard."

"My point exactly."

"You don't understand. I have so much at stake. This career I've built, my entire family. They barely talk to me, anyways."

"I can't imagine why. Did you molest my sisters, too?"

That wounded him. I could see it in his face. "I would never touch them. I would never think of it."

"So you're a situational pedophile."

79

"No. I'm not attracted to children. It was Augusta, and Susan. She looked so much like Augusta, but she didn't have a heart. She terrorized my girls when she lived with us, and I never believed them. I thought they were jealous of their cousin. Only when she left did I learn that she even burned Vera on the stovetop, and my own daughter didn't tell me what happened because she didn't think I'd care." The tears were welling back, now, and he vanquished them with fingertips pressed to the corners of his eyes. "I love them. I want to make amends with them, and I could never do that if they knew the truth of what I did. If Bernadette knew the truth."

"Don't you think they deserve to? Don't you think I deserve to meet them?"

"What good would it do you? It would only upset you more. It would rub your face in the family you can't have."

I shook my head, examining my shoes and trying, for now, to tuck away my fury. "For someone who cares so much about being a good person, you have a vested self-interest."

"That's what it means to be human."

I snorted, withdrawing into the room and slamming the pane behind me. "You know the worst part of all this? I'm not sure I'm angry at her. I'm astonished. She wove a tapestry. Something requiring a degree of skill, a sense of aesthetics. I'm not sure I will ever know another person like her. Do you think I'll love anyone else?"

"You'll grow out of asking yourself those questions, feeling like that."

"Have you?"

My father smiled, the expression of a beaten man, and said nothing as the wall clock rang the hour with the sound of wind chimes.

Some time passed before our next meeting, because the most recent one did not sit well with me. In private, I fostered my indignation. A child molester did not think me worthy of the family I deserved. To name him my enemy in light of all he'd done (and hadn't done) felt cathartic. The shame was not mine to bear, but his, and I did not deserve to be punished for it. But he did; this man who did not care what I was doing so long as I stayed away from my own family.

One evening, after class, I found myself parked across the street from his office. I waited. I told myself I was just curious, that I would drive away, but I knew this was a lie. I didn't have much time to question it, because soon enough, here came Julius, climbing into his Benz at seven-thirty to crawl home in the dark. I hung back a block or two, and though I thought he'd lost me more than once, soon I sat across the street from the Vasko residence. The well-lit house was large as one might expect, and well-furnished from what I could glimpse without getting up close, similar to the equally large, semi-distant houses sprawled upon wide lawns. I remembered all the times Evangeline had confided in me our money woes.

At ten after eight, the living room light flickered off. An hour later, at nine, one of two upstairs lights. In the still-illuminated upstairs window I saw bookshelves and took this to be his study. Working, even at home. Not a warm relationship, Julius and Bernadette.

The light was on until ten-thirty. Then, the house was quiet. I returned to my dormitory and did it again the next night, and again, neglecting my classwork and social responsibilities. I was hyper-focused on my prey: Julius, and the family that should have been mine. Two weeks in, I hit the place, and the lock was good but worth no more than a minute of work. The quality of their door made sense when I took stock of the lavish contents, and I realized then that Susan's tastes were not a widow's *nouveau riche* absorption of her late husband's, but rather a lifetime cultivation. Photos of family were oddly few. I did find upon the mantel a few photographs of the girls when they were young and in school. Blushing Ada, boyish Vera, and a vibrant nymphet with a shark's smile. I turned away as soon as her face registered, my chest aching with loneliness.

Their fridge was trim, unsullied by so much as a drop of liquor. I took a few bites of leftover lo mein, then made my way upstairs with camera at the ready. By two, it seemed they were both asleep, and quite heavily judging by the snoring. Indeed, I got four shots before Bernadette stirred in her sleep to turn her attractive-if-severe face away and hide it with a head of graying blonde. The fourth included Julius, old and gape-mouthed and helpless in sleep.

No outside help was needed to develop, as there was a large lab we were welcomed to use for class. As far as anyone knew, I was working on a project—and, of course, I was.

After scheduling an appointment with the good doctor, I sealed the photos in an envelope with no return address and mailed them to his office. I was not clear on my aim in doing this; I suppose resentment inspired me to show him that I did not need his permission to be around his family. Nothing constructive could come through my actions, but I confess I have never been good at seeing consequences as more than abstractions in the face of a bit of sport.

Though there was no clear advantage to be gained, my spirits were lifted to be the conductor of such a thing as this. In fact, when the day came for my appointment, more than one classmate saw fit to comment on my sunshine disposition. I informed them that it was a surge of inspiration. The truth, enough.

In the office, Julius was at his desk, hands folded with his pen between his woven fingers. He got right to it the moment I closed the door. "Someone broke into my house."

The amount of effort required to maintain an expression of shock was Herculean. "My God, is everyone okay? When did this happen?"

"I don't know. Recently."

"What did they take?"

"Pictures."

I scoffed. "Why would anybody steal some photographs?"

"I mean they snapped photographs." Julius regarded me from beneath heavy lids as if enduring a child's unfunny joke. He jerked open his desk drawer and withdrew a quartet of familiar photos, which he dropped upon his calendar. "Awfully artistic work."

I rose to examine them. "That wouldn't be my foremost concern, if I were you."

"Did you break into my house and take these pictures of my wife?"

"I don't know how you got that idea."

"Cut the bullshit."

"Why would I do a thing like that?"

"Who knows why someone like you does anything?"

I touched my chest, brows lifting in mock offense. "Like me?"

"Yes, like you. Like your mother. What are you doing this for, huh? Do you want money?"

Snorting, I straightened, my hands sliding into the pockets of my slacks. "You would rather garnish your salary than introduce me to your family."

"Absolutely, you little animal."

Heat rushed up the back of my neck and into the base of my scalp. "You're as guilty of shutting me out of your family as I am of any crime. These pictures could have been taken by anyone, but you pin it on me because you want an excuse to keep me away."

"Then maybe you should stop giving me excuses."

What would Susan do? I stood, my muscles tense, my mind hot. There were fleeting fantasies of murder which I did not seriously entertain. "Fine. Nine hundred a month."

The blaze in Julius' eyes began to die. "I knew it would be this way," he said, his words dense. "As soon as I saw you, I felt something terrible in the air. I've done awful things, you know. But nobody, not even me, deserves to deal with people like you or your mother. At least I try to make up for the things I've done. Here I am holding evidence of what you've done, and you can't acknowledge it."

"I can acknowledge everything I've done. That I was a child troubled by my father's absence, that I was changed by my mother."

"But do you think that change is for the better, or the worse?"

I grinned at the tea party. "I think it would be fair to categorize her effect as positive overall. She has had tremendous influence on my sense of direction."

"So, what—you're a helpless victim, with no accountability in your behavior because you've suffered?"

"Of course not. My accountability is my signature." Hands braced on the desk, I leaned forward as he drew further into his chair. "I am a force of nature. Just like my mother, and just like you. Nature's accountability is to itself. It acts with no sense of justice, or fairness. Only of itself, and what it must do. You know," I straightened, "you can't hold me responsible for my alleged crimes until you can hold yourself responsible for yours."

"Of course I admit responsibility for my mistakes. One of them is standing in my office right now."

Somehow, his words brought a flash of heat like I hadn't felt since Evangeline's death. Glad for the desk between us, I stepped back and exhaled. "I'm not a mistake. I'm exactly the son you deserve." When no retort came, I crossed my arms and repeated my demand: "Nine hundred a month for eighteen years."

"Five hundred."

"Nine."

His nostrils flared. "Five-fifty."

"Seven hundred, and I won't darken your office again."

"Fine. Let's put this deal into immediate effect."

"Fine by me. You have my address." Trembling, I stormed through his office and into my car, where I sat for ten cold minutes in the Chicago dark, because he would only see me at the end of the day. Breath billowing before me, I returned to school and started the process of getting drunk. This bender lasted only three days, but after I sobered I remained locked in the double room of which I was the only inhabitant; a stroke of fortune brought by an absentee foreign roommate and my failure to mention the situation to administrators. There I was alone but for the Woman, who kept me company into the late hours while I drew brushes aimlessly across the page for projects I did not intend to finish, about things that did not inspire me.

So, I stopped doing it. I stopped seeing my friends, I stopped painting, I stopped going to class. I had an empty dormitory, an empty house, and a figment of my imagination. What was I going to do from here? Surely no man could see his future, but I felt blinder than most, and my talent was not enough to prevent my faith in my artistic abilities from shriveling.

For weeks, I left only to shower, or scavenge for food. My classmates did not bother checking to see if I was still alive. The stipend began arriving and I was supported through the end of the term, at which point, tired of coping with this shaggy dog joke, I packed my things and returned to the place I wished was still my home, tall and empty in the countryside of Ohio.

Chapter

13

After attending to the matters of the water and electricity, my first order of business was to call the Patrokolis brothers.

"Jesus, Vasko," said Gavin, shoving past me into the empty foyer, "who'd you kill to get someplace this swank?"

"Some old lady," I said, and Mark laughed.

"Your girlfriend, huh?"

"Something like that. Anyway, she's gone. So this is my house until she's back."

"No shit," said Gavin, weaving into the living room. He ran a hand over one dusty end table, then, from the sitting room, shouted, "Jesus Christ! These books are just for show, right?"

I laughed, but as Mark and I joined him, I realized from his face that he was serious. I may not have seen them in a while, but had it been that long? Had they always been like this? "No, they're not for show," I admonished. "These are—she read them, but there were far more she took with her. I have books too, you know."

"Yeah, but I mean—that's a lot of books."

"A lot of stuff," corrected Mark, blowing dust from a 1992 Gustav Klimt calendar still on the wall. "You thought about selling this furniture?"

"Of course not. It's hers." I scoffed. "She'll be back."

As Gavin rifled through a drawer, his brother, the eldest of our trio, sighed. "Rick, I hate to break it to you, but a lady with this kind of money? The kind of money to up and leave a place like this? She's not coming back. There are billions of men on this planet and she can have any one of them. Why you?"

"Because she's—"

I stopped myself and looked at the mahogany box which once held her drugs. "She'll be back for me."

In the corner of my eye, the boys exchanged a piteous glance. "Look, man," said Mark at last, "at least don't let this place go to waste. Have a party!"

"We could fit half the town in here." On instinct, maybe, Gavin slid open the drawer of an end table which contained my letter from Susan, and my one photograph of her, nine months before she had me. I slapped his hand and slammed it shut. Had they always been like this? Invasive, ready to defile a space sacred as this one?

Then I realized—my God, of course they were. They were burglars. But that didn't change the nature of the space they now defiled.

I had never met these people in my life. She was right. There were no people but us. But I had no one else to go to, so I nodded and said, "Sure, a small party, I guess."

The most appalling thing about the first few years on my own is that I should have listened to my mother. She warned me away from drugs and the brothers, so I embraced both and much else besides. At first, I was keen to play out games of seduction as she had with me, but found that not many girls in town were interested in the thrill of the hunt and chase; at least, none that I found. Bear in mind I did not have a large pool to pick from, for even those who were not teen mothers were looking to have a child, or were addicted to hard drugs, or had dropped out of high school at fourteen, or were hardcore Christian conservatives. I also awoke in Susan's skeleton every day, and our reputations began to precede us in the town. I soon itched to leave for good.

So, I took the tattered remnants of the tuition check, (by winter 1994 down to the high end of four zeroes) and moved into a Columbus apartment on First Avenue which many years later became a short-lived gallery. (I managed to get one show in it before it closed its doors, just before everything happened with Delilah and Susan and I.) Then it was full of cockroaches, with a basement that could have belonged to Dennis Nilsen.

There, I found solitude and freedom. I got to know myself. I painted long into the night. I spent much on drugs but more on paint and rent. I even got a job to support my habits and 'blow the stink off of me,' as Evangeline sometimes said. But there, alone in the city, I did not know what I could do. I knew no one, and did not want to know anyone. More school seemed a waste of money. Other people seemed a waste of time. She had given me a taste of ambrosia and snatched it away. Then, I was bitter. Now, I understand she was motivating me. Because I did not keep friends, or want to, and because I did not engage in casual sex, or want to, I filled the aloneness with not just painting and labor, but also daydreams and literature on subjects that interested me. All of it fueled my fantasy relationship with the Woman, and, of course, my work. There were hard times; long periods when effort felt worthless. But the highs were good, and better than drugs. And, left alone, my fantasies were vivid as waking life.

The problem with powerful imagination, though, is the law of diminishing kicks. Soon a goddess demanding human sacrifice, a fascist officer torturing a beautiful spy—these cartoonish scenarios to be painted and entertained in idle moments weren't enough. The fantasies simply became too dark, and too realistic, and too thorough, and when the redhead sacrifices inspired by women on the street weren't enough for my appetite, it always came down to slaying the Woman. Her death (never less than gorgeous) completed the cycle of a doomed goddess: a sacrifice to herself, and to me. Because, in the end, the Woman was always a part of me.

Soon even these fantasies' excitements were diminished, and I was left on my own, bored, in a dry spell with a blank canvas. I could not reasonably expect reality to be better than my fantasies, so it almost seemed there was no point in carrying on healthy relationships. I receded, and regressed, and broke into another house, and because I was caught with a deadly weapon (a knife in my pocket, just for self-defense), I got five years.

What may I say about prison that has not been said better elsewhere? It was a speed-bump in my life. The government put me in the corner to think about what I'd done. So, I thought. I thought about what I had done wrong, and how I might do it better if it happened again. I would not get ahead of myself, for one (I had cased the home for only a week before breaking in). And I would not go to the home of someone from work. (Did that detail slip my mind? No matter—she was new, a beautiful brunette from Delaware, and I only wanted to see how she looked asleep.)

That was the reason Evangeline was such a problem when she died. I was her relation, I knew her, so it was my door they came knocking on. You can do anything as long as you don't get caught, so if nobody can identify you, why show restraint?

Prison helped my lying, too, and my charm. A particular guard read to me (and others) as a closet homosexual. With guards risking a sexual assault charge, the most that happened was a little flirting for a few cigarettes, but it was a valuable trade and welcome practice. The other inmates did not trouble me for the most part, although I have always had a tendency to run my mouth and earn a black eye for it, and this was true in prison as it had been in school. The library was sad and under-funded, so I drew. I sent letters to Mark and Gavin, and to Julius. One foolish day I sent one to the PO Box, and six weeks later a postcard arrived from Kyoto with the words, *Thinking of you* written on the back. This, I threw away.

The Woman was fine company, then. Prison was not all different from where I had been before, in my apartment. The cockroaches were louder. The food was worse. The sky was still gray. I was alone and would be alone when I was free. That came at two years, early for good behavior and reha-bilitation as demonstrated by my artwork, which at the time was primarily biblical: the Crucifixion of St. Peter wowed the parole board, themselves Evangeline's brand of guilty Catholic.

Upon release, I wrote to Julius, who resumed my stipend so long as I never contacted him again, which I agreed to conditionally. Of course, I was not able to inform him of my conditions, as he had asked me not to write. On the street, I found an apartment and another job, now in a mortuary office as a paper-pushing clerk thanks to the owner's beneficent heart, and in 1999, I resumed my schooling at CCAD. Now, after learning from the mistakes of my fellow prisoners, I studied people on a level deeper than the surface. I wanted to know what made me different from others down to the smallest traits, and to learn how to hide these elements of myself. I wanted to see how different events made normal humans react, what they looked like when they reacted and what the long-term ramifications might be. I read books intended to educate on body language, psychopathology, relationship building, and trauma. Educate they did.

I am by no means an actor, but I am my mother's son, and the artistic temperament lends itself well to all manner of creativity. This time, I stayed in school, and both made and kept friends. Here and there I kept girlfriends a little younger than me, who were only sexually exploratory to a point and (Are you bored yet? I hope so. I was bored of the whole joke. You might be so bored that you almost miss Susan. I did. Even you, formless, you're half-comprehending while you wait, as I did, for something to happen without a true sense of what 'something' might be. Some great tremor in the universe, perhaps, to signal a new turn of life. A woman, walking into a butcher's shop.) unwilling to be choked, which was a pity with the redhead because she had a lovely neck. I tried heroin, too, but as I grew older, my drug use cycled to what it had been at the start: alcohol and marijuana. I went to all the clubs and parties and knew all the people because one got places by knowing people. For two years I was back in Chicago pursuing the short MA program there. Away from Ohio, my work blossomed, the sum of tens of thousands of hours spent with a pencil or brush in my hand finally beginning to manifest. During the same period I became celibate because neither women nor men excited me, and I was left with the Woman if I wanted to avoid incarceration for indulging my appetites to their fullest extent. After six years of growth it would come at high cost to throw my life away, and so I sublimated my urges into fantasy and the newfound voice of my work.

All these elements combined to cultivate an air of some mystery when in 2005 I reunited with those CCAD students trying to make a name for themselves in the Columbus art scene. While I began my career as a restorationist, I also began contributing to small shows and entering competitions. A particular rendition of *The Lady of Shalott* drew a great deal of adulation. Now and then I received a commission, which I took, though I did not care for them. At the time, becoming known was the issue of importance.

But my small victories left me hollow. I craved more, was capable of more. People the world over needed to see my art, to be moved by my art. (Why, I ask myself, asked even then?) It was not enough for me to know my greatness: so must others. My work was my one outlet aside from drink or smoke. My fantasy life still sizzled, even into the age of thirty-two. My apartment was full of books, my fridge was empty of food, and, in retrospect, I was something close to lonely. I did and didn't know what I was waiting for. The idea of her return hung over my head in a titillating shadow of dread. I did not want it. I told myself I did not want it at least once a week, more often twice. She had infected me with something that sixteen years of distance could not cure.

So it was that, at thirty-three, still pining, my disease was brought into remission by a letter left at a gallery, which was how I met Delilah.

Act Two

Chapter

1

I first perceived Delilah's orbit on January 10th, 2008, when I read the first love letter as fresh snow sparkled in the sunshine beyond the frosty kitchen window. It was not intended to be a love letter, or it was, perhaps, in the way a little girl loves with all her heart the singers to whom she sends notes with no expectation of reciprocation. Such a thing from an adult woman was fascinating.

I had never received a love letter before, discounting Susan's final note to me. After the *Sins* show opened, I was called to the gallery to pick up some mail. The curator—a lovely, Spanish-Egyptian woman with whom I'd slept several years ago and since maintained an amiable friendship—presented it to me with a bright smile between lips like Irish cream.

"She was very cute."

I looked at the letter front and back. "Somebody dropped this off?"

"First thing this morning, a few minutes after we opened. I've never seen a girl go so red, the way she did when she asked me to give that to you! You're developing fans."

"If only they had money," I said, chuckling, and she slapped my bicep.

"There's more to life than money, you know."

I not only knew, but I knew because I didn't have. Never once did I think the missing element could be heralded by a fan letter. All the same, at home I was mesmerized by the glossy stationary and rounded cursive, cheerful as the morning sun.

Dear Mister Vasko,

Thank you for opening my letter! You must get a lot of them. I've never met you, but I wanted you to know that your work moves me. I have gone to a lot of shows downtown, and while I am no expert, you are the greatest artist I have ever seen. If I could afford to, I would buy you out of paintings.

I have been to three of your exhibitions. The first work I ever saw, The Lady of Shalott—*that painting changed my life. The longing in her face as she reaches towards Lancelot ... I want to feel that way about somebody. Is that what you want? Somebody to reach for? Or do you want somebody to reach for you? Something in your work tells me it's the latter. You're waiting, not for someone to save you, or change you, but for someone to return the passion burning inside you. The passion you pour into your paintings.*

I do not mean to gush, or pry. I just wanted to tell you how I admire your work, and the fearlessness it must take to put your soul on canvas. I hope you'll receive the acclaim you deserve, and not because you change for your critics, but because you've made them understand how important you are.

Thank you again for reading my letter. Maybe next show I'll get up the nerve to shake your hand!

Sincerely,
Delilah Delacroix
PS. Is that you in Pride and the Mirror? *I'll bet it is.*

Astonished, I reread it three times. Each word had an insight like I'd not experienced in years. At each show, the contemptuous creatures pretending to be people projected the themes of their own works into mine, or some generic political or social criticism, or commentary on gender, or the state of modern art. They had no respect for me, did not know me well enough to know that all my works were me. But this woman burst with understanding, this Delilah. This woman with a letter kissed by cinnamon and vanilla. This woman, who, in hopeful hint that she might welcome correspondence, included her return address despite having dropped it off at the gallery. Intrigued as much as indulgent, I wrote her back that night.

Miss Delacroix,
You flatter me. I am not sure if everyone would agree I deserve such acclaim. I am not sure I do, myself. My work still lacks a certain intangible quality. But all good artists are forever growing, and I appreciate your praise.

Your powers of perception are quite keen. It would be a pleasure to meet you in person at my April show. You are no expert, perhaps, but surely you must be an artist of some kind. What has you going to galleries so often otherwise?

Whatever you are, I would love to see your work. I can already tell you to be intelligent, and tasteful. What else are you?

Warm regards,
RJ Vasko
PS. 'Richard' is just fine, Delilah.

Six days later I received another letter, along with a package of crème brûlée. No, she wrote, she was not an artist, but an avid lover of art. Instead, she was a chef, and baker—an accomplished one, judging her gift. Once upon a time she owned a failed restaurant with her ex-husband, but good food wasn't enough to keep them afloat in the floundering economy. To Delilah, the failure brought relief, because the whole thing was his idea, and it felt like selling out. Now, she only cooked for the people she loved.

If these crèmes brûlée aren't art, I wrote back, *I don't know what is. Do these mean you love me?*

I'm afraid I'll scare you if I say 'yes', she replied.

To be fair, little is more repellent than someone who falls in love right away. But I ate nothing but custard until the cups were all empty, and her insightful adoration had a constant flow of adrenaline cycling through my veins. Someone out there connected with my art; with me. No doubt her feelings of love were a residual effect of my paintings and would pass in time. But for now, it was so novel I had no choice but to humor it.

I'm not a man to be deterred by a thing like love, I wrote her. *Especially not if it tastes so exquisite.*

When she didn't reply for a time, I thought she had lost interest, or I had misspoken. But one afternoon two weeks later, I arrived home to find a fragile box upon my townhouse porch. Within was most assuredly fine art: a marble cake, whose perfect circumference was enclosed by flat shards of dark chocolate. The mound of raspberries and blueberries on top were dusted by sugar and recalled a frosted lawn. It was a tragedy to eat, but all beautiful things in this world must end with time, and the raspberry filling oozing with the first slice annihilated my regret.

There was no letter with the cake. It required none. Moved, I shut myself in my studio to nurse the alien glimmer in my heart. How many bodies had passed through my bed after Susan? Too many to count, each more tedious than the last: mannequins who loved me because I presented a lovable front for a few months at a time before intimacy melted my mask and boredom moved me on. Many were starting to see through my charade by then, anyway.

Yes, before my period of celibacy I made every effort to fill what my mother had torn open. I tried to cram it with possessions, drugs, sex. Somewhere along the way, work began to fill it, and I realized that all this time I'd been no better than a hick whiling away the day with the warm holes of his flocculent ewes. I forswore the whole business and had become resigned to the notion that the only women who might understand me either did not exist but in fantasy, or were the object of sublime loathing. My imagination ran wild, and my Woman had been my company for five years.

Here, now, was a woman who inspired a quiver. Something in me was stretching awake, roused by the scent of potential. Using old studies, I painted Apollo struck by Eros' bow upon seeing Daphne, her distant back turned, a mound of dark hair crowning her pale neck. The Woman was my stand-in for the Delilah I had not yet seen, and I noticed then that my figment had become curiously quiet with the coming of Delilah's notes. The focus required to fantasize was elsewhere, and the energy along with it. I took this as a sign.

Upon the painting's completion, I added it to the April show, and tried to wait. I could not. After three days, midway through March, I found myself on the porch of a corn-colored cottage on Stafford Street, the sweetest of all the suburban homes in that particular annex of Columbus. Its lawn was covered in snow, but I could already imagine lilacs and daffodils growing from the mulch. I rested the painting against the front door and, as was habit, examined the lock to find it newer than the house. It had been years since I'd picked one, but such observation was by then second-nature.

Other forms of observation were second-nature, too, like noting most of the neighbors were gone for the day, and that Delilah was safety-conscious enough to draw the blinds when she was out. The porch was home to a small structure labeled "The Cat House", quotes and all, overflowing with blankets and currently unoccupied. An Easter wreath hung upon the violet door. Everything was darling, and I, hot to see the woman in this yellow house with talented hands and a generous heart, retreated to my car, parked around the corner, and settled in with my camera. It snowed as I waited, bundled and sketching six hours from noon on, until a plum Nissan cruised around to stop in the distant driveway. I cracked the window, aimed the camera, and lost my breath as the Woman climbed out of her car.

Stunned, I snapped pictures and examined every feature, from her great, smiling eyes to the rounded, dainty nose above bowed lips. Black hair blew in the wind beneath her red beret as she mounted the porch to see what awaited her, the breadth of her grin exposing dimples of childish glee in her heart-shaped face.

I looked out from behind my camera and understood the agony which Apollo had grown to demonstrate. To be sure, my dream-image of the Woman had been a series of glimpses from the corner of my vision, half-clear even with closed eyes, but I had never been surer of anything than I was of the fact that I was seeing her in the flesh.

A shriek brought me from paralysis, and I looked again through the camera to see Delilah tear away the paper and reveal my declaration. One hand clapped over her laughing mouth. She hopped—actually hopped, my Woman!—and clapped her hands, and looked around, and when she did not see me she held herself instead, bright-eyed and grinning. Then, as if waking from a dream, she looked around once more and ushered her gift in from the cold. Deprived of the sight of her, I descended into hysteria. I laughed all the way home, and in my studio examined the photos, which I kissed, and admired, and wondered over even as I began the studies. In one glance, the Woman was dead, and more alive than ever.

In return for the painting, I received a batch of art deco cupcakes, but engrossed as I was in my work I ate only a few in the lead-up to the show. For four days and much of their nights I worked on my piece, which sizzled upon the canvas without intervention: Pygmalion, clutching the half-marble robes of giggling Galatea. Their likenesses were striking. As I hung it on the gallery wall, Patricia, the proprietor, stood over my shoulder to smile.

"You know, when I look at your work I don't know whether to think 'Sargent', or 'Goya'."

"That's because you should be thinking 'Vasko'," I said, pausing to admire the suggestion of bluebells outside Pygmalion's window.

At home, I shaved for the first time in a month and spent more than a few moments ensuring not a thread of the burgundy shirt was out of place. There was always the possibility that she wouldn't come, but if she was my Woman, the question was not 'if', but 'when'.

The first two hours of the show were an endurance challenge of greeting, thanking, and remembering names. It was impossible to avoid the clock, and more than one invitation to go drinking was turned down in favor of four plastic cups of wine, each half the size of any respectable glass. The scene was more of the usual: crowded with people buying cheap prints, nobody shelling out for pieces. Everybody who loved it couldn't afford it, and nobody with the money connected with the themes. Pygmalion and his creation were the talk of the show, and colleagues were up my ass about it. I was less eager to endure, and was about to sneak away for the seventh cigarette of the night when a glint of sunshine pierced my eye.

In a dress made for summer, the color of her happy house, there stood Delilah, riveted by our likenesses. As the crowd moved around her, she froze, awed, one foot lifting just an inch out of its shoe, her delicate hands clutching her black coat to her heart.

My present conversation was abruptly ended, because all things in existence vanished but her. Through the crowd, I breathed nutmeg, vanilla, and soft, sweet skin. Suddenly I was inches behind her.

"What do you think of it?"

"I think it's a beautiful work of art, by a beautiful man."

I chuckled. "A little disturbed, isn't he? Did you see *Prometheus and the Eagle*?"

"It's not that he's disturbed. He's passionate. Look at this passion, all this love."

Now she turned to face her opponent, gesturing toward the painting as she did. Her stalwart expression snapped to excitement, or panic, or wonder: I am not sure which, even now. A red-hot streak fell across her cheeks, then speckled her chest. Up close her eyes were a brown so rich they looked black as her hair in the gallery lights. When it all passed, (quicker than a second, but a second I savored in slow-motion), she laughed, and her hand fluttered over her mouth.

"I've waited so long to meet you," she said, lowering her fingers.

"Not as long as I have. It's good to meet you, Delilah." I kissed her cheek, the sound of her inhalation charming as a mouse's squeak.

"I'm so happy. This is so beautiful. Apollo is so beautiful, he's in my living room."

"You can hang Pygmalion in your bedroom, then. But you must promise to show me how it looks sometime."

"I can't." She covered her face with her hands, daring once to peek back at the painting. "Oh, Richard, I love it, but I couldn't."

"Why not?"

"It would feel like taking a child from its home."

I laughed, a true laugh like I hadn't in years. My hand found her shoulder, warm and soft. She half-tensed under my touch, a feral cat allowing a human's affection. "I'm sure it will be happy in its new home. Besides, I'll see it plenty."

Bright red, she burst into a spell of giggling, her hands clasped before her. In all of ninety seconds, animated Delilah became the most sincere woman I'd ever met. Perhaps she was excited to meet the artist she admired, but emotions overflowed from her. She did not censor or mute her reactions in the way of most adults. "Thank you, Richard, it's incredible! It even looks like me!" She laughed and faced again the figures, her left foot poised to leap from her lavender kitten heel. "And Pygmalion looks so joyful. I was right, you are Pride."

I spread my hands. "I'm many things."

"Yes." She squinted her smiling eyes to better assess my face. "You're Pride, and Lancelot, and Pygmalion. You're all of your paintings, and when your face isn't there, the feeling of you is."

I kept smiling to avoid showing how she rocked me, my thumb jerking toward the door. "Do you want to go someplace else with me? You're the most interesting girl I've met in a long time, maybe ever. I'd like to get to know you better than the Delilah I think I saw in the letters."

"I haven't seen the whole show yet."

"You'll see them one way or another. Come on." That elbow was made for my palm, the way it fit. She allowed herself led through the crowd until we were on the street, where we could breathe. I helped her into her coat so my knuckles might brush the supple highway of her clavicle and my nose the fragrant hair I remembered from dreams. The April nighttime still had the crisp snap of an apple, but, surely, that was not why Delilah shivered when I stepped around her to straighten my collar.

"You really wanted to get out of there," she said to divert attention from her fluster.

"I can't stand shows. They're too crowded. Nobody can take anything in, it's meaningless. By the time a piece is hanging on a wall I've written it off. Most of the attendees grate on my nerves, anyway." I could not suffer myself to call them 'people'. Delilah's presence further diminished them, and now on the sidewalk it seemed we were alone in a world of wind-blown ashes. "They make me feel sick. Obsessed with wanting to be 'artists'."

"What do you want?"

"To make powerful art."

She smiled in perfect comprehension. I offered her my arm as she asked, "Was it just a coincidence Galatea looks so much like me?"

"I don't want to lie to you on our first date," I teased, and she laughed, but pressed on as she did.

"How did you know what I look like?"

My tongue darted across my lip as I weighed the advantages of honesty, remembered she might be my Woman, and finally said, "I waited outside your house the day I dropped Apollo off. You're just as I imagined you." My eyes narrowed as I scrutinized her beautiful face and found no trace of discomfort, but instead, girlish delight.

"And you're how I imagined you," she said, her nose wrinkling with the breadth of her grin. "Charming. And wicked."

"Wicked!" Though I struggled to maintain an expression of mock-offense, soon it was for naught, because I laughed, too.

"Yes, wicked."

"What makes you think I'm wicked?"

"Your face in *Pride and the Mirror*. That's a different face from the one I'm seeing now, but it's almost the same. Haughty." She smiled and touched my cheek.

I turned my leer away to brush my lips along the heel of her palm, which dropped to my hand to tug me forward. Her pace increased to a canter. "Let's go to Grove Park!"

She pulled me half a block, and as we wandered down the path, she pushed against my arm in case I might disappear. I had offered it in case she might do the same.

"Delilah, why aren't you still married? I can't imagine the fool who'd give you up."

She lowered her head as intrepid joggers trudged past us, down the snow-sludged path. "I never should have married him. I didn't love him, but we were friends, and he loved me so much. I thought I could grow into loving him."

"Why settle?"

"That was what I thought people did. What I deserved."

"What do you deserve now?"

"To feel like the Lady of Shalott, reaching for Lancelot."

My mouth brushed her hair. I wanted to dive into it, into her, push her down on the snow and have her there in the park. I wanted to read the future in her entrails, bind books in her flesh, drink her holy blood and ascend beyond mortality. I resisted. "When did you divorce him?"

"December, 2006."

A handful of months after the premiere of *Lancelot*. I smothered my grin. "You look young to be a divorcée."

"We met in culinary school. I couldn't drink at my own wedding. I'm ashamed of myself for hurting him like that. He was so confused when I left. But my father had just died, and my head wasn't right."

"Don't be ashamed. You only wanted to be happy."

"But I was cruel."

"And I'm sure he grew for it."

Finally, we found an empty bench and I stooped to dust its snow away. She watched me, smiling. "Have you ever been in love before, Richard?"

"Do you really want to know?"

"I must."

We sat, her shivering until I wrapped my arm around her shoulders. "When I was seventeen, I had a short, intense relationship with an older woman. When she left, I tried to rebuild, but I had nothing. It got so bad that later, I was arrested for breaking and entering."

"Why would you do something like that?"

Appraisal of her expression revealed no judgment; only interest. I should have expected as much. This was not any woman, but my Woman. "I wanted to see how people lived."

She smiled a thousand-year-old smile. "Are you lonely?"

"Yes." I said it without thinking, surprised at myself. Before she named it, I hadn't known what to call it.

She squeezed my hand. "Me, too. But I think it's because I've been waiting for you."

I couldn't stand it. Could you? On those full lips, pink like cherry blossoms, I kissed her, breathed her. Though she assented at once, her kisses were the tentative gestures of a girl easing into a cold pool. Never had I felt a tongue so soft. I clutched her, captivated by her solidity. Yes, she was real, and I had found her at last, my Woman!

Chapter

2

Exhilarating as she was, our magnetism seemed somehow queer. More than once I had found myself with a woman who moved fast in her relationships, and in some ways Delilah recalled them. But this was different, and the possibility I might find my fantasies in her sparked just as urgent a need for intimacy. It was as if we were making up for lost time, rather than getting to know each other the first time. For our first true date, Delilah arrived on my stoop at eight with her coat buttoned to her chin and a basket hanging from her arm.

With a glance at the damp weather, I asked, "Isn't it a little early in the season?"

As she kissed my cheek, she said, "It's never too early for a picnic! I want to feed you and show you all the things that are special to me, and what better way to do that than with an outing?"

"I suppose so."

Never the outdoorsman, the idea of a picnic, with all the ants, wet grass and rain hazards, had the appeal of a mid-July dumpster dive. But what man hasn't sacrificed his principles for a woman? Just this one consideration would delight her, I was sure. Besides, I told myself, it was hardly as if I was going to bend over backwards all the time. (You're not laughing at this yet, but you will.)

Conversation on the way there, at least, was easy, and quick to take coincidental turn. Delilah provided most of it, asking me about myself, my work, the books I liked and didn't, movies, music; all of which she seemed well-equipped to discuss. "You read often," I observed, pleased. She smiled.

"I'd better! I manage Minos Books for the nice family who owns it."

That was a place I'd been a thousand times; a twisting old house converted into a book store which was a fire department's worst nightmare. The things they had in there were amazing. "I love that store," I said, and she smiled. "I can't believe I've never noticed you."

"You notice me now, and that's what matters." Her smile was for herself, now, and we pulled into a parking lot before the green slope of a dam we climbed, black water rippling just beyond the sidewalk. We settled on the hill, Delilah laying out a blanket, then arranging wine, various cheeses, sausages, cucumber sandwiches and tiny raspberry tarts for dessert.

I laughed. "When we grow up, I'm going to marry you."

She blushed and covered her giggling face, then gripped my hand. "I hope you'll want to. I mean—I'll bet you're used to fly-by-night type girls," she said, staring into my eyes, now resolute in her sparkling expression. "You're too smooth."

"I admit I have something of a past with women."

"Well—I'm not interested in that. I want to know you." She placed her hand on my heart. "There's something so beautiful in your paintings, amid all the atrocity. I've never seen a more beautiful Saint Theresa, but I've also never seen a more visceral one. And framing it as Lust!"

"I love that piece," I said with a proud grin. "I may have used a model, but I like to think of that one as a self-portrait."

"How so?"

"It's about being stricken by the cosmos—annihilated by the divinity of creativity." I clutched her hand upon my chest, saying, "Each painting is a love story with itself. From the moment I envision it to the final brush-stroke I am bound to suffer and delight. And there is a moment, a wonderful moment, when the work flows so well you wonder if you're even creating it. The painting, the act of painting, of creating, expression, it becomes all that exists in that one timeless moment where there is only the work."

Delilah leaned forward as she said, "That's beautiful."

"That's art," I replied, helping myself to some cheese.

On our way back, we found ourselves on one of the many two-lane high-ways crisscrossed between fields and farms. Some doddering fool toddled before us in an Oldsmobile, doing fifteen miles below the limit. Huffing, Delilah drummed her thumbs upon the wheel. "Come on! What are you doing?"

"Pass him."

"No, I hate passing. I never pass."

"You never pass?"

"Never. That was what happened to my dad. He was trying to pass a car and drove his truck into a tree while avoiding oncoming traffic."

"How terrible." I stroked her thigh and watched her shiver. "No woman your age should have to lose her father."

She shook her head. "The worst part of it was that I was sad, but kind of relieved. He wasn't a nice man. Not that he was evil, he just had problems." Then, at the vehicle before us: "Give me a break! There isn't a lot of time before my car turns back to a pumpkin!"

I laughed, and as I did, I grabbed the wheel and jerked us into the oncoming lane. Delilah's shriek was my soundtrack as I advised, "Hit the gas."

"Richard!"

"The gas!" Less calm, now, headlights appearing on the horizon.

Screeching, Delilah responded with a stomp, and the car with a groan forward. We were clear five seconds before the truck barreled past, and her cries dissolved to laughter. As I settled back, she struck me in the chest. "Don't do that!"

I said, grinning, "You passed and survived. And now we're at the speed limit. You should thank me."

I could see her hiding a smirk. "Maybe. That was kind of fun, I guess."

Though she was already turning as if she'd memorized the directions on the Internet, I advised her where to go, and once at my house, invited her inside for wine. She glanced at the clock, and was inside a few seconds later. Comfortable as you please in my favorite armchair, Delilah regarded the nearest cherry bookshelf with a keen eye. She seemed absorbed in it a moment, then asked, "Who do you think was the most interesting?"

I followed the tip of a pointed finger to the section designated for men and women of homicidal proclivity throughout the ages. I hummed my consideration. "I suppose that is difficult, because if they weren't interesting they wouldn't be on my shelves. That said," I pushed into the depths of the shelf the volumes on Son of Sam, BTK, Zodiac, and, after hesitation, Jack the Ripper, "these are the pretenders of the bunch."

"How so?"

"They were in it for the attention. A pathetic reason to end a life."

"Is there a good reason to end a life?"

"Ask the government."

"All right—aside from self-defense, and war, and executions, how can murder be anything but bad?"

"It depends on the individual's outlook, influenced by culture, experience, genetics. Morality and ethics are social artifice." I stood beside her, one hand on the back of the chair while I lifted my glass with the other. "Murder happens in nature all the time. To paraphrase Nietzsche's ideas, is it evil that wolves should prey on sheep? Or that chimpanzees should engage in cannibalistic infanticide?"

She tapped her chin, like a girl in a black-and-white movie showing at four in the morning. "It's not evil, but it's not self-aware. Animals don't have the same faculty for cause-and-effect reasoning we do. They don't have souls."

"Ah, a soul. Is that the difference between humans and animals, then?"

"Maybe. There has to be something." She touched her heart, then mine. "Something distinguishes us from the rest of the species on earth."

"Indeed: our capacity for telling ourselves we are distinguished. We have languages so complex they have inspired profound transformation in the human mind. They adjust how we see the world, and everything in it. We conflate the thing with our label for it. This isn't a shelf, it's just—" I patted it to demonstrate. "But we're convinced it's a shelf, wrapped up in the word. Nothing is taken at the face value animals find, and at times we even poison animals with our conceptions of language."

"Animals have languages, though. Dolphins and ravens."

"Dolphins enjoy murdering other animals, and ravens use their language to communicate information about grudges and warfare. Are those things cruel?"

"You can't really hold an animal to the standard you'd set for a human."

I waved a hand, and my drink, almost spilling wine and laughing as Delilah flinched, expecting a splash. "That's why when it comes to psychopaths and murderers, the term 'evil' is misattributed. Their brains function in a different way from those of the normal human population, have smaller amygdalae. Their brains are literally different. Historically speaking, it once so happened that man was a gentle creature with a large frontal lobe and large amygdala."

"The Neanderthals," she confirmed, engrossed as she gazed up to me, wine forgotten.

"Exactly. And then emerged modern Man, with a smaller brain; and though the two coexisted for some time, soon Neanderthals were bred and beaten out of existence."

"You think psychopathy is a kind of evolution?"

If she was still this hooked, there was something wrong with her, and it was just my sort of psychosis. I'd might as well go in deep now to weed her out if she didn't really have a chance of understanding me. So I said, "What else could it be? Individuals carrying the traits lumped under the dubious umbrella of psychopathy are better-equipped to propagate their genes. Philandery and risk-taking beget many children, after all, and empathy deficiency brings increased success in every arena from white-collar business to personal power."

Delilah nodded in consideration, emptying her glass. "You wouldn't be unfaithful to me if we were together, would you?"

"Here we are, chatting about killers and psychopaths, and what you worry about is adultery. Wouldn't most women be nervous about other penchants?"

"I'm not scared you'll hurt me physically." She smiled, still all daisies and sunshine. "I'm positive you're capable of it, but I'm also positive you wouldn't do it unless I gave you a reason to, and you can bet I never will."

With those words, Delilah's aberrant thought patterns and all their sugar-sweet potential revealed themselves to the dozing beast of my heart. Her mechanics fascinated me. Best, for all the joy she exuded, whispers of anguish lurked in her smiling eyes. I had no doubt she had endured her fair share.

My thumb brushed against one dimple as I asked, "How do you do it?"

"Do what?"

"Be so happy."

Yes, there it was, that white-toothed mural of emotion. Would that I could steal it from her face. "I don't know. I'm not. I'm really not."

"You don't show it."

"Because people get along with you if you're happy," she said, her gaze sloping toward my knee. "Depression is an illness but people say you wallow if you show it. After a while, I learned not to show it. Sometimes I do feel happy, until some little thing happens, like washing mom's elephant mug. Then one sadness leads to another, and I just spiral until I'm lying there wondering why everybody has to suffer through this."

"'This'?"

"This, life, everything." She gestured around as she spoke. There was a glimmer in her eyes, the tension in her throat outlining in exquisite detail her esophagus. "I feel like I'm lost in the woods. I used to think about killing myself but I was afraid of the pain, and I'm even more afraid of what I don't know than what I do." Her chin dimpled as she turned her head. "I'm sorry. Most people don't think it's very attractive, getting like this."

"Do I seem like most people?" That got a little smile out of her. I knelt so I could better see, then sat upon the floor. My hands engulfing hers, I bent forward until our eyes leveled. "You don't have to be happy all the time, Delilah. Not with me. You know what I want?"

Quivering, she returned her focus to me.

I placed my hand upon her cheek. "I want Delilah. You. All of you. In fact, you're already mine, and I'm already yours."

Her eyes batted away tears, and she grinned, now, true and flushed. "Oh?"

"Yes. You just don't know it yet, that's all."

It was as if I had slapped a hungry lion: she pounced, mouth to mouth, her body wriggling into my lap, every inch of her torso a perfect complement and fit to mine, warm and soft, toned, sweet-smelling without artifice, kind without theatrics, loving without deceit. Every form of the Woman imagined and every woman slept with—yes, even Susan—was eclipsed by Delilah.

Soon our clothes were gone. Upon the floor, we became ravenous beasts. Any inhibition in her dissipated once she was nude, and I found to my delight she was not only reactive, but proactive. Most women I'd known since Susan had a penchant for lying still as a corpse in comparison, but Delilah knew her body from her hips to her mouth and used every part as if at once embracing me, yet fending me off like I was her attacker. She screamed and clawed and tore her hair, and I, my God—I lost my mind.

Once she placed her hand upon my cheek. "You're so present," she said, wonder in her voice and smile.

I said, kissing her brow, "There's nowhere else to be."

The mystery of sex had by this point well worn off. For years, I had not managed without some minor sadism, nor completed without more intimate methods (asphyxiation, violation, humiliation, a veritable station of -ations like trains ready to be ridden to a satisfying miniature annihilation) that some might deem misogynistic upon learning of my crimes and my relationships with women. I will not spare much thought to this notion, however incorrect, because you may take from my work as you will. Art is a gateway not into the artist, but into oneself.

Delilah was a gateway into the both of us. I had never wanted to spare the mental effort required to learn about the women I was with. Now I wanted everything. It was a pity I was not Delilah's twin, or perhaps her left hand, so I might have known every second of her existence. I kissed that hand as we lay on the living room floor amid scattered sketches. There was more I wanted to know, and too soon it was time to go, and she looked as heartbroken as I felt as she kissed me goodbye, saying, "Goodnight, goodnight, please call me tomorrow, goodnight, goodnight."

Chapter

3

Picking a lock is simpler than one might think—even you could do it with a bit of practical understanding, assuming you have something like hands that is. I won't bore with details, but suffice to say after a certain point it can (and often should) be done in the dark. I was limited to broad daylight for Delilah's house, but neighbors who minded their business and a practiced set of fingers had me through the door in ninety seconds. Since her departure some six hours before, each moment had been spent planning. I craved to know her better, and couldn't stand to wait. Now, in her house, I grinned as I untied my shoes in an entryway where the scent of a bakery entangled with the aroma of tender woman.

Hands in my pockets, I moved through the carpeted living room, where I sat in a brown leather sofa, circa 1979, and admired her vast collection of albums and books, constrained by neither genre, nor quality. This eclectic element I appreciated, because I wasn't capable of it myself, having been for most my life an admitted snob. Black shelves overflowed with cracked and new spines, some stacked upon others to create more space, no doubt the cost of managing a bookstore. I imagined my books mingled among them, then looked upon the furniture with greater scrutiny. Yes, that green armchair would go, and this sofa. They wouldn't mesh with my furniture, which was newer and higher quality anyway. Emotional attachment, I guessed, was behind the furnishings, present also in photographs of her parents upon the mantel. At least she'd torn up the muddy carpet and repainted the white walls; the ones in the room where I stood were now violet, save for a goldenrod accent wall which was home to *Apollo's Ecstasy*. She had, I discovered, a record player, and a collection of vinyl albums. I dropped the needle on the one already there and found it a warm, dreamy folk piece by some band I'd never encountered, but would hear of in excited passing throughout the next six years.

Down the hall, I discerned from other photographs a sketch of her childhood: not happy, but not entirely tragic. Her father's humorless disdain for the camera elicited a certain affinity, as did his features, dark-on-pale like mine. Of course, in some ways my Woman fit the prototype of Evangeline, so Delilah was not alone in falling victim to the adage about marrying one's parents.

The three bedrooms were her master suite, a storage room, and a guest bedroom. I began with the collection of treasures. Old clothes and purses made up much of the horde, but soon I picked out more personal keepsakes: a red dog collar faded by age; a Jake Delacroix's bowling trophy from 1994; the hats of a woman born two generations before me; the suit of a man sixty pounds heavier than I. In the closet space beneath that suit I discovered with a cry of joy a motherlode of photo albums. Taking mental note of their orientation, I explored her life to prove beyond shadow of doubt that she was a real person.

Each image felt less new knowledge and more the same brand of affirmation one receives when a helpful friend fills in the details of a now-foggy shared memory. Here, *la infanta* herself; big grinning mouth and doll's eyes. (I have never cared for children, but confess my heart was stolen by the pudgy blob.) A toddler, black hair curlier than now, crying at the camera with such indignant force I could hear it decades later. Here, at four, that impish smile kissed by dimples. Six in overalls, nine and visibly uncomfortable in a dress for school pictures, ten and swimming, sixteen and driving. Throughout the photographs were those more or less faceless adult figures in whom I observed mutual weariness no doubt sparked for complimentary reasons: he hated her, and she hated him for hating her, all of it evidenced in detached body language and big, fake smiles. Her mother's conspicuous absence beginning in 1996 was marked with the inheritance of weariness by her daughter. There it was behind Delilah's smile as she tried on an apron for her birthday, or graduated from high school. The book ended, then, the back page inscribed: *Happy Graduation, DeeDee! Never forget where you came from once you've gotten where you're going! Love, Nana.*

The next book was a binder of letters—friends or relatives, never lovers. Never her ex-husband. I had no doubt she had received many gestures of romantic intent, but it was clear she had not thought enough of any to keep them. Excepting, of course, Apollo. Were I a cat, I could have washed my face, so contented I was by my star-crossed darling. There was much to pare down, but the room looked upon the back yard and would make a perfect studio.

The master bedroom, I admired one inch at a time. The air was perfumed with her. Warmth, sweetness, sex. I stood over her unmade bed, bent over her pillow to inhale a fortnight of hair. That scent snaked into the bottom of my lungs, gripped me. She formed beneath me, before my third eye, then rippled away as a dream.

Above her bed, where the faithful might hang a crucifix, there hung a familiar print: *The Lady of Shalott*. I basked in the implications and meandered through the room, running my fingers across the clothes in her closet and dresser to discover a set of red lingerie, tag still attached. They almost matched the walls, a burgundy I was pleased to note I would not have to change. After pocketing a pair of black panties from her hamper (the very same from the night before), I took stock of the dust-coated guest room, which bore no resemblance to the fuchsia little-girl's room of so many of the photographs.

It was in the kitchen I found her very heart. These appliances were not showpieces like Susan's, but well cared-for throughout their productive lifespan. No dishes in the sink, not a spot on the floor. She would have been appalled by my bachelor kitchenette, and my fridge, which compared to hers was desolate. Hers was gleaming new and stuffed with meats, vegetables, a bowl of rising dough, milk and wine and cheeses, and a freezer overflowing with some pre-made meals like frozen soups and bisques, each carefully labeled in lime green Sharpie. The peanut butter cookies on the stove caught my eye. This woman would fatten me if I wasn't careful.

It was while in search of a fork to try the pasta salad that I came upon her spare key in a drawer full of half-used spools of thread and other odds and ends. Less important quests abandoned, I took it (with a few cookies) and made my retreat. My first stop was a department store, which produced a copy of the key in all of two minutes, no questions asked—every hardworking clerk is accomplice to some crime in this age of convenience. Next was the florist, who eagerly inquired as to the occasion of my purchase. Somehow, I was almost eager to share it.

"I've met the Woman, and I want to show her how crazy I am about her."

She smiled while arranging poppies into a mushroom cloud. "I see a lot of men in love. There's a twinkle in the eye."

In the card, I wrote, *In lieu of a more personal surprise. Yours, Richard.* When I dropped the bouquet off and replaced the original key, I took her copy of *The Crying of Lot 49* to read at home until clutched by dreamless sleep. What stirred me awake some hours later was the sound of girlish laughter, and I came to and found I'd answered the phone in my sleep. It was gleeful Delilah on the other end.

"How did you do it?"

"Do what?"

"Shut up. I love them, they're the most beautiful flowers I've ever received." I imagined her glowing the color of the poppies she clutched. "I can't wait to see you."

"The feeling is mutual. What are you doing on Saturday?"

"Volunteering at the animal shelter, but I'll be free at five."

I laughed along with my reflection. "Of course you volunteer."

"Of course." I heard the smile in her voice as she asked, "How did you get in?"

"Why? Are you frightened?" I'd expected her to call in a fit, at least a little disturbed. Instead, her reaction was amazing. The further I pushed her boundaries the more eagerly she responded, and I was beginning to wonder if she even knew what boundaries were. I'd only learned the term myself five or six years before, and still had trouble understanding its point in certain contexts.

"I'm excited." Her sweet tone was enriched by something lower. "Your passion excites me."

Yes, passion. I was passionate about Delilah the same way I was passionate about my work, the same way I was once passionate about Susan. I leaned against the dresser. "I have the feeling you are an important person in my life, Delilah."

She exhaled, one deep, soft breath. "I want to see you sooner than Saturday."

"Me, too."

"I'll think of something," she said, and the line went dead before I could respond. I kissed the phone.

In my studio, I selected one of several canvases about the length of my body. Upon my easel, it held the promise of untrodden snow. What form that promise would take, I couldn't hope to know. But it would be for her, whatever it was, and it would be great.

It was as if I was a boy again, waiting for the week to end so I might visit my lover. But Delilah could not stand to be apart from me any more than I her, so each night she would email asking about my day, send another to chastise me for not eating properly, and a third to tell me good-night. She wove magic with her words as Susan once had, but where Susan's were venom from the fangs of a snake, Delilah's were ambrosia from the mouth of a goddess. Everything she said was meant with her whole heart, left bare to my teeth.

For a handful of days I filled the hours with my job, working on the restoration of a water-damaged family portrait which I had evaded for as long as possible. The piece was boring and the style was boring, and the longer I looked at it, the slower time crawled. To battle it even ten minutes drained my resolve, and when I remembered I was doing it for the dollar and not myself, the task became even more miserable. On Thursday, I stumbled into the house, dropped my keys on the coffee table, and navigated a field of sketches on my way upstairs. In the bathtub, I considered the melody of Delilah's holy voice. I wanted to hear it whenever I pleased, but a call might suffice. The phone rang four times before, incredibly, it went to voicemail. Flabbergasted, I just managed to clear my throat by the beep.

"Delilah, it's me. I was hoping to hear your pretty voice. Saturday is too far. Won't you call me back?"

Disappointed, I left the tub soon after, and once in pajamas, went in search of something to eat. Wouldn't you know, I found just the thing the instant I turned on the light—albeit, not in the kitchen.

On the living room coffee table, there stood a cake box. It had not been there when I arrived home. Nor had I ever seen the thing before, noting now its resemblance to one of Evangeline's Sunday hat-boxes. My keys had been moved aside to accommodate it. Once opened, it revealed a masterpiece of lemon drenched in chocolate ganache and roasted almonds.

That little minx. Either she had gotten in and out of the house during the thirty-minute window in which I soaked, or, more likely, she had been home before I was. No wonder she hadn't answered the phone! Almost trembling, I called her again, and when I did, my friend, I discovered a thing more remarkable than the cake: not only had my reverse-burglar failed to turn her cell phone all the way to vibrate after my first call, but she was also still in the house. The soft jingle chimed twice before I traced it to its source, the same source as that of sudden rustling. Amid the winter coats and boots of my hall closet huddled Delilah, who responded with the naughty grin of a child caught with a fistful of cookies.

The discovery required more than a few seconds to process through my brain, and in the interim, Delilah's grin melted into a gasp of panic. "Don't be upset, I just wanted to leave you a present."

The words grazed me over the pounding of adrenaline. For all the times I've invaded the lives of others, I'd never dreamed of it happening to me. I admit, I was jarred. How long had she been here? What had she seen, where had she pried? Had this been any other person, I might have pulled them from the closet for a sound beating before (begrudgingly) calling the cops. But this was Delilah. Delilah, my Woman, who was here not to take or snoop, but to play my game with me. I understood the uniquely feminine impulse to crush that which is tooth-achingly adorable. Laughing, I pulled her from the closet to kiss her mouth.

"How long have you waited?"

She nibbled her lip. "Just a few hours."

"In the closet?"

"It's nice. It smells like you."

"Why didn't you leave once you put out the cake?"

Blushing, Delilah leaned into my arms. "I wanted to watch you enjoy it. Then I was going to leave."

She described all this as if her behaviors were commonplace acts of courtship. In reality, they were grander gestures than I had imagined receiving. Here I'd been for years, drifting along without a clue I was waiting for someone to do unto me as I had once done so eagerly unto others.

"Don't dream of leaving." I shooed her to the couch. "There's no escape from me, not until you tell me how you managed this."

"Promise you won't be mad?" When I nodded, Delilah slipped off her coat, and from its plum pocket produced a keyring. One by one, she passed through the keys, until she stopped at one which was eerily familiar.

"No," I said, laughing like the victim of a prank so cunning he wished he'd thought to orchestrate it. I examined my own keys to find them unmolested, and a cursory examination beneath the sink revealed the spare key taped where I had placed it years before. Hands on my hips, I returned to Delilah. "That just raises more questions."

"I will answer two." Ah, that twinkle of mischief!

"Two?"

"Well, three. But I want a piece of cake, I didn't get to try it."

"That's a hard bargain." I retrieved two plates and a knife. My grandmother once warned my weakness for sweets would devolve into heroin addiction, and she was right for a few years, but between Delilah and her baking I had no fear of relapse. Only a new, more potent craving. "So, how did you get in to make the key in the first place?"

"You left your patio door unlocked."

Puzzled, I tried the slider and found the lock solid. When I offered no response but an arched brow, she giggled. "Well, not recently."

My brow arched higher. "When?"

"Sure you won't be mad?"

"Positive."

"September 5th, 2007. You went to a party right after taking a call about it on your deck, so I locked it for you on my way out."

"That was ... eight months ago."

"Yes."

"How often have you been visiting my home?"

"A few nights a week. At first it was a couple of days a month, but I couldn't bear to be apart."

Now, my friend, I must step aside to address your proprieties. If you have proprieties, anyway—you are no doubt baffled by what one might term her 'quirks', and by my favorable reaction. But I've heard it said humans do not adopt feral cats: rather, feral cats ready for domestication then adopt a family. Sometimes this is so literal that the humans discover the cat inside, already making itself at home. So it was with Delilah, who had been my shadow longer than she had existed within my self-contained reality. Until that second, she had been mere curiosity: an improbable dream. But she was better than my dreams. Her secret was not cruel, as Susan's; instead, symptomatic of devotion. Here was her insanity before me while she sat, cake untouched as she awaited my stones. As if, after all this time, she did not know my glass house!

"Why did you take so long to write me, then?"

"That was three questions." Grinning, Delilah at last nibbled her dessert, and I remembered to follow suit until she rose again. "I got you milk, too. I knew you didn't have any. Your fridge is in such bad shape." I observed her while she moved with eerie familiarity in a kitchen where I had to think twice to find which cupboard contained the cups not intended for alcohol. "You're so thin because all you do is drink your calories and puke them up like a sorority girl. I would love to see you eat something healthy."

"A-ha, so you bait with pastries, then close a trap of chicken and rice. That's your con."

She laughed, her nose wrinkling as she examined the glasses. "There's no con. I just—I like you so much."

"It's all right to tell me you love me, you know."

"Oh, God, yes, Richard, I love you!" She clapped her hand over her chest as if to contain her slamming cartoon heart, breast heaving with the effort. "I loved you the second I saw your work, I've loved you more with every new one. And I love you even more now that we're together, really together, and I'm not just some sad, crazy girl playing pretend."

"So come here, then."

She did, a glass in each hand. When they were upon the coffee table, I pulled her into my lap and observed the tremor of her body. "It's all right," I said. She exhaled, nodded. I turned her gentle face towards mine in time to see the blossom of her pupils. "How well would you say you know me, Delilah?"

"Not well enough. I have ... impressions of you. I know an imaginary Richard, I guess. But I don't think he's far from the real thing."

"What is your imaginary Richard like?"

"Well, he likes to be alone. He is social, sometimes. But he comes home earlier than his friends do most of the time. That's how he wants it, because they're not really his friends. The way my friends don't feel like my friends, sometimes." There was that whisper of yearning in her eyes. "But he's a passionate man. That passion has to go somewhere. So, he pours it into his incredible art. His art that's violent, and insidious, and sexual and wrenching, just like he is. And even though he has his art, and his pretend friends, he's restless. Waiting for something, though he doesn't know it. Sometimes he feels lonesome. But he keeps painting, because it's more than just work to him—it is him."

I grinned, flattered. "That's not so very far off, though I've known I was waiting."

Her eyes curled to crescent moons. "Have you?"

"Yes. But I didn't realize I was waiting for you to reveal yourself. Why didn't you approach me directly?"

"I'm too shy." Even the admission reddened the tips of her ears. "I couldn't just walk up to you. What if I wasn't interesting to you? Or it didn't go well? You would have no reason to like me if I were just some fangirl, so I wanted to understand you from afar because that was all I dared ask. But when I saw your *Seven Sins* show, I couldn't sit in silence. I needed you to know I exist."

"And do you ever, Delilah." I ran my hand down the column of her throat. "You're better than anything I've imagined. But surely by now you've stolen a few glances at my true face. Doesn't its arrangement trouble you?"

"No. Because it's your face, your perfect face. And I don't care."

"Good." I kissed the curve of her jaw, my lungs filled with the scent of sugared femininity. "What do you want, Delilah?"

"To be happy."

"Do you think I'll make you happy?"

"No. I think we'll have an easy time being happy together."

"Good. Because I think I love you, and so I intend to spend a great deal of time with you, whether you want to or not."

Her being stilled like a calmed lake, face luminescent. She kissed me, desperate, as if she might wake up any time now. How long had it been since I kissed Susan that way? I did not remember Susan anymore, not then. Then, my universe focused to a pinpoint, and all I knew or saw or remembered was Delilah.

Chapter

4

Though I once treasured the thrill of the hunt, however short-lived and banal the prey, I was quick to settle in to what I had with Delilah. She wasn't interested in games or censorship. She wanted all of me. Though it was easy enough to suppose our attachment to projections, we sensed that maybe we belonged together. The notion purged caution. I fell into an old pattern of longing for her company every second I didn't have it. Once, at seventeen, it had been acceptable to moon over a woman—but at thirty-two, I had the power to make her mine, and didn't have to sit around tearing out my hair.

For a single woman lacking a large network of friends, she was well occupied. Our hours together were between seven and midnight at first, so one Tuesday in the middle of May, with little else to do, I relieved Delilah of her old sofa and coffee table. When she came home and made a game of not noticing my pieces in their place, I introduced my bookshelves and modern lamps. Next, the dining room table, the armchair, and in her room there appeared my dresser and bookshelves, and by June I returned home only to paint.

Does this seem fast? Perhaps it was. I admit Susan instilled a habit of early cohabitation, but the company Delilah granted seemed somehow vital to my spirit. She was so different from me. Her universe shimmered with a million vibrant atoms. An invitation in was an invitation to Faerieland. Is it any wonder I put such energy into obtaining my future studio, if only to have no excuse to leave her?

One Saturday afternoon, when Delilah returned from the shelter with her aroma muffled by the stink of hounds, I decided the time for action was now. The issue required a delicate approach, and once she declared her plans for *filet mignon*, I made a show of disappointment.

"You know I'd love to stay, darling. But I've got quite a bit of work."

A shadow fell across her face, which cracked from a smile to heartbreak. "I can't have filet mignon without you."

"You can. I'll eat what's left over when I come by tomorrow."

"You're not staying the night, either? Oh."

Had you seen her face you might have thought I had murdered a puppy in front of her. I almost felt badly, but there are clichés about eggs and omelets for good reason. I held her hand. "You know I'd like nothing better, but I'm going to be working late. You don't want to be woken up by my coming to bed at two, three in the morning, do you? You volunteer all day again tomorrow."

Lower lip vanishing behind her nibbling teeth, she looked to the closed rooms. "I love when you paint, but I hate when you leave. I wish I could spend every second with you."

"So do I, but you're busy. Tell you what," I said, standing, "why not call tomorrow when you're finished? I'll drop whatever I'm doing and come over."

Pouting, now, Delilah clung to the loops of my jeans. Her forehead rested against my chest. "Can't you stay a while?"

"I would if I could."

"What if you had a studio here?"

"Then I'd have no reason to leave."

Jaw working over the problem, Delilah sprang from her seat and, fingers still hooked in my jeans, led me down the hall. "There's three rooms, but I'm not using them all."

"The best room for a studio is full of your parents' things," I said, the picture of innocence.

"Yes." Frowning, Delilah turned the doorknob and stared from the threshold of the cluttered room, her sweatshirt slipping down to bare one shoulder. "I know none of this does me any good, but I'm attached to their stuff."

"Why?"

"What if I forget them?"

I wove her throat a necklace of kisses. "You won't."

"How can I know?"

"We remember the important things. What in this room isn't in your mind?"

"Do you remember the important things?"

"I have many fond and terrible memories of my mother." I turned on the light and waded into the sea of stuff. "I was adopted, you know."

"I didn't."

"Well, now you do. Briefly, I met my birth mother. She was no more cut out to be a mother than I am to be anyone's son."

She frowned. "You shouldn't say that."

"No, it's true. You know what they say, darling, about the way a man treats his mother?"

"It's how he'll treat his wife," she said, grinning.

113

I examined Jake Delacroix's dusty bowling trophy, score of 291. "I was not kind to my adopted mother. All she wanted was my love, and I couldn't give it. But I loved my real mother the instant I saw her. She was like a queen."

Delilah appeared at my elbow to whisper in my ear, "I know you'll treat me well."

"How do you know a thing like that?"

"Because you've been waiting for me, like you said. I'm not silly, Richard. I know you're not a nice man. Or a good man. You're okay with that, so I'm okay with that. All you have to do is tell me if I've upset you, and I'll make it better."

"I doubt you could upset me."

"Like I said."

After a moment of silent contemplation, I tapped the trophy and confirmed, "Your father?"

"Yes."

Having become enamored with the pale gouges healed upon her back, I found them with my fingers. The scar tissue was silk. "Why did he become a parent?"

"I don't know. It wasn't so bad. He stopped beating me once I figured out how to be a good daughter to him. Mom never knew what to do. Sometimes she didn't leave her room at all. But he was nice to me sometimes." She smiled, her fingers running over the engraving. "When I was little we'd walk to the corner-store for his cigarettes. The clerk was this nice old man with one hand that didn't work. He always had biscuits for our dog."

My head lowered against her shoulder while we swayed amid the dusty past. "It's a good thing he took care of himself," I said. "If he was alive, I might feel the need to protect you."

Her father's trophy in her hand, Delilah shared a tarnished smile with her reflection. "I don't blame him for hating me at the end. I've been ashamed so long. My mom was just so sad, and hurting so much with her cancer. I was fourteen and afraid, and after a while, she'd lie in bed begging me, 'DeeDee, bring me my morphine, please.'" Big tears welled in her eyes, proof of how wholeheartedly she felt her pain. I admired her, hardly daring to touch her lest she flutter away.

Pawing her red nose, she said, "One day, I did. I put them on her bedside table, but at the end I had to help her take some of them." Her voice glimmered. "She told me I was a good girl, gave me a kiss, and went to sleep."

Now that her shoulders trembled, I placed a hand on her back. She lowered the trophy and buried her face in my shoulder. "Dad came home and knew what happened as soon as he saw us. He beat me right beside her body, but then he told me to hide the bruises, and when the responders came, he covered for us. For me."

"Don't think that makes me like him anymore."

"It doesn't have to. I didn't like him very much, either, but I loved him. He was my dad, and he protected me from jail even though I—killed her. Even though I would have deserved it."

"That's ridiculous. Assisted suicide is different from murder."

"But I took a life. My mother's life."

Incredible, this commonality bridging us. Her act was the other face of mine, rational compassion against incendiary rage. If there were ever a time to open up, to reveal the significance of our symmetry, it would be now.

"Would you like to know something only two other people know?"

With curious, reddened gaze, she peeped up at me, and I said: "I killed my mother, too."

Her face flushed. Now she gripped my hands, more certain of our kinship. "What happened?"

"She lied to me about being adopted. When I puzzled it out, I was furious. Hurt." I affected a wounded look and stared through the window, where a tree I was soon to paint lazed in the summer breeze. "I came back to myself and found I'd strangled her to death."

Now Delilah's tears welled for me. "You must have been so afraid. What did you do?"

"My real mother helped me."

"Poor Richard." She placed her hand upon my cheek. "You couldn't help what you did. In a situation like that—that's shocking. Anyone prone to anger is going to snap with that kind of news."

"I only hurt myself. Evangeline was sad, and lonely. She was the only person who cared about me for my own sake, even if she was afraid of what she saw."

"Well, she's not the only one anymore. And I'm not afraid." She drew herself up. "I know you, and I love you. No matter how red your hands are, they'll always be beautiful to me."

"Even if the red was yours?" Now I was being playful, but the erotic idea lowered my voice.

She smiled, wanly, and I dreamed a hint of leer into those lips. "I love you."

"Because you think I wouldn't?"

"Because I know you would."

"What gives you that idea?"

Laughing, Delilah sorted through a box of miscellanea. "The shelves full of books about serial killers? The way you look at yourself in the mirror? The way you look at me?"

"How do I look at you?"

She straightened, the faded red collar gripped in her hand. "Like you're going to eat me. Like a dog looking at a big, juicy steak."

My hands settled on her waist. She seemed so small I fancied I might crush her. Perhaps she had a point. "Wouldn't I love to. How scrumptious. Your delicate ears," I nibbled, "your soft breasts," I touched, "that sweet rump," I squeezed. "No meal would be the same after a bite of you."

She squirmed and giggled, more excited than disturbed. "Do you ever think about things like that?"

"Sometimes." Never had I admitted such a thing, but there we were. "Cannibalism isn't the focus. It's that moment of death I think about. Do you ever think about it?"

Her lips pursed. "I think about my own death, sometimes. I used to more often, but now it's just ... I don't know, background noise. But every now and then, I ..."

"You?"

She was blushing, laughing, covering her face in her hands. "I don't want to say it, it sounds stupid. You'll think I'm weird."

"What if I told you my favorite fantasy was slowly torturing and murdering a beautiful woman?"

We stared into each other's eyes, Delilah all but trembling. Her voice was a near-whisper. "Sometimes, when I touch myself, I think about being raped, or kidnapped. I wouldn't ever want something like that to happen in real life. I don't know what's wrong with me, I have such sick thoughts."

I caught her face. "There's nothing wrong with you. Nothing wrong with fantasies. Have you done much experimenting sexually, Delilah?"

Maroon, she shook her head. My hand tangled in her hair. "I suppose your husband was too soft to give you what you needed."

"He never wanted to hurt me. He was a nice man."

"Well, I'm not a nice man. I want to hurt you." My nose brushed hers. "I want to make you feel good, and bad, and everything in between."

"Richard?"

"Yes?"

"Are we healthy?"

I laughed as I kissed her. "No, my darling. We are not healthy. But that's fine, as long as we're aware of it."

This seemed to please her, or placate her, at least. She smiled against our kiss. Then, squirming, she said, "Let me get some garbage bags. Will you help me clean up?"

"Of course. It's my studio, after all. But won't you be tired tomorrow if you spend all night cleaning?"

Delilah paused on the threshold of the room. "I love those dogs so much, but I came home, and saw you, and felt like I wasted my day. We could have flown kites, the weather was perfect. Maybe I'll stop going. I had the dogs because I didn't have anything else. But now I have you. I don't want to keep busy when you're right here. Feeding the stray cats is enough kindness. I want to save the rest for you."

Then she left me in the mess of her memories. Why, I even felt a few pangs of my own. In private, I studied again the bowling trophy, the golden figure frozen mid-roll. She was generous, Delilah. She saw through faults, to the qualities of the soul, even if she had to invent them. I couldn't do that. One slight, and I remembered forever.

But, perhaps it was time to take advantage of the opportunities given by life. My father, after all, was not dead. He was very much alive. And wasn't this the best time for a man to see his father? At the peak of life, of love? If he were me, he might do the same thing. I can hardly be blamed for trying to reconnect, however it turned out for him.

Chapter

5

How simple the Internet makes the process of finding anyone, let alone a psychiatrist, with a vested business interested in an accessible name. I booked an appointment a month out and bade my time with Delilah. One half-sunny morning when she left for work, I drove to Chicago.

I confess I did not tell Delilah about this trip. Being with her full-time was intense. She was always excited to see me, please me. But it had been a long time since I'd fucked anyone, let alone been part of an actual relationship which might last longer than a few months. It had been even longer since I had loved—though I had never loved like this. She made me wonder what it was like to be kind. I did not want to be a kind person, despite having spent much energy pretending to be one, but I envied Delilah's ability to thrive on kindness. Being kind made her feel good; it didn't make me feel anything. Cruelty, victory, power did. I sought them not for their own sakes, but to fill in me that collapsed sun. Being kind to Delilah also filled it, but I must set aside the rosy lens of love to admit that even kindness towards her was an act of power. I had the power to be unkind, after all, and instead I was warm, even generous. That took strength.

But there were still moments of unkindness, and perhaps it was unkind to go without telling her I would be in Chicago for twenty-four hours. I wanted air to process my feelings of attachment, and to deal with my father in private. It might hurt her more to know she was uninvited. Besides, it was a day trip—driving, an appointment, more driving. She wasn't missing anything good.

His new waiting room had a decidedly modern aesthetic, with a new secretary who asked if I was a relation of the doctor.

"If I am," I replied from behind last month's *Esquire*, "it is distantly."

After twenty minutes, a woman came out, and after thirty more the front desk mannequin said, "You can go in, now."

The office, books and furniture were all new, but the layout was identical down to the old man behind the desk, who, at seventy-one, now looked every bit his age, as if he'd lived thirty years in the past sixteen. Was I responsible for that, I wondered?

"You've lost your personal touch. What happened to greeting patients in the lobby?"

"You're not my patient."

"Oh, good, so I'm finally your son? Let me correct myself to your secretary. I thought we were still playing our game."

"The only one playing is you. I want no part in it."

"You chose this. By the way, why haven't you retired? Surely my pension hasn't left you that hurting."

"My work is too important to just stop. Will you retire from painting?"

"Fair." I made myself comfortable in the therapist's chair, hands folded upon crossed legs. "How have you been, Julius? It's been so long since we last spoke."

"Do you care?"

"No, but I'm curious."

He snorted at his desk phone. "I'm alive."

"Bernadette?"

"Fine, I suppose. Look, what do you want?" Only now he dared look at me, hands spreading. "Am I not giving you enough money?"

"It's always about money with you. Can't a man want his father?"

"So it's male bonding you want. What should we do first? Fishing, or working on cars?"

"I'm sensing a lot of defensiveness. Could it be you feel guilty?"

He brushed lint from his lapel. "Every day."

"I'm giving you the opportunity to absolve some of that, and you're not taking it."

"Because I'm not interested in discovering the catch."

"Is it so hard to believe I'd like to forge a relationship with my father? I'm thirty-three in a few weeks, you have one foot in the grave. Don't you want to know your only son? It's been sixteen years, Julius. Who's to say I haven't grown a little?"

My father exhaled through flared nostrils. "I'll humor you for a few minutes. Why the sudden interest in having a relationship?"

"I met a woman." Already I was overcome by a grin. "The Woman."

"Have you."

"Her name is Delilah."

"I'm sure you'll be very happy until the money or drugs or whatever it is runs out."

"Why are you talking to an eighteen-year-old? He's not even here. I was a different person when we saw each other last, you know."

"Oh yeah? So what's your angle with Delilah, then?"

"I love her, that's the angle."

Julius looked as if I were trying to convince him of Santa Claus, his mouth slanted beneath his lowered brow. "Really?"

"Why is it so difficult to believe if you don't even know me anymore?"

"You're your mother's son."

"Indeed, and yours. You've said yourself our family is full of poets of one medium or another. And who feels more than the artist? Why, you yourself know what it's like to have his heart gnawed through by two women."

To this, he had no argument, and I know because he asked, "How long have you been seeing this Delilah?"

"Since April. But we've written since January."

"Prison?"

"Fan of my work."

"Oh. Oh," he said a second time, drawing out the syllable as he made a connection. "I see what this is now."

"Just like that?"

"Analysis is a gift. The answer comes in minutes, and for fifty more you sit and listen while the patient justifies it for you. At least, that's how it's always been for me. More often than not, I'm right."

"Psychiatry truly is more an art than a science."

He smirked, but I saw in his eye a light amid the ash. It was not a far cry from the one in mine when channeling my work. "Tell me about Delilah."

"She sees my work. Me." I touched my chest—gripped it, truly. "She's beautiful, and kind. And a chef of tremendous talent."

"Sounds wonderful. Are you living together yet?"

"Actually, yes. I just severed my lease last month."

He nodded, his forearms poised upon the desk, hands folded. "Is she a professional chef?"

"No, no, she manages a bookstore in Columbus. Very nice place. She finds restaurant work stressful and unfulfilling."

"Out of curiosity, has she ever been the victim of abuse?"

"Her father was cruel to her. More an infamous Grandpa Dick than lonely Uncle Julius, though."

My snide remark didn't faze him so deep in the flow of our streamlined therapy session. "And how does Delilah make you feel?"

"Like I'm high." I laughed, covering my forehead with my hand. "I've hardly been painting, though I need to. I feel powerful. Masculine. I can't focus on anything but her."

"Because she's feeding your narcissism."

"One must love oneself and let others follow suit. You can't tell me love is pathological."

"It can be, depending on how it's demonstrated. Just look at me. I loved your mother. It was like a knife in my chest, and when she left, she didn't pull it out. She twisted it, and I still loved her. It took that to realize how sick I was."

"I'm not sick, and neither is my relationship. Now, I admit, perhaps we're a bit enmeshed. But what does anyone's business matter if it's consensual?"

"Consent can only get you so far. If a person is unstable enough, they're not capable of giving consent. Can anyone consent to being the source of a narcissist's emotional sustenance?"

"Your eagerness to label me is astonishing."

With a heavy sigh, Julius said, "Fine. What do you think it is?"

"Destiny." Though I heard his scoff, I went on. "Since I received her first letter, I have felt the strangest pull. As if I cannot picture a future without her. Such a small woman casts a long shadow."

He leaned back in his chair, arms folded now. "What do you want, Richard?

"Her."

"And you have her. So what now?"

"Be with her. Bask in her."

"I think we both know there's something more."

There was, but it was only luck that his softball of paranoia sailed in the correct direction. At the time, I denied what I wanted from her, because once I acknowledged it there would be no chance to turn back. "If there is," I admitted at last, "it is not a conscious drive."

"Most are not." A gentle look, almost sympathetic, became his face. Again, he sighed. "You really think you're in love?"

"I know I am."

He chuckled humorlessly, the wave of his hand almost regal. "Well, fine. Have your fun as long as you're kind to her. We'll see the man you are in time."

On the way home, I applauded myself. The meeting had gone well, antagonism aside. And even though I'd been out of town, I hadn't so much as entertained the notion of hiring a call-girl or picking someone up at a bar. Once upon a time, that would have been all I could think of while away from my current lover. I really had grown, and I was so busy self-congratulating that I failed to notice the living room light was on at one in the morning.

As soon as I was through the front door, I was assaulted by a torrent of pillows. "Where the hell have you been?"

Though I used my forearm to protect my face, I heard her tears just fine. "Chicago."

"Chicago! You went to Chicago and didn't even tell me?"

"I didn't think to."

She stood on the edge of the living room, cheeks tear-stained, teeth bared, singularly attractive in only my shirt. "Why wouldn't you think to tell me you were going two states over?"

"Do you know how long it's been since I've had a relationship? I've never cared about anyone I've been with—it was a mistake, Delilah. I'm not used to sharing my comings and goings."

"What were you doing there, then?"

"I saw my father."

Her face and body both relaxed. "Is that all?"

I nodded while hanging my coat. "Where did you think I was?"

"I didn't know." The sob she emitted had me turning back to hold her, and as I took her into my arms, her tears became full-blown. "Your phone was off, I kept trying to call you. I was afraid you were dead." She wept into my shirt, her hands moving over my back to affirm my existence. "Why wouldn't you just tell me, or call me?"

"My phone's had battery problems. I needed some time to myself, anyways."

"Well, you need to let me know that. I'll buy you a new phone if that's what it takes. But if you need to be alone," the very idea brought new tears, "tell me. You scared me. I didn't know whether to kiss you or kill you when you came through the door."

I wiped away her tear. "How about we start with one, then work on the other?"

"Promise you'll never do something like this to me again. I've never felt like this. Don't you care about how I feel at all?"

"Of course. I didn't upset you on purpose. I suppose I didn't know how you might feel, so I avoided the whole thing."

"Well, don't do it again." She shook her head. "How could you not know? What if I disappeared a day and night, then just strolled in at one in the morning, all la-dee-dah casual?"

"I would be angry. And suspicious."

"So why wouldn't I feel that way?"

I spread wide my arms, frustrated, miserable because nothing was worse than a conversation about feelings. "Why and how people feel is a mystery to me, Delilah. I observe, note, and adjust accordingly if the behavior in question merits adjustment."

"Would you say it does?"

Stroking my chin, I said, "In that you find said behavior upsetting, yes. Some compromise is called for."

"Compromise, huh?"

"I'm never going to stop needing occasional solitude, but I will endeavor to keep you informed."

She nodded as she stroked my cheek. "Okay. Do you want breakfast, or do you want to go to bed? I'm going to call in today, I haven't slept a second and can't work on four hours."

"I am famished."

"Me, too."

So it was that we, sleep-deprived, our conversation unfinished, shuffled around the kitchen at one-thirty to make ham and eggs and biscuits and gravy. Delilah did not speak and her silence was louder than any shout. At last, I dared ask, "Is there something still wrong?"

"I just wish that you trusted me enough to talk about your father with me."

"It isn't that. It's a complicated thing, our relationship. I resent him. He hates me. But still, I'm drawn to him. Like there's something to be gained, though I don't expect there is. I avoid thinking about it. Why are you so interested?"

"Because I want to know you." Her hand flattened over my heart. "I want to know every thought you've ever had, and why. I wish we were twins."

As did I. "You want me to tell you about my meeting with my father?"

She nodded; so, I did.

Chapter

6

It was not much later that I first attempted the Piece upon that blank canvas once selected just for her. Sprung from Julius' snide condemnation and Delilah's craving for communication, what began as a sketch of *Echo and Narcissus* began to outgrow its medium. At the outset I produced it as practice, but returned to it again and again. Delilah glimpsed it from over my shoulder one day and emitted a gasp.

"You like it?"

"I love it."

"I'm thinking of painting it."

"Please do!"

"I'll need a model, you know."

Bouncing, she clung to my shoulders, then climbed over the arm of the couch and upon me. "That would be incredible! Please, I'd love to."

Her enthusiasm warranted a storm of kisses, and after it passed I stripped her down and began immediately. In my vision, Echo was inches from laying hand upon her beloved's back; I asked Delilah to reach as if to touch me while I slept, and the tenderness with which she turned her palm stirred my heart alongside my brush.

For some time, it became my sole focus. As Delilah made a comfortable amount and I still had some years left on my stipend, I took a break from anything unimportant. Although she encouraged me to keep an active social life for the sake of my work, my interest in networking had been in steady decline since I was first forced to attempt it. The way I saw it, everyone loves the hermetic poet, the shut-in artist, the deafened composer. Let the world miss me a time, and come upon me in my prime.

This Piece, I felt, was prime. This was going to be my breakthrough. Every brush-stroke reverberated through my arm. When I worked on the Piece—a few hours at a time, often, but sometimes an entire day or more—my heart-rate sped. My face grew hot. Its nuances were unclear, but I mixed the pigments and moved the brushes and trusted the work to reveal itself in time.

But, dear friend, I am a man given to odd turns of mood, and it was with delight that Delilah consoled and coddled me through them. I think it appealed to her maternal instincts, and this variety of Richards (melancholic, alcoholic, manic, insomniac, maniacal, criminal) upheld the novelty of her romantic experience. Whatever might sustain you until the end, my daisy!

It was December when I took leave of my studio to meet Delilah at work and take her to lunch. Minos Books was a labyrinth of a store, so much so the stack of maps upon the front counter came well advised. I found Delilah was not at the front counter and squeezed up a narrow flight of Escher steps. Every section was floor-to-ceiling, each room increasingly claustrophobic, the hallways themselves overflowing with books, and after turns through coffee-table books and twists past romance novels, I found her in the children's section. Well—I heard her before I saw her.

Her laughter was at once welcome, and the precursor of a snag of jealousy. This irrational folly of nerve was revealed as instinctive when I rounded a shelf to see her perched on a stepladder, stocking books passed by an olive-toned young man who might have warranted at least a friendly leer in any other context. Now it was he who leered, examining Delilah's curves each second her turned attention gave him the opportunity. How might his nice, white smile look a few teeth lighter?

But she turned to greet what she took to be a customer, and her face clicked bright as a light. If she was aware of the boy's interest, she did not care; the moment I appeared I became the center of her universe. She sprang from the ladder with my name on her lips. I kissed her, the store and the boy fading until she leaned back for air. "I'm so happy to see you. Grayson was just helping me finish so you and I can get lunch."

The boy—a young, Greek sailor, or so I imagined him beneath his dusky curls—bounded to shake my hand as if I were her father instead of her lover. Amid his gregarious show, I sensed his dreams of seduction. He would have been lucky to lick her shadow. I imagined snapping the bones of his fingers as he offered a dumb smile. "It's great to meet you. Delilah talks about you all the time."

"I think everybody's going to kill me if I don't shut up about you." Giddy, she kissed the back of my neck.

With a sideways glance for the child: "I'm sure they're glad to hear you so happy."

The boy whose name started with 'G' offered a delayed smile. "Sure we are. Delilah's the best. How long have you guys been together?"

"A year in January," she said.

"Really? The way you talk it seems like you've been together a lot longer." Though I bared my teeth, oblivious Delilah carried on, overjoyed. "I feel like it's been longer. Eternal. He's just the most wonderful man, he makes me feel alive."

Her intention was not to harm her young colleague, but I recognized in his dulled eyes the effect all the same. With tightened expression, he mounted the ladder to continue her work. "You guys have a good lunch."

"We will! Thanks for helping, Gravy."

"Yes, Grayson," I snorted at the nickname, not attempting to match my eyes with my smile, "thanks so much."

With a wary look, he resumed stocking. Satisfied for now, I tickled Delilah's ribs until she darted off, a startled sparrow with a wake marked not by feathers, but giggles. I chased her through the twists and turns of the bookstore until we skidded to a stop at the front desk, both of us breathless and laughing in spite of the stitches in our sides. It was the same stitch, no doubt; dancing the thin border of perception separating us, one end of it in her and the other in me. I kissed her until she extricated herself to claim her purse and lead the way outside.

Arm-in-arm, we strolled down the narrow brick passageway leading to a side street in German Village, an area of Columbus whose bricks-and-mortar architecture always struck a few lovely notes in my sensibility. I could not admire it today, troubled that when lunch was over, she would return to the store, and the boy, and his absurd fantasy.

"Friendly young man."

"Grayson's a hard worker. He invited us to a party today, actually."

Bitter heat surged through me. I squeezed her hand. "Would you like to go?"

"Oh, no, I'm so tired, and that isn't my scene. They're all going to be college students."

"When he extended this invitation, did he mention me specifically?"

"Well, no."

"That's because he's in puppy love."

"No way."

"He's flirting with you." As I helped her into the car, I said, "He's a hard worker because he's sweet on his boss. He's in his early twenties. It's a dangerous age because one has the responsibilities and expectations of an adult, but the decision-making capacities of a retarded teenager."

She laughed as I got in. Her hand found my leg, where it was most at home in the car. "I wonder what you'll think of yourself in ten years."

"God willing, I'll hate this self, too."

"Why?"

"Because it means I'll have grown." I took her by the scruff of her neck and kissed her forehead, her mouth. "You make me want to grow, my daisy. I want something better, for me and for you."

With a bite of her delicate lip, Delilah leaned her head against my shoulder and sighed, sighed. "I want to be better for you, too. There's this idea of the perfect Delilah, but she's so distant. I don't know what she's like." The bite transformed into a delectable purse. "I don't know. Maybe you've got a point. About Grayson, I mean. I guess I've always seen it but I've been trying to ignore it. It upsets me."

"Why?"

"He doesn't have the right to look at me like that. Nobody does but you. He doesn't know anything about me, just that I'm nice and pretty. He doesn't see me." Frowning, she crossed her arms. "I wish we lived on a deserted island, and nobody could see me or think about me but you."

Often, this sculpting felt less a labor and more a product of teamwork. A statue shedding marble before its sculptor lifts a finger. Delilah was never a victim; the Delilah who wrote to me, the Delilah born to Jake and Silvia Delacroix in 1981 and brought home to a white house which wouldn't be yellow like sunshine until they were dead. The deceased Delilah, who died mere moments before I did the same, breathing in the syrup of her blood. These were the same woman. The only difference between these Delilahs was that one had craved my influence; one had not known to; the third absorbed it. And me, I loved them all.

Chapter

7

Adept as I am at self-analysis, some answers evade even me. That in mind, I would attempt to address a few associated questions now, rather than suffer future interruption.

It is possible you view my love for Delilah with skepticism. You know enough about me to suspect my every word. Wise—but I mean my love for Delilah more than I mean my love for my reflection. It is a love that has grown each year, and while I confess I loved her less then, I assure you this was because time had yet to unveil more glorious facets for my worship. Then, I was obsessed with Delilah, but did not appreciate her. And, while enmeshed, I was not entirely sure she understood me.

Once, at eleven in the evening, at a truck stop diner outside of town where the night waitress' hands trembled so violently it seemed an aberration of physics a drop of coffee never spilled, I noticed from the corner of my eye a red-haired vixen who smiled as she paid her bill and swept to her feet to leave. For a heartbeat, I imagined she was Susan, then imagined what her face might look red as her hair with my hands around her throat. Delilah's swift misinterpretation of my leer, I was soon to realize, was evidence of issues to which I had been ignorant for almost a year and a half.

Lowering her pastrami sandwich upon the plate, Delilah wiped her fingertips and followed my gaze. Her petulant cough snapped me from my fantasies in time for the question, "Do you like what you see?"

"Not as much as I like what I'm seeing right now."

With a scoff, she attested her love for me, then took another bite of her sandwich. This, she worked on for a time. She washed it down with a sip of Sprite. She smoothed the hem of her jeans in the crook of her knee. I watched her, too hypnotized by every delicate movement to look away now. I had to look at other women because I could not imagine killing her and losing this— her self-brewed storm in progress as she collected the courage to make a

Statement, like a little girl working herself up to a dive off the board. At last, we were drenched with the splash.

"You know, I don't appreciate it when you look at other women right in front of me. It hurts my feelings."

"Would you prefer I hid it from you?" When her look took an infinitely more sour turn, I sighed. "It isn't as if a look means anything."

"How would you react if I looked at other men like that?"

"Aggressively towards the man in question, of course. But not to you. Why, we might even look at them together. That would be fun."

Arms crossed tight, food forgotten, she said, "You don't even like that I have friends. Like Grayson. You hate Grayson, and he's never done anything to you. He's just a boy with a crush. He just wants to be friends, and so do I."

"Hell, Delilah, I don't like me to have friends. Are you lonely?"

"Of course not," she said, quickly, then softened. "You're all I want. But sometimes I get scared that I'm not all you want."

"You are. Men are hardwired to look, and so are women for that matter."

"But I don't."

"So I shouldn't, even if it's harmless?"

"It's not. I just told you it hurts my feelings."

Feelings, again. I couldn't handle those, and spread my hands. "I love you, my darling, but I am not responsible for your reactions."

Her scowl was charming, but in my growing irritation, appreciation was difficult. She glanced around the diner. "I'd like to continue this conversation in private."

"That might be wise."

It took seven and a half long minutes before I was able to catch the waitress and obtain our bill: the tension grew a tumor between us. In the car, Delilah settled with a huff, but we said nothing until the off-ramp, when she cut me.

"You'd tell me if you wanted to sleep with other people, right?"

"I don't, Delilah."

"Okay. I believe you. But if you ever do, please just tell me. We can figure something out." Her glistening eyes turned to her window. "I couldn't bear to lose you."

"And I would never forgive myself for chasing you away." I squeezed her knee. "I have no reason to see other people."

"Come on, Richard, I know you better than that. You don't need a reason to do anything."

"But I don't want to. If my mind ever changes, I'll ensure you're first to know."

She nodded, mollified, for now. "I just love you, is all. And I'd do anything for you. Even share you."

Yes, this I knew to be true, and, being no fool, drew the conclusion that bearing such a burden would wound my fragile flower. I could stand her discomfort no more than she could my wandering eye. When through the front door, she wrapped her arms around my neck and buried her face in my chest. My fingers burrowed through the long black curls pluming to her shoulders, falling across her face, that velvet curtain with a brown-sugar smell which served as backdrop to her alabaster throat. The wave of it crested into the point of her elegant jaw, upon which sat the lips I kissed, hot with repentance, as my hands pawed the curves of her warm, wide hips. But on my end, performance took some time. My mind drifted to the girl in the diner, but on second look, it was Susan, and the thought of tying her up in a hotel room and making new orifices in her body sent me to a dizzying climax that produced a mewl of perhaps too-intense pleasure in my sensitive other half.

As she slept, I lay awake. What was I to tell her? That I hadn't thought of fucking the girl, but rather of strangling my mother? Something prevented me from disclosing this detail, though she knew of my fantasies in an abstract sense. My foremost concern was that it might seem too 'real' to Delilah, and I felt then the need to maintain distance between the dream of me, and the inevitable reality of me. And, a worse detail yet, in order to explain the specificity of my desire, I might have to acquaint her with the depths of my relationship with Susan. Without that background, she would have little context aside from that displayed in a library of Baudelaire and true crime. Though the murderous and cannibalistic devotions slipped from me in the heat of passion had served as a litmus test for her level of tolerance, I was not sure how open-minded Delilah really was, and never in my life dreamed I would tell anyone about what passed between Susan and I. Yet here we are, too, talking about this, in a sense, or sharing it in some way beyond words—I suppose this is afterlife, isn't it? My life, and my self, separate from my life—I lived my life, didn't I? Lived this—but you haven't lived it, not as I have. To you, I must not seem real. If you perceive me at all, you must be something more, perhaps of another dimension, omnipotent, something. You know what you are, mostly, probably, and I'll bet that means you know what I am—an illusion, a soul, a spirit, a character in a play, as Susan often put it. But I don't suppose you have any way of trans-mitting that information to me, or that I would even understand it if you could, or that it would matter, whatever the answer really was. Do you know, at least, what will happen to me when I've finished telling my story? I'm terribly curious. Just as you're terribly curious of the lengths to which I went so Delilah might see reason when it came to the odd harmless glance at an admirable body.

At the end of a March workday, I called the Vasko office and managed (through secretarial incompetence, perhaps) to be connected to the good doctor, whose sigh was audible as he picked up.

"What is it now? My secretary books the appointments."

"It might draw attention if we booked a session for couples' counseling. You're not generally known for it, are you?"

"Has it already fallen apart?"

"Actually, this is the longest relationship I've had." Saying it out loud gave me pause. "I thought it might be good for my father to meet the woman I love."

"Is this so you can have an audience while you pick apart the mistakes I've made?"

"Keep being defensive, and that will be just the reason."

Julius rustled some papers. "Fine. If you need something to do that badly, I'll be here Saturday."

"Then so will we."

"You plan on making me regret this?"

"No more than you regret any other choice you've made."

We left it at that. One can count on a man full of poisonous secrets to keep his mouth shut, lest they all escape. When I invited Delilah to see my father, she set to baking immediately. Why, I was very nearly jealous.

As expected, Julius was fine an actor as his spawn. The locked front door burst open to reveal a bright-smiling man whom I recognized only in context—had I passed this smiling Julius on the street, I would make it fifteen feet before recognition arrived. The effect was not unflattering, nor entirely artificial, but it wasn't Julius.

"Richard! This must be the Delilah I've heard so much about." With both hands, he enveloped her paw, then embraced her, probably to hide his face. Shock brightened his eyes. Perhaps he was not expecting her to be as she was, petite and scrumptious as anything out of her oven. Even after six hours of fretting about first impressions, Delilah was a radiant spirit who cracked the walls of cynics.

"I'm so happy to meet you!" After hugging him around the neck with one arm, Delilah used the other to thrust upon him a box of coffee cake." I hope you don't mind, I didn't know what you like."

"How could I mind? This is perfect." Julius shut the box and ushered her into the office, trusting me to follow, or hoping I wouldn't. "You know, when Richard told me about you, I couldn't believe it. But I guess it takes a certain quality of woman to interest someone like him."

We grinned for different reasons, she and I. As Delilah flowed into a comfortable place in the sofa, Julius and I stood side by side, and for once, neglected to stare each other down. Instead we shared silent admiration, and this time the unabashed gaze of another man did not inspire aggression.

In that office we were two men bound in a communion of contemplation, side by side, in the presence of a soul-moving work of art. We exchanged a sly look, then turned pleasant smiles toward her as she twisted at the waist to see us. "I love your office. The big windows make it so airy."

"Smoggy, maybe." Julius strode to his leather armchair beside the couch, and out of courtesy I allowed him to lead the way. My hand upon the nape of her neck was all it took to remind him of his place, anyway. "I'd like to get out of the city," he continued, "but it's where my patients are."

"You do a noble service. I was in therapy once. Saved my life."

"What made you go?"

She placed a hand on my knee. "My mother passed away. But I've healed, with time, and effort."

"And now you've found Richard."

Ever-bashful, Delilah lowered her blushing face to hide the breadth of her grin. "Yes. And now, I've found Richard. And I'm so happy."

"So there's that much wool over your eyes, huh?"

We chuckled together, a goddess and her shadow. She shook her head. "He doesn't have to fool me. I don't think Richard is a perfect man; I wouldn't love him if he was. There's a corrosive quality to him, I'll be the first to admit, but that's what attracts me. His rationality, and his honesty." Her smile wilted. "So, of course, I have to believe the things he's told me about you, Julius."

The old man nodded. "I hope he hasn't embellished much."

"Some realities require little embellishment," I said, sitting forward.

The ticking clock filled our silence until Delilah took his hand, which had become his point of focus. She squeezed it, saying, "Everybody's done things they regret. Some are worse than others, but they don't define us. That's what my doctor taught me. And it sounds to me that, despite everything bad you've done, you've done many more good things. I didn't bring this up to judge you; I wanted you to know I know, so we don't have to pretend."

Julius nodded, smiling without his teeth. He glanced at me, wondering, perhaps, if I'd filled her in on the finer details of my side of the story, and knowing of course that I hadn't. "I appreciate your saying that. It's hard for me to deal with what I did some days. There were a lot of consequences. There still are. But I try, day by day."

"That's all anybody can do, isn't it. Are those your daughters?" With an elegant turn of her head that sent her hair and earrings swaying just so, Delilah observed the photograph I once admired, still in the same silver frame, still with the same Bichon and the same cream shoulder of a precious demon. My stomach quivered; Julius and I looked away, each with the same dark look. I knew his to be of anguish. Mine was of simmering disdain.

"Yes. My daughters, and my niece."

"They're beautiful. Do you ever see Richard's mother?"

A laugh barked from him and he rose to busy himself, cutting coffee cake with plastic utensils. "No, thank God. I haven't spoken with her for almost seventeen years. I don't think my heart could handle it."

"What do your daughters do?"

It went on like that. I imagine it's a similar experience for most people introducing relatives to significant others, though my relative seemed far fonder of my significant other than of myself. Not that I blame him. In immediately draining the pus, she freed the wound for welcome air. It was a smashing visit—until both my father and I were caught unawares.

"Can I get some opinions on some things, Julius? Since you're a psychiatrist and all." She smiled. "I know it's silly to ask you to be objective in this situation. Richard is your son. But you might see things from another perspective."

He and I exchanged looks, his too pleased now that Delilah was using our session for actual therapy. He leaned forward, elbows on his knees, hands folded, glasses in his breast pocket. "What's on your mind, kid?"

"Well—and I don't want Richard to feel cornered, here—but I have this friend. Grayson." As I sighed, she smeared her palm across my mouth to silence me without having to interrupt herself. "He's a nice boy, and I think he wants to be my friend, but Richard thinks he has a crush on me. Maybe he does, but he doesn't want to get in the way of anything."

"What he claims to want is immaterial," I said, jerking my head away. "He knows what he wants, and he's willing to go to some lengths to get it."

"You don't even know him!"

"That doesn't mean I'm blind."

She crossed her arms, fingers curled beneath her elbows. "Well, I'm not, either."

"I thought it made you uncomfortable to know his romantic intent."

"It does. But I don't have many other friends, do I?"

Observing with the eyes of a man riveted by a tennis match, Julius tore himself away enough to ask, "Do either of you have many friends?"

"No," Delilah and I said together before I added, "But that's not abnormal."

"Of course not, not necessarily. But when two people are very, very invested in one another, sometimes it is good to keep at least ... one foot outside of the relationship, in a sense. A separate hobby, maybe, or a pet, but certainly at least a friend. What isn't healthy is such opposition to the notion of friendship. Why don't you want friends, Richard?"

"I'm not interested in other people. I'm interested in Delilah."

She squeezed my hand. "That's sweet. But having friends doesn't lessen my love for you."

"I think you view them as a threat, Richard," Julius said, the glint of his eyes revealing just how much he enjoyed this opportunity. "Not only a threat to you, but to this isolation you've built."

"How dare you accuse me of isolating the girl. If I isolate her, I am also isolating myself. Delilah is mine, she—"

"Absolutely not." The slap of his hand on the arm of his chair caught me unawares. I straightened, surprised, perhaps closer to impressed. "Delilah is not yours. Delilah doesn't belong to anyone, no more than you belong to anyone. You told me once you felt Susan was trying to own you. How do you think Delilah feels?"

"That's neither here nor there. Nor appropriate conversation in front of Delilah."

"If I'm your doctor, it's my job to push you out of your comfort zone from time to time."

"You can't push me if you're wrong. My relationship with Delilah is nothing like my relationship with my mother."

He gave the look one gives a homeless man in lieu of pocket change. "We'll talk about this another time, since I see it's upsetting you. But remember how you would feel if somebody constrained you."

"They are. Tell me, doctor, while we're at it," I shot a stinging look to my darling, who hid at once her petite scowl, "are fantasies unhealthy? Passing fancies? Delilah took my observation of a woman in a diner quite personally."

"Was she right to?"

"Only if it is wrong to entertain a fantasy."

"There's nothing wrong with a healthy fantasy life. But it's not respectful to ogle people in front of your partner if they're uncomfortable with it. How would you expect anyone to react?"

"A look is meaningless."

"Obviously not to me," she said with the fierceness of a lion cub trying out her roar.

"And friendship is not meaningless to me."

"So, compromise," said Julius. "Either cut out both activities, or allow both within reason. If you really want to be together, you need to understand that compromise isn't changing for somebody. Compromise is just two people striving to grow together and trust each other. Don't you ever see people you want to admire, Delilah? Why not point them out to Richard? You could both talk about the people you find attractive to make it seem less secretive, threatening. And why not invite Richard out with your friends sometime?"

"I have no interest in spending time with a bunch of twentysomething kids, all due respect to my twentysomething sweetheart."

"Well," said Julius, hands spread, "then you'll have to make peace with her visiting friends by herself. Accept your trust issues with Delilah are irrational unless you have actual evidence of infidelity."

We regarded one another, Delilah looking refreshed and myself, no doubt, somewhat haggard, and found between us both warm palms and tender fingers. Compromise, compromise. I supposed I could for a time, but nothing in the world, I knew, could make me accept any friendship of Delilah's. Certainly not with a man. That, I knew, could only end in heartbreak. So I would have to save Delilah from herself. But perhaps there was a point in all Julius had said. Perhaps I might try, and she might do just the same.

Chapter

8

Following the ambush, things were briefly better. I minded my gaze before Delilah, and she did not discuss Grayson. But a lack of communication about the boy did not indicate his absence. It was unavoidable that she should see him, this of course being work; but she was the manager, and could easily invent a reason to fire the child.

The root of the problem, then, was not dealt with; merely the symptom. I was still sickened. I could not help it. She was all I thought about when alone, and on days she was delayed, every second was an agony. I paced the house, stared through the window. Outside, the semi-stray cat she fed each morning waited with twitching tail, accustomed to her usual arrival time, awaiting her attention. From time to time I found myself alongside it, both of us on the porch swing, commiserating over our inexplicable love for just this one.

One night when she arrived home a half-hour behind schedule, she announced plans to meet several work-friends at the coffee house. I sat up from my comfortable place against her side, stricken. "When?"

"They want to meet at eight-thirty, so I'd better get going pretty soon."

I opened my mouth, shocked she should be leaving the house. Then the anger came, and the paranoia. I wasn't good enough for her. She needed to go see Grayson. "Don't you see enough of those people?"

"I do, but Rebecca is such a sweet girl. I'd like to get to know her better."

"Oh," I said, no doubt icily.

"I'll only be gone a couple of hours."

I looked at the clock. "I hope you have fun."

"I hope you do, too. Why not paint a little?"

She was gone ten minutes before I tailed her to her favorite coffee shop in downtown Worthington, barely around the corner from our house. In the golden window lights, I made out Delilah's hair, and some blonde a bit younger than she, and that pathetic little boy, and all three of them, laughing. I retreated, boiling, unable to feel my fingers.

I could not pinpoint why I was angry. I did not expect infidelity on Delilah's part. I did not think she even liked his attention that way. Julius did not realize my trust issues were rational, because Delilah was an irrational type of woman. And if Susan, the almost rational woman left, Delilah too might someday be gone, following the will-o-wisp idea of someone, just as my spark had led her from her husband. I was desperate to grasp every second I could with her, and she with me—at least, she should have been. I was beginning to think Delilah did not understand the urgency with which I acted. She did not perceive the wall of black smog barring the way of the future, coming not now, but soon, and formless. I was panicked because her time was taken up by these life-sized dolls. This couldn't go on. If it did, they might make an impression on her. Some influence I might never manage to shake.

Such a small amount of influence had already altered me, after all. In my studio, I put away Echo and Narcissus, knowing Delilah would not wait for me to speak. Mere words would not suffice. I needed action: a grand gesture, or, at the very least, an ultimatum. If she was testing boundaries, or trying to expand her own, fine. She would discover mine soon enough.

With my tender heart so at the forefront of my consciousness, it should be little wonder I was soon to wind up on my father's couch.

"So what you're saying, Richard, is you want help in isolating your girlfriend?"

"No," I said, exasperated enough to regret the journey. "I am concerned by the nature of Delilah's friendship with this boy. You know, were this Delilah asking about my friends—"

"Hah!"

"—you'd have already given her a pamphlet about how to end relationships."

"Great idea," he said, jotting in the margins of his calendar, "write pamphlet."

"Do people actually pay for these sessions?"

"Most people are asking for help in sorting out their lives, not looking to control those they allege to love."

"If I didn't love Delilah, do you think I'd be this agitated? Look in my eyes, Julius—this red isn't drugs, it's insomnia. I haven't slept in four days. Imagine my mind."

"I'd imagine it's stressful, watching your control slip."

My hands shot into the air and landed on either side of my skull. "It's forever the same! Are you so convinced Delilah is a pure angel subject to my heinous machinations?"

"Nobody's an angel, but she's better than you."

"Well, then it'll come as great surprise to learn that she's known me twice as long as I've known her."

"What are you talking about? Of course she has, she was your fan, wasn't she?"

"My biggest. The girl broke into my house and made a copy of my key a year before I knew she existed. She's lucky she was stalking me, and not somebody who might misinterpret her intentions."

For a few seconds, Julius stared. Then, as he closed his eyes, he pinched the bridge of his nose. "Jesus Christ."

"I know. She's marvelous."

Outside, his secretary answered the phone. Then, he laughed: explosive laughter, heavy and hacking and painful. "It's not funny, it isn't funny at all, my God, but all I can do anymore is laugh." And he did, he laughed until he cried. I waited for him to finish, smiling, polite. For some reason, I thought of Susan. How often had she dealt with him in similar manner?

"I'm glad I gave you a good laugh today," I said as he wiped his eyes. "Now would you consider helping me?"

"No! No, my God, Richard. That girl is sick and you want to keep her that way. You know she's too attached to you to even dream of cheating. You're just a child having a tantrum because other boys like your toy as much as you do. You can't accept that she has a separate identity."

I spread my hands. "I don't want an identity apart from her." Always a surprise, the things I said in his office.

"Richard, you're a smart guy. You know that's not healthy. And if you don't, I'm a psychiatrist, here to tell you it's not healthy."

"I see how it may be perceived as, or even become unhealthy; but some self-sacrifice is normal in a relationship."

"There are degrees. However you rationalize it, this relationship is unhealthy. Delilah is more troubled than I knew, and you're doing nothing but exacerbating her problems. You're gratifying each other now. But some-day, it's going to get out of hand. Someday, one—or both of you—will pose a direct danger to the other. You'll get bored, or she'll get paranoid, and then you'll see what this measures up to."

Still as my heartbeat, I glanced out the window. Delilah's warm hands wrapped around my throat. Reality, fading. My last sight, My Woman's wrathful face. I smiled in a dreamy haze.

"Then I suppose we'll have to make the most of it."

I returned home, still hounded by the threat of Grayson whenever I looked at Delilah. For some time, I struggled to come to terms, as he sug-gested—the modern man, secure enough to pay no mind to his lover's male friends. Still, I felt the gulf. Surely she was the Woman, but she was real, and

I might lose her outside imagination. I foresaw a long struggle, but she was worth it, even as we communicated less and spent less time together. I thought I could handle it, and that I ought to give her room to run. Then, one afternoon, I found her making a cake.

Drawn to her active kitchen as a bee to sprays of spring lilies, I hovered behind her, awaiting my chance to plunge a fingertip into the batter. I kissed her neck. She smiled and cooed. When she glanced away, I made my move from behind her shoulder. She swept the bowl away just before contact, her backside settling against my groin as she said, "That's not for you, mister. It's for a birthday at work. I'll bake you a cake tomorrow if you want."

The smile dropped from my face. "For Grayson?"

As she bent to slide the pans into the oven, she said, "Yes, Grayson. He's twenty-one, everybody wanted me to bake a cake."

"I'm sure they did." The sour note was unavoidable, and as Delilah turned to wash the dishes, her head lowered.

"I guess you're mad."

"You may do as you please," I said, kissing her cheek, "so long as you accept the consequences."

She stopped the water as I settled at the kitchen table. "I know you see something in it, honey, but I don't."

"That doesn't mean it isn't there."

She only baked for people she loved, after all. She loved this boy, and regardless of the innocence, I was stung. Was I meant to sit by as she drifted away?

A terrible thing, though, if the boy were to meet with some kind of tragedy. Things happen every day, after all. Delilah might be heartbroken. She might never make a friend again, knowing the wounds left in their absence. When the dishes were clean, she sat beside me. "What are you thinking?" She shrank an inch as she spoke.

I plucked a recently emptied glass from the table and rose to pour a scotch. Her flinch irritated me. "I'm not your father. I'm not going to hit you unless we're getting off on it." The meekest smile showed on her face until I asked, "Do you really want to know what's on my mind? I don't think you'll appreciate it."

"It's important for me to hear. I wish I could read your mind. I can never guess what you're thinking."

"Well," I said, leaning against her side of the table, "just now, I was thinking about murdering Grayson."

Her silence deepened like night after sunset. I realized she had stopped breathing and went on, absorbing her body language. "I don't like him. I don't like what he represents. Right now I am not able to do it—not because I do not want to, or cannot, but because at present I have no way to do it cleanly."

Gray was the color of my true love's face as I continued, "It does not have to be this way. I do not have to spend weeks fantasizing about his death. You do not have to face any serious moral dilemma. You have a choice. Either have done with me—"

"Never."

"—then let him go on Friday, or be his friend until he turns up dead."

Any other woman would run to the police, but I knew by then that she would not. A frown driving furrows into her cheeks, Delilah turned her glassy eyes toward the window. "So close to his birthday. It's cruel."

"Far crueler to force me to act."

She looked over her shoulder, then at the hem of her lemon-cake dress, which she tugged over her knees. "I just wanted a friend," she whispered again. "I didn't mean anything by it."

I pushed her hair from her face. "I understand. But we're together, and if you are my Woman, you will understand why I say I want us to be so close there is no room for Them. Only Us, together. I want to love you so intensely there is none left over for anyone else. Yes, that's it—to nullify myself in you."

Flushed, she kissed me, a kiss fiercer than her kisses had been in some time, and soon she clung around my neck.

Not a normal woman, my Delilah: but a great one. I pulled her into my arms and sat her upon the table, devouring her mouth and neck. I saw in her eyes the reflections of my desires, saw our wants and hopes as mirrors. As I pushed her dress to lay kisses across her ribs, she gasped and murmured, "But you can, though."

"Can what?" My tongue darted against her navel.

"Hit me."

And, well, she said it with such a wicked grin, I couldn't very well refuse her. Could you?

Chapter

9

On Friday, Delilah returned fifteen minutes early to report she'd let the boy go. ("Budgetary issues".) We never again spoke on the matter except for a chuckle, and things went back to normal. She had proved herself again. I'd been a fool to doubt her. Not very long after, we had a breakthrough. We sat in a bar in downtown Columbus one evening; a place notorious for its confectioneries as much as its cocktails. Out of, yes, respect for Delilah, I diligently avoided observing the slender creature with a short, red bob, who lounged like a pearlescent housecat in the corner of my eye, there amid some colorful shadows filling her round booth with her, chatting, laughing, and I didn't dare to look at the woman lest I upset my Woman, but I supposed it was an acceptable sacrifice. Delilah was absorbing enough that night as it was, her eyes a smoky focal point in the middle of her face, just as the steep cut of her black velvet dress provided a fine focal point for her svelte figure, her arms swaying through the air as she spoke, sloshed her drink, laughed and leaned into me.

Three drinks deep, she lifted her head to whisper into my ear, "Do you see her over there? She's so beautiful."

"I don't know if I'd say beautiful. You're beautiful," I said, running my lips across Delilah's cheek, back to the crest of her ear. "She's just—sexy. There's a difference."

My darling threw a petulant look my way, though there was tipsy humor in it, and we both giggled as I mocked it back to her with a cartoonish lower lip while she loudly insisted, "I can be sexy."

"You are, though, but that's the thing. Beauty encompasses that. Sexiness is inherently banal. Fleshly. Beauty, though, is the realm of the mind. It can take the fleshly form," I giggled at the combination of words and stroked her thigh, which made her giggle, too, "but it's so much more than that. It's intangible, this kind of attraction." My damp lips brushed hers as I murmured, "I want to maybe fuck her once. I want to fuck you until I'm dead."

141

She cooed, laughed, as her hand slipped beneath the table to land upon my thigh, then slide between my spread legs, so she could discreetly knead the bulge in my slacks. "You're such a romantic."

"Aren't I just."

"That grin." She laughed, covering her mouth with her free hand. "You look so evil."

"That's only because you know me." My gaze skipped like a record across the redhead because she happened to be glancing my way when I looked, and I would hate for the stranger to feel ogled and find an excuse to hop bars.

Delilah observed this, comfortable with it when liquor was in her, and whispered, "What would you do after?"

"After what?"

"After that one time, with her?"

I knew just what she meant, but played coy, bending my head to correct her. "It's not so much a matter of after, darling, as it is before, during, and after." My mouth opened to exhale a sigh against her ear as she gripped me through two layers of fabric, pawed and groped me.

"But what would you *do*," demanded Delilah, lifting her hand away from me to rest against my chest. I sighed and turned my head to kiss her.

"I'd make sure she was tied down. It doesn't matter how, just that she is." I barely had enough blood left in my skull to string a sentence together, let alone dodge the question. "I might talk to her a little. Get to know her. Hear how she's feeling about what's going to happen. Then, after she's gotten hopeful that I see her as a person, I'd start with my hands. A slap or two. Maybe a punch. The stomach, though. Not the face, I wouldn't want to ruin her face."

Suddenly, I was staring somewhere very far past our booth, the wall, the world, and saw only a ghost. Delilah didn't notice because I whispered in her ear while she nibbled my neck. "Then I'd take a knife to her. Make art out of her. I'd fuck her in the ass with blood as my lube and force her to come, and then I'd strangle her."

Against me, Delilah shivered, and I only half-realized my hand had crept up beneath her dress to brush the damp lace hidden there. She turned her head up to whisper, and I heard the smile in her voice. "I'd help you bury the body."

I remembered Susan's words, and chuckled, and turned my head to kiss her. Between the kisses, I asked, "Would you watch?"

"I don't know, I might get jealous."

I laughed as I rose to pay the tab.

For some reason I felt at her mercy, and reveled in it. They were tender mercies, anyway. We didn't make it home that night. Instead, we fucked in my black '69 Camaro on the top floor of a parking garage, then fell asleep for two hours. I awoke first, just sober enough by Delilah's standards to drive us home. I watched her make-up-stained lids flutter in her sleep as I buckled her in and felt like a sparkler was lodged in my chest. It hurt me—literally ached me—to see her in that moment, pure, natural, beautiful. I was so proud of her. Every day she emerged further from her proverbial shell for me. Every day she gave me more and more. Who knows why she decided to start looking at women with me? Perhaps she felt as if she needed to get back into my good graces, a patent untruth. Perhaps she thought if Julius and I had both suggested something, it merited some consideration. I can never be certain.

But even with all her progress, the Piece looked dismal as ever, there, in the closet, so I arranged to see Dr. Vasko again. Before I went, Delilah asked, "May I come?"

"I'm sorry, daisy," I said, pecking her brow. "You know I'd love you to, but I need to shake off this block."

"Oh," was all she said, but it so deflated her I asked, "Why?"

"I don't know. I was just hoping to see him. I like your dad," she said, a grin spreading across her face. "I love talking to him. He reminds me of you."

I snorted. "I'm nothing like that clod."

"You're both intelligent. You have a penchant for sarcasm. And you're each highly principled. Getting to know him is like knowing another side of you."

"I suppose."

"Honey," she asked after a time, her head in the fridge, "if I baked a pie for Julius, could I trust you to bring it without eating more than a piece on the way there?"

"Perhaps."

She smiled as she shut the door. "And what if I wanted to talk to him on my own some other time? Would that be okay?"

This might be worth some consideration. After all, it was clear Delilah needed a friend, of sorts. Though I might not trust Julius, it would be good for her to make a friend over whom I had some small influence.

"We'll see," I said in sing-song.

In his Saturday-emptied office, Julius responded to news of my conquest with little more than a twisted mouth. "I'm sure you're proud of yourself."

"A little. And she's interested in coming to see you."

"I can't blame her."

I smirked. "If I allow her to, are you going to fill entire sessions with useless sarcasm?"

"No. I'll help her."

"By alienating her from me?"

M. F. SULLIVAN

"I'll help her understand why she thinks she needs you."

A battle between the two of us might be entertaining. The amount of time I had with Delilah seemed endless, but Julius was a persuasive man, and the nature of his profession forced him to hone his art to sixty-minute sessions. Delilah was right: he was very much like me, but his cunning was disguised by an ostensibly good nature and the diplomas for all to see.

"Do you think you'll turn her away from me?"

"I think trying is better than sitting here, listening to you gloat about how you took away the girl's only real friend."

"Very well. You may try—conditionally. The moment she comes home saying you told her something you shouldn't, I'm pulling the plug."

"Don't worry."

"You're smart enough. I don't expect I have to." I flung open the nearest window, situated between two towering bookshelves and above a telephone table. The city of Chicago sprawled before me, a limitless wasteland of homeless and pigeons. "I loathe this city," I said as I smoked, half-sitting on the table. "Why don't you move someplace less gray?"

"Why don't you? Columbus is just as murky."

"I would if I could manage the energy for a project short of suicide."

Julius snorted. "Turn that into a genuine threat of self-harm. I'd be tickled for an opportunity to call the cops on you, even if it was to prevent suicide."

"You know I paint in hyperbole," I said, tipping a candy jar full of stale mints for use as an ash tray. "I'm feeling bleak, that's all."

"Subconscious guilt?"

"Guilt is a waste of emotion. This is just ... almost disappointment." I scratched my grinding jaw, thinking of the Piece, its blurred and mangled figures, its feelings, impressions, lost. Life lost. For no reason at all, I thought again of Grayson. "A missed opportunity."

"Where?"

"In satisfying whatever this is inside me. What is it, Julius? Why can't I rest? The world finds what it loves and is happy, isn't it?"

"Not always," he said. "Not even often. Life is long and full of much joy and strife. Our failures have more to teach us than our victories."

"But I can't move forward now that I've failed. This thing in me—I have to put it on the canvas before I can produce anything else meaningful."

"What makes you feel you can't complete another piece while this one comes around?"

"I know I can't. I've tried. Everything else is a misdirection of energy."

"What makes this one important? Is it going to be your breakthrough, do you think?"

"It's the feeling I get when it's good. When I'm thinking about it, planning it, painting it. But I set it aside awhile, and when I came back, it was all wrong."

144

"How so?"

"The wrong story. Wrong perspective and meaning. There was practically no meaning now that I think of it." Grim, I took a drag on my cigarette. My throat always stung when I smoked but I just never seemed able to kick the addiction. Talking to Julius, though, it always helped. A few seconds to stop and think, something to steady my focus. "I can't call it finished before it's perfect, and I don't know if I'm ready to make it perfect yet."

Julius rocked back in his seat. "Do you realize the depths of your issues with self-esteem?"

I scoffed. "What issues? I'm fantastic—the greatest living artist nobody's ever heard of."

His brow knit; his sympathy always looked too close to pity. "What have you done when you were blocked in the past?"

"I don't know if I've ever been blocked like this. Usually I take a lot of drugs, fill a notebook with sketches, and move on. The work comes back. But this is for Delilah. This is about us, it's too important to be abandoned."

"Invested as you are in this painting, you may not be able to put it entirely out of your mind—but you can set it aside a little longer, gain better perspective on it. Or, as I told you before, you would both benefit from a hobby."

I flicked the cigarette out of the window. "Let me rush out for some tennis shorts."

With a sigh and a roll of his eyes, Julius spread his hands. "Or, you can lie around the house in your underwear, brooding and drunk and miserable. What do I know?" He rested his fingertips on his chest. "I'm only a mental health professional."

"A glorified drug dealer," I said, fetching my coat. "When Delilah comes, would you give her a prescription for something cozy, Xanax, or Klonopin?"

"Feeling anxious?"

"Something like that, maybe." I patted the corner of his desk after buttoning up, and said, "You'll probably see me again in another month or so."

"Oh boy. Another hour of Richard. Tell Delilah to call me soon, please."

"Hey, right." The peach pie. "Walk me to my car. I have something for you."

In the end, he got about two thirds of it, which I think is pretty good. I didn't eat much the rest of that day, so a few missing pieces couldn't be helped. Unwilling to stop for food, on my way home the lining of my stomach felt ready to dissolve, doubling my irritation. My conversation with Julius resonated with me. So much of it seemed so typical I made no effort to hide my sneer. Why, then, couldn't I shake it?

A hobby, he'd said again. After all, when Delilah was not at work and I was paralyzed by hopelessness, my time was spent browsing the Internet and drinking. Delilah cooked and cleaned and lit the house like sunshine, but more and more I was bored. She was mine. She would be mine. There was so little challenge that I fantasized increasingly about murder. And while Delilah responded to my sexual sadism with delight, I was sometimes reminded of an old joke:

A masochist and a sadist are at a party. The masochist walks up to the sadist and says, "Oh, hit me, please won't you hit me?" The sadist, a twinkle in his eyes, replies, "No."

I was listless. While once my listlessness would have translated to philandering, now it translated to smoking and drinking on the couch, starting at eight-thirty while watching Pink Floyd's *The Wall*. When it was over, I switched to cable news and found I'd been missing out: a shooter was terrorizing the campus of some university, and the talking heads didn't disguise their enthusiasm.

Now here was something entertaining. Most men had sports, but I followed acts of violence with equal sofa-bravado. I'd tuned in at the perfect time, because a mere thirty minutes had elapsed and the shooter was still loose. There was no telling what the toll would be once SWAT got him. The report went on with wild speculation over his identity, courtesy of smash-cuts to reporters feverishly theorizing with words like, "allegedly," citing that ever-nebulous source within law enforcement whose oft-false word would be treated as media gospel until the fog lifted. It was a circus, and I was riveted as one is to a lame movie.

School shootings hadn't been interesting since Whitman climbed that Texas clock-tower. He must have been so at ease up there, the tumor in his brain inspiring a state of grace. Anymore it was case after case of teenage angst appropriating bloodsport to get attention. The high ratings made these boys into stars, and made more boys want to be stars. School shootings were part of the need for attention cultivated by reality shows and YouTube. Privacy meant nothing in the face of potential stardom. Eerier each day, Warhol's prophecy.

But worse than the daddy issues and need for attention, mass murder just lacked that personal touch. Where was the intimacy? Why kill, if not to be intimate? Power was a reason, I supposed—Susan's favorite drug. One received that from death. But it was the closeness that appealed. I had never been closer to Evangeline than the moment I was elbow-deep in gore. Was death not as significant an event as birth? Why, then, should it be less intimate? Less personal? It was my greatest fantasy, often floating across my mind as I watched her sleep, that Delilah might kill me once I had outlived my use. I hoped she would eat me when it was done, make soup of my bones, bury them in some fairytale yard, and tell no one. A private ritual to reflect the public one; the one attended by nurses and midwifes and cab drivers throughout the ages. There was no reason it ought to end that way. No reason it should be less beautiful, even if it did not seem so; tender, though it often appeared its very opposite; and bloody, which it usually was. Murder makes a mother of us all.

Once, the intimacy of secrecy was valued. Instead of a melodramatic mission of suicide, people lived and killed in the dark. Sure, some serial killers drew attention any way they could, but far more were artists working in the medium of control. With prudence, a man might spend his whole life killing and never face questioning. People disappeared every day. With no trace, no crime. Only pure emotion from the survivors. The horror, the frustration and confusion. And in the event of a discovered body, an acute reminder of mortality. In short: art.

What happened to those brilliant artists? Men like the Mad Butcher of Kingsbury Run, or Jack the Ripper? Men who knew the value of art is higher than that of acclaim, who evaded capture because they harbored no subconscious wish to die with fanfare at the hands of the State. It seemed more and more that the suspense of the long-term killer was replaced by the instant gratification of seventeen-year-olds on the march with daddy's AK. Though I had read before the FBI's estimation of 30–50 serial murderers active in the United States at any given time, the American media always had too short an attention span to follow them.

Not to say that some don't hope their anonymity might be lost after death. But it is only with the condition of his death while free that an artist might define his life's work as such. Undiscovered, murder is an art. Discovered, it is a crime. Murder is a medium different from any other, yet much the same. Dickinson, stuffing her drawers with poetry. Goya, painting black the walls of his dining room. Vasko, dismembering bodies and burying them in the wild.

For the first time in years I thought of my lost work, Clytemnestra in brassy blood; then of the Woman, and my need to produce for her something more than great, something stunning, a Piece of myself. A sacrifice. The compass of my life pointed in one direction only, and Delilah was a part of it all. A grand work, true art that would mean more than time. More than the ego that came with conventional success—which, no doubt, I would find in tandem.

Delilah and I wanted to grow together, and we would. I could coax her along with me, though I was certain she wouldn't bite immediately. I had much to consider. The medium, for instance; disposal. It was increasingly difficult to get away with murder, but I have long been a proponent of the virtues of negative examples. So, others failed: good. Let them. Artists of all colors, creeds and heritage went nowhere, died fools' deaths. I would look them over and learn again all they had to offer me. With a bottle of wine, I consulted online archives for captured murderers, and reread Ian Brady's Gates of Janus alongside Carl Panzram's prison memoir and the death-row conversations of Ted Bundy. All of them were in one way or another certifiably genius, but they made serious errors. Though I took copious note of these in my head, I refused to write anything. But I suppose I have a confidant apart from Delilah now, haven't I, friend?

Overconfidence was the root of most failures: Bundy using his real name and distinctive Volkswagen, Brady and Hindley attempting to involve her brother-in-law, Nilsen and Gacy stowing refuse in their homes till neighbors complained about the smell and the neighborhood plumbing. To do such a thing at home in the first place was a fool's errand. Sound carries, after all. We lived in a quiet neighborhood where neighbors didn't seem to talk to one another, or, at least, not to Delilah, but even they might question a scream.

The aspects of study and planning came easy. Murder had been on the periphery of my thoughts for decades. A chance to enact my dreams thrilled me to life. During the day I kept a tidy house and greeted Delilah with unfettered enthusiasm, ensuring she was on my arm as we made our reemergence in the art scene. People had to keep me in mind, even if I had nothing yet to show them. When I could, I sought supplies. It was never difficult to pass them off as necessary for my usual work. Quicklime, for instance, was not only a caustic agent that would become my dear friend, but was pivotal in the production of paint.

After a month of preparation, I was ready. I excused myself a few days by explaining to Delilah I would be seeing Julius. After about twenty hours, I would call her and report car trouble, and tell her I was forced to spend the night elsewhere a day or so. How I longed to bring her with me! My darling was too meek to jump into the pool on her own. I would have to coax her in; but before I did, I needed to test the waters.

It's funny. The sordid deed was one which had incubated my whole life, and in the end its timing was arbitrary. I wanted a reason. Now I saw the clearest one, and, eager to get on with it, I made my way to my mother's empty house in the countryside.

Though I had not been in years, the place held up. The fence I installed around the property sometime before meeting Delilah had not hurt. But, I had not maintained the house aside from that, and it towered, faded and peeling in the sun, amid a field of overgrown grass, the tree behind it tremendous, extending one wooden arm to caress the roof.

Inside, the furniture was draped in dust. As I moved through the house to place battery-powered lanterns, I half-recalled the dream of a dead boy and a poisonous woman. Upstairs, the old studio, still full of his old drawings. I knelt before one, found it to be a study for Clytemnestra, and moved on.

The bathrooms were as disused as the rest of the place, and clean-up would be a challenge. I had purchased a great deal of water and rope at a camping supply store, and some tent poles. With a pair of buckets tied to each end of one pole, I went out back and discovered the well was dry, and so ventured to the woods where I knew a creek about a mile out, the very same which drove me to tears in my post-Susan fugue. The walk was longer than remembered, but then I was young and staggeringly drunk and so lonely it didn't matter how far I wandered, or how cold the snow. Now I was in the middle of my thirties, and though that was not old, I was a consistent smoker who endeavored to avoid physical labor. Hauling the water was certainly that, so I settled for the two I filled on one journey as enough extra for now, and turned my attentions to digging six four-foot deep holes spread amid the forest loam. Only three were finished once I exhausted myself. Three days was not enough time to do much of anything to any degree of acceptability. Next time I would think of a longer excuse.

As I unwound to sleep (a joke, truly, excited as I was), I went through the assortment of tools collected over the past months. First, there were practical pieces: a knife (a fine little out-the-front switch number), rope, and duct tape. In a science experiment guided by the Internet, I combined acetone and bleach to make homemade chloroform. I wasn't sure it would work, so to better my odds, I ordered an experimental benzodiazepine, Phenazepam; an unregulated and ultra-powerful drug whose active dose I'd read to be smaller than the head of a pin. There were pliers, and matches, and proper butcher's tools; a bone saw, a boning knife, a cleaver. And, of course, a sizable pitcher to retrieve the pigment.

At nine, I called Delilah, no effort required for her to perceive my agitation.

"What's the matter, honey?"

"The car stalled on the highway."

"Oh, my gosh—where are you? Are you okay, do you need me to come get you?"

"I'm fine. I got a tow, I'm at a hotel here in Gary. The driver thinks the garage should be able to look at it tomorrow."

She whimpered, a puppy in the cold. "When will you be home?"

"I don't know, darling. Sunday, or Monday, maybe. I'll keep you updated."

"Okay." Voice soft, she lamented, "I miss you."

"We'll see each other soon, daisy. Don't fret. Watch some movie you love that you know I won't like. I'll think of something nice for you when I get home."

"You don't have to do anything for me. Just hold me."

We hung up soon after, and I got in the car. I knew just where I was going. Findlay was a town about an hour northwest of the place I'd grown up, had a reasonable population size, and, like most US cities, a dedicated population of prostitutes to keep the sex-starved content. This was ideal, as whores were barely treated as human by most police departments until a serial killer was suspected—and a serial killer was unlikely to be suspected until multiple bodies were found.

Have I offended your sensibilities yet? Do you hate me? Or do you refuse to expend the energy? I am but a man taking advantage of a system. Prostitutes make easy targets in their black market industry, wherein, as Bataille might point out, they make themselves a means to an end. They become things, parodies of people. There are things in every industry, to be sure, but they are abundant in the sex industry, which provides the clearest example by making the body—and the spirit inside—a commodity. I suggest this not as justification, but as food for thought, for a thing's status as such does not give me any right to kill one, I'm told. That is half the fun on its own.

At eleven-thirty, I trolled downtown for prey, my heart hammering with the thrill. Here a blonde, there a haggard brunette, a Latin mama rife with cellulite, a skeleton no more than sixteen if she was a day. After midnight, I found want I wanted: maybe my age, worn enough to look older, with dark red hair and long legs. She was alone, so I crawled down the street beside her a few feet before rolling down the passenger window.

"Heading to a party, baby?"

She looked over her shoulder and in the semi-dark I projected on her the haughty calm of another. "Maybe I am."

With my sweetest grin (the 'little-boy grin', Delilah called it, which carved in my cheeks' long-lost dimples echoing Susan's), I unlocked the door. "So am I. And I'm looking for somebody to go with."

Her eyes lit up at the smell of money, and she unquestioningly got in the car. "Fifty the first hour and a hundred every hour after."

"New customer rates?"

"I like your face." She smiled. Missing one tooth in the left side of the mouth, near the back. There was a certain charm to it, or so I convinced myself, until she asked, "You're not a cop, right?"

"Of course not. Would a cop have this?" Slowly, so as not to startle her, I reached into the glove box and produced the vial of Phenazepam to shake before her glittering eyes. She almost squealed.

"Coke?"

"You done Xanax?"

"Yeah, daddy, yeah."

"Well, you've never done this before." I took her left hand and turned her palm up, uncapping the vial with my other thumb and tipping it. "Want to try? I'm no pusher, I'm just new in town and could use some friends to share with."

"Sure," she said as I tapped out the rough visual equivalent to a 5mg dose, which of course means it was much more than that. She licked her hand clean, reacted to the taste with a face which forced her features into a severe series of once-hidden wrinkles, then offered almost eager directions to a nearby motel, anticipating a fun john for her night ahead. She asked, "First time?"

I affected a sheepish look. "I don't know what I'm doing. I have a girl-friend, but sometimes I want more."

She smiled, her hand on my thigh. "What she doesn't know won't hurt her."

"As long as you're clean."

"Of course. I always use a condom."

I nodded as we pulled into the parking lot behind the motel, an area with one visible camera I was careful to park away from. With the car stopped, I took a breath and reached into my jacket. "You want a smoke?"

"I'd love one."

Smiling still, I slipped open the plastic bag containing the chloroform-soaked rag; I said, "Let me put it in those sexy lips," with my other hand on the back of her neck. She smiled, and closed her eyes, and I crammed the rag over her nose and mouth. She coughed, eyes widening while her body twisted and her lungs began immediate, panicked hyperventilation. Her hands flew in all directions: one jerked the handle of the door, then the peg of the childproofed lock; the other bashed at my wrist, my arm, face, eyes, anything it could find. She got a good scratch on my temple and I made a mental note to cut her nails while I tightened my grip and practically jammed the rag down her throat.

Just as I was getting concerned with the potency of my untested concoction, her eyelids drooped and her body stilled in my arms. I released it, nudged it, and, satisfied it was under my power, bound its limbs and pushed it into the back seat of the car. Then I drove, calm, as delighted as I'd been by my very first painting. How easy! No pimp to chase me down, no sheriff to pull me over. But, there was no such thing as too easy when one's life was at stake.

If I might have but a few memories to keep, one would be the beauty of night-time Ohio as I chauffeured my first, deliberate victim to slaughter. The state highways were a crisscrossed web of growing corn and soybean. There was peace, quiet, not a person on the road, a patrolman who didn't spare a second glance, the sky glittering with stars broken by looming black telephone poles and drooping, fraying wire. The labored breaths behind me, angels of light gracing my radio with hypnotic voices, pregnant moon glowing behind the edges of charcoal clouds. And beyond: black, infinite black, interrupted only occasionally by the street lights, and the distant luminescence of

151

shimmering cities which waved as though mirages, until, through the spell of highway hypnosis, I stood in a cold foyer with the thing draped over my shoulders. I dropped it, and it stirred with a terrible gag. My lip curled as it vomited on the once-shining marble. Delirious from the inhalant sleep and the potent drug, it slurred the words, "This isn't my apartment."

"No," I said, "it's not."

Now it was harder to imagine it as Susan, who was never as confused as this thing looked. Still, if I squinted, it was my mother cowering. If only Delilah were there! If only I could be sure she would understand that this, the foundation of my passion, emerged bubbling because of her. I wanted her to feel what I did, and to feel her feelings in return. I thought of empathy, and the distance between people. I tried to imagine being this whore on the floor beneath me. How a regular person, that distant illustration made of crayon reds and charcoal blacks, might feel. Would I feel any closer to this creature if I had a different brain? A different childhood? What if I were in this thing's place? After a moment of consideration, I finally suggested:

"If I were you, I'd try to run."

Chapter

10

Have I cheated you? Here I thought you so much better than I! In truth, I neglect the sordid descriptions so you may suffer as I did. If you are more like myself than I perceive you to be, human, in fact, or something like it, have you ever spent months awaiting some event and found how quickly the ecstasy of the moment gave way to memory? How instantly you hear the applause, see the credits, stand in an empty living room amid abandoned bottles and plastic red cups. There you are, a fistful of fresh memories, somehow unsure if it was better or worse than you'd dreamed, but desperate to relive the experience.

There was begging, screaming. I saw in the fresco strokes of a struggle, replete with gnashed teeth and whipping body. I called it Susan, and felt good.

"That's not my name," it slurred.

"I don't care what your name is." My boot smashed upon its ribs, the flesh giving and slick beneath the tread. "You are what I say you are."

In the colors and motion, the viewer perceives a child's giddiness in indulging his most favorite game, or perhaps discovering his passion. Yes, I had picked up a pencil for the first time and felt this. Met Delilah, and felt this. The artist has renewed himself with his latest work, and it shows. I laughed as birds must laugh when first they fly. After, in the stillness, I patted a cold, swollen mass of flesh.

"You did great."

Then came the immediate setting about of work, because it wasn't over. When I was a boy, Evangeline had been as much burden in death as in life. But this was playful. I had touched something greater and more terrible than myself, kissed its feet, saw the universe expand, contract. After feeling that, dismemberment was simple. I was out of practice, but butchery is like bike-riding in many ways. I removed fingernails, fingerprints, pulled out the few teeth I hadn't when it was alive, and sliced off more than a few flash tattoos.

Without electricity, the greatest challenge was keeping the blood cold. I made use of the basement again, this time as a root cellar. I dug a hole larger than the circumference of the pitcher, enough to tightly accommodate it in the cool earth. It would do for the time I had. Once each of the six pieces was contained in its own plastic bag of quicklime and bleach, I dragged them to the woods in a sack. With a new surge of energy, I finished three more holes, and in the warm glow of dawn deposited one piece in each. The process of filling them was much faster and easier, and by nine I was compacting the earth, disguising the spots with natural detritus, and then, for the first time in my life, bathing in a stream. I laughed at the frigid water, admiring the shapes of breathing trees, the sounds of birds, as I never had. I did not yet entirely understand the glory of the universe, but I knew that I was beginning to. At the house, I cleaned, rinsing away stains with water and bleach, scrubbing with the stamina of a boy half my age. In the end, not a trace was left, and I stowed the tools under the floor, where Susan had once stowed drugs. Then, phone off, I read mildewed collections of Rimbaud, and discovered, in the back of some Huxley volume, pills which were still good, and lay on the pool table, caressing my memories of a black-eyed creature begging for mercy.

For a solid seventeen hours, I slept, and the drive home was gay as the last morning had been, confidence mingling with euphoria as I returned at nine to an empty garage, an empty house. I took a proper shower for surety's sake, then threw away both my clothes and the thing's, burying them at the bottom of a garbage bag before I did Delilah the favor of cleaning out the fridge. Then, still alone, I brewed the paint.

The actual process of producing gouache calls for a large amount of water to be bound with several hundred grams of Gum Arabic. I, obviously, had a more innovative base. The boiling blood had a peculiar smell—rich, not unpleasant, though metallic. I confess I dipped a fingertip and tasted it, but, of course, it was for the satisfaction and not so much the flavor. Upon combining it with Gum Arabic and clove oil, I secreted it in the very back of the fridge, did the dishes, and slept again, my rewired brain demanding time to settle in.

My awakening arrived with a comet's impact. "You're home!"

My dreams were stuck to me—hadn't I been debating the definition of umbrellas with a fox mere seconds before?—but the sight and slight weight of my darling inspired a paroxysm of lustful joy. I clutched her to my body, inhaled deep the smell of her hair, and felt it was for the first time. "Yes," I mumbled against her ear between heavy kisses, "yes, I'm home, and I don't want to be anywhere else for a long time."

Though locked in my arms, Delilah contorted to remove her stockings under the warm affection of my leer. "Poor thing. Is the car okay? What was wrong?"

My mind shifted into frantic forward gear. "Something with the transmission," I said as my hands drank their fill of soft breasts and hips, invading her clothes to do so. She wouldn't inquire too deeply about the car's details, I knew. "Did you miss me?"

"Every second. I hate it when you're gone." Lashes like dark folding fans batted toward me while her teeth nibbled her plump lower lip. A familiar flush grew across her face, and the effect it inspired was more enthusiastic than ever. "Did you miss me, Richard?"

"The way I'd miss my ear if I cut it off." My kisses trailed over her neck while she half-moaned, half-squealed. "There wasn't a second I didn't wish you were with me."

It didn't take long before we were both naked and burrowed in our blanket cocoon. To be sure, Delilah has always inspired great virility, but I felt like Mars himself. Now more than ever I realized how she loved me, needed me, deserved me. I wanted to protect her as much as love her. Cain might not have suffered the pain of his mark had he a woman to understand it. No mark then, but a badge, as it was to me. An honor to share with the beloved over whom I relentlessly doted.

It must strike you as odd that an act of such depravity should inspire wholesome cravings of home and hearth. You, after all, think me a pervert, and I admit I am. But perversion is a deviation from nature, and to me the only thing more natural than murder is painting. Am I to blame for nature's love of sin?

To me, the most curious effect of murder was the way it transcended sex, yet restored the novelty of the sex act. To be fair, it restored the novelty of every act. Brushing one's teeth, for instance, or strolling to the corner store. Or watching Delilah get dressed for work in the morning. And from the fluid of my rejuvenating act there would spring new life. My perversions, my works, my themes had all been passed through time. I knew that now in the peculiar electricity I felt with every sensory experience. I wanted to penetrate into the hearts of the symbols used, grasp within the real meanings and evolve mere transcendence into ascension.

As she fastened silk stockings around her thighs, I sat up. I considered the paint in the fridge, considered Delilah, the center of my reality. I slithered behind her, my hands upon her taut waist.

"Don't go to work today. I feel I haven't seen you in a year."

Whimpering, Delilah snuggled against my chest. "I shouldn't."

"Isn't business slowing down this time of year?"

"Yes. But it wouldn't be responsible."

"Are you going to lie on your deathbed lamenting your irresponsibility, or will you wish we'd spent more time together? Call in."

With her mouth in a moue of mischievous guilt, she stared me down, until, suppressing her smile, she called in. The sound of her forced rasp reassured me. I had brought her this far. Was it insane to dream further?

To bed we returned, and I might go so far as to say I was tender. Delilah was my Woman, after all. Violence against the other served her well. In time, she would see that. I would pull her into my underworld, my Persephone. After, I stood to get dressed. "We're going for a drive."

An hour later, at the dam where she had first brought me, she was on her knees in the damp grass. "How do you want me?"

Behind her, I placed one hand on her neck. The other gripped the fabric of her red silk dress as she gazed up at me, adoring, awaiting instruction. "Now fight me," I said, and she laughed, but I stared in anticipation. First, Delilah offered token shoves against my head. In response, my grip tightened, and the hand on her shoulder dropped to the hem of her dress. She gasped.

"Stop it, honey, there's people down there."

"You'd better fight me off, then." As my hand cut a path to her panties, she began the squawk-and-flutter routine she reserved for being tickled. Her upper half doubled its density, and after some wiggling she was halfway out of my arms, hanging out of them, stretching to get further.

"Freeze," I said, and once she did, I stepped away and sat before her with the sketchbook in my hands. Persephone poured from my pencil, and the Piece throbbed on the page. It was alive in me like a fetus, and after the studies were finished, we lay in the grass to admire the clouds.

"How much money would it take for you to kill someone?" I asked her, suddenly. "If you knew you couldn't be caught, and the richest man in the world offered you a blank check, how much would it take?"

She laughed. "I don't know if I could ever do that."

"Why's that?"

"I'd be too scared."

"Of what? There's no way to be caught."

"Sure, but what about God?"

I hadn't heard her touch upon religion much recently, and propped myself upon my elbows. "I thought you were done with your Catholic nonsense."

"I am," she said, plucking a few long pieces of grass. "But if the organization is wrong, and you don't believe in Him, none of that proves there isn't a God to judge me. Or to punish me, once I've judged myself."

"So don't judge yourself."

"How can't I judge myself if it's murder?"

"'The most cowardly of murderers is he who feels remorse,'" I said, recalling Sartre. "God can only judge you if you judge yourself. If you are acting against your morals, your deepest inner self, then that is a crime against God. But if you are in the right, if you are natural, why would murder be any different from a wolf running down a deer?"

"Because wolves are meant to run down deer. But people aren't supposed to kill other people. Kind of like with God. He kills in the Bible, but it's different when He does it. It's—I don't know, stepping on an ant. I don't want to step on an ant, but sometimes I do by accident. It's not murder, though, because I'm so big it's amazing I perceive tiny ants."

"Exactly. If God perceives us, it's amazing He does. So do you think He's going to judge us for the things we do? Imagine you are the ant-God. The same Delilah, but now you have ant omniscience, and know their every thought and feeling. Each of the millions of tiny insects, all across the globe— and if there are ants in another part of the universe, you know what those ants are doing and thinking, too. Do you think you would take the time to punish every ant who killed his brother? Who gorged on the colony's food? Are you going to think about their sins, or will you instead view it as a tapestry of emotions, white and black, good and bad?"

"I love all the ants, if I'm the ant-God. Why wouldn't I be upset if they were hurting each other?"

"Because you're still human. You have other concerns. And you love all the ants, you just explained. Wouldn't you love the murderers as much as the victims? Wouldn't they be just as much a part of you?" I sat up further, spreading my hands. "God is not good, or bad. God is a spectrum, if He is anything. But that's the problem—He's not a 'He'. He's not anything. People try to personify a being they cannot comprehend. A being so far above them they are less than ants. They are atoms which make up the universe. It is insane to think God would personally judge each one. And people call me egotistical!"

Delilah laughed, running her hand up my back. "That's because you are."

"Because I know there's only one difference between me, and God."

"What's that?"

"I'm here." I waved my hand in front of my face. "I'm me. And I couldn't be anyone else. I can't imagine what they feel, what they think. God is not bound by that. Not bound by the morals of a short life. God is the infinity of being. Don't insult the Universe by binding It to the same laws to which we bind ourselves."

She was quiet, scrutinizing without disagreement, her eyes hungry to fall away from mine. I gave her the privilege, lying back beside her. As I lay my cheek upon her breast to listen to the beating of her heart, she said, "Twenty million dollars."

Chapter

11

The problem with being the creative type, artist or killer or what-have-you: cyclical moods. This, I think, is caused by self-reflection. One gains perspective on one's accomplishments to find them lacking more often than the average accountant, say. Worse, creativity serves the same master as perversion: diminishing kicks. A touch of greatness whets the appetite for more. What was lived once, we crave to live again. And our cravings bring truer frustration, for we tell ourselves we shouldn't want what we've already had. But despite the thrill with which Persephone and Hades emerged, in six months I was again grasping for meaning. This time, there was no distinct catalyst. Only the necrotic hand of time, which withers the most shining genius. How was I to grow when so comfortable?

Are you the sort of person who needs an excuse to do something? I never was, but such ceremony required saving until I became claustrophobic. This next happened when outside a dressing room where Delilah talked herself out of some party dress. Looking across at an overweight, mustachioed husband and probable father of too-many, I was asphyxiated by the fancy that I could spend eternity awaiting her. Eating the same gourmet meals together, however rich and delicious. Painting the same reincarnated work forever, no matter how beautiful. By the time Delilah stepped out, I was aghast at the trap I'd allowed myself into. My time would only come once, and it was being wasted.

At home, I began swift preparations, and was soon explaining to Delilah another appointment in Chicago.

"You haven't been in almost ten months. Are you feeling okay?"

"I'm in a rut."

She accepted it, and I thought everything was normal. Before I went on the hunt, however, I called her, as last time, which was my mistake.

"I'm afraid Julius didn't have time to see me today. I think he should at the end of the day tomorrow, though."

"Oh."

She said nothing after this, and when five seconds or more had passed, I asked if she was there.

"Yes. I'm here."

I sensed danger. "What's wrong? You'll see me soon enough."

"I know I will, honey. I'll be okay. Have a good night."

Striking was the absence of affection—no 'I love you'. Now I faced a decision: go placate Delilah and miss out on the ceremony, or stick to my story so both of us might be happier overall.

Though a proponent of risk, I know when I am caught. I fled after four hours of disappointment to buffer my hour-long drive home. The lights were on, and Delilah was in tears upon the couch.

"I'm home. You can stop crying now." I dropped my keys and as they jangled upon the phone table, peeled off my jacket to let it fall on the floor.

"Where have you been?"

"What do you mean?"

"I talked to Julius. You never planned on seeing him."

I have no doubt the color flushed, then drained from my face, the surge brought on by naked fury. "You make fine use of your friendship with my father."

"If you don't want me calling your father, don't tell me lies."

Now was not the time for statements of logic. Working on the edge of my brain to support my lie, I scrambled with, "I wouldn't do a thing like that."

"You're doing it now, you windbag. Why won't you just tell me?" She hiccuped back a few more tears. "Is it another woman?"

"No, Delilah. I am not cheating on you."

"But how can I believe that? I love you, Richard, oh God. Don't you understand the way it tears me up when you lie? What are you hiding? Why can't you be honest?"

"How am I to predict your reaction? I wish I could open your head and pick out each exquisite thought, absorb them. But I can't. I can't predict you. And any lie I tell you would only be a result of that unpredictability."

"Nice justification."

"Don't act like you don't know me, haven't known me since before we began. If anything, your advantage at understanding me is unfair. I'm blind." I waved a hand before my eyes. "You are so much my contrast, Delilah. You're Technicolor. I want to be like you, but the best black and white can hope for is gray. I understand your gradient, but in translation, the truth of the colors are lost. You know that. And you've always known that. I'm what you want, what you love. If I felt any differently, I wouldn't be your Richard."

Delilah's mouth wrenched, as it often did when she was beginning to shift blame to herself, or at least question her conviction. She wiped her hand across her eyes. "That's no excuse for lying. Nobody knows what somebody else is thinking. Instead, they treat other people with kindness and honesty, and don't do things that might hurt them. Especially when it's somebody they love. It should go both ways. I may have had extra time to know you, but you've seen me since the start, all my ichor as much as fresh air. You can't claim complete ignorance of my feelings. You can observe, and I know you might not visualize consequences, but you're smart enough to understand cause and effect."

Yes, I knew that, of course, I knew all that. But what was I to do? How was I to consider Delilah's feelings when my dreams lived, when the Woman lived, when I killed for fun and so far got away with it—you tell me how I could be expected to manage her feelings! Yes, it's terrible, I know, but there's no point in lying now, and that's simply the way I am, and I do not love Delilah any less for it and did not then, but still I crossed my arms. "I don't know what you want me to say."

"The truth."

"I've told you that."

With a sob, she darted for the bedroom. "Then you shouldn't have bothered coming home."

The door slammed and locked behind her. I stood in the middle of the room, almost trembling. As the air stilled, I shoved a favored lamp from the table to see it shatter, gave one hard rap against the bedroom door, and left when she didn't open it.

This time, the whore was from Columbus, and I put it out with a bag over the head. As it was not my first effort, the house was well prepared when I arrived; kits of toys packed beneath the floorboards, along with tarp and mops and plenty else. As I arranged the objects before the creature already bound to a chair, its eyes grew like a cat's in the dark. It leaned against the back of the chair, screams muffled by the gag to which it had awoken in the car.

"That's in your mouth so I don't have to listen to you." I waved the first knife I drew. "You're not going to contribute to conversation, so why bother?"

As I approached, it shook so hard it vibrated the chair legs upon the floor. My empty hand found the back of its head. Tears streaked its cheeks with black eye-shadow. When it emitted no sound, I saw in its face shades of Susan's to inspire the heat of rage for her, for Julius—even for Delilah, now, for not understanding. For not being here. But to do harm to her in the mind's eye would be blasphemy. That was what my mother was for.

If the surrogate cried out when slapped, it screamed when I pressed the knife to its cheek. "Nobody's going to find you. If they do, they won't know it. A toothless skull, a femur. But they won't find you. It'll be as if you never existed. That's okay, though."

I crouched to look into the eyes of its hanging head. "You're going to be something great. You're important to me, and Delilah, and the world of art. You're doing a good thing here with me. Better than anything you'd have done if left to your own devices. Given this, or a hospice death at seventy, I'd choose this."

Wet eyes squeezing shut, it took a few ragged breaths. The tip of the knife pressed against its stomach. "Will you be quiet, now?"

It nodded. I nodded, too, but felt hollow. My body was here, but my spirit was home with Delilah and our fight. I wanted to tell her the truth, but couldn't. Perhaps I could manage some small gesture to console us both. The sound of her joy was all I needed to ease my restlessness. I took a breath, braced myself for the effort of an apology, and patted the thing's wet cheek.

"I'll be right back. Don't go too far, now."

The signal in the foyer was weak, but a bit of wandering toward, then halfway up the stairs got me a bar. When the call got through, I listened to one ring, then two. And then, I realized that, though Delilah learned from her mistakes, and remembered to silence her phone this time, it was on vibrate, and probably leaning against something solid in her purse, and that solid object's reverberations now echoed through the gaping foyer. With it, bounced that familiar intake of breath.

I whipped around to seek the source of the noise. The buzzing ceased without trace. I ran down the stairs, my phone my flashlight as I caught the frame of her ankles mid-run. I pushed myself, smokers' lungs seizing with the effort as I tailed her out the door, around the massive house, close to the woods, so close I might lose her, but now—first a few hairs tangled around my knuckles, then a dress, a yelp, Delilah on the ground, me collapsed upon her. Panting, I said, "You need to let me explain."

But Delilah kept fighting, her eyes wild with real terror. She slapped me, punched me. I tried not to enjoy. As I got her arms under control against the ground, she gasped, "Please, Richard, please don't hurt me. I love you."

My grip relaxed a little. "I'm sure this looks like a strange situation, but I promise you are the only woman I've slept with since well before I knew you, and I wasn't about to fuck that one."

Her darting eyes making drive-by contact with mine, she whispered, "I know. You were going to kill her."

The air between us fell cold as corpse breath. "Why would I do something like that?"

"Stop it." Her teeth gritted. Somehow, those wrists slipped free so her little hands could beat upon my chest. "What makes you think you can treat me like I'm as stupid as all the other girls you've dated just so you could get one over on them? I've given you my heart, my soul, my house, my money. I let you throw away my parents' things, I gave you a place to paint. I gave you my body. I gave you all my secrets, even the ones about Mom. I've never asked for anything but you, and the truth is a part of that. But you don't respect me, or trust me, or think about me. You can't even answer a yes-or-no question. You can't do anything for me that won't benefit you more."

Each word was like another slam in my chest. I had to look away as she mentioned secrets, because I could not look Delilah in the eyes as I did the rest of the world at a time like this. Yes, she was different. Yes, I owed her more than this. "Yes," I snapped, still hot from our argument, overcome by new adrenaline. "Yes, I was going to kill her. Are you happy?"

"Of course I am." She shouted the words, then almost relaxed. "Thank God you finally said it. Thank God." Her chest pumping for rabbit breaths, laughing softly, crying, "What kind of person am I?"

I laughed, too. I knew just what kind of person she was. It was as if I was meeting her all over again, a little boy discovering a little girl hidden in a book of terrible possibilities. She was more than a lover—she was my true friend, whom I had been a fool to doubt. Delilah's face glowed in the dark, an earthbound moon and two lovely craters in which swam my reflection.

We blinked at the same time. "Richard?" Delilah touched the corner of her mouth. "Are you crying?"

"I'm sorry," I said—and just then, when first I reached toward a spark so hot my spirit dares not touch it even now, I meant my apology. I kissed her, and the strange warble of the world ceased as my hands moved over her warm body.

As we separated, she smiled the way Evangeline sometimes had when I came home late but didn't reek of mischief. "Can we go inside to talk?"

After helping her up and dusting us off, we entered through the kitchen. Delilah looked around, awed, and I lead her through to the dining room, intent on avoiding conversation about the previous owner. I sat her at the head of the table, kissed her, and said, "Excuse me a moment."

In the sitting room, the chair had tipped over, but the thing in it was no closer to escaping its binds than it was when I'd left it. It had, however, succeeded in breaking several nails.

"That's a good idea," I said as I sat it up. "We'll get to pulling your nails out soon. Just relax. This is a moment of peace. Enjoy it."

I took the lantern with me and, to my pleasure, it illuminated the glow in Delilah's cheeks, beneath the tear-stains. I sank into the seat to her right and took her hand. "How did you find me?"

Delilah toyed with her phone, her fingertips tracing the grooves of the case. "I followed you—saw you get off on the exit you've pointed out to me before. I parked about a mile away and walked."

"We've driven past this place all of once."

"I never forget anything you tell me," she said, placing the device face-down. "You showed me once when we were on our way to the museum in Cleveland, and I told myself I'd remember it if you ever disappeared again. One more place to check." She swallowed, cleared her throat then looked through the kitchen toward one sitting room entrance. "I found your tools, everything you have in there. And I knew what it meant, but I made myself pretend it didn't mean anything. You'd show up by yourself and there would be some other explanation." Her eyes watered. "But I was right. You're a murderer."

"Delilah, you cannot honestly say that you had no idea this was coming."

"Yes, but—it was just a fantasy. I knew you were a bad man, that's what I like about you, because you're still good to me. But killing her—why?"

"Art," I said, gripping her hand. "Art, and you."

"Me."

"Yes, my God, my inspiration! If it wasn't for you, none of this would have happened. And that isn't a bad thing," I hastened to assure her crumpling face. "It's real art, wretched and stirring. A spike of emotions for so many people—and you know that paint I made last year?"

She stared, nodded slowly. One moon-white hand loosened the top button of her blouse to ease her breathing.

"This is big, Richard," she murmured, tracing her thumb over her suprasternal notch. "Do you think you can get away with it?"

"I already have, twice in my life."

"Your mother—and another one like this."

"That's right."

Her fingertips drummed upon her clavicle. "Why all of this? It's more than me, or art."

The question quieted me. "I am not sure. A way of coping, perhaps."

"With what?"

"With—" I tapped my fingers upon the table, and suggested that nebulous cause. "Life. Murder is a beautiful thing. A powerful thing. It gives me the strength to keep my head up. Because I am close to death, I am grateful for the life it affords. I've wanted you to experience it with me for so long. The fresh breaths after I've finished are unlike any breaths I've taken. I'm so glad you're here."

"You should have told me sooner."

"Would it have made a difference?"

"It would have been nice to know what I had really gotten into."

Her words echoed ancient ones of mine. I remembered the humiliation of being in the dark. Empathy, once so foreign a concept, became simple in the empty house with Delilah and a sacrifice. Gripping her hands all the tighter, I said, "I was afraid you wouldn't understand."

"I don't know if I can understand," she said, pulling away to rustle through her purse for a bottle of pills, "but I don't have to condemn. Or maybe I do, but I choose not to."

My hands were cold without hers. I watched her take one of the pills, then, with consideration, a second. The remainders rattled in their bottle as she struggled to re-cap it. When she did, she dropped it to work her hands over her temples. "What am I going to do? I love you so much, Richard, but how am I supposed to live with this?"

"By knowing it doesn't make you a bad person."

"It's murder, Richard, for no reason."

"For every reason. For art. Are you going to let the rest of them dictate your life?" I waved to the window behind us, to the room at large, as if we were at that very moment surrounded by a jury of so-called peers, or, at, the very least, a spectator such as yourself. "They don't know you. They aren't living your life or mine. They can't see the higher purpose, can't understand that this is because I love you."

Her eyes lifted. "Do you mean that?"

"Yes. Yes, of course. My love comes bursting out of every pore—if I were a cat, I'd leave dead animals on your porch each morning. Instead I do this, my love, to paint for you. To produce something transcendent."

The curl of her eyes indicated that no matter how faded her smile, it was still a true one. Now it was she who reached out, her thumb tracing the peak of my cheekbone. I cradled that hand, saying, "I know it must take a lot to be with me. I am not emotional, I'm challenged by showing love in ways which involve neither words nor money. This is what I have for you, instead. All I have. It is not what you've always wanted, but this is what we are."

Licking her lips, Delilah admired the dusty grandfather clock. "Is it me you want to kill?"

"No," I said, maybe too quickly, struggling as I was against an influx of sublime imagery. I pulled her out of the chair until she made the transition into my lap by herself.

"No," I said again. "I do want to know your every molecule, inside and out. I want to smear myself in your viscera. Drink and bathe and paint in your blood, you avatar of the divine. But I couldn't live without you now. I couldn't kill you unless you wanted me to. And once I did, I'd have to kill myself, too."

Delilah rested her forehead against mine, flushed, almost smiling. "Never say that. I can't stand the thought of something happening to you."

"Nothing has to." Her eyes caught me, held me, darkly glittering onyx stones adrift in opal pools. My arms wrapped around her so I could better kiss her softly gasping mouth.

"Do you think less of me?"

"No," she breathed, "never."

"Will you stay with me tonight? I want you to see it."

With a hint of feral terror, Delilah's gaze whipped to my face, then to the distant door of the sitting room. Moment after moment, we sat in the silence of a gallery, the type laden with a thousand opinions. I could only wish to know. Agony, that silence. Such agony I decided she wouldn't do it, so I'd have to slowly convince her to accompany me to the next and though I had no doubt I could—

"Okay," she said at last, "I'll watch."

Like a boy on Christmas morning, I crushed her to my breast and laughed. "My Delilah!"

"I don't know how this will affect me," she said against my shoulder, "but I can try to relate to you. I know I would kill for you, if anyone tried to get between us."

"Woe unto those who would dare," I cursed. "However it affects you, you don't have to cope with it alone. I'm here. Come on." I ushered her from my lap with a kiss on her cheek. "Let me show you my work."

Hand in hand, I pulled her to my secret burden, which made me a happy outsider still desperate for company in his isolation. My heart bounded with love, and by the time we were at the door I was so suffused with adrenaline that I burst into the room with a theatrical slam.

"Surprise!" I shouted, and the thing emitted a cry, shrill despite its gag. "We have a special guest! Oh." I registered somewhere in the rev of mania the sound of metallic clattering across the floor. Then I noted the overturned chair, and the ropes frayed around wrists bloodied by hysterical effort. I slid my gloves on and bent down.

"I gave you tons of that stuff to put you out! You must do a lot of drugs to be awake like this. Valium? Xanax?" I looked at it as I picked up the knife, examined the sheen of barely stained metal against leather. "Probably Xanax," I said to Delilah, who was frozen in the doorway with fascination in her eyes and repulsion (or terror, if there is a difference) on her pallid face.

The thing in the chair wrenched back its head to see Delilah. Then, its shoulders trembling with its sobs, it looked her in the eye. My darling's watered, then squeezed shut, her head turning towards me.

"What am I supposed to do when she looks at me?"

"You don't have to look at it if you don't want to. I will. Just try to remember it's not a person, Delilah." I crouched before it, obstructing its view of her. The smell of perfume was faded by sweat—musky and foreign. It regarded me with pupils stretched to hide blue irises, snotty nostrils flared. I remembered the first day at Martin's place off the highway, when he invited me to attend the slaughter of a fine Hereford to ensure I was broken in. Both animals had wet, dumb, wretched eyes, and both served the world better dead. "If you want to keep your eyes, you won't look at her. You'll look at me. Do you understand?"

The thing nodded, matted eyelashes batting. For the second time that night, I did the courtesy of setting its chair upright. Then, tut-tutting, I knelt behind it. Behind Susan.

"The mess you've made of these." With one hand, I gripped the wrist, and folded back the initial layer of duct tape. It had gotten a fair nick in itself and blood welled across a blue vein. It tracked that road, then spread upon the duct tape, and I saw upon her flesh what looked like roots. I was entranced.

"What a lovely idea," I murmured. "And a good night for it. I'm so glad you're here, Delilah." I pressed the tip of the blade to the whimpering creature's forearm. "Nothing, after all, may be said to be art until it has an impact on an audience. Otherwise," I dug in, and here came a shriek, "it's just a tree falling in the forest."

Delilah hugged her shuddering frame. "That would explain the noise."

"Put on *Tannhäuser*, then. I'm feeling operatic tonight." I waved to the boombox in the corner, the CD already set to go. She did, lingering beside the source of music, and I carved the thing's arm while it howled against its bit. A pattern of furling red like the fractals of reality blossomed before my eyes. Its flesh was worn, but yielding beneath the metal. Once or twice—mostly on the edges—I slipped and cut to the red rind of meat. Each time, I thought of pumpkin carving, a treasured tradition of mine. This was much easier, and I only had one person to awe, rather than a neighborhood.

"What should we do for our Jack-o-Lantern this year, daisy?"

"I don't know." Though her voice was so soft as to be otherworldly, I realized she must have moved, and found her just behind me. She stared, entranced, a dazed look in her eye. I grinned.

"Do you like it?"

"It is—it's beautiful. It's horrible. I feel like I'm going to throw up but it's like this—I don't know." She put her hand to her forehead and half-fell into a sitting position upon the floor behind me, studying my face. "You look so happy. Like we've met again for the first time."

"We have, don't you see?" I put aside the knife to the tune of relieved gasps from something far away, something I heard beneath the chorus of pilgrims. After stripping off the gloves, I took Delilah's soft face in my hands. "We have just met, because you are here, and I want you to be here forever, with me forever, so we can show each other who we really are for the rest of our lives. Will you marry me, Delilah?"

The words flew out of my mouth on their own, but I meant them. Of course I meant them, my Woman! And oh, her eyes, suddenly shaking off her daze, bright Delilah peering through her drugs, big white orbs like the china in her mother's cabinet. But best, that smile of flashing dimples, smiling with her whole body, arms around me, a sweet mouth on mine, Wagner's chorus crashing around us as Wolfgang watched Elizabeth ascend to Heaven, the heat of Delilah, the smell of terror, oblivion, woman, death.

Chapter

12

Delilah became Mrs. Vasko several weeks later, in a civil ceremony featuring a broken air conditioner and thick July humidity: but her smile so glowed, we may as well have been at Notre Dame. The roar of her beauty stung my chest like a collapsed lung. Of course, the days before the wedding were somewhat rockier.

The morning following that first night, (I say 'morning', though in truth it was late afternoon) surprised me, because she had ended everything in a fine mood, all considered. But by her awakening, she was quiet. She did not look at me, did not get up. During the hours in which she lay staring out the window, I sat beside her reading *The Flowers of Evil*, mostly silent but sometimes aloud to her, to the sunshine, to all our furniture and future together. This was how Susan once dealt with my teenage fugues, rather than how I dealt with my mother's, my technique being one of resentment and retreat. After four, as I read to her, 'Invitation to the Voyage', she sat up and said, "I think I'll go to Mass."

Now, I knew, was not the time for questions. I kissed her rumpled hair. "As you like. I'll be here."

"Thank you." In the bathroom doorway, she hesitated. "I won't—I'm not going to—you don't have to worry," she settled on at last.

A smile crossed my eyes. "I know."

She nodded, then showered and dressed in a gray gown. On her way out, she stopped to kiss me. And that, then, was the last I saw of her for forty-eight hours.

Things were fine until six, when I received her call. In a fluttering voice, she said, "I think I need some space to just—process things."

Helpless in my studio, I froze. "What do you mean?"

"You go off whenever you need to. Aren't I allowed?"

"Well—yes, but—"

"I don't think I owe you an explanation. I love you. I'll be back. But I really need to think about some things. By myself, please."

I couldn't stand to entertain further conversation on the subject. Seeing as my warm-ups were in vain, I set aside my pencils as I asked, "How was Mass?"

"Strange." Her voice softened so I strained to hear it. "After my mother died, whenever I went to church I felt so sad. No matter the denomination, my throat would close up, my eyes would water. But today I felt nothing. Just a bunch of judgment as people returned from communion and wondered to themselves why I wasn't taking it. It used to be I felt God's absence—but now it's neither absence, nor presence. It's like He never existed at all." Slowly, Delilah exhaled. "I'll be back soon, honey, I promise."

"Be safe," I said as we parted, and that was all we spoke until Monday. The house was sucked of life, and I was disappointed. We were meant to spend the weekend basking in afterglow. Instead she was off sulking. Ridiculous. Sullenly, I brewed my second batch of paint, which was something I had wanted to share with Delilah.

But I supposed it wasn't unreasonable of her to require time to think. Murder, while not commonplace to me by any means, was nonetheless accepted in my mind. It would take her much more adjusting, as she had bought into a lifetime of cultural messages about good and bad and the meaning of death. Perhaps I might ease her transition. Make it as magical an act for her as it was for me. I knew in part I could rely on cognitive dissonance to do the job—she already loved me, deeply, and now saw artistic merit in it, so she could more easily see how murder was an acceptable thing. But more effort was required, and I was grateful Julius had prescribed her that Klonopin, which he also seemed to believe Delilah might legitimately need. Those pills intensified her clumsiness and made her forgetful, but they kept her calm, and happy, and helped her sleep through the night. At least guilt couldn't keep her up.

The trick was filling her hours. When she got home, I would distract her with comfort and love. We would not talk about it unless she was the one who brought it up. And then I would explain my views. I had no doubt I could make her understand my point in a debate, but when emotions get involved, logic becomes lost. Little inspires emotion like death.

For a time, I tried to imagine myself as Delilah in this situation. I couldn't, really. First I had to imagine being Delilah, and that required knowing what it was like to feel a spectrum of emotions which were distant to me at best. Instead I imagined myself in her situation, and I would be terribly enthusiastic if I discovered my lover had an interest in murder. This was where we were different, she and I, but I think it is largely due to our upbringings. While I more or less ignored things like The Golden Rule and empathy from the time I was old enough to grasp the concepts, Delilah took them as gospel because she had no other choice. She was burdened by her feelings, by

169

kindness. And she understood what I said when I explained that we were people and others were not, but I knew she did not feel it.

What I would give to show you into Delilah's head just as my own—what I wouldn't give to see! But that's life, isn't it? In life we live through two eyes only, and sometimes fewer, but never any more. Delilah's story is a different story, and I cannot tell you how she came to terms with the people we were. I am not even sure she ever did. The structure of another's mind—their reactions, their emotions—is all the result of guesswork. We know the person projected before us, but seldom do we see the person doing the projecting, and I am not fool enough to believe Delilah was totally open with me. She repressed so much that sometime after our second murder she had problems with a stomach ulcer.

I do know that when she was away the two days, she at some point saw Julius—an impressive drive for a woman who hated passing and interstate driving in general. I know this because early Sunday evening he called me to bark, "What the hell are you doing to that poor girl?"

"What are you babbling about?"

"Delilah! Explain to me why Delilah just spent two hours on my couch, either manic or in tears?"

I sat up, looking for whatever reason at the clock, then the window. "Delilah came to see you? What did she say?"

"That you asked her to marry you, for starters."

"That's where you say, 'Congratulations, son! I'm proud you're starting a family. Please name your first grandchild after me.'"

"No, that's where I say you have no business dragging that poor girl into this—awful family. You give her this name, you're taking steps towards permanently ruining her life."

"Now you sound like a superstitious old drunk."

"It's just the fact of the matter, Dick."

"Don't you ever call me—"

"That's what you are. You're a dick, and you're walking, talking proof this family is evil. You're the product of two generations of incest, you know. I'm surprised you're not a full-blown schizophrenic yet."

"Oh no," I said, coldly, staring out into the empty street. "No, my psychosis manifests in different ways, I think."

"Like thinking it's a good idea to drag this girl through your muck. She wouldn't even tell me what was wrong. She just kept saying she's scared, she's in love with you and she doesn't know what to do."

I thought on my feet and, after a few seconds, said, grimly, "Perhaps she's dwelling on what happened to Evangeline."

"I don't think I can blame her for being upset to discover after all this time that you're a murderer."

"Well, no, but it wasn't murder. It was—it was a crime of passion."

"It was murder."

"And it never would have happened," I snapped at last, gripping the phone so tight I thought it might explode in my hand, "if you had told me then in your office what I was. If you had told me the truth, nothing like that ever would have happened—I would have known. I would have known the crimes you brought against me from birth, against my mother. I would have had time to cool down before I saw Evangeline. Her death is on your shoulders, Julius—not Susan's, not mine. You don't get to hold it over my head. You don't get to applaud Delilah's skittishness about what I've done. If anything, you owe me this. You owe me your help in getting her over this death."

The line was quiet. I checked the face of the phone. He was still there. After ten seconds he said, "I am not responsible for what you did to your mother."

"Keep telling yourself that. You call Delilah right now and ask her to come back. You talk to her and make her feel better about being with me."

The 'or else' need not be said. He understood, and hung up. I stared at the slab in my hands, then sketched in the womb of my studio, where I did not have to think about anything but my work.

At four on Monday morning, Delilah arrived home, called in to work and slipped into bed beside me.

"I got you a ring," I mumbled in my half-sleep, unsure if her face was another dream, almost certain it wasn't when she kissed me while I added, "Onyx like your eyes."

"Even though I ran away?"

"You didn't run very long. Did you have a nice time?"

"It was okay. I got some things sorted out."

"Did you?"

"Uh-huh. Passion—passion makes us do things. Incredible, strange, terrible things. And passion is what I love about you. What I've always loved about your work. All this is your passion bubbling up to the surface. Sometimes you can't help yourself. And it doesn't mean you love me any less, or that you're a bad person—by society's standards, you are, but I have my own standards. You're more important than morals. I love you more than I want to be thought of as good by other people."

"Who are those other people, anyway?"

"I don't even know," she said with a smile, and that was that.

The next order of business, then, was the wedding. Most of it was easy, but I was given pause. A little pang of something washed over me. Marriage was a tremendous moment in a man's life—I couldn't take this so lightly. I wanted proof that I had undergone this, a witness to assure the doubtful that I was loved. The trouble was we knew no one, particularly no one we wanted at our private-as-possible ceremony, which I hoped to get over with soon.

That was where Gavin and Mark came in. For the first time in seven years, I went to Marion and found them living in an untidy apartment, still together, one particular wall covered in scribbling to which Mark furiously added upon my arrival. "Vasko, shut the door, we're toking in here."

"What are you doing to your wall?"

"I'm planning."

"Planning?"

"My to-do lists," he said as Gavin walked in, still in pajama pants at four in the afternoon.

"Rick! What's going on?"

"I'm about to be a married man," I said, and Mark dropped his marker to spin around and shout, "Shut the fuck up!"

"It's true," I said as the brothers looked at each other and laughed. Mark picked the marker back up just to hurl it at me.

"What planet is this where Richard Vasko gets married? What happened? How many 'shrooms did I take?" Gavin felt his forehead and looked at the clock.

Both were paler than I remembered. When last we spent time together, they were planning a robbery. Evidently they had recently gotten out of jail. Not best-man material, but I figured I could toss them a few bucks for their time and shoo them along after the ceremony. It was only to assuage my paranoid mind, to ensure I was not delusional and that all this was truly happening. "I fell in love. What can I say?"

"She must be a fox," said Mark, holding out his hand. "Pictures, please."

I relinquished my phone. Both ooh'd and ahh'd, and Gavin made as if to pocket the device until I snatched it from his hand. "What a girl," he said. "I can't seem to keep one for more than a month."

"I couldn't either, but then, I didn't want to before her."

"What makes her so special?" asked Mark.

I looked at the phone, then around, and leaned in to half-whisper, "Think of the most insane thing you've ever gotten a girlfriend to do for you."

The pair looked at each other, then responded with a simultaneous, "Yeah?"

"Well, she does that, and more."

It was the only language they knew how to speak, and it was half-true in my case, anyway. They gave high-fives and Gavin said, "That's beautiful, man, no joke. I'm real happy for you."

"I don't know anybody I'd rather have at my wedding than you guys."

"We'll blush," said Mark.

"He says the sweetest things," said Gavin.

I grinned. "Could I convince you to put on a shirt and tie if I bought lunch and gave you a week's warning? It'll take twenty minutes, I promise you."

"Oh, shit," sighed Mark, retrieving his marker to add 'VASKO WEDDING' in block letters onto his to-do list for the week, which overlapped with countless old ones. "Why the fuck not?"

"Mark," I said, trying to stifle my grin, "can I offer you some paper? I have some paper at home."

"No, no, this way is best. I can't escape it. Keeps me sharp. Every time I walk into the room I check myself, and ask, 'Am I being as productive as possible?'"

"I truly admire your attitude. Maybe someday you'll start a self-help course and con millions out of money and time."

"Dream big, Vasko. Dream big."

"And this, then?" On a side wall, in tiny print, was scrawled the phrase: *I'm tripping alone.*

Gavin grinned. "That was me. I was freaking out a little."

"Gavin, are you going to do shrooms at my wedding?"

He scoffed, and scoffed, and huffed, and scoffed, and said, "Why would you suggest such a thing?"

"Don't worry," said Mark, "I'll keep him under control. You tell me when and where and I'll make sure he's decent."

"Thank you," I said. "But who's going to make sure about you?"

"Go fuck yourself, Vasko," said Mark, turning back to his endless wall of tasks. "And congratulations, or whatever."

To their credit, they looked quite nice and were polite at the wedding, though they might have put less lascivious an emphasis on the word 'congratulations'. But I was grateful to them, and so was Delilah, and she was happy to see me with friends—of course, she was just happy. Happy and beautiful, and calm, and understanding. And as we exited the courthouse back into semi-sunny Columbus, I felt as if we were entering a golden age.

Chapter

13

As fine a fit as we were before, Delilah and I were in perfect sync for the next two years. I toiled on the Piece and began a more meager series of nymphs which showed at a local festival and won small prizes along with a few sales to acquaintances. Delilah worked and we were happy, and each spring the Piece began to fail, as it would, inevitably, until I was ready for it—and I knew I would not be ready for it for some years. I began to accept its failure as part of something greater, a life-death cycle surging in and out. Each failed Piece taught a lesson, and the lesson was that the story was not right. The figures, after some time, would lose their sense of self, and become insipid and empty. After Delilah discovered me, I began a new, larger Piece with the two of us as Eros and Psyche, the latter gazing upon her sleeping lover's face in the dead of night. By that December this had failed, and I spiraled until March of the following year, when I announced to Delilah my need for a new revolution of the cycle and a more ambitious work.

"Oh," she said.

"This is for the painting."

"Oh," she said again, and continued washing the dishes with only the barest half-glance toward the pill bottle on the counter nearby. "May I come along?"

I smiled. "You want to?"

"Yes. I want to see you like that, again. You seemed—natural. Honest. You've seemed so honest since I found out."

"Because I have nothing more to hide from you."

"I'm glad." She touched my wrist with her wet hand, squeezed it, smiling still. "I just want you. Your honesty. I want you to be happy."

I kissed her fingertips. This was the life she had chosen for us; the life she allowed. Of course she wanted to be a part of it.

"How do you get them," she asked suddenly.

"They're prostitutes. They get lost in the system more often than not."

"That's so sad," she said, and I nodded.

"It's a terrible thing. But I can't help myself. When I see an advantage, I take it."

"It doesn't seem fair," she said, wiping a knife free of suds. "It's almost—I don't know, too easy. And it gives the wrong impression in your work."

"How so?"

"Well, like Gary Ridgway. He had a prostitute fixation, they were all he killed. What if, someday, they talk about your work like their profession had something to do with it?"

I tilted my head. This was a fair point. "But they're such easy prey."

"Yeah, but it's a pattern. We should strive to avoid patterns. It's okay if all the girls look the same, or whatever, but they need to be unconnected in every other way—including profession."

I drummed my fingers on the counter. "What would you suggest?"

"I don't know. I guess maybe pick some girl up at a bar. That can't be too hard." She grinned at me, almost blushing as she dried her hands. "You could get any girl you want."

"I only want you."

Giggling, Delilah snapped the towel at me before hanging it. "But really, I don't know. That or a sex club. There's one in Cleveland, I think, one of those swinger places? They advertise in *The Alt Paper* sometimes, and lots of regular party-type ones there, too. That's nice and far, and crummy enough that bad things happen to people all the time. If you really want to stick to prostitutes, then, fine, but we should get them from someplace out of state. And I don't like it—what you do with the bodies."

I almost laughed at how vocal she was becoming on the subject, the way any other wife in the world might criticize her husband's housekeeping. "What's wrong with it?"

"They're so clustered. It's scary. If somebody finds one, the police will turn over the whole area and they'll find everything. It's only dumb luck you haven't been caught that way yet, leaving them near the house. We need to spread them out. And not just each body, but each piece. There's a whole lot of state, a lot of roads and farms and woods."

"You've put some thought into this."

"I can't keep you from doing it. All I can do is make sure you won't get caught or killed. I don't know what I would do if something like that happened."

"It won't."

"No, it won't, if you listen to me. And no more cell phones," she said, crossing her arms. "You know they can track you with that. Google knows where you are all the time, don't you even look at the privacy settings?"

"Well—"

"What if the police were investigating us and subpoenaed our phone records—or Google—for our location or search records? It's 2012, honey. It's not as easy as it was when Bundy and Dahmer were running around, and even they got caught eventually. I've read that drug dealers get prepaid phones, they call them 'burners'. We could do that. Do it from whatever city we're ... working—"

"Hunting," I suggested, and she almost cringed.

"... whatever city we're hunting in, paid for with cash so they can't be traced. And if we go to clubs, there will be cameras, so maybe at least I should look into wigs."

I squeezed her close to my breast, kissed her head and said, "We make a fantastic team."

Fuzzily, she smiled. "We do."

A month later, I was fucking her on the floor of the dusty sitting room in front of a terrified thing we acquired at a questionable bar near Cincinnati called The Lodge, presumably due to its proximity to a firing range. The outing had gone fine, if not a little clumsily: Delilah's grip slipped while we were incapacitating it, and for a few heart-rending seconds it was nearly able to free itself. But I managed to hold its dress, and gave Delilah a chance to regain her grip on its wrist. With it bound and gagged, we stuffed it in the back seat, where it lay awake the whole journey.

Delilah trembled in the passenger seat. She had done beautifully in the club as I observed from a distance—bright, charming, she convinced it to come with her to a different club after a few drinks. I retreated to the car just before them and waited inside, and it was over when the passenger door opened. I rewarded my darling with kisses. Halfway back to the house, while cutting through one of a thousand anonymous small towns, we slowed by a side street garbage can and disposed of three phones after wiping them clean, removing the batteries, and removing the SIM card from its device. Then we were in the sitting room, the thing splayed upon the pool table, half-naked and screaming terrified.

Delilah sank into a covered arm chair and inhaled deeply. "She's between jobs," she said, hand cradling forehead, cheek, neck. "Her name is (blank)." I do not remember the name. It didn't matter.

"Forget its name," I soothed, inclining her chin. "This isn't a real person. It's just a thing. A means to an end."

Her lips pursed. She nodded, slowly, then watched the creature I approached, knife in hand. As I worked, I stole glimpses beneath its hiked skirt, and what I saw was sure to be soft and warm as the flesh marked with slits and blooms from my knife. I could do whatever I wanted to this thing, and there was nothing it could do.

"Come here, daisy," I crooned, and slowly, Delilah did, arranging herself behind my elbow. I gripped the back of her neck to consume her with a kiss, one which probed the top of her throat and sought her spirit. I dropped the knife and clutched her while she whimpered, then sank into me. On the floor, I bit into her neck to screams of pleasure, felt her insides, and while penetrating Delilah sank the knife into the thigh of the thing, where I left it, stuck. We had to take a twenty-minute break to recover before I could resume work. Delilah dozed on the floor, then awoke as I broke its fingers.

Tongue darting against her lips, she asked, "Does it excite you?"

"Immensely."

On her knees, she fondled through my pants as I worked. The fact that I had just had sex seemed for once to escape me, and I felt energized for a second round. But now there was only the idea of inflicting sexual torture on my prey. If only Delilah was a bit more open. My body's potential as an erotic weapon was wasted in her jealousy. Then, I noticed the pool cues. Not as easy to snap in half as you'd expect, but very useful.

As I rammed the makeshift stake between its legs, Delilah covered her eyes with a cry. "Oh my God."

I twisted the cue. "What else did it want tonight?" Someone else writhed on the table, someone a few years older but with the same toxic sexuality as this thing. "Nobody comes to a club without hoping to get laid. So, it's getting laid."

In the end I slipped and the cue drove too far, piercing its abdomen. It died of a stomach wound and wasted blood, but it was a good time. Exquisite, like Saint Theresa. But on the way home, Delilah was quiet, and when I asked her what she thought, she said, "You wanted to have sex with her."

"No, I wanted to sexually humiliate it. There's a difference."

Still, Delilah fumed. "There's not a difference," she said after some miles. "It means you're putting her—it—whatever into the role of a sexual object. It hurts my feelings. It's not enough that you kill them, you have to want sex with them, too."

"I wouldn't want them if they weren't attractive. But that's not what it's about. It's like models for painting."

"You don't jam phallic objects into models, and if you do then I have serious questions about your work."

I squeezed her thigh. "I can't believe you're jealous of that thing, darling."

"I can't help it. I want your attention, all of it, good or bad." Delilah hugged herself around her seatbelt, her head against the window. "There's something wrong with me."

"Why?"

She pressed her nose against the glass. "Because when I saw you there, hovering over her, pushing that cue into her, I wished I was her. I want—"

She lowered her head. "No, I don't want you to kill me. I don't want to die. But I wish we could be that intimate."

"We are that intimate. In sharing this, we are more intimate." I gripped her hand and kissed it. "This is a private world, a secret for you and me. Something to bind us. Their roles are fleeting, but ours are steadfast. We alone bask in the secret. The dead have none."

But still, she frowned, and frowned again a week later in Julius' office, saying, "I know it's a silly thing to be jealous of."

Julius tented his fingers and, after a fashion, offered, "I would expect on some level it's natural for a wife to be jealous of her husband's artistic models. Nobody likes to think of their spouse looking at competition all day."

"It's just—I feel ridiculous, because sometimes I wish he wouldn't paint anyone but me. And I know that's not possible, but it's so important to model for him. So special."

"But she's involved in every Piece," I added, "even if only for early opinions."

"Well, Delilah, I hate to say it, but Richard has a point. If he's not doing anything inappropriate with the models, there's no harm in it. I know you want as much of his attention as possible," he said, gently. "You love him very much."

"Yes," she whispered.

"Well, I think he loves you. And the fact that he finds other women beautiful doesn't mean he loves you less. It just means he thinks the female form is worth immortalizing."

"I suppose that's true."

I squeezed her hand as Julius said, "Now, does that mean I think you can stop feeling jealous?" He glanced right while squinting his eyes and screwing up his mouth. "Probably not. But you can reality-check your jealous feelings. Stop and ask yourself, 'is it rational for me to feel jealous in this situation'? So, say Richard is flirting with another girl—that's rational. But if he's painting a model for his work—"

"Not rational," said Delilah, and Julius nodded.

"Right. Think about that. But everything else is okay?"

"Perfect," she sang.

Really, I cannot thank Julius enough for his help in those days of our marriage. Although he was loathe to support our union, he did, so long as I pressed him with unspoken threats. And, too, I wonder if there wasn't part of him that wanted us to succeed—wanted me redeemed. He refused to see I was more than the boy I had been. Still, credit lies with him, because he helped Delilah see murder was simply a method of my love for her. He even kept her drugged for me. And, perceptive as he claimed to be, he had no idea.

Once, he even said, "You know, Richard, maybe you really have turned it around."

"It's only taken you, what, four years to realize it?"

But then another year passed, and another Piece, and there came time for another murder. One night, I'd had a tremendous idea, one that flew me out of bed and into the studio—Hypna and Thanatos, a play on the Greek twins, the two of us, intimate and sprawled, my love, forever on the walls of a crime museum! Richard Vasko and his wife, Delilah Vasko (née Delacroix) murdered, etc., etc. Better than a headstone, I think.

I confess that, in these two years, drunk with the joy of Delilah and the love of blood, I lost sight of the Piece. I had given up trying to know what it was about, resigned to failure before each variant. During the worst of these periods I kept clear of my studio but for one or two afternoons a week. It seemed pointless to keep painting when I was just as happy killing with Delilah. Where could I hope to go with my painting, with anything? In my depressions, my odds of success seemed impossible; in the upward swing following a murder, it seemed impossible to fail, but the upward swings diminished in length and intensity with each occurrence. The dreary Ohio winters stretched far longer than they had when I was young. My Christmas came each spring, when the ground thawed for planting. Everything was new and colorful, and the possibilities limitless.

"But what about the blood from the last one," Delilah asked when I posited our next venture while she, sleepy and drugged, wove a crown of dandelions from our back yard. "Isn't that paint still good?"

"It needs to be fresh. Real. I need to feel the power of the creative process, the movement of life and death."

"Will it ever stop?"

"When the Piece is finished."

"Do you even know what you want it to be?"

"A testament to you."

She quieted, but I still saw stress in her eyes even as she went along with it, somewhat satisfied that I didn't sexually terrorize the fourth one as I had the third. This was a prostitute from Craigslist, used at a public library with Tor and a throwaway e-mail. Of my victims, she least resembled Susan, and I learned a lesson that night about shopping online. To prove I was only after its blood, I slaughtered it as one would a pig, after waterboarding and rede-signing the bone structure of its arms for a few hours. The blood splashed upon Delilah's feet as it drained. I washed them clean with distilled water and kissed them dry.

It was around this time that the 21st anniversary of my agreement with Julius came around, and I wouldn't have noticed it if the checks hadn't stopped. Three weeks into May I realized there had been nothing, and called him on a private cell number given to Delilah a year or two prior. He sounded chipper, so I took advantage of his good humor to inquire, "Have you sent my check this month, Julius?"

"Why, what do you mean?"

"You know what I mean. Or is your wife listening in?"

"No, no, I'm in my office. I just don't know what you mean. It's been eighteen years, not including those two and a half you were in the system. I've thought about this day every day since our deal, and now it's here. I don't owe you a damn thing."

I almost panicked. I had rather expected him to expire before the end of our agreement, and here it was, having crept up on me because I had forgotten it existed. A lifeline yanked away. Delilah made a reasonable amount of money in her position, but what was I to do? My work was coming, but it wasn't as if I immediately sold every painting I produced. That money would be slow to trickle in, assuming it came at all.

"Just like that?"

"When you finish paying a debt, Richard, that means it's finished," he said, and then, with the nerve of all nerves, he hung up on me.

I lowered my phone, and calmly announced to Delilah, "I need to have a word with the good doctor tomorrow."

"Is everything okay?" She reached for me until I came close enough for her kisses.

"There's just some confusion. We're trying to have a conversation over the phone that we need to have in person and," I laughed at the absurdity of it, waving the device in my frustration, "this isn't working. We need to be face to face."

Uneasy, perhaps tuned to my intent, Delilah kept hold of me until I kissed her hand into releasing. I went to bed early, and was in Julius' office by noon. And I do mean, in his office. After he hurried his previous patient out, he hissed, "No."

"Yes."

"This is my lunch."

"What are you, a banker? Get the door." I realized he had shortened an inch in the past few years—so seldom did he come within even a foot of me, it was just then I noticed.

As he slammed the door behind us, he ran one hand through snowy hair. "I suppose you're here to break my legs?"

"I'm going to talk to you."

"Yeah?"

"Yeah." I sank into the seat behind his desk and found the room had a different atmosphere from his position. It seemed more enclosed. Comfortable. All one saw was books and soft blue walls. The patient's perspective was exposed to the elements. I kicked my feet upon the desk. "Who do you think runs this relationship, Julius?"

He said nothing, so I pointed helpfully to myself and asked, "Do you know why?"

"Because you're a coercion-wielding coward."

"No. It's because you're a coward who can't own your mistakes." I smiled as I took the tea party from its place. If only Susan could see Julius getting it from me. After all—squeezing him for money had been her idea. "If you could admit your crimes, you would find it easier to live with yourself."

"I have admitted. I admit every day to myself. Just because I don't broadcast my guilt doesn't mean I don't feel it. But you can't admit—you can't even see what you've done to that girl."

"We're in harmony."

"You're in control of her," he barked. "The times we're all three of us in a room, you watch her the way an abusive parent watches their child talk to CPS. That same piercing stare while waiting to hear what they say next. Well, what is she going to say, Richard? What have you done to make her like this? How can you possibly justify it?"

"I'm not sure you should hear the truth, Julius. It might upset you."

"Enlighten me."

A vein throbbed in my temple. If he wanted so badly to know my business, maybe I would tell him. To me, his litany of regrets was not palpable, and I craved the assurance of his suffering. There was only one weapon in my arsenal capable of such destruction, but using it was a dangerous order. I would have to gracefully frame the issue. "This isn't fantasy, Julius. Doctor-patient privilege doesn't extend this far, so I want you to wait, and understand you shouldn't get excited. At first, what I'm about to tell you will seem like an opportunity to go to the police. It isn't."

"What are you talking about?"

"My hobby, of course. As you suggested. It began as an outlet, but it blossomed into an art of its own." I reached into his desk drawer and switched off the tape recorder there. "Delilah had no idea at first. But she was always meant to. I wanted to share something with her. Something tremendous and holy, but foreign enough that I had to coax her in. You helped. Your role, in fact, cannot be under-emphasized. When I was laying groundwork, you gave her drugs which reduced her anxiety and made her more accepting. Gentler." I smiled at the thought of her. "When she discovered what I was doing, she came to you to reconcile her discovery with her love. You aided her with only a little prodding."

His face was slowly graying, a corpse on time-lapse. I went on, "When she was jealous, you helped her come to terms. And now she's doing better than ever. She's happy, and does everything she can to help me, no matter what she's helping me with."

"What is she helping you with, Richard?" So soft it was almost gentle, his question.

I smiled. "My art. There've been four such Pieces so far, and three wouldn't have been possible without your help. You've been so good to us, Julius. That, you see, is why you can't go to the police. You've aided us in this, even indirectly. Giving out prescriptions so freely, just because I told you to—did you catch that conversation on your tape recorder?"

Slowly, Julius sank into his couch.

"Say something. See what happens to your career, and see what happens to your family when the truth comes out. If you so much as sneeze in my direction, I can destroy your life with a letter and a blood test." I leaned forward, hands folded upon his desk. "I am in charge of this relationship. You've done this to yourself. I am the embodiment of all your evil. I am your cruelty and your selfishness, walking, talking. You might think I'm worse than you'll ever be, but I think Delilah has a point when she says we're much the same. We differ one way, though. I can face what I've done, the true gravity of it. If you had never raped my mother, never been so weak and obsessed over a child, four people would still be alive. Five, including Evangeline," I added after a moment, glancing toward the window.

This lecture was a gambit. I knew exactly how much I was risking, but it was satisfying to see him shrunken and dark. I said, "I could threaten your family. But that would be clumsy, and I don't have to do that anymore. Your crimes speak for themselves, I think. The weight of what you've done—in the end, it's you who has to live with it. People can pull your license, leave you. But you can never leave you."

I rose. "I don't care about the money anymore. You can keep it. Get yourself something nice."

Madness glinted in my father's eyes; the bright terror of an animal, and now I saw the seed from which I emerged. What poetry to leave him there! I began to, my hand almost upon the doorknob, until:

"Hey, Richard."

I turned to find him standing by the desk with flaring nostrils and all but foaming fangs. "You remember how your mother came to me the second time she left you?"

My scalp prickled. He bared every tooth in no smile I'd ever seen.

"We fucked that night, one last time on this desk. That's why I moved it with me." He patted it; a man showing fondness for a favored steed. "I finished on her face. Your mother cleaned herself like a cat, ate every single drop, then put on her clothes and left me, too. But that memory," he met my eye, smirking, "that one's kept me warm for twenty-two years."

I knew exactly what he was trying to get me to do, and still, I came close to doing it, anyways. The distance between us sucked shut. My hand even rested upon the side of his face, the muscles straining to smash his skull into that precious desk. How good it would feel—I tasted it on the edge of my tongue.

But I heard her. Susan. I heard her say my name from the tar pits of my mind. Not my name; an old name. The name of somebody dead and buried: "Dick."

So, I did as my mother would have. I leaned forward, eye to eye, and kissed my father on his hollow cheek. Tranquility washed over me with the kiss, and I stepped back, turned around, and went home without looking back: but I can well imagine now that Julius, upon my leaving, sank into his chair to weep.

I worked all through the night and the next day, and no police arrived. That evening I brought Delilah to the Amish ice creamery she loved, where she enjoyed a sundae and visited with cows, and on the way to and from we passed the isolated old house and saw no activity around the scene. At home we made love, read to each other, fell asleep, and I did not think of Julius.

The note came ten days later, and said upon his stationery: *I won't give you the satisfaction.*

Bemused, I called. It rang through to voicemail, so instead, I called his office, and his harried-sounding secretary answered the line. "This is the office of Doctor Julius Vasko," she said, brusquely.

"I'm trying to get through to the doctor—could you have him call me when he gets out of his session?"

The girl faltered for a few long moments. "The doctor isn't in a session right now."

"On lunch, then, and refusing to take calls?"

"No, it's not— I'm sorry, sir. Doctor Vasko is dead. I'm taking care of his business here at the office, writing referrals."

I faltered, almost laughed, and managed instead to say, "What do you mean, he's dead?"

"I mean he's dead, sir. I'm sorry."

My hand over my mouth, I stared across the street as a tomcat dashed in time to avoid an oncoming car. Bristling, it cleaned its tail on the sidewalk while I said, "My God. Do you know what happened?"

"May I ask who's calling?"

"A former patient. And a friend of his."

"Listen," she said, "why don't I give you the date for his funeral when I have it? I'm putting together an email list—give me yours and we'll notify you for the public visitation."

"It's rjvasko@gmail.com," I told her, adding, "like the doctor's name."

"Oh. Yes, sir." She connected my name with my face and seemed to hop to it slightly, and I remembered only then all the lingering smiles she had cast my way while I waited across from her. "I'll let you know as soon as I have something more. I'm sorry you had to find out from me."

"I'm sorry I had to find out at all."

After the call, I sank into the corner of the couch and held the edge of the phone to my lips. So that was it. It seemed a farce, his death, delivered not in action, but words. He killed himself. I reread the short note, then placed it upon the coffee table.

Once upon a time, I had thought my father to be dead. I remembered this feeling, but it was different then, because I thought I had something to lose. Now all I had to lose was a nemesis, someone I enjoyed spending time and energy tormenting. There was a kind of pleasure all its own in such a relationship, a sustained surge of power, and now, like that, it was gone, and I was cold, and I would have to explain to Delilah when she arrived home that she had lost another friend.

I held her while she wept, and felt myself as if nothing had happened at all. It was disappointing then, but I realize now that Julius' death was only a tool. An important step toward the looming black sea, and a calling home of the creature within.

Act Three

Chapter

1

As though nature conspired to set the mood with the eerie plucks of a tuning orchestra, rain enveloped Chicago the day of Julius' funeral. While dressing in the hotel bathroom, wallpapered in noxious green and yellow, I consulted my reflection for escape plans. I had no reason to appear. I knew no one (no, one). I had been the cause, or Delilah, or both (the satisfaction of seeing him in the ground). She might very well be there (She might very well be there).

In the mortuary lobby, early, awaiting the director, a wilted Delilah asked if I ever imagined my own death.

"Often, abstractly. Sometimes it feels closer than my shadow, but just as often it feels it will never happen. That I'm immortal."

She hugged herself, drawing tight a scarf of burnt charcoal around her shoulders. "Do you wish you could live forever?"

"It's my greatest nightmare."

"Do you want to die?"

"Sometimes. Not actively. But I often think, 'it had better be sooner than later.'"

She squeezed my hand. "I couldn't survive you."

"You won't have to."

"Aren't you afraid of death at all?"

The wall across from us resembled porcelain, smooth and almost gleaming in the sallow light. "I'm awed by it. Life is a fractal of perceptions which exists only by benefit of eventually not existing. 'Afraid' isn't the right word."

She followed my gaze, my fingers losing feeling in her grip. "I'm afraid of it. I wish we could live together forever, no fears. Just joy."

"But that's the beauty of it." I lifted her chin toward my face. "Someday we'll be dead, it's true. But as our molecules remember they once were stardust, so too will they recall the force with which I love you. And centuries, eons from now, when a rabbit chews a leaf, or a seed from a tree lands in a particular patch of dirt, our reincarnated molecules with brush together and the universe will quiver with the fleeting memory of us. That is quiet, Delilah. That is joy. Forever."

She was stirred, large eyes glistening and squeezing shut to hide from the emotion. As I kissed her, there appeared in the periphery of my vision a slim blonde attendant with a gold name-tag the sole fleck of color on her black jacket. As she ushered us into the chapel, a toad wearing a suit greeted us. "I understand you are the doctor's son," he said in Eastern bloc English.

"Estranged," I qualified, the hand not around Delilah slipping into my jacket pocket.

"I see. Mrs. Vasko was insistent. Immediate family only for viewing."

"I am immediate to him, even if I'm not immediate to her. It's his funeral, not Bernadette's. We came early so we wouldn't bother her, or be bothered by her."

The man considered this, then waved us through. "I can give a few moments."

Alone, Delilah and I walked arm in arm the length of the chapel, where the cherry casket opened amid a field of flowers. A wax sculpture of my father had been laid in the casket, eucalyptus tie and white collar pulled high around its neck. So the noose, then.

Delilah squeezed my hand, but I had no reaction. This was mere consummation of the expectation I'd had of him in my childhood. This was where I expected to find him in the first place, and finally I was here; but in his place, a duplicate, the fiend, denying the pleasure of gloating, disappointing with some thing incapable of conversational skirmishes, empty and preserved for the ground. No satisfaction, indeed.

As my wife bent her head to cry against my breast, I drew her through the chapel step by step. We left the mortuary to avoid the rest of the visitors and cruise the steely city with no word exchanged until the way back, when a churn in my stomach alarmed my intuition enough that—poor me— I asked her, begged her one last time, "Are you sure you want to go?"

"Yes."

The end of it, then. Delilah sealed our fate—I told you, darling, nothing good could come of your friendships! Let me be your only friend, you mine, let us head south now, now!

Instead, we entered the half-full chapel, sat in the furthest pew, buried our noses in programs, and waited. Though Julius had been a flighty Catholic, the family selected a Presbyterian minister to officiate. I was considering this with amusement when I smelled it, a ghost's announcement, worse than any rattling chain: the scent of frankincense and rose. A perfume I knew, which brought me back to seventeen, my head in a warm lap while a warmer voice read Roy Campbell's Baudelaire:

Rest on my heart, deaf, cruel soul, adored
Tigress, and monster with the lazy air.
I long, in the black jungles of your hair,
To force each finger thrilling like a sword:

Within wide skirts, filled with your scent, to hide
My bruised and battered forehead hour by hour,
And breathe, like dampness from a withered flower,
The pleasant mildew of a love that died.

I lived the moment again, I swear!

As the vision arrived, so too did it vanish, and I was shaken as the service began.

Vera, the younger, shorter-haired of my sisters was the first to speak, and highlighted her father's generosity, though did not seem to mean it. I was still putting myself together as she finished, and half-listened as maternal-soft Ada expounded upon his compassion, showed to not only family, but patients and the needy. Bernadette spoke third, with brevity, her silver hair pulled tight at the back of her head. She had the tender voice of an old woman who had shouted and sung to at least two generations of children, one which no doubt could tell some interesting stories. What would she have thought of me had she known me as a child?

"I loved Julius. He was my best friend. If we needed anything, he made sure we had it. Money. A house. Beautiful children. But I don't think he was ready to give us himself." She looked into the podium, smiling in private catharsis. How much did she know about him?

"He wasn't good or bad. Julius was human. I think I speak for all of us when I say we loved him despite his faults, because in the face of them all, he made the effort that most people never do—to be kind. We will all miss him."

Delilah's breath hitched as I slid the umbrella from beneath my seat, ready for the closing statements and the procession out. But when the minister stepped up and instead began to apologize, I puzzled over the meaning of his words as though they were a second language. There was an error in the program, he said. One more speaker.

My stomach lurched. His lips moved with a name I couldn't hear above my ringing ears, but as the speaker rose from the front of the chapel opposite the Vasko women, I heard again the voice:

Rather than live, I wish to sleep, alas!
Lulled in a slumber soft and dark as death,
In ruthless kisses lavishing my breath
Upon your body smooth as burnished brass.

To swallow up my sorrows in eclipse,
Nothing can match your couch's deep abysses;
The stream of Lethe issues from your kisses
And powerful oblivion from your lips.

As Susan Vasko took her place at the pulpit, I gripped Delilah's hand to keep her from disappearing along with the rest of the room. Pale fingertips furled around the edges of the old wood, and the toxic eyes of the high-headed woman behind them swept row by invisible row to the back of the room, where they stopped, because they had found me.

"Most of you have not seen me in years," she said to me, her relentless gaze breaking only for a moment, so she might offer the sweetest of crocodile smiles to Ada and Vera, wherever they were. "But there is no finer occasion to reconnect than that of such tragic passing. An event like this reminds us we must never squander the relationships we're blessed with. When cool heads prevail, we must rebuild old bridges. When people grow, and change, we must evolve from regret to re-establishment. It would move Julius to know his death brought us together.

"My uncle was many things throughout his life, and knew better than anyone the importance of change. I regret not knowing him in his later years. He was good to me, once, and though not everyone did, I loved him. He was responsible for making me what I am today, and he has affected many others, each in some unique and drastic way. He never meant to be, but he was an important man, Julius."

With a broad grin that began with me before blossoming, along with her spread hands, to the room at large, she said, "Let's make use of this opportunity: the last gift from a man who moved us all."

One hand stroking the cherry of the casket in a caress that left me cold, Susan left the stage. If only it had been my hand to put him down, my jealousy might have been settled. But now he was martyred; a tragic tale of depression and not the monster I saw. Perhaps that was the root of my disappointment. I glanced toward the exit of the chapel, and when I looked back I had lost track of Susan. Once more, I perceived the pews of mourners. Delilah squeezed my knee.

"Is everything okay?"

I settled into my seat while the minister resumed. From the unmoving corner of my mouth, I confessed, "That was my mother."

Eyes growing, Delilah's focus raked the thinning crowd. She may not have known what transpired, but she knew its effects. "Do you want to leave?"

"Not yet. She saw me."

"I'm sorry."

"Stop apologizing. You never need to." My nose brushed hers, enough to coax a smile from her before we joined the other attendees.

During the ceremony, the storm had receded to a drizzle. The cemetery was flush with blades of emerald, not grass, the marble statues gleaming pearl. We kept to the procession's rear, though I could not track Susan. I was so busy searching backs for reddish brunettes and brownish redheads that I missed the moment my father's symbol disappeared into the ground, but he had become old news when he kicked away his chair. Something new and old presented itself, something which stood apart from time and parodied the movement of others through it. Delilah and I held each other while mourners tossed roses after the casket, and then, again, I saw Susan. The back of her, at any rate, and the slit of her black wobble dress (more fit for cocktails than internments), the end of a tan stocking, the beginnings of pale thigh. I looked at the still-heavy clouds for fear of blaspheming, and again, when I gathered the calm to look back, she had evaporated.

As the crowd dispersed for the wake, my mind flooded with panic. I was going to see her. I couldn't see her. I crushed Delilah to me, kissed her wet eyes and urgently said, "If we hurry now, we can make it to the car."

"Now, Dick," crooned that voice behind me, lower, older, still the same, "you aren't trying to dodge your mother, are you?"

The panicked climax of a nightmare: that moment, however brief, when the mind's eye conjures the face of the Other hidden in the Self. I felt her hand upon my back, and slow-motion-turned to face her, finding as she slid into vision that she had aged as an actress wears make-up to look ten years older. That is, the inevitable lines kissed her features so each was more ornament than wrinkle. The mouth of a woman who smiled often, the bright green eyes of eternal inquisitivity. Even her hair, though graying from the temples, still shone with rich red vitality.

I felt small, and terrified, and knew I had no hope of protecting us. It was freeing, that hopelessness, as much as it was terrible.

The ruby curtain of her lip fell away to reveal her teeth. "I'm so happy to see you, darling. You look well."

"So do you." Stiff with *rigor vitalis*, I bent forward to kiss her cheek, and could not discern whether it was her kiss which lingered, or the ghost of it. "That was a beautiful eulogy."

"It was." Delilah, from my elbow.

"Why, and who is this charming creature?"

"This is my wife," I said, urging her forward, shielding myself. "Delilah Vasko, meet my mother: Susan."

"Goodness," the apparition gasped while extending her right hand, "I have been gone quite some time, haven't I?"

"Twenty-two years."

The old, sly glint crept into her eyes. "So you kept count."

"At least this time I knew to."

Her automatic smirk twitched into a frown so quickly I might have imagined it. "I suppose I can't expect forgiveness. I'm sure you've needed me in your life."

"Not particularly. If anything, I've flourished. My wife, my work."

"You're still painting?"

"I'm still breathing, aren't I?"

Her smile was self-satisfied, and I knew she applauded herself for my accomplishments. "I'm so pleased to hear that. I would love to see your work sometime. You know," she deigned to address Delilah, "I still have the most beautiful early Vasko. Orestes slaying Clytemnestra. Wherever I live, I must hang it in the bedroom so I may think of my son."

Delilah smiled right back. "That's sweet. Do you move often?"

"Reasonably often. There's so much to see and do, I just couldn't stand to stay in the same place more than a decade. Certainly not a lifetime." Her gaze flickered in my direction. I felt a quiet snarl of anger but had no time to retort as she continued, "Have you seen much of the world, Delilah?"

"Not really. We had a trip to Quebec in high school, and I went to culinary school in Pennsylvania. My internship was pretty short but it was with the most beautiful restaurant in New York: Calvaire."

"Oh, I adore Calvaire. A chef! No wonder you tamed him. I'd love an opportunity to taste what he lives on."

"I'd cook anything for Richard's mother," sang my wood-sprite, too sweet to catch the lurid implications I was only half-sure of myself.

"Invite me over sometime, then. I'm considering moving back to Columbus—you two are in Columbus, aren't you?"

Before I could prevent the release of sensitive information, Delilah cheerfully confirmed. I bared my teeth as Susan extracted from her clutch purse a pair of ivory calling cards, one for each of us.

"That does it, then. We must visit each other. I've missed you, Richard." She gripped my hand, staring into me as she had the first time, all those years ago. "What a marvelous man you've become."

"You don't know anything about me yet."

"Of course I do. You're my son."

With an air-kiss for Delilah, Susan left us. Now it was just me, Delilah, the internment crew, and a familiar hollow in my chest. Teeth chattering, I took Delilah's hand.

"She seemed nice, considering how little you talk about her."

"She certainly seems that way," I said, tracking my mother until she disappeared over the hill. When she was gone, I tore apart my card (already softened by the sweat of my palms) and crossed to the open grave to scatter the pieces over the flowers.

"I'm not telling you what relationship to have with my mother," I said, observing the conflict in Delilah's features as she studied her card, her furrowed brow telling me all there was to know. "I just advise you don't have one at all. For your good, and mine."

Delilah nodded, and I led the way back. We resolved to leave the city immediately, though it seemed every light turned red just for us. Only a few extra seconds, minutes—but these extra seconds, minutes were full of rosy Amouge Gold perfume and seaweed eyes. The visions chased us across the states, and I could do little to dispel them, save to touch and kiss and breathe the honeyed air around my wife. It might not cure the illness, but affection could comfort me in my final hours. It was as if I'd been sucker-punched in the middle of my hyperventilating chest. Everything had seemed so clear a few hours ago, hadn't it? Perhaps the murkiness I once felt merely disguised itself as meaning, the way a newspaper, observed enough by a schizophrenic, may carry a secret message.

To have allowed her to keep that card was a terrible mistake, I realized. Tantamount to keeping heroin around a recovering addict. Now that Julius was gone she was desperate for a friend, and thought Susan might be one of whom I could approve. I dared not tell her my reasons for protest, therefore I dared not protest. I dared only to throw Delilah's card in the first trash can I saw while she looked the other way.

If only I could tell you disposing of the card helped me sleep that night. I knew, though, it would only buy us time. Now that she had seen us once, she would find us again, and we would be at her mercy. As we passed the old house on the way home, I began to relive her voice recounting the final two Baudelaire stanzas, and because I could not bear it, I turned on the radio.

Chapter

2

For a final few months, things were peaceful. We discussed neither the funeral, nor Susan, which Delilah knew to be a festered wound. Instead we made good use of our time, jump-started by Julius' death and the terror of infinite futures. Though stalled on the Piece, I set to work anew, churning out quick and small pieces meant to pander to audiences who might spread my name. By my August birthday I appeared at every show I could, and managed an interview with *The Alt Paper*, popular amid local artists and art aficionados. I felt incomplete without the Piece, but trusted it to come in time, and filled the interim.

Those three sweet months—if I could pick any to keep with me after moving from this life, it would be those. Every weekend, we were on another trip to one of many charming landmarks around the state: parks, festivals, local attractions. But it wasn't about doing something; it was about being together, and seeing these things through her eyes. Forging a shared existence, evidenced in a lifetime of joyful memories. I was settled. How could I have been happier? How could I have been fool enough to hope it might last?

Mid-October, our peace came to an end on a crisp Saturday spent with a highly recommended model. Because nude women in the house discomforted Delilah, I visited the girl in her apartment to begin a watercolor of Europa. By three, she was fidgeting, and at four we called it a day. On the way home, I stopped for a bottle of wine, and five minutes later let myself in at home, too spirited to note the red Cobra parked across the street, or to recognize that Delilah's laughter rang in harmony with another. From the living room, she caught my eye, and sheepish guilt danced across her expression before it steadied into a smile. "Honey! Guess who came to visit."

There is a moment after settling into one's seat on a rollercoaster—sometime between the click of the safety mechanism and the baleful approach of the first hill—where one realizes with a delightful thrill of horror that there is no escape. Cause-and-effect has come into motion, and all one can do is hope the next day's paper won't include photos of a derailed cart spilling over with dead bodies. In those precious seconds, Delilah's words still fresh in my ears, I scrambled through my psyche in hope of producing someone, anyone we knew well enough to invite home. By the time the intruder's dark head emerged around the corner, the terrible reality of metal screeching against metal rang cacophonous in my ears, and one by one the boxcars crashed over the edge of the track, and Susan slithered full and evil into view.

"Darling," she said, with that same smile I had loved and loathed before, "I hope you don't mind my dropping by. Delilah invited me and I couldn't refuse an opportunity to visit her. I was planning to sneak away before you returned."

My fist tightened around the bottleneck. "Why is that?"

Impassive green eyes flickered between my hand and face. "I didn't want to upset you."

"Why would I be upset?" Teeth gritted in a smile, I half-slammed the bottle on the kitchen counter and snatched the opener from the drawer. I imagined smashing her skull open, a mess of red wine and red blood to lick from my fingers while I clubbed her to death with a jagged bottle. But the carpet cleaning would be murder.

As I jerked free the cork, I caught the women exchanging a silent look accented by a half-rolled eye from Susan and a drooping smirk from Delilah. I asked, "Already developed telepathy?"

"No, my darling. We're laughing with you, is all."

The women tittered. So even Delilah betrayed me under Susan's sway! I poured three glasses and, after shoving one into the hands of the banshee, retreated to my fickle goddess and enrobed myself in a shield of intoxication. "How did you two get in touch?"

Meek Delilah admitted, "Facebook."

"In her defense, it was I who sought her out, not the other way around."

This glass was half-empty already, through some trick of the light. "Never would have pictured you to have a Facebook." I had checked dozens of times.

"I wouldn't either, but I have been quite intent on making amends with my estranged son. And, of course, his blushing bride. How ever did you manage to find a girl like this? So sweet. Poised. Why, were I ten years younger and six years earlier, I'd have tried to get her for myself."

The white ringing of tinnitus muted Delilah's giggle, but I still saw her face flush, and jealousy rattled me. Susan's every interaction was a seduction, from chats with shop-clerks to conversations with clergy. I could never trust her with Delilah. I wouldn't be killing Susan for satisfaction if something happened between them. Of course, it was not just Susan who had my envy. The attention she gave Delilah had me just as green in the face.

"So," I said upon finishing my glass and helping myself to a second, the bottle returning with me this time, "what have you been up to these decades?"

"Too much. A lot of travel! Argentina, Germany, Japan. I was just telling Delilah about the smell there. Poor plumbing in rural areas."

"You don't say."

"Oh, yes. Let's see, what else ... oh, I married. Twice."

"Did you. Thrice a widow, then?"

With a contemptuous chuckle shared by her vinous reflection, she said, "Very nearly. Dimitri tried to kill himself, and Victor tried to kill me."

As Delilah gasped, I laughed. "I couldn't imagine why."

"I'm afraid I attract a certain personality type."

My wife smiled in misplaced sympathy. "I do, too. It's because we're such open and giving people. That's what my friends used to tell me, anyway." For an instant, she looked sad, then forced a bigger smile for it. "Are you moving back to that nice old house in the country? Richard's shown it to me once or twice."

"Oh, I don't know. These days I'm not sure I have the get-up-and-go for a renovation project. I did drive past it on my way from Cleveland, though."

"It's beautiful," Delilah breathed.

"It was, once. Maybe it still is, but that's for someone young to see. But it still has the same feeling it did all those years ago."

I humored her. "What feeling is that?"

"Like it needs company." Her glittering gaze lingered on me a heartbeat before turning back to my wife. "I found a marvelous apartment downtown, though. I'd love to have you for dinner sometime to repay you for those scrumptious scones, Delilah, darling."

"I'd love to see your apartment!"

"Wouldn't you like to come, Dick?"

My face seared with the heat of a thousand memories, not all (or many) unpleasant. I snapped, "It's 'Richard' now."

"You'll always be my Dick," she said with a dismissive wave of her hand, unknowing or unconcerned by Delilah's visible discomfort in the face of brewing conflict. My mother drained her glass, rose, and slid over her bare shoulders a black leather jacket with leopard-print lining. "At any rate, I fear I may be overstaying my welcome. You will come, won't you?"

"I'll talk him into it," Delilah said with a grin as she walked her to the door. I lingered on the couch, unable to approach.

"Keep him out of trouble, won't you?" Oh-so-European, she kissed Delilah's cheeks and wrapped her into a hug, shooting a sly look to me over her shoulder. Ah, the money I'd have paid to peel off the woman's face!

When she was gone I trembled in my seat. Delilah watched me, hands curled into fists. "We had fun." The same tone of pre-emptive apology used anytime she decided I was owed explanation. I like to think just then I was.

Carefully, slowly, I arranged the words in my head before I spoke them. "Whatever relationship you choose to have with my mother is between you and her, I tell you again. I'm not fool enough to think I can prevent it. But it's a bad idea. You must remember you can never trust her: the moment you do, she's about to destroy you."

Frowning, Delilah lowered herself beside my feet to rest her head in my lap. "I'm sorry she abandoned you. I'm sure it's hard to trust her."

"It's not that," I said, maybe too quickly. My fingers wove through Delilah's hair as I tried to fathom what commonality she might find in Susan to form a friendship. I only saw myself. "I know you want friends. Why not go out with the people from work?"

"I tried that once." She was smiling about it by then, a little 'oh, well' grin-and-shrug.

"Girlfriends, then. Old friends from high school."

"I don't know." She sighed, her face vanishing beneath hair. "I feel guilty when I spend time away from you of my own volition. I don't really know any of them anymore, anyway; Janice has a baby, Allison parties all the time. It's all they post about, and I haven't talked to them in person in years. And I'm so tired of work. Why would I want to think about it in my off hours by hanging out with my coworkers?"

"You should quit, then." A weary smile, a little hope, Delilah, couldn't you feel it coming?

She laughed. "Yeah, right, bad influence. What would we do if I quit my job? You spend money like it has an expiration date."

"I don't know. Buy an RV and drive around. Bonnie and Clyde, Mickey and Mallory."

"I love you, silly man." After a moment of silence in which I set aside my glass, she said, "We don't have to go to dinner if you don't want to."

"I don't, but I don't have a choice."

Chapter

3

Susan's company loomed with the inevitability of death, more now that dinner hung over my head. But I've always thought it preferable to meet death head-on—to direct it, rather than await it. That in mind, inviting death is no small summon, and it took a week to call the number she'd sent Delilah over the Internet.

"I thought I'd never hear from you," she said when she recognized my voice.

"We need to talk."

"In person. Won't you come see my apartment?" She recited the First Avenue address, reading 'Ave' as if it were its own word. Morning traffic kept me from arriving for almost an hour; sixty minutes in which my bones buzzed with anticipation while thick drops of Columbus rain pelted the windshield. I cringed as much as thrilled at the thought of her. Not to mention the effect of such a betrayal upon Delilah—I knew better than to think she might adjust to our perverse consanguinity. What, then, excited me? What sparked this hyper-awareness, as a dreamer gaining lucidity? The sunshine future presented by Delilah split into an infinitude of paths, too many without her at all. An end to our union, I was sure, meant an end to my life.

In the lobby of the high-rise, I was confronted by a doorman with a barrel chest and shadowed eyes. "May I help you?"

"I'm here to see Susan Sinclair, apartment 703."

"There's no Sinclair here, sir."

"I see. She's going by Vasko, finally? Or did she keep the name of the last poor fool she married?"

Beaded eyes took stock of me. Ex-military if ever I'd seen one, that man. The type to get drunk and show off. Loyal as any hound, and intimidating in his black uniform as a pup grumbling behind the fence. "Your name, sir?"

"Richard Julius Vasko," I said, peeling my coat from my shoulders while stealing a glance at his nametag. "May I go see my grieving mother, Mister Hansen, or do you need my license?"

Maintaining an even stare I returned twice as coolly, he plucked up the desk phone and said to me, "No, you're more or less how she said you'd be," then to the phone, "Susan, how are you? Good. I have Richard here. Shall I send him?"

A few seconds later, he thanked her, hit the call button then hung up. My upper lip twitched. "Quite casual, aren't you."

"I like to be friends with the tenants."

"That's how she gets you," I said as I entered the elevator. Behind its closed doors I contemplated my reflection. It would look strange if I simply came back down and walked out. Not that the opinions of strangers troubled me, but Susan would hear of it. Delilah would get a phone call. I'd look weak. But was looking weak all that bad, considering what awaited me?

The elevator doors opened with an old-fashioned chime, and I identified 703 not by its number, but rather by the palm billowing a fountain of leaves beside the unlocked door. Inside was the type of apartment described as a 'pad', replete with conversation pit, burgundy carpet, and permanent bar where stood the smiling hostess, her teeth and blouse glittering in equal measure.

"Would you believe my heart skipped a beat when the boy said your name?"

"You should get that checked out," I said, locking the door and avoiding eye contact by admiring her assortment of oriental knick-knacks; fans and masks and scrolls and such, decorating red walls and shelves which seemed to float against their supports. "At your age, it could be a condition."

She chuckled, wafting to my side as I slipped from my shoes. "Perhaps, but old age comes upon the spirit as much as the body. I'm afraid you'll find I've softened."

"I'm afraid I might believe you."

"Still don't trust me?"

"Less than I ever did."

"Good. I love a challenge." With one hand, she took my coat, and with the other, she gave me a vodka tonic. Then she clicked on the floor lamp beside the door, and stepped back. "Let me look at you now that we're alone."

I stood a little straighter under her scrutiny, I admit. My chin lifted; my shoulders, too. She hung my coat upon the rack without turning her back, then began a slow, cautious approach. "You're taller. And a little thicker, maybe, but not in a bad way. Healthy. Those circles, though." She chuckled, touching the ones beneath her own made-up eyes. "It's hard to say whom you most resemble."

Then, her fingers extended towards my cheek. I stepped back, chest puffing. "I don't know if that's a good idea."

"Why?" Her gaze bounced against my ring finger. "Because you're afraid you can't control yourself?"

"Because I know I can't." Her swan's neck appeared lengthened by the shadows spilling down its milk surface. Brief fantasies of kissing it bled into ones of sinking in my teeth and tearing out her throat. Susan against the wall, gushing blood until she died. I slid my hands into my pockets. "This is dangerous."

"Then why did you come today?"

"I didn't have a choice."

"But you do." She smiled, practically purring as she lowered into her settee. "There's always a choice. You chose to come to my party all that time ago. The funeral, too. Today you chose to shave and wear that dapper crimson shirt. Free will is a burden for which we must admit culpability."

The drink was strong as ever, and for some reason made me realize the apartment didn't smell of cigarettes. The ashtray had only a half-burned joint. Maybe I'd quit smoking. Delilah hated it, after all.

"I had no idea you'd be coming to the service," I lied behind my glass.

"Just as you had no idea who I really was?" She smirked, re-lit the joint, and blew at me a dismissive ring. "Then you were stupider than I imagined, or more naive. You knew. If you didn't, your atoms did. The same way every molecule in me trembled each time I held you." She leaned forward. "I'll bet you weren't even surprised by the revelation."

"I don't recall being surprised, as such. Angry."

"Are you, still?"

I spread wide my hands. "Do I seem the type of person to hold on to my anger?"

"So much so, I'm surprised you haven't already killed me."

"You do have a doorman now. I might be hard-pressed to get away with this one."

We shared a smile which was not a smile at all. Perhaps against logic, certainly against expectation, it warmed me to see her. Rather than the empty red leather armchair, I sank into the cushion beside her, arm draped across the back of the seat. She was so close I daren't breathe. At once, I was back, 1992: she read Foucault and I pretended to read Hemingway but only marveled at the effortless beauty of her focus. My chest ached with a developing cold. "When will you leave me this time?"

"Whenever you choose. Just the same as last time." She faced me, pushing back her hair. I was distracted by the silver streaks, like fingers of death slithering down her skull. I realized she'd had bangs when I first knew her, a detail I hadn't copped to, but had absorbed in the same way I had the freckle on her jaw or the shadows down her throat, ones which showed her age in the alpine slopes and equine tendons.

199

"I wanted you to stay last time," I thought to say.

"You would have killed me if I had. I wasn't ready to die then."

"And now?"

"Come what may, though one might hope you'll have grown a bit." She lowered mossy lids lined with brown, nodded her smiling head, waved her delicate wrist. "I want very much to be in your life, my darling. So, I defer to your terms."

"You could have come any time," I said, half-laughing. "Could have written. I have a website, for Christ's sake."

"And I am most excited to see your new works in person, from the looks of it."

"You can't. I can't. Look—" I set the drink upon the glass coffee table. "I don't know what you want from me. We can't do this. I'm married. I'm happy with Delilah, we're trying to be happy."

"Are you succeeding?"

"Very much. She is my other half."

With an indelicate snort, Susan looked askance and said, "Your father used that term while rhapsodizing about my mother. What sickening puppies Vasko men become when smitten!"

"You've returned to mock me, then?"

"No, my heart. I've returned to be your mother."

"That ship sailed thirty-nine years ago." I was at the drink again. "You can't expect to be my mother after what we had."

"What we had was the best I knew how to do."

"Evangeline was doing her best. You deceived me into being a pawn in your power fantasy."

"Would you have chosen to know from the start, if you could?"

"Yes. You could have told me what kind of choice I was making."

"I all but did. Recall our conversations, or the stories I shared. And, sexual though I am, I have always treated you like a son. My son." Ferocious with pride, her words, her smile. "I'm so tickled by what I've seen. I must see more. This brilliant artwork, this sweet Delilah. And oh, my, how sweet, Delilah." Leering Susan fanned herself. "I could just eat her up."

A quiver bumped through my pulse as all manner of fantastic images flooded my brain. Aroused in more ways than one, I snapped, "If you come near her, I'll skin you alive."

"You won't stop me from befriending her, surely. I want to see what makes her special enough to shackle you."

"The minute I catch a whiff of something off, I'm ending it."

"At your discretion."

Stretching my legs, I placed aside my now-empty glass. "So what's your ulterior motive this time?"

"I was wondering if you might paint my portrait. It's been ages since I've sat, and longer still since I've done it for myself. You were the last to paint a piece meant for me and only me."

My gaze flickered over her body, from soft breasts to tight thighs. A terrible idea. "I don't know."

As her legs crossed, her black satin skirt crept further up her thighs. Her hand landed upon the hem, weighing either pulling it down or further up. "As hard as you've been staring, it seems you'd appreciate the opportunity."

"Painting, mother, is the least of what I'd like to do to you."

Glittering eyes crinkled. Pleased, perhaps, by the epithet. "I'm sure I can't imagine."

"You can't."

"You ought to tell me, then."

I hesitated, then remembered this was Susan—still, no doubt, unshakable. Tongue darting across my lips, I said, "I'd like to push you down on this couch and fill your throat so you can't run your evil mouth."

She grinned, my grin, the same in many photos with Delilah, the same in the mirror when admiring myself. She leaned forward. "I can imagine that just fine."

"When I'm finished, I'll put my hands around your throat. Like this." How inviting her flesh, and after all this time! "And I'll strangle you. Not until you're dead—just so you black out. And when you wake up," I bent towards her until we were so close that I saw every complex line upon her face, felt the radiant heat of my mother's flushing cheeks and mouth, and said, "you'll be in a different room. Tied to a table. And I'll fuck you again, but it won't feel like fucking."

"Won't it, though?" On she smiled, eyes narrowed and devious. When her lips parted, I hoped as much as feared she might kiss me.

"I suppose I shouldn't put it past you."

"Not at all."

We breathed together, her every inhalation echoing into me through my hand.

"Did you miss me at all, Richard?"

My jaw worked uselessly. I wanted to kiss her, felt myself doing it in some other place and time. Instead, my hand relaxed, and I wrapped her up in an embrace. Her body against mine, I buried my face in her mane, the crook of her neck. I took deep lungfuls of frankincense and graceful age. Each was a breath deep enough, sharp enough, to resemble sobs. Susan nuzzled my ear, her fingers curling through the hair at the back of my scalp.

"It's all right, baby. I'm right here."

As we held one another, the slow rocking of her body penetrated my awareness. Her heartbeat, soft against my cheek, was the metronome that kept the time of her sways. The relief I felt inspired repulsion, and soon I pulled free again. "I need to go."

"I understand." Her smile faded to an impassive expression of disappointment. "When will you and Delilah come to dinner?"

"That's for you two to decide. I'll have no part in facilitating your relationship. But I'll see you next Sunday for your portrait."

"Come by any time."

Almost free, I made it to the door in seconds, wrapped my hand around the knob, and—

"Richard."

"What?"

"Your coat."

Mechanically, I grabbed it, croaked, "Thanks," and made good my escape. I flew past the doorman and trembled in the car for ten minutes to calm down, empty and oozing as I dreamed of plunging my fingertips into Susan's prefrontal cortex. Then, floating somewhere above myself, and now better grounded to the depths of my shame, I drove home, resolved to forget my promise to paint her, and knew my resolution to be hopeless.

Chapter

4

I never did bring dinner up to Delilah. The effort required to broach the subject of my mother was too costly. If Delilah knew I was visiting her, she might interpret it as permission to do the same. But if I could hide some visits and minimize the rest, I could not help my violent shifts in mood. One day might be spent churning out a pair of paintings; the next, lying on the couch while bemoaning the nature of existence to a half-listening, now more-or-less indoor tomcat. They swelled without evident pattern, these melancholic tempers, but certain elements were consistent: mostly, total artistic impotence.

So that was it for this iteration of the painting, already weak to begin with (*Hypna and Thanatos*, whose process was delayed somewhat by Julius' death). Barely a few months, and already over, given way to restlessness. Now knowing the cause, I was all the sicker. All this time I awaited Susan, but now I had her and daren't end her. Not only was it a death too easily traced to me, but I could only do it once. Every murder had been a rehearsal— but with opening night looming, I panicked. What might happen after? No death would be the same unless it were the unthinkable deed I entertained while sucking air from Delilah's pretty lungs. What would I do with myself?

Delilah would lose her mind in prison if we weren't successful. Worse, she might end up a self-defensive liar, hoping, maybe, to get off like Homolka, rather than Hindley. Or, rather than the dignity of execution, I might be condemned to life in a cage. But all that in mind, even if we got off clean, I would not be the same man after a second, more meaningful matricide.

Susan was safe, then, until I solved these problems, but still, I craved death. I was mad. Once I had felt I was leading us to something, and only just recognized we were wandering through the fog, hands clasped, both equally lost. Death was the one beacon we had, so we beat a path towards it, together.

Suffused with Wagner and whiskey, I surprised Delilah one evening by cooking dinner. Observation served me well after almost six years, so the result was neither burned, nor unappetizing. She was thrilled at the meal as much as the state of the house, but seemed perturbed. When pressed, she said, "Just work. I have nothing but long days and nobody to help me."

"So, quit."

"You keep saying that."

"It would be good for us to get out of here. I've never left the Midwest, you know, except once to the beach with my—Evangeline." The admission deflated me. Why, in thirty-nine years, had I not once managed to leave the region, the country? Of course, the answer was the same as ever: Susan. Grim, I polished off a glass of wine and obtained another under Delilah's concerned eye.

"Did you paint today?"

"No." My skin seemed an ill-fitted suit. "I think I need to take a break from my work. This work, at least."

Her lips twisted into a frown. "Stuck again?"

"It's not what I hoped it to be. I'm swimming upstream. I know one day I'll manage to finish it, but my God. I'm just tired."

"You put so much pressure on yourself."

"Because I want to create something perfect for you."

Delilah pushed her cheek with the tip of her tongue, and my heart sang with adoration until she said, "I love you, Richard. I love your paintings. I don't care if you think they're not perfect. They are to me, because each one shows a different way you feel about me. Nothing can really be perfect. You think you're Odysseus, but you're actually Penelope."

I chuckled. "Unweaving my tapestry by night? But I have no suitors to escape."

"Exactly. So why are you doing it? What do you think will happen when you finish it?"

"I don't know. Some great ecstasy, maybe. My third eye might open." I laughed at myself, head shaking. "I don't know. I expect to never produce anything like it again."

One warm hand settled upon mine. "You are great, Richard Vasko. And as long as you're alive, you'll keep getting greater. After you know what you want out of this Piece, you'll usher in a new era for your work. For us."

I lifted my head, flattered despite myself. "Maybe so. I want something better for us."

She nodded, all at once appearing immensely tired as her other hand joined the first. "Do you think that maybe once you've finished it, we could stop?"

I engulfed her fingers with kisses light as birds' feet. "Yes, my darling, anything for you."

She smiled, and nodded, and then asked, still smiling, still sunshine, "So when should we have dinner with your mom?"

I rubbed the bridge of my nose at her sharp diversion. "Please, call her Susan. I don't know. I'm leaving the social niceties to the ladies. I'm just a chaperone."

"How Victorian." Giggling, Delilah leaned to see the kitchen calendar (Gorey's *The Loathsome Couple* that year. I recall because I had been tickled to find it, though its ending saddened her). "Friday?"

"Whenever you like."

"You really don't want to see her, do you?"

"I do, and that's the problem. She's evil. But there's no avoiding her; she's commissioned me for her portrait."

My wife's whole demeanor brightened. "Oh, how great! I'm glad you're getting work."

"Yes, it's every boy's dream to work for his estranged mother."

Delilah chuckled, one cheek stuffed with pasta. "Work is work," she said after swallowing. "She didn't have to commission you, but I'll bet she did because she wants it to be special, and because she wants to spend time with you."

"I'll bet she does."

"Don't be mean to her, Richard. We both know moms don't last forever."

"No, but you keep guilt-tripping me and you'll be in the running for mom of the year all the same."

She laughed, shook her head, and again assaulted her chicken with gusto. "This stuff is great, honey."

"You must be rubbing off on me."

Three days later Susan was grinning across a very different table: one of black glass set upon needle-like legs which provided the impression of Kubrick's monolith, hurtling through space.

"This lamb stew is marvelous, Delilah."

"I couldn't stand to make you do all the cooking."

"Well, it goes perfectly with the theme. An Aegean feast—I've been in something of a Dionysian mood lately, you might say."

My wife laughed, perhaps blushing, her whole being bright. "Should we cut off your wine?"

"Only if you want me to die. Speaking of—Richard, could you open another bottle?" This, as Susan emptied the first into her glass. I did, glad to avoid being part of the conversation.

"You certainly look the part," Delilah carried on to her.

That, Susan did, her hair curled and arranged in upon her head, woven with orchids and ivy. A few silver strands curled near her temples, drawing attention to the elaborate palette upon her eyelids, green

205

and purple and dark, bloody pink. "You'll make an old lady blush, Delilah."

"You're only as old as you feel."

"I disdain that cliché. I prefer, 'you're only as old as others perceive you, and only if you care.'"

Delilah pondered this a time. "But our self-image is based in large part on the way people react to us. And we help decide what they feel, so it's cyclical, anyways."

"For some, I suppose that is true. Were I trapped on an island with no human contact, I would know what I am. Who I am."

"I'd have a nervous breakdown in all of three days," said my laughing darling.

"I'd find you," I said from my glass. "Hone in on you like a pigeon."

Delilah cooed, as did Susan, mocking. "You two," she said with a tut. "Haven't you fallen out of love yet? Normal married couples hate each other by now."

I arched a brow at Susan. "When have you ever known me for normal?"

A depraved twinkle shone in her eye. "A fair enough point. Still, as the veteran of three loveless marriages, I must know the secret."

By this time there were nearly three glasses of wine in me, you understand—but, I admit, I would have been possessed by the same urge if sober. Drunk, I was smitten with my opportunity, and leaned forward. "You really want to know, Susan?"

She leaned dangerously close, and I suffered the urge to kiss her. Instead, I said, "We murder women together."

We stared each other down, my mother and I, her eyes scanning me as Delilah's heel stabbed the toes of my shoes. In my periphery she drained her glass while focused on Susan, who, after a few intimate seconds, burst into a cackle I was quick to echo. With a sigh, she waved a hand and said, "No, but really."

"Good communication," I said behind my sickle-grin.

Delilah smiled, relieved but shaken. "We're always up-front about our feelings."

"True," She mused. "I am seldom up-front about anything."

At that moment, unfamiliar patent leather and smooth ankle grazed the shin of my slacks. Though I recoiled, sitting straighter, the damage was done. Her touch lingered with the sear of a brand.

"Why, Susan," I said, clutching the bottle to pour a fourth glass, "self-awareness. Maybe you have changed, after all." Each word over-enunciated to maintain the appearance of control. "Next you'll tell me you've stopped baking the children you find gnawing on your house."

Delilah struggled against her laughter, squeaking out my name. Susan smirked. "But they're delicious. You haven't lived until you've had ginger-bread *foie gras*. Particularly if it was a clever child, my clever boy."

"Not clever enough." I drained the fourth glass, ignoring the meal in favor of efficient intoxication. By this point I'd cleared most of a bottle in all of twenty minutes, and the room lagged so brutally with each turn of my head that the food wasn't appealing. "Tell us something interesting: why did that husband of yours try to kill you?"

"Try not to sound so jealous, darling," said my mother. "I know it's difficult for children to accept their parents' love-lives, but that business is long over."

"I will bet," I said, pointing the empty bottle at her, "it was because you can't answer a question with just one word."

And that rotten witch, sitting, smiling, mischief in her eye like a hint of gold on a Granny Smith, asked, "No?"

Delilah clapped her hands, and even I managed a smirk before excusing myself to the first of several brief escapes to the bathroom.

In the end, it was a fine dinner. It was as we readied to leave, though, that Delilah asked the direction of the bathroom. The room and my stomach spun in one direction while the rest of me wrenched the opposite way. I, a drunken mess, was to be left alone with Susan. Stupid, desperate to have her out of my sight, I swung away from her, to the coat rack, to reach for what I found wasn't there. In a maelstrom as I was, I didn't feel her behind me until her breath caressed ear. "You look like you could use some help."

Susan lifted my coat over my shoulders, the fabric's weight somehow alien. Half-glancing over my shoulder and seeing the curve of pale cheek against rich hair, I plunged my arms into the sleeves one by one. Susan's hands followed them while her nose brushed my ear, along with maybe the tip of a tongue as she gripped my hands and somewhere whispered, "You know it's going to be your idea in the end, don't you?"

The toilet flushed. By the time the door opened, Susan was on the other side of the room and my hand was on the doorknob. As Delilah tarried to hug and cluck, I opened the door and lurched back with its swing, then out into the hall, breathing air which didn't smell like my mother's perfume and thus calmed somewhat the spinning world. It didn't work as well as I'd hoped, and I began to sweat, and at last when Susan said, "Oh, Richard," my answer was half-roared amid my torment. "What?"

"Give Delilah your keys. You're in no condition."

As I thrust the keys toward my wife, I snapped in juvenile outburst, "I'd have given them to her, anyway. You needn't police me."

"Not policing, darling. Parenting. Drive safely, Delilah."

The door shut before I could get a last word in.

In the elevator, Delilah and I observed our reflections—hers, smiling and flushed, mine glistening and pallid—and each seemed to take no notice of the other's condition.

"What a nice time," she said at floor five.

The worst part about Susan, I thought, was that she was right.

"I know you don't get along, but she's a neat lady." At floor four.

When the time came, I would be the director of my undoing. My liver groaned.

"She's admirable in so many ways. What a survivor." Floor three.

My mouth watered all the way back to my throat. What if I became so hypnotized I turned my back on Delilah?

"And so cool! She sang 'Sweet Jane' for me that day she visited." Two, now.

My vision blurred as my esophagus filled to my chest. What had all this been, if Susan could so easily return to destroy it? What could I do? What could I do?

One, doors opening: "Richard? Are you okay?"

I nodded in time with the chime, grimacing, hot, darting forward, seeing only the goal of the revolving doors, a cruel architectural decision through which I tumbled, gagging, and as momentum hurled me toward the bushes, I ejected into them a full bottle of wine and a few bites of lamb stew. A phantasmagoria of bloodlike vomit, Delilah's voice echoing the words, "Poor sweetie!" and the feeling of hands leading me to the car are all I recall of the rest of the night; but I do remember at home a warm breast, and the assurance that it belonged to Delilah, along with the terror that, too soon, it might not.

Chapter

5

Saturday saw me ill past noon, an omen as much as a consequence. I would not go on Sunday, did not. Though all I did for a week was sleep, I was more exhausted each time I awoke. Then, on Thursday, Delilah asked in a tune of forced innocence, "Are you still going to paint for your mom?"

And, recognizing the weight of the conspiracy against me, I croaked, "This Sunday."

I arrived at one in the afternoon without bothering to call. The doorman did that for me, and dawdled before summoning the elevator, favoring chummy chat. "Feeling better?"

"Much."

"Looked like you were having a rough night last time I saw you," he continued, now hitting the button. "Groundskeeper had a conniption next morning. But don't worry, Dick. We strive for discretion."

How I loathed him, his familiarity, his presence. He'd no doubt had his paws all over Susan already, which was why he always condescended to chat with someone who clearly had naught for him but contempt. I blanked my face. "Good," I said as the elevator opened, and I carried him up with me but when Susan opened her door, I forgot all about him.

"Good to see my efforts were not in vain this morning," she said, appraising me with eyes painted like smoldering embers. Around her body wrapped a black yukata embroidered with silver trees and laughing dragons. I couldn't look at it, couldn't stop!

"That dinner had me sick two days."

"A liquid diet isn't healthy."

I waved my drawing board at her, the other arm overburdened with a retinue of supplies. "Am I including the apartment number in the background?"

Expressionless as the *noh* mask on her wall, Susan let me through. As I set down my ream of paper and case of miscellanea, I said, "You realize if I'm painting in here, I'm smoking in here, right?"

209

"A poor excuse, but I'll allow you on the condition you share them with me."

"Here I thought you quit."

"I have." She hefted my abandoned supplies and led me to the bedroom. I reluctantly followed. There it was we found ourselves again, similar, yet new, parallels run between two lives, past and present. But was there a distinction? Hadn't we always been here? Trembling, I remained on the threshold to absorb the mossy walls above mahogany wainscoting. Sunlight filtered through saffron drapes, echoed in the curtains of a wood-carved bed so dramatic it became, as many of Susan's possessions, self-referential. A parody of a bed. From behind an amber dressing screen, she said, "The other day I realized we haven't discussed pricing."

"Christ. I'm a whore."

She tittered, her curved eyes peeking above the screen. "Of sorts. But imagine the kind of talk that will get around when an unknown genius is paid half a million dollars for one portrait."

I swear I felt my pupils dilate. "Half a million?"

"I have high expectations." Her head disappeared and there came a bit of bird-like fluttering. "Besides, I must compensate your lack of creative control."

"We'll see about that." As I flicked the latch of my case, something moved in the corner of my eye, where she emerged in a black gown which hung by her ankles with a velvet shimmer. I half-resented its implication of her pale limbs, yet stared all the same. She smiled, turned, and said, "Could you?"

Backed into money's corner, I tugged the zipper between her shoulder blades and stared down the track of her spine, fingers burning. When I stepped away, I applauded my self-control, for I had managed without touching her flesh.

Before a vanity with legs carved like the trunks of trees, she appraised her reflection. "Hair up or down, do you suppose?"

"Down," I said. Most women seemed powerful with hair back and a rich wardrobe; Susan was at her peak when nude with wild hair. She would never accept a portrait without some symbol of her power.

As she arranged her mane, she said, "You just want to get out of painting my old neck."

"Your neck is beautiful." There was no disputing that, but it did reveal her age in a way her made-up face did not. "It's honest."

"Something about me must be, I suppose."

Weary, I clipped a few papers to the drawing board. Half a million, my God! "How are we doing this?"

"Rather *Madame X*, I think." One hand rested upon her bedpost as the other gathered excess fabric from her dress. Shoulders back, she adopted a sullen moue. My heart quivered against my stomach, and I recalled her awful prophecy. I dragged a chair across from her, far enough that I wouldn't seem so much lower. Then I worked, already spending my money: wholesale drugs, a new oven for Delilah, a new car for myself. It was already in front of me and all I had to do was finish a painting. But it wouldn't be so simple, I knew. Somewhere, there was some string attached, and I'd only find it once I swallowed the bait.

My suffering was immense as I toiled for her, silent, professional. On the page, though, I savaged her. First the proud swell of her breast, then the wide span of her hips. As I channeled the firm thighs beneath her tight dress, she was first to speak.

"Are you really so bitter?"

"It isn't that."

At her knees, she asked, "Would having the knowledge to make your own choice really have changed anything?"

"Evangeline," I said, adding, "maybe."

Dryly chuckling, Susan said, "You were just a boy, then. It did you good to be shocked awake. A boy can't make decisions without influence, Richard—but a man can."

Her gaze charred my flesh. Before I began her throat, though, I realized something was wrong. Setting aside the board, I rose to correct her. As I prowled near I noticed a new color in her clavicle. A foot before her, I reevaluated her figure, and the angle of my chair. An inch before her, our eyes met, and my fingertips slid along her jaw. This, I tilted up, up, and saw her lips part. The breaths lapping at my face weakened my resolve, but I remembered the money, and the chance to build a home with Delilah, who cooked gourmet and helped hide bodies and curled around me all night long. Breathless, I murmured to Susan, "This man is married now."

A faint smirk creased her cheek and I ordered, "Follow me with your eyes."

She did, her chin inclined and gaze downcast in an expression of sensual scorn. At work again, I said, "Yes, that's right. Just like that."

On it went: not right, but righter. Her idea didn't jive with me. At home that night, I nursed the hollow in my chest while replaying the day. After my gentle admonishment she had grown reserved, but surely the fire in her eyes wasn't my imagination. Sketching her was still the finest leisure known to man, however reserved she was. And, if I was honest, her reservation only brought fresh fire to my blood. I wanted to chisel to the woman beneath the marble.

What was I doing? I was in too deep, as they say, wanting to plunge into the pool and never resurface. Delilah was wonderful, but Susan was exciting and fresh, and the prey whose death I imagined on the edge of sleep each night. Yet, I could find no way to it without hurting Delilah, who was baffled when she returned from the store to find me lying in the dim-lit living room, hand on my forehead.

"Are you feeling depressed again?"

"It's not like before." I took her hand. "Let's go driving awhile. I'm boiling alive in here."

"First help me put away the groceries."

With a sigh, I consented, and did the work under her supervision. Only then would she allow herself led to her little plum car, allow me to drive us to the edge of suburbia, where she lay her hand on my thigh to ask, "What's wrong?"

Tongue wetting the roof of my mouth, I said, "I have a talent for self-sabotage."

"Self-sabotage in what area of life?"

"Any of them. All of them. You, my work. Even living at all. I make things harder for myself."

Delilah stroked my knee. "Would it help to know you could never sabotage your relationship with me?"

"You'd be surprised, darling. I can be a stupid man."

She laughed. "Don't worry. If you do something stupid you'll know, and I'll know, and you'll regret it, but we'll get over it. I love you. No matter what happens, I want to be with you."

"But why, my darling? Me and all I am, why?"

"Because I love you. I love the way you screw up your face when somebody in traffic is making you mad. I love playing in the snow with you in winter. I love the way you sigh when you hold me. You make me feel indispensable." She smiled. "Like I'm the best person, the only person, and that you really do understand me. I love you," she said again. "We don't get to pick who we love."

I nodded, more to myself than to her. That was more or less what I had expected her to say, but I couldn't count on her temper. She had explosive potential, and never had I imagined it unleashed by adultery. She would kill me, and I would deserve it.

Could I avoid adultery, though? The vision returned, Susan's throat in my clutches. One of few acceptable outcomes. The idea of killing Susan was natural, but not easy. Even if it was easier than letting her destroy my relationship with Delilah.

Why, though, this struggle? Because she was my mother? Because of her mystique? The notion of killing her felt difficult in the way the Piece felt difficult. At home I did not enter the studio because I knew what I found there wouldn't please me. Better to start again. Maybe I would do well to take some time away. Refresh without planning something new. The painting would arrive when it was ready to. It always did.

Susan's death would be like that. By coming into our lives, she had chosen an end to hers. But I did not know when or how that end would arrive. I felt it might happen spontaneously, as the mystical experience, bound to be so pure it would rival the ecstasy of Theresa.

That night, I lay in bed reading *Sons and Lovers* by Lawrence, awake until Delilah whimpered my name.

"I'm here, Delilah." I placed the book aside.

She nuzzled against my shoulder. "Can't sleep?"

"I've got a lot going on."

"Do you want to talk about it?"

"Not now. I love you."

"I love you," she mumbled. "Don't worry me."

Chapter

6

After a few days to rationalize the situation in a certain light, I realized one might call me a victim of Susan. My wife no doubt would have, had she known our history. If I were to take Susan of my own free will, Delilah would be devastated—but she might understand, were Susan the instigator. If you had a face (perhaps you do and I cannot perceive it) it would no doubt be contorted in a sneer at this mockery of genuine suffering—and I agree. I prefer my excuses impeccable, but Susan was just beyond the garden wall, so I was forced to grasp. We saw each other once a week, six hours a day. Six hours a Sunday in her room, suffused with sex and perfume, one long hair upon the pillowcase. And on the wall, an old painting I struggled to avoid as one does an ex-lover.

Before our third sitting, with professional a tone as you please, I announced the painting wasn't working the second I placed it upon the easel. "There's nothing in it. It's static. You want a self-portrait, not a response to *Madame X*, but all the same you're making me respond to a work which requires no comment."

"Hm." Her expression hardened, mouth now a quivering line. She stepped *en avant* until a warm breast grazed my back. Then, near my ear: "I see what you mean."

"I've been thinking," I said, trading brush for cigarette, "something more *Olympia*, if we must have a theme."

One hand had, at some point, settled on my shoulder. "Weren't you just saying the other month you are a married man?"

"This is art. Besides, you're my mother."

"Indeed I am. A mother quite impressed by what her son managed to make of even her static concept. May I keep it?"

"Half-finished?"

"I'll have a finished one, eventually. But I like the look of this, in spite of its turgid conception. Oh, darling," she said suddenly, almost girlish, pirouetting, "unzip me, won't you?"

My head swimming, but all the same determined to prove my strength of will, I did. The dress shed from her like old skin, abandoned to pool around her feet. She slid away her lace bra, her panties, both of them bright, brick, firehouse, devil-flesh red. But when she faced me, I was the only one who was naked, and full up with a vision of seeing her splattered by a car. I wasn't driving it, mind you, but watching, and a bit of brain stem almost flecked my cheek before I remembered I was dreaming and begged her to lie on the bed.

Once she granted my plea, I smoothed sheets beneath the ribs which curved to echo soft breasts and the tawny areolae crowning them. To kiss them, to lay my head upon them and listen to her heart—how I hated her, how I loved her, how I trembled before her!

As I propped her up, my hands on her ribs, I breathed, "Tilt your head towards the canvas." I shifted her hands: one upon her stomach, the other behind her head like *La Maja Desnuda*. My palms swept down her thighs to draw them together, one leg just bent at the knee. Upon stepping back, I was swept by a wave of doubt that I might not be able to forge a reproduction fine as the live work before me, but with a glance at my reflection, I steadied myself, and set to work.

It was true, time had only kissed her. My fingers itched to touch her so they ran now and then over the flat lines of her effigy. After a time, she murmured, "What is it you see in Delilah, exactly?"

"Her whole being."

"Yes, but what is it that makes you crave her so? Certainly she's charming, very lovely. But there must be more."

"She makes me feel carefree, like we're children living alone in the woods. Sometimes I can get away with staying in a whole week at a time. I keep the television off and pretend we're the only two people on Earth, and she's not at work but instead off foraging."

"And what have you done while she forages?"

"Nothing."

Susan clicked her tongue at me. "You expect her to sustain the household by herself?"

"Not entirely. I sell some things, sometimes—I made almost nine thousand dollars this year," I said, chin lifting. "Most of that was in prints and prizes, but I sold some originals. And, before that business this summer, I had a pension coming in. I've had to step up marketing and production now."

Susan offered a serene smile I leapt to capture on the page. "That poor man."

"Poor man! After what he did to you."

"Don't be angry on my behalf, darling. I already have all of society telling me I am a victim: Et tu? Didn't you care for him at all? I did."

"No. He was a coward and a liar." Sneering at the mention of my dead rival, I botched her upper lip and struggled to mend it. "What he did, what he was, was pathetic."

"Of course, I agree," she said slowly. "But I can't claim his crimes were that bad in the end. After all, look at you."

I ached for her, screamed inside of myself, and at home when I fucked and choked and kissed Delilah, it was really Susan. Even then I was barely able to finish, and knew I'd been destroyed so utterly that I had no choice but to rush my cycle. When I proposed the idea, Delilah voiced an abbreviated series of mousy objections ("Two a year? Doesn't that seem a bit much?") but soon obliged, and even consented to come hunting again.

By now, we had a routine. Our separate arrivals at some trendy Cleveland glow-stick dance club were staggered by ten minutes. I got an overpriced whiskey, then prowled the floor to pass the time until the prepaid phone buzzed with the message, *By the bar*.

Soon I was there, my gaze skipping amid the crowded figures. Three sweeps revealed Delilah's tilting head, her distinctive plume of black curls and milk flesh rendered almost blue under the lights, and beside her, a woman of middle age, a redhead with high cheekbones and a carefree smile. What fine taste my darling had! And how well she knew mine, because she was mine. Completely mine. We belonged to each other as a pair of limbs. I could never feel such a thing with Susan. There could be no partnership with her, no reciprocal possession. She would possess me, but I could never hope to possess her. Her whole self would be forever just beyond my fingertips.

As I came from behind, I finished my drink, dropped the glass on the bar, and then placed my hand on the base of Delilah's neck. She jumped, then smiled and reached for my face. As I bent my head to slip my tongue into her soft mouth, my eyes explored the tribute. Yes, quite beautiful up close, a bit heavily made-up, perhaps, but I'd found I liked that once they got to crying, especially when they'd really caked on the mascara, as this one had.

"Honey, this is Chelsea."

"Wonderful to meet you," I said, taking the stranger's hand to kiss a few seconds longer than proper. After, I stood with one hand on Delilah's shoulder and said, smiling, "I'm not interrupting anything, am I?"

"Don't be silly," said Delilah. "We were just talking about going back to school."

"A student," I said.

"Not yet," said our tender Texas lamb. "Right now I'm working at a beauty parlor. Funds. It's just around the corner."

This worried me. "Are you out with friends?"

"Nah, I was, but they wanted to get club-hoppin', and I just want to see if I can find some fun here for once. What do you do, uh—"

"Julius," I supplied, then explained, "I'm an artist."

"Are you! What kind?"

"I paint," I said, regarding the bone structure of her face and struggling a little to morph her features into Susan's. They seemed closer to Delilah's, so I glanced away as my wife lauded my work. Then I said, "You'd make a beautiful model, Chelsea."

"Oh, she would," Delilah said, so excitedly it was as if she had forgotten our mission.

Our prey smiled, lingering on my face before admiring my chest. I turned to get myself another drink, and ones for the ladies while I was at it. As I did, grinning Delilah leaned into some conspiratorial exchange with her fair-weather friend. They giggled, and my thumb traced the base of my wife's spine.

The colors of the club shifted to orange with a change of music that came as I distributed drinks. "I love this song," I said in genuine surprise to recognize the remix of a heavy bassline. It hadn't stopped playing on the radio since its release some months before, and I'd finally adapted to liking it, mostly when I was drinking, which seemed to be more often than not since Susan came to town. "Who wants to dance?"

Both looked up from their conversation, smiling. "Hell yeah," said the Texan, "that's what I came for tonight."

"Then step right up," I said, offering my hand. The dupe took it, allowing herself led to the edge of the floor where her body set into near-instant motion. I slipped my hands over her waist and adjusted to the beat. Her tight hips ground against my groin, hair against my lips. From the top of her head, I watched dark-eyed Delilah, well aware how she hated moments of the hunt like these. I watched her until, in the slowing beat of the song, I twirled the woman towards the crowd and brushed my lips over hers. No sooner than I did, I felt a pressure on my back, soft breasts, hands wandering over my chest. Over my shoulder, I saw Delilah's focused eyes. To the beat, I slipped out from between them to guide Delilah toward the woman. They danced close, then touching, my sweet Woman slipping her arms around our temporary play-mate. Her nose brushed the girl's as they moved, skirts riding up with the grinding of hips. The tentative brush of lips, of tongue, then again the shared smile.

Clearly they had hit it off even before I arrived. Unsurprising, the way Delilah inspired people to open up. She had a chemistry that appealed to every type. She thought so little of herself, my Delilah—but how very much the world thought of her!

It was soon we all decided to leave, a collage unfolding for the next hour of alcoholic adrenaline: whispered voices, suggestions, blue and pink lights and white legs, a glimpse of a fox fur coat worn by someone near the door, the sounds of shoes on pavement and giggling women, car doors slamming, driving, my voice warning it that we were in for a bit of a haul, getting to the countryside and putting it under for the duration of the two-hour trip, Delilah's trembling voice, husky with excitement ("I just want to spend time with you,"), the ache of my throat after too many cigarettes, the relief of the last green exit before the house, the cold of the night—or, more accurately, the dimples prickling along Delilah's arms, which reminded me it was cold.

As I worked on the thing, I was hyper-aware of my wife, watching me, drink in-hand. Last time she hadn't seemed tense—but perhaps Julius' death, or the change of pattern, brought the tension of tight lips and lightly crossed arms. I felt a kind of fear. She seemed on the other side of the house, no doubt in large part due to a breach in hunting protocol. It had agitated her, that kiss I gave, but like a guilty child, I couldn't own my lack of self-control and instead shifted blame to the first scapegoat I found.

As I carved a tableau of trees growing and dying and rotting and growing again, I considered that, were it not for Susan, we would not have broken our cycle. She had driven me to this point, made me irritate Delilah, which irritated me, and now the night was half-spoiled by atmosphere alone. Susan: capable of ruining even Death for me!

Near the end of it, I set down the ice pick and said to Delilah, "Come here." She did, wearily, eyes firm upon me and not on the bloodied, half-dead cripple behind us. I took her hand.

"I am sorry we've got to do another so early."

"I know," she said, half-sighing. "It's okay, honey. I just don't want it to be more of a habit than it already is."

"Of course not. This is for my work. My real work." I squeezed her hands. "You're a victim of my proclivities as much as I am, darling."

"No." Twisting my ring around my finger, she said, "I'll never be your victim. I won't let that happen."

Her spirit brightened me. No, she wouldn't. She always surprised me with her strength, and I think she was surprising herself, too.

After we cleaned up—now a three-and-a-half hour process with the two of us working in concert, excluding internment—we buried the dis-membered limbs in the cellar, because the frigid earth outside was caked in frost, and snow, I knew, was mere weeks away. The thing went where Evangeline had upon her death, beneath the furniture (by now aggressively musty, each jostle unleashing a plume of allergens; twice I stopped for a sneezing fit, Delilah petting my back each time). Bundled against me later as we integrated upon the couch, Delilah filled the vaulted ceilings with echoes of breathless panting. She clutched me, rocking against me, above me, nuzzling as though to climb into my chest. Moonlight illuminated her skin with the mystical cerulean of impending dawn. As she shivered with the comedown, she stared through the tall windows, to the flat landscape, and said, "Let's move someplace with mountains."

"Fine by me. Where?"

"I don't care. The desert. Let's live in a patch of cacti at the base of a mesa. I really do want to go away from here. Even if it is in your fantasy RV." Wanly, she smiled. "We can't stay here much longer, I don't think."

"Why not?"

"Don't you get a bad feeling?" She studied the empty fireplace. "I hate to give the thought energy, but I feel like the longer we stay in Ohio, the greater the odds of something bad happening. I feel something awful looming nearer all the time. I don't know what it is, but I know it's there, and either I run, or I prepare to face it."

This, I knew too well, and was relived as much as frightened to know she felt it, too. "What will facing it entail?"

"I don't like to guess. We don't have to find out. We tie our loose ends and go. Everything new. Safe. A fresh future."

"What future do you see now?"

"I don't. Do you really see one, Richard?"

She was right. I knew she was right. I had said it myself, felt myself how we should go. But I also knew I couldn't. I stared beyond the window, beyond the fading starlight. Bobbing on a boat at sea, we clutched each other amid the waves and slept entwined in the pale blue morning until it was time to go home to brew the paint. As it simmered, I noticed my real phone, left upon the counter, blinked with a voicemail. Upon checking it, I realized how small the state was. Or, perhaps, how cruel fate:

"How funny," began Susan's recording. "I'm in Cleveland of all awful places and could swear I saw you and Delilah leaving this club with quite a fine specimen."

This caught me so off-guard I couldn't understand the rest of the message and had to hear it a second time.

"I can't imagine what you're doing here," she continued, "but if you two aren't exhausted after making your new friend, give me a jingle. Manuel and I have a hotel room. Oh, and remind me to tell you about Manuel."

The message ended there. I swayed in place. In the pan, sanguine bubbles grew and burst. It was one thing for me to joke about murder while drunk, because my sense of humor loses friends; it was another thing for Susan to see us leaving with our victim. Paranoia cast an immediate shadow over me. The more she knew, the faster shrank my odds of escape. All those years for nothing. All the ways Delilah and I had changed each other, for nothing.

I wouldn't let it happen. Everything was made for nothing by death, but in life I might preserve beauty and meaning until each reached an end of its own accord. Soon after receiving the message, I sat smoking on the back deck, where I was exiled by my addiction so Delilah's drapes might smell less like her father's. From behind the screen door, she said, "You look peaked, honey. Are you okay?"

"I just don't care for this business with Susan."

"Why are you doing it if she bothers you so much?"

"I'm doing it for what she's paying me. Us. Doesn't she talk to you? I'd have thought she'd mentioned it by now."

Shadowed as she was by interior lighting, the nuances of Delilah's face were lost, but still I fancied it darkened by a flash of blood. "I don't like to talk to her about you."

I tilted my head. "Why not?"

"I'm not sure." She turned, frowning, then said, "Anyway, what is she paying you?"

"Half a million dollars."

Her posture jolted from bow-headed to steel-spined in a second. She slammed open the screen, and the tomcat, until that moment prowling across the fence, startled and fell into the bushes. I got my first good laugh of the day, and Delilah was now so bright it was as if the whole recovery process was skipped. "Half a million dollars! Five-hundred thousand dollars!"

"I didn't want to curse the outcome by mentioning it, but you asked."

She collapsed into the seat across from me, winded, teary-eyed. "We really can go away. Richard, this is wonderful! This is the best news I've heard in too long." She put her hand on her cheek in wonder. I said nothing, too engrossed in the simple perfection of her features. After a moment of dreaming, she shook her head. "How much money does that woman have?"

"I've never dared ask. But she's too shrewd for anything less than a hundred million in this economy, I'm sure."

"My God. All that money, and nobody to share it with." My little wife frowned at her feet. "Poor Susan. It must be lonely. No wonder she wants to make amends."

I didn't correct Delilah. I smoked my cigarette while the cat clambered back atop the fence, where he cleaned his haunches with great dignity, shivered head-to-tail, and strolled onward as if nothing had happened at all.

Mercifully, Susan did not mention the Cleveland encounter that Sunday. Instead she ruminated in the self-satisfaction of a woman working out a puzzle. That's not to say we didn't talk around it, of course. As she let me in, she asked, "Feeling tired?"

"Never better." I took her in my arm to kiss her cheek. "You look ravishing."

"You are in a good mood, my, my. Been getting up to mischief, no doubt."

I squeezed her, then stepped away. For now, the urge to murder her subsided. Now there remained only a few other urges, ones whose edges I might playfully skirt. With a kiss for her forehead, I moved ahead of her into the bedroom. "So, Manuel? No doubt chosen for his raven hair." I swept my fingers through my own.

She laughed while disrobing. "Don't flatter yourself. I don't pick men for their resemblance to my son."

"No doubt because you already have your son at arm's length."

Nude, now, and effervescent, Susan pressed to my back to regard the studies in progress. "Who said anything about arm's length?"

"And you say you want into my life so you can be my mother," I said with a derisive laugh.

"Not a conventional mother, but the type you respond to. Remember when we were together. Can you name a time I was unmotherly, unloving? All our time reading, talking, working, dancing. Playing," said with a lewd drop in tone. "Why, I even bought you clothes, and tried to pay for your education." Patting my shoulders, Susan finally moved away, and flung herself onto the bed with an unabashed grin. "I was so happy to take care of you. I knew it couldn't last, but perhaps now it can."

"I'm a man. I don't need taking care of."

"What a silly thing to say. Delilah doesn't take care of you at all?" She scoffed. "Men are so quick to forget what states they'd be in without their women. And women, too, forget where they'd be without their men."

I reflected on that time together in Susan's house. No, it had been wonderful—but as she herself had said, it couldn't last. What made her think it might now?

I asked her, and she said, "Nothing can truly last, darling. But I could make you happy until it's my time to bow out."

"I'm happy with Delilah."

"Because she lets you walk all over her?"

"Our relationship isn't like that. I help her."

"And how do you help her, then," asked Susan in a tone so odious, with so sneering a caste, that I nearly felt the return of those murderous urges.

"I clean for her. Sometimes I cook."

"Do you think that's all she wants, her man's help with her woman's work? Hasn't she hopes? Dreams?"

"Of course," I said.

"So what are they?"

"Well, she'd like us to go away. Stay together through thick and thin."

"Of course she does, she's a puppy! But she is also a person if ever I have met one, Richard, struggling and decent. If that girl were born centuries ago she would have been a pretty little martyr saint. Instead she is here, with hopes and ambitions which surpass you. Just as you have your painting, Delilah's heart is pulled by a greater calling. But you see her as a woman, first and only, specifically your woman, and define her wholly in relation to yourself. You have given her these dreams of yours, but her own still smolder. She is on this world to do one thing, and she has told me so, herself."

I daren't entertain the notion that Susan might know something about Delilah I didn't, but I couldn't let this pass me by if I truly didn't know. Paranoid, I ventured, "What thing is this?"

"To perform acts of great charity." Susan smiled at me, long and hard. "I think she will. She may surprise herself with the form it takes."

I didn't like our subject. It implied my knowledge of Delilah was imperfect, and made me remember our looming black wall. I returned to work. "You're awfully eager to defend her. I thought she was your rival."

"I have no rivals, darling. You'll come to me in time. Until then, I can't stand to see that silly little girl mistreated."

"Admit you love her."

"She's quite endearing. Somewhat exhausting. Always so high-spirited."

"She must be, to balance me."

Susan smirked. "She is a lovely creature, though, isn't she."

"Oh, yes. I swear she glows when she's nude."

With a tigerish smile, she stretched and squeezed her thighs together. "I'm sure it's an enchanting sight."

"Meek and shy." I grinned, pleased by the effect Delilah had telepathically. Susan flushed, eyes wanting and breathless, lower lip drooping.

"It almost sounds like you want me coveting your wife."

"Of course I do. It's a sign of my immaculate taste. Make no mistake," I said cheerfully, setting aside my charcoal, "if you ever did lay a hand on her, I'd have no choice but to cut it off. But the fantasy—well, there's nothing wrong with a fantasy. Maybe even toeing the line. Delilah might do with some broadening."

She practically writhed as I came to her side. "You might not care for her once I've broadened her."

"I'll never stop caring for Delilah. She's not so weak as to be changed."

"Oh? Surely you've changed her."

"Not changed, so much as brought her into finer relief." Matter-of-factly, I lifted her hand from her stomach and moved it to the apex of her parted thighs. As I curled her fingers into position, my knuckles brushed a glimmer of moisture. My mouth watered with the dream of descending upon her as instead I lifted my head and met her vulpine gaze, full of sex and filling me with helplessness. Her other hand I moved upon her breast, my thumb brushing just so a downy curve which brought the years rushing back.

"Quite a risqué pose," she intoned as I stepped away.

"You're quite a risqué woman," I said to my board, beginning again, again, again.

Chapter

7

The broadcasts started about two weeks later: Chelsea Daniels, missing from Club Russo in Cleveland. Police sought witnesses who may have seen her that night, as she was thought to be captured on video leaving with an "... as-yet unidentified couple." I found it exhilarating. Delilah did not.

"I told you no good would come of doing this with regular women," she said, tugging the sleeves of her sweater. "At least you didn't rape this one."

"What are you talking about? It was your idea we go to a bar, rather than prey on whores."

Her brow furrowed. "It was?"

"Don't you remember?"

She looked away, her thumb brushing over her lower lip. "I don't remember that." She touched her forehead. "My memory must be going."

"Klonopin has nasty effects on long-term memory. It's good we got you off that stuff, even if only because the old man died." I tucked her hair behind the shell of her ear which, once exposed, became the focal point of my kisses, my teeth. "Just relax, Delilah. It's going to be fine. Nobody knows us in Cleveland."

Somebody, of course, had known us, and that somebody regarded the affair with bright-eyed and good-humored speculation. Susan reminded me of Evangeline, thinking aloud her Christmas list:

"Just the other day I saw on the news how some pretty Texas rose was plucked in the dead of night. Could have sworn I'd seen her before."

"Oh?"

"Can't recall the circumstances, though."

"Funny thing, that."

"Very funny. That's what drink and drugs do to an aging mind, though. Details slip. But what could have possibly happened to that poor girl?"

I smirked despite myself. "What do you think happens to most women who disappear?"

"All kinds of things. Rape, murder, sex trafficking. The world is full of depraved individuals. If you were so inclined, what might you do with such a girl?"

I glanced from my canvas, piqued, and said, "The imagination of an artist is disturbing, indeed."

"If I were that sort of person," she offered, "I might begin with rape. Loosen them up a little."

"How very unfeminist of you."

"Rape isn't about gender, or feminism. It's a tool of power, like any torture, but far superior due to its inherent sexuality. It is physically, spiritually, morally violating. And once one intends to cross the line of murder, what's a little rape? They won't live to feel the long-lasting trauma, anyway."

"You callous creature."

"Well, I only saw the girl. It isn't as if I know her. Am I supposed to feel for every person in the street? Imagine how exhausting that would be. You couldn't manage it either."

"No, but Delilah does. And I love to see it."

"I'm sure you do—but you know you'll tire of her someday, Richard, or she will have a change of heart, and it will be for just cause. That's how those people are. You have the impression everything is perfectly fine, and you might go on for years. Then one day their conscience gets the better of them, and they behave like fools. They're fine people to be with for a time, but at some point you have to realize you can never have something like that long-term without destroying it. People like you and I should forge our partnerships among like-minded individuals, for everyone's sake, least of all our own."

"And all this is why we ought to be together?"

"No. This is why you ought not to be with Delilah."

"Surely you don't think I'll alienate her based on your advice?"

"You can suit yourself, my boy," said placid Susan, batting her eyelashes. "I only think of what's best for you."

What she wished was best, anyways. Still, her poison worked: all was not well at home. Even with the promise of five-hundred thousand dollars for a fresh start, and even though no new leads were made in the Daniels disappearance (but for sloppy sketches which looked so unlike us it was embarrassing), Delilah was frightened. She gloomed from room to room on evenings and days off, and though for some weeks I maintained an immaculate house so she wouldn't have to, she seemed drained. Cornered. At times I heard her softly weeping in the kitchen or bathroom and listened helplessly, unable to invade her privacy. Now I wonder how much she already knew, or foresaw, at least, as I sometimes did when we lay in bed, mouth to desperate mouth, egos dispersed amid the universe. But we had no way to know what we truly dreaded.

One morning, lying beneath the apple tree in the back yard, the ground cold and our coats and gloves covered in snow from winter games, I took a crisp breath to ask, "What do you want to do with your life, Delilah? What do you want to leave?"

"I don't know." Her head rolled away from me, towards the frozen-over bird bath near the bushes. "I just want to give all of myself. I want to make people happy. Someday I'd like to start a charity. Maybe one for children of abusive homes. When I was little, I used to pray someone would come and save me. I want to be that savior for somebody else, just once. But it would be even better if it was lots of people."

"You've never told me that before."

"I don't know. It'll never happen, so I don't think about it much."

"Why not? There are plenty of abused children and vibrant art communities in South America. We could go there."

A spilled wine glass, her smile, sad and empty, tipped to the side! My chest ached as she changed the subject by saying, "Aren't you going to use that paint?"

"Eventually. It'll keep. The idea will come soon, but I can't start without it. I'll know when it's ready."

"How?"

I squinted, waving my fingertips over my heart. "It's a kind of excitement. Suddenly my whole being is set, exists for nothing but the production of whatever piece is in front of me. I feel the ecstasy of flowing work, lose myself, forget what and who and where I am. Then, I know it's a real Piece. One that means something. One that comes from someplace deeper than inside of me."

"That's beautiful." Rising, she dusted snow from her cherry-red pea coat. "Come on! The hot chocolate will be cool."

Inside, having shaken off the snow and settled into the couch to warm her flesh, Delilah murmured, "You're too kind to me, Richard."

"Because I love you."

"Of all people, why me? I'm not interesting."

"I find you fascinating. You're clever and fierce and silly. My sprite. I could put in you in a jar."

She smiled just a little. "When we go away, where do you want to go?"

"I'm not sure. Venezuela, maybe. We could live in the rain forest and eat psychedelic plants all day."

She giggled. Then, with tender hope brimming in her eyes, she asked, "Do you think that, someday, maybe a long time from now, we could adopt some children?"

"Maybe someday," I said, and she nodded, resolving that this answer was better than 'no'.

"Let's go to the zoo. They've got the Christmas lights up. I'll bet they're beautiful."

"I told Susan I'd be over tonight. We keep losing time because the painting keeps changing. You're welcome to come."

"No," she said, thankfully, "I don't want to disturb your work. I'll stay home."

Just a little, I saw the martyred quality Susan noted, and resented her for it because I could not see the same quality in myself. If only she knew of her own strength! If only she would take a stand, not ask, but tell. I dreamed of that day as the condemned dreams of the liberation of the noose.

So, then, for months it went on. Susan and I, so close to the line we were very nearly on it; and Delilah, hopeful and quiet, perhaps aware something was amiss but all the better at blinding herself to it. From time to time, she would go shopping and return with bags and bags of new clothes and make-up, not a penny poorer. Although I did not think it was safe to let her spend so much time with Susan, the choice was not mine to make. Delilah gathered some strength from her meetings with my mother. I could hardly begrudge her idolization. After all, I was just as much a victim to it. I had worked on her portrait for months and it was barely half done, and that was at least a little intentional on my part.

On the whole, things were just fine, and I was satisfied I'd found at least a temporary balance. Then the April thaw came, and I returned to the house to re-intern the remains of the fair Miss Daniels. In the basement, I rearranged the furniture and removed the five pieces buried beneath, formless in tremendous sacks of quicklime, bleach, and, when anatomy allowed, full of bacteria-rich yoghurt. One by one, I began the tedious process of hauling them up the stairs, and indeed I already had two sitting at the top floor when I recognized with a white shock of flu-like nausea that there should have been six in total, not five. Panicked, I recounted, and confirmed with a symphonic swell of horror that the head was missing.

The head. The head, where could it be? I took up my shovel and dug another foot down to find there was nothing. The head was gone. Vertiginous, I sank beside the torso and struggled to fabricate an explanation. Had I put it someplace else that night? Of course not. Nor had Delilah, who detested the notion of interacting with the dismembered parts, and insisted I deal with them.

But then there was Susan. The owner of the house. I recalled her voicemail from that night and pounding blood throbbed a headache to life. Of course she knew where to look. And of course she'd have no problem doing a thing like this—but why? For control? For a lesson? I had to find out, but I couldn't admit to anything in the process.

So, searing with rage, I buried what I could in a patch of woods between

Marion and Columbus and called on Susan the next evening to find her in the red leather armchair with all the bearing of a queen.

"It's been too long since you've come without pretense of business," she said, legs crossing beneath her black pencil skirt. "I'm glad you called first. I'd have gone out."

"This is more interrogation than social call." From the sofa across from her, I radiated loathing toward the cleavage peeking from her white blouse, towards the emeralds of her earrings, towards the silver nails of her manicured hands. "I'm looking for something."

"Ah." Her eyes shone so instantly that I was certain now of her guilt. The curious tilt of her head was dirt rubbed in my wound. She wanted my reaction, waited for it just as I would were I her. "What are you after?"

"Innocence is the one thing you've never pulled off well."

"I'm quite sure I have no idea what you mean."

I closed my eyes and exhaled. "I don't have the patience for this."

But she did, and the glow of her features was that of a girl playing a game. Always having fun, my mother, and always at others' expense.

"I'd love to help you, darling, but you have to tell me what it is you've misplaced before I can."

"I don't need to, when you know very well. Tell me where it is."

"What?"

Fuming, her gaze tracking me, I looked through the fridge and freezer. When both doors shut again, she smirked. "Perhaps it's some of Delilah's Tupperware you're after?"

I was back across from her, all but blowing smoke. "Tell me," I snarled, on the edge of real panic, powerless before her self-satisfied little smile.

"I can't tell you what I don't know."

The fury of twenty-two years flooded back. I wanted to crush her face until her skull was a soup bowl of brains and shattered bone. I wanted to tear out her tongue and jam it down her throat with my cock. My boot smashed through the glass coffee table, which gave and shattered into a field of frost.

Susan barely blinked. A single brow arched, and, lips in a curt curl, she tsked. "You do have your mommy's temper, don't you, baby?"

"I swear to you, Susan," I said, glass crunching under my Doc Martens as I crossed to fit my hand against the Grecian slope of her throat, "if you don't tell me where it is, I will kill you right here."

"And the doorman will identify you, and the police will find you and your precious Delilah, and whatever other sordid businesses in which you and that girl engage will no doubt come to light."

I squeezed her throat, my teeth bared. "Fine. I don't need to kill you today." I jerked her to her knees on the glass-covered floor, watched as shards bit her pale flesh to extract a gasp of pain.

"Where is it?"

"You're letting this get you quite upset, Dick." She gazed up at me with parted lips. Her hands, almost plaintive, ran along my chest. "Why don't you talk to mommy about it?"

I stepped aside and shoved her forward onto her palms. She uttered a sharp cry that seemed practically a moan, and became just that as I jerked up her skirt.

"You want to play games," I said as I knelt behind her, swiftly unbuckling my belt and pants, "then, fine. Here's my favorite."

As I tore away her scarlet lingerie, I forced her shoulders down to the shards. Her face resisted, but her chest and ribs ground into the snowy field. And as I forced my way in to find her more inviting than ever, I realized this was no more a rape than, say, tickling Delilah. Whether by the act, the reunion, or her own machinations, Susan was as aroused as I and sure to verbalize it. Nor could I help myself from the same, my knees stinging, head pounding, whole self drained in this storm of sadomasochism, all of reality and time and death disappearing in this, then Susan tightening and half-screaming into the glass, "Does it make you feel better to fuck your mommy?"

I yanked her head towards mine just to spit in her face, right in the corner of her eye, which shut as she moaned. As I punched her in the back of the head, then gripped her neck, she groaned, "Give me what I deserve, baby."

Those words put an end to me, because what she deserved was to be pushed out of a moving ship and left to be baked by sun and eaten by sharks. I cried out, gripping her shoulder with one hand while the other fell into the glass to steady myself. For some moments, we lay panting. Then, I rolled back onto my haunches to pluck shards from my palms. Susan began a similar, more involved process, a soft hiss sometimes quivering past her lips.

When more or less free of crystal thorns, I set to work on her shimmering shins. In the aftermath, I felt a miserable wretch. The full impact of what had happened was yet to settle on me, but already I felt the ache in the pit of my stomach. There was no way to win.

"What do you want from me? Why are you doing this?"

Susan glanced up from where she plucked glass from her bust. "Why can't you believe I only want you?"

"Because even if I believe that, I'm afraid."

"Why? Think of all I can give you. Do for you. What can that little girl do that I can't?"

"She makes me happy."

"Do you know what else brings happiness? Security. And how does one buy security?" She winced as I slid a piece from the edge of her knee. "I want to secure your future, Dick. I can't trust some girl to do that."

"Can't you tell me where it is?"

"Only when you can tell me what it is," she said, smiling. "Now come and shower with me, sweetheart. If I don't take one soon, I'll look like Countess Bathory."

Chapter

8

It was now clear that there had only ever been one way to free myself, and with my new mistake, I was more in in her hands than I'd been my whole life. She was right: her death would uncover the head, and the head, then, would unveil me. Thus, there was still one barely feasible mode of escape, which required deliberate timing. I would wait until the portrait was finished and her check cleared. Then, I would make some invitation to lure her from her house. With her dead, Delilah and I might flee.

But, with my plan fomented, I felt sick. The sudden burst in the dam of our deviant relationship heralded the potential of a river I had forgotten. I did have a choice. I remembered I was not literally bound to Delilah, to this path which filled me with dread. Perceiving as I did the paling of passion between myself and my anxious wife, and suffused with the dissatisfaction of obscurity, Susan might own me, but she would push me, and in a few decades she would be dead, at any rate. But with her claws in me so long, would death free me? Would I spend my freedom mourning all I had missed? Which path, if not taken, would inspire the keenest longing?

Through the early morning hours after that glass night, I blocked out a new work which instructed my fingers how to move. Three forms in a Grecian marble womb, an old story revisited, all the figures intact. Clytemnestra, baring her breast in plea for clemency; Electra, clutching gauzy gowns over her eyes in the midst of a cry driven as much by horror as by vengeance; and Orestes, towering over his doomed mother, silver sword in hand. She wanted a painting: I would give her one. Susan would see its magnificence just as I did. She might even understand, then, and nothing more would be necessary.

So why couldn't I stop thinking about seeing her again? Why did I recall our glassy tryst with fondness? I brimmed with excitement and only regretted that I had to keep it secret from Delilah. In deepest dreams, I possessed them both, openly: but such a reality could never manifest, and, at any rate, I would be swiftly worn by the ordeal. No scenario allowed for an escape without casualty in one form or another.

At eight in the morning, my work was disturbed by a knock at the door. Delilah slipped inside, frazzled to have woken without me. "Honey? Didn't you come to bed at all?"

"No, darling. I've been working."

Seeing her, bleary-eyed in rumpled pajamas, I felt a shadow fall. I remembered the taste of Susan's blood and, aching, folded my little wife into my arms to relieve the pain. With her there, I could hardly imagine having anything different. Suddenly the solution to my dilemma was clear, and would remain so until she was at work. Then, in solitude, I would be lost. But for now, in the corner of the sofa, I clutched Delilah to my heart. My lips pressed kisses to her neck and ear, seeking private penance. Even in her ignorance, I felt unworthy. Against my tender goddess I had committed the foulest sin. In doing so, I tore her down and now saw no deity, but a delicate girl who would be destroyed to hear what I had done.

So, quiet, I plunged my face into the waves of her hair, and struggled to think of nothing.

For a man with two women, I felt desperately lonely. At any second my tenuous grip on one or the other might slip. Susan could send us to prison with the wave of a hand, or Delilah might leave and there would be no more 'us' at all. Lost, I kept my head down and managed my days in piecemeal. Whatever kept me busy was welcomed. For Delilah's birthday, only a few weeks after my failure, I finally brought her to the zoo. Glowing on tiptoes, she watched the animals reverently, as if each in its turn was the bearer of some secret delivered in whispers. By the elephants, we rested, her head against my shoulder.

"How much longer," she asked, weaving her fingers through mine, "until we can go?"

"Soon," I said, though I had no way to know such a thing. Since that night, I'd hardly touched Susan's portrait, and the notion of letting it ride forever was too tempting.

"When's 'soon'?"

"I'm not sure."

"I'm so tired, Richard." She looked it, too, her eyes dim with the drained affect which had grown amid her features since Julius' suicide. "I keep seeing that girl's face. Some nights I wake up covered in sweat because I've had nightmares about turning us in and you hating me forever."

This startled me. Delicately, I asked, "Do you often think about turning us in?"

"I would never. But sometimes I dream I'm sobbing and I can't stop, and I find my way to a police station. Then I see they've already brought you in, and your face—" Her eyes glazed over, so she squeezed them shut and buried herself in my neck. "I just don't want you to hate me."

"I could never hate you," I said, kissing her brow. "Even in a cell, I wouldn't have it in me."

"I don't want to be taken from you," she whimpered. "I don't want you taken from me."

"Nobody can separate us."

"But sometimes you're so far away. What can I do? After the murder has stopped, you'll be bored. What if you try to leave me then?"

"I won't," I said, but the words rang hollow, because I knew it as well as she did. "I'm right here, Delilah."

"But you're not. You're getting further away all the time. You're so quiet and brooding and you won't talk to me about anything."

She was right, but there was little I could do to fix the problem. This was something I had to solve on my own. Rising, I took her hand.

"I know it's not very reassuring, but I need you to trust me. It's under control."

"Is it? Really?"

Her scrutinizing gaze forced me to break eye contact by kissing the tip of her nose. "I promise."

No matter what I said to her, though, I was more out of control than ever. A bloody fantasy life courted me day in and out, and every second I was home alone was another hour spent resisting the urge to drop in on Susan, or to drive to the house by the highway with a prostitute in my passenger's seat. Though I could hardly stand the weight of my single breakdown, I craved to repeat it, or any vile deed. I even started thinking about heroin again, and it had been a decade, at least! In response to my infection, I quarantined myself in my studio and worked endlessly on a piece for which both women separately posed. I succumbed to that euphoric phenomenon of the painting pre-existing, as if my work were a summoning, not a creation. But then, again, a little more than halfway through, the bliss of production seized up. I was paralyzed. Fear of failure inhibited me, but more likely I knew even then that the end of the painting would herald irreversible action.

The Sunday after the zoo, Susan, as if nothing had occurred between us, said, "Did Delilah like her birthday flowers?"

"She loved them," I answered without thinking, only after realizing Delilah had told me they'd come from coworkers.

Upon hearing this, Susan merely smiled. "Perhaps the poor girl feared criticism for spending time with me."

"I don't criticize the company she keeps."

"That isn't what I've heard."

"So you're her new therapist?"

"Well, the poor girl needs a friend. A woman can't expect her husband to sympathize with all her problems. Particularly not a husband like you."

My nerves wracked, I rested my forearm upon my knee as I read her face. "What problems are these? What has she told you?"

"Is there something in particular she shouldn't talk about?"

"There are any number of topics she'd ought not to discuss with you, ranging from weather to philosophy to any and everything in between."

She scoffed. "You would have us do nothing but sit around discussing you all day?"

"Of course not. I am the most taboo topic of all."

"How are we to spend time?"

"Ideally, you're not."

"Why are you so opposed to our friendship?"

"Because the only thing that could come of it is a wedge."

A chuckle, divine and condescending. "Oh, darling, no. That's not what I'm doing with her. That's what we're doing here."

I bristled. "You'll never manage it."

"Then why am I still picking glass off of the floor? Be realistic, darling. If you were so dedicated to Delilah, you wouldn't be coming to me at all."

"I'm here because you're waving a check under my nose."

"Were that true, you'd have finished my portrait months ago. But here you are, with work your excuse. You've really gotten yourself fooled, boy."

"Don't call me 'boy'."

"Then take responsibility for what you want. You mope over your indiscretion, when you've been just as much a lout ever since you suggested we move from *Madame X* to *Olympia*. I've given you every chance to refuse me, ignore me, but you know what you want and can't help it—can't admit it to yourself, or to her. That girl can't last with you, my dear, and if you don't see it now you won't see it until I'm gone for good. You're lying to yourself as much as to her, and it's pathetic."

She bolted upright, hair tumbling over her breast. "How do you think it will go once you have the white picket fence, darling? Working some drudgerous job; subsidizing your painting, day in, day out, no freedom allotted, total loyalty demanded. Working and working each day the same, until, white-haired, you die, accomplishing nothing but a wasted life and a wife who could never truly comprehend your ennui. But I understand your ennui, Richard—your terrors—because they are also mine. I know how much to loosen the leash, and I can give you the life you dream about. After a few years with me, five-hundred thousand will mean nothing to you."

I hid behind the canvas, half-snarling each word. "What would I be to you? Some toy to be discarded when you're bored?"

"No. You would be my son, for me to love as best I can. My partner."

"You say partner now, but you couldn't stand to live without controlling me."

"I don't need to anymore. You've done all the difficult work for me." Smiling Susan slid her legs over the edge of the bed to light one of my cigarettes. "From here, my dear, your spiral will hasten. Soon you'll be in my arms for good, and I've barely had to lift a finger. I only lay the tools before you, and you destroy your life on your own."

Behind a translucent plume of smoke, she tilted her head. "You think I'm cruel. Heartless. Someday you'll look at your life and understand why I've done this for you."

"What makes you so sure Delilah and I will fail each other?"

"I've told you before. You cannot imagine the toll a conscience takes on a person—and one look in Delilah's eyes tells me hers weighs heavily, indeed."

Exhaling, I recalled our zoo conversation and permitted for only an instant that most pessimistic of daydreams, where my heart was broken by a guilty girl. Soon, I resented her as bitterly as if she had already turned us in. I rubbed my eyes with the heel of my palm and sat at Susan's feet, forehead pressed to the cool porcelain of her bent knee.

"Why couldn't you have come back sooner?"

Immaculate nails combed my scalp. "Because we're only just ready for each other, my love."

"Why can't I have you both?"

"I'd happily involve myself in such a fine arrangement, but you know Delilah could have no part in any such thing. She loves you too much, or the you she convinces herself to see, at any rate. She can't see how you're hurting her. Chipping away one bit at a time until there's nothing left of the person she really is. There is a Delilah you want her to be, I think, but it is not the Delilah she is, and to expect her to change for you is cruel."

The agony of reality twisted my joints. Eyes clenched shut, I lifted my head to kiss her, the both of us tumbling back upon the bed. After, with racing hearts, we lay examining each other's healing wounds. At one point, with my eyes closed to the blur of reality, I heard low and tender singing and felt the strokes of fingertips against my temple. Wracked as I was, I only pretended to sleep.

Chapter

9

Our final argument, our worst by far, began with a question which seemed practical enough on Delilah's part: "Did you take out the trash, honey?"

As the exhumation had been at least a month before, I stopped to consider her question with a glance toward the kitchen.

"You know," she said with an eye roll, and I gathered.

"Oh, that. Yes. I took care of it."

"So it's all gone? And you buried them separately, right?"

"Yes." No need to worry her about the head, since I didn't know where it was, but knew whom it was with.

"Good." Then, dipping her head once more over her tattered copy of *Lolita*: "Richard?"

"Yes?"

"I love you."

I kissed the corner of her eye, which fluttered me away—Monsieur H. Humbert might appreciate the pain it caused my heart just then, if only in principle. On we went with our day, and the next. On Sunday, I visited Susan, as usual, and for once I accomplished something. Her commission was nearly finished now, and glowing on the canvas, much as, at home, Clytemnestra's re-death pulsed alive with the fruits of a cold case. Her figure was alive for me, at home and at work, and she responded to my labors with praise, saying over my shoulder, "You flatterer. I think I'm under-paying you."

And then I went home. I thought Delilah might have lain down for a late nap, as the lights were off, and so I went to make a drink. Just a few more visits, and then I'd have a check from Susan, and we might move on. But how realistic was the notion of escape, even with money?

That was my last coherent thought before I opened the freezer door and discovered the answer to at least one of my questions. I almost started upon meeting a pair of frostbitten eyes, but any surprise was swiftly purged by anger. Deep, white-hot, dangerous anger.

Silent, I shut the freezer door. With the flip of a switch, I uncloaked Delilah, who sat on one of two steps into the living room. I lowered upon the other. "Delilah," I said, almost whispered or else I would have shouted, "What is that doing in our freezer?"

A sullen mound of animate gloom, Delilah stared at the kitchen. "I thought if I hid the head, you might panic. You'd insist we'd need to leave. At the very least, you'd confide in me to keep me aware of the risks. But you just lied to me instead."

"I didn't lie," I said, still the eerie calm of the storm's eye. "I didn't mention it because I didn't want to frighten you. I didn't realize this was some kind of silly test."

"It's not a test."

"A ruse, then. A gambit to goad me into moving us before I'm ready to."

"Will you ever be ready?"

Her question, so barbed, yet poised in such mouse-like manner, only stoked my rage. "I keep telling you I will, goddammit."

"Please don't swear at me."

"I'll say whatever I fucking like when I find out it was you who stole the head. Oh, Christ." My stomach lurched as I placed my hand upon my forehead. "It was you, Delilah. I can't believe it was you."

"Who did you think it was? Why didn't you tell me if you were scared?"

"Because I was certain it was my mother," I said, voice raising now. "Because I was certain—"

There would be no taking this back. But in the heat, the bitter anger of having been tricked, of having fallen into Susan's arms because of Delilah's anxieties, I wanted badly to hurt my little wife. And to seize the opportunity to come clean.

"—I fucked her, Delilah. I was trying to rape her, anything to get her to tell me where it was, but we ended up fucking, instead."

She squinted up at me. "You—but she's your mother."

"We have a complex relationship."

In seconds, I knew my mistake. In seconds, she settled into the pallor of chalk, her face an exquisite and temporary work upon the blackboard of her hair. Her eyes darkened. She trembled, my darling, as if her molecules underwent transformation. I, under a cloud of my own, could think of nothing further to say and awaited her explosion. Instead, she whispered, "Why?"

"I wanted to humiliate her, the way she always seems to humiliate me. But it's out of hand, now."

"Were you like this the first time you met?"

"Yes, we had a sexual relationship. That was why that business with my adopted mother came about."

The chill in the air reminded me of putting Julius in the ground. I reached for Delilah's shoulder but felt my heart blacken as she jerked away, violently, like I was a stranger and she wasn't kidding around the way she sometimes did, pretending she was a girl I picked for my next prey, or making believe she was some frosty Diana eluding the hand of a hungry mortal hunter (my favorite, as she always lost in the most breathtaking ways). I digress, I evade, I do not wish to remember that awful fight at all, do not wish to remember the wet tremor in her voice as she begged, "Please don't. Please, please don't touch me, don't."

Slowly, I withdrew. "Daisy," I began, but her hands clapped over her ears.

"No, I can't stand it. I can't believe it. Why am I so stupid?"

"Don't say that."

"I am!" Delilah hugged herself and gasped, "I believed you loved me."

"I do love you."

"If you loved me, you wouldn't do this to me."

Bitter, now, and pushed, I snapped, "I wouldn't have done it at all if you weren't feeling tricky."

"Don't you blame me for this." Her voice raised a note each second. "Don't you dare say this is my fault. You know you've been waiting for an excuse since she came back—and you never told me. We've been together six years and you never told me about her." Tears blossomed in the corners of her eyes. "Oh my God. You knew she was coming back."

"I hoped she wouldn't."

"Stop! Stop lying." She snatched a brass bracelet from her wrist to hurl it the close distance at my head, and I ducked with no time to spare. "You've been waiting. You've never been with me at all—you've always been with Susan. Is that all I am to you? Filler?"

"No." I almost shouted it, and despite her protests, snatched up her hands. "You don't understand. I've always been with you. Maybe at first, when I didn't realize what we had, I might have been waiting for her. But if I could send her away now, I would."

"Why are you seeing her, then!"

"Because I'm compelled to! Because I want her money so I can make you proud of me, because I can't rest until I know she's dead."

"And having sex with her is going to help you do any of that? You're terrible. You can't take responsibility for your actions. It's her or me or anybody but you. This is you, Richard. You've done this to me and to yourself, and I think if you love her so much—"

"Delilah, I don't."

"—you can't even admit that! Well, why don't you go spend some time with her?" The sneer she wore didn't fit her face: a wholly new person stood and crossed her arms. "Since she's so important to you and you don't realize it, maybe you should go figure it out."

I rose to try and touch her one last time, and again, she recoiled. The blister of fury burst within me and I narrowed my eyes, at last growling, "Fine. You enjoy burying that thing by yourself."

"Just go!" A pleading note rose in her voice, and I saw again the overflow of tears. "Please, Richard. Go away."

So I did. Without my coat, barely remembering my keys, I slammed the door after me and went to a bar down the street from Susan's, where I drank until I vomited. How I made it to Susan's, I do not know, but the next memory of that night is slumping into my mother's arms and feeling her lips on my forehead.

The next morning, I awoke to the scream of the sun pouring in through a picture window. Disoriented, I sat up, reached for Delilah, and hit an empty mattress. My churning stomach sank and I stumbled from bed to vomit again, aware of only the frigid porcelain on my forehead and the waves of heat flooding my body. I straightened when something clammy touched the back of my neck, and found Susan with a glass of water in one hand and half the contents of a pharmacy in the other.

"Poor ragged pup."

Though I accepted the pills, I regarded them with suspicion until I recognized one as a B vitamin. The second they hit my stomach, it objected, and while I willed them to stay down, Susan said, "Why don't you tell me what's happened? You were incoherent last night."

As I leaned against the cool tile of the wall, my eyes slid shut. "I owe you an apology."

"Oh, my. Should I call Satan and ask how the weather is?"

"I'm sure you have his business card somewhere."

Chuckling, she perched upon the edge of her tub. "To what do I owe the dubious honor of an apology from Richard Vasko?"

"I jumped to conclusions."

"You don't say. What conclusions are those?"

I turned my face so my cheek might be swathed in the cool of the wall. Dismissing her question, I said, "Delilah knows now."

"No wonder you're such a fright. I imagine it was tiring to deal with her overreaction. No wonder," she said again, smoothing a few hairs from my forehead.

"She threw me out."

"Did she really?" It was no doubt impossible for her to suppress the tone of approval.

"She told me to go to you, so I did."

"So you did. Well, come on." Smiling, she sprang upright to turn on the shower. "Get yourself cleaned up. There's coffee, fruit, and medical marijuana in the kitchen."

"No such thing in this state yet."

"Well, then, I have superb dope that will pick you right up."

Dry-mouthed and still nauseous, I used the toilet tank to drag myself to my feet, my right arm assisted by Susan. Her scorching touch was unwelcome in my condition, but, too tired to object, I allowed her to strip me and nudge me into the shower, where I remained until it ran like ice. Solitude was welcome, but fostered self-reflection for which I was not ready. Delilah's heartbroken face emerged constantly from the miasma of my mind. My entire body and spirit were raw, wearing at the edges where something vital had torn loose. Yes, that was it, that sensation of missing something; the inky blackness of rot in your stomach upon waking in a bathtub full of ice to a new set of stitches and a note telling you you're down one kidney. In the search for a way to soothe the agony, my mind only doubled it: after all, my natural source of comfort was Delilah. But I couldn't lie in her arms, now, couldn't eat her food and unburden my woes. Every pang of longing came with a flash of resentment for her inability to understand that I, too, was a victim—but in light of morning, even I noticed the title wore thin on me.

What happened now? Was that it? Had our life together been so quick to implode? If so, was it worth anything in the first place? I felt ghostly, and after the shower shared a nasty glance with my reflection, still angry but too drained to admit at whom.

The sound of a slowly plucked piano was what eventually coaxed me from the bathroom. As Susan's fingers made their nimble way across the keys, I slid into the empty kitchen table to roll a joint and pick at the selection of fruit arranged upon a plate—not with a chef's eye, but an ad-man's. No, none of that; plastic fruit anyway, no doubt. The music trickled through me as I smoked. I didn't know the tune, but the melody was soothing, and soon the music and the reefer had me focused on the present. So, Delilah had thrown me out. No point in lying about.

Soon enough I was next to Susan at the piano. It turned out to be a sonata by Scarlatti, though I don't remember which one. The dexterity displayed by her fingers astonished me. Painting is wonderful because it can generally be done with one hand, the other doing nothing, holding something, pressing down paper or flesh. Piano is something on a different level entirely.

"How old were you when you started playing this thing?"

"I began when I was seven," she said, both hands bouncing, or brushing, really, the keys, each at its own tempo and part of the duet. "Julius insisted. The Vasko women have a history of musical talent, particularly in my case. The men, too—did you know your father played violin?"

My eyebrows lifted. "I didn't."

239

"I don't know if he still did as he aged, but for most of his life, until he was about your age, he did. He was beautiful at it, Dick. You could hear his soul in his music. He looked like a man captivated by the spirit of what he was doing—much as you do, engrossed in your painting. A beautiful thing, isn't it?" I nodded, and she asked, "Do you play any instruments?"

"No. I like to listen to music, but we have nothing to do with each other professionally."

That low, honey-chuckle; the exquisite dimples of time appearing in her cheeks and eyes. Until now, I had avoided looking at her body as something beautiful rather than something which deserved to be conquered, so I drank her in as she conceded, "I'd suppose you've spent too much time mastering one craft to dabble in others."

"I'll blush."

"Hah! Now that, I'd pay to see."

"How much?"

With a roll of her eyes, Susan leaned around me to strike a few keys. "You seem to be feeling better."

"What choice do I have? I don't know how upset Napoleon really was when they exiled him to Elba."

"The first time, or the second? Given all I know of your temperament, I expected a few days of sulking."

"Not right now. Sure, in a while. It'll come and go. But right now I'm here with you."

"Do you want to be?"

"I'd rather be here than anywhere else."

Susan smiled to herself as though reflecting on a daydream. "When I got my second divorce, I spent some time in Peru. I tried Ayahuasca there, more potion than hallucinogen, and the vine brought me back to you. I could touch you—did touch you, then, in my hallucination, or memory, dream, and then you rippled away like a pond, and I felt the most terrible anguish. All I sacrificed ... I can't have it back, and if I did it all again, I'd do it the same. Still—sometimes I wish I had come to you sooner. Seen you grow up, felt to you as normal mothers do towards sons. But this is simply how it is, how it always is. There is no choice in the way it is. I always come back to you late. The sun always rises in the east. You are always an artist. We are always living this. And I, for one, am happy with this, as much as it is. I can't know you, love you in the right way, and so I love you in mine."

I swept her hair behind her shoulder and leaned in to kiss the corner of her jaw. As I did, I remembered Delilah's beaten eyes, and recalled, too, how ill I felt. I puffed on the joint again, and once recovered, stuck it in the corner of Susan's mouth. Now she lifted a hand to manipulate it, the music a shadow of itself.

"Do you want to know my favorite place, darling? The Sedlec Ossuary."

How I envied her as I dreamed a painting of svelte young Susan wandering a cathedral of bones, her oil figure gliding, enraptured, across her bony backdrop. "I'd love to see it."

"The design is exquisite, and there are such echoes in the air. Murmurs of life. Why don't we go see it together?"

I laughed, and only knew she meant it when she didn't laugh with me. "When?"

"As soon as Monday, if you're up for it."

"Maybe," I said, thinking of Delilah.

"Do you think she's going to want you back?" As if I'd thought out loud.

"Yes," I said, sure of it now that I was calm.

"How long are you going to wait for her?"

"I waited for you for two decades. She won't take half as long to come around."

"It isn't as if I haven't wanted you. It's that I couldn't be with you when we were young. I know a pattern when I see one. I did not want to linger in its formation."

"Why do you return, then, if you know there's a pattern?"

"Because I have precious little else to lose, and wish to live out my life with my son."

"What pattern is it that you fear so much?"

She smiled, an ancient and mysterious affect becoming her face. "I cannot say."

"Has Delilah ever told you anything about me that I should be upset about?"

"No, dear, but even if you weren't an open book to me, I would be able to discern something just off about her behavior. I do not know how others perceive her, but she reminds me of a skittish bird. Frightened. She becomes hyper-aware of police presence, as any good criminal, with as subtle a double-take as possible and maximum distance when credible. I should know: I do the same. But she does it out of flight more than prudence. You have gotten her into something, Richard—or guided her, perhaps—and she may seem happy, but there's real terror behind it."

I rubbed my jaw. "I keep telling her there's nothing to be afraid of."

"There's never anything to be afraid of if you have an exit strategy, but it must be foolproof. Or you can walk away before it reaches fever pitch." She closed the lid of the piano and propped her elbow on it. "If you could go anywhere in the world, where would you go?"

"Amsterdam."

She laughed. "Then we'll go. Fake passports aren't difficult to get these days—you can literally buy them on the Internet. That Bitcoin currency is miraculous."

With some reluctance, I agreed, "If Delilah hasn't come around in a month, then we'll go."

"Very well," she said, smiling. "Let's finish that painting, say, now that we have so much time."

'Let's' and 'we', as if she were painting it with me. I kissed her elbow as I stood and said, "I'll finish it when it's ready."

Chapter

10

My most pressing concern the first few days after the schism was a potential visit from police. One of the key factors in Delilah's refusal to call them came from fear of our separation, or so I believed. After sending her a message to ensure she had taken no rash action against her own well-being, I received one saying, *Thanks for checking in on me. I still love you. I just need to be alone.*

What choice had we? In case she might have a lapse of judgment and call the police, Susan convinced me to drive her to Virginia Beach a few days. Her noble profile glowed in the golden light of dimming evening, as beautiful as it was when last we drove—west, then, not east, with all that country and future still before us—but I noticed at rest stops the aches stayed longer in her gait than in mine, and her jaw ground as she unfolded from the car, and she napped for thirty minutes or so more than a handful of times, something she'd once told me she hated to do on road trips.

"You're getting old, lady," I told her as she rubbed her knees in our beachfront hotel room.

"Isn't it terrible? Someday it will happen to you."

"Sometimes I wonder," I said. The sky was dark, and the ocean was dark, and the waves hushed upon the sand some twenty feet from the pre-set lawn chairs, all unoccupied, the crooked one on the edge host to several fat, satisfied gulls. I pictured walking over that second floor balcony, dying with the smell of sea salt I remembered only vaguely from one visit with Evangeline at the age of ten. Then, in a shock of innocent, crystalline memory, I remembered she had once been beautiful. Almost happy, never quite. It had been years since I'd thought of her. The distance of time warmed me to her. I saw her smiling face as she helped build a sandcastle. She even destroyed it with me when it was time, a part of it, but in the end she gripped my wrist and told me to stop before the demolition was complete.

"Leave some for the ocean to take away."

243

I don't know why, oppositional a child as I was, but I obeyed. It felt nice for the ocean have part of it: we had taken our share. Later, she was enchanted by the concept of Buddhist mandalas, and indulged a phase of childish sand art on our back patio, to be blown away when finished. I remember being disappointed when she gave it up. It was nice for her to have art the way I did. Not so many years later, I washed her away. I hadn't thought of her because her death hadn't seemed like a tragedy, merely an incident. But once, she was alive. Absently, I wished I could have loved her as easily and wholesomely as she had me.

That hotel room was more cabin than hotel, truly. Upon our arrival, we had been ferried to it via golf cart and provided a map, as well as a number to call should we require a lift to our car or the restaurant or the bar. The place was a duplex-style building with red brick and two upstairs bedrooms. I felt out of place, like she'd smuggled me in. In a black wicker chair on the balcony, a modern masterpiece of licorice, I smoked and watched as Susan, poised before the foot of the bed, wiggled out of her slacks and lay them upon the checkerboard comforter.

"I never expected to become old," she mused while trading blouse for dress shirt purchased and packed for me. It fell around her thighs, only just hiding anything and making me utterly sick with want.

"You told me once you wanted your poolboy to put you down. I may not clean pools, but—"

She ducked her head to release her hair, which plumed around her like mahogany smoke. "After all this time, you're still thinking of murdering me? Near eight months I've been back with you—"

"And twenty-two years gone. A lot of time for fantasy. I can't help but imagine it now that you're here."

Head cocked with those wry, narrowed eyes, Susan sat in the chair opposite. "That reminds me of something I was thinking just today. You ought to confide in me more."

I snorted. "So you'll have more to use against me?"

"No, because I'm your mother. And because I'm interested in you. I think I see, but I don't want to think. I want to know."

"Know what?"

"About how, and whom, and why. Certain things, I am quite sure of— that you and Delilah were not bringing that woman home for sex, for example."

I spread my hands. "Why would we bring anyone home, then? Assuming we would in the first place."

"Indeed, why would you?" She totally dismissed the possibility of misunderstanding. But I can't expect her to mistake anyone for me but me. "What could you have been up to which so rattles Delilah and inspires in you such paranoia? Something that drove you to ravish me in a fit of anger for stealing something you're too afraid to name"

"I regret it," I said. "At least, the consequences are regrettable."

"Are you going to mope this whole trip?"

"No. I'm here with you. But I once had my future. Now I'm not sure what I have."

"More a future than you ever had before. I am what you are, Richard. I am your self. I am you." She smiled and touched the center of my forehead, just between my eyebrows, and a wave of bliss swept down into my neck.

"You're not me."

"More than you could know. More than I could know. Be with me and we will make each other stronger. I'll spread your name, whisk you someplace safe. And if you should find yourself possessed by—urges, I suppose I can tolerate a hobby so long as you maintain discretion, and keep me informed so that we may make arrangements."

"Delilah wants me to quit."

"I'm sure she does. But I have no moral objections to what you do, so long as I am not the immediate target of interest." Her once-gentle expression, then, grew narrowed and stern. "I would humor you," she clarified, "but I would not wish to observe such a thing."

I scoffed. "I thought you were a progressive woman. A hedonist."

"I confess I am. But I have seen Death: have summoned it myself, when I was small and afraid. It does not interest me to toy with it as you do. A Death cult is just as absurd as one of Life, my boy."

The soft waves lolling against each other called my attention. If I put her in the ocean, her end would be beautiful, but my definite undoing. I watched the water to hide my humiliation at her faint disapproval of my unspoken passion. What a nice night to swim—but not with Susan, who would either not swim at all, or be too elegant in the water. Delilah, now—in water she was graceless, but that didn't stifle her grin as she splashed and paddled in circles around me. My inept little naiad!

Susan was here, and so was I—but Delilah was not, and that seemed the most crucial element. What if she came to collect me in the five days we were at the beach? Would finding us gone push her over the edge?

"How long do you expect this to last?" I asked Susan, finally.

"Longer than you would with Delilah. Neither of us should engage in a relationship with a sensitive. Not for longer than a few years at a stretch. We're too intense, too intelligent and easily bored. But I think we can keep each other interested, don't you?"

She bent closer, as if to share a most intimate secret, her hand upon my knee. "Because we understand one another's burden. This loneliness. We suffer no illusions—just as we might intellectually speculate on the emotions of others but cannot feel them, we are all too aware there can be no true connection here. I touch you, but really our atoms can never touch. All we feel is a glass barrier defining the reality we've come to accept. And we are lonely in this life. But we can be lonely together." Her hand was soft, and the air was cold. A gull screamed, then took off from the chair and startled its companions.

I rose. "I'm very tired."

"I understand," she said.

In bed, she slipped beside me, naked and cold, her limbs always having had curiously poor circulation. Once, when we were young, I asked her about it and she joked that she was dead. I wonder if it wasn't a condition of the spirit in some ways. When I wrapped myself around her, she was almost small against me. One hand sheltered the back of her neck, the other gripped icy fingers.

Out of the darkness, she said, "Will you promise me something?"

"What's that?"

"I know that sooner or later, it is going to happen."

She paused, waiting for me to deny that it would, and I made not a sound. There was no point in lying about it. Yes, we both knew better. One way, or another, Death would come for Susan in the form of her son.

"If I have any say at all, I have always preferred the idea of drowning."

I still said nothing, not even mentioning the thought had crossed my mind mere minutes before, and only kissed her forehead as I reconsidered the notion. It did seem satisfying, the idea of drowning her. Watching her struggle and splash and fight for air. And after, she would be no less beautiful. No wonder she wanted it.

"Do you want to die, Susan?"

"No. No more than one wants to be born. But it is—fair, say, for me to die at the hands of my son. How would you do it, if not by drowning?"

This, I had no answer for, because any answer was incriminating. She tilted her head to see my face better in the moonlight streaming through glass doors. With narrowed eyes, she studied me, and then, smiling, said, "Ah, of course," and guided my other hand to her throat. My heart began to pound as I felt her say, "Your first instinct whenever we fuck. The first thing you thought to do when you barreled in, making cryptic accusations. After, of course, breaking my coffee table."

"You'll go to your grave talking about that coffee table."

"I loved that table," she said, playfully put-upon.

"You're more upset with the table than your own death."

She smiled and lifted her chin, exposing herself for my hands to better encircle. "It's not that I have never mourned the idea of my own death, but now I see through it. This is just a stream of consciousness. We are not even actors: merely parts, played by the same cosmos. We are each of us splinters, cogs of an infinite machine so complex it resembles the neurons of the brain, because what else could it possibly be, the Universe, when all we perceive is an electrical impulse? The Universe resides in a brain which resides in the Universe and on and on.

"A stream does not stop, Richard. A stream flows out, out into an ocean, into a pond, where it evaporates, then rains, and then returns, sometimes in that stream, sometimes in this stream, sometimes in no stream at all. But it does not vanish. If I am wrong, and my self disappears for good, then so be it, but," she smiled, "after what happens every time happens again, and the stream reaches its end, it will evaporate and return to where it started, more or less. And it's been such a long time since I've seen my father."

The vibrations of her throat hummed into the bones of my hands and I shifted my grip to squeeze—but it was gentle, and came with kisses, which were not as carefree as the kind I gave to comfort Delilah. Susan still smiled, and rasped something I couldn't hear, so I slacked. "Be careful not to bruise me. We have a party in a few days."

"So wear a turtleneck."

She laughed, then gagged as I choked her harder. But her smile hardly faded, even in her sleep.

Now, I can try to convince you I moped and pouted and wished for Delilah the whole vacation; that I was but a captive at mercy of Susan's money and spell. In truth, I enjoyed our trip. Each morning we roused ourselves, slathered on sunblock and began a day spent doing nothing but reading, drawing, swimming and dozing on the sand with a drink always nearby. In the afternoon, we would wander in to the restaurant, which served fresh sushi and strong margaritas, and then, after a nap, amuse ourselves by going into town and taking the trolley to various sites around the town.

It was different than it might have been with Delilah, though. Susan had no patience for the kitsch littering many of the boardwalk stores, and so we searched for galleries. One in particular had some attractive work reminiscent of the impressionists, and I paused before a painting of a girl wandering in a swamp, her hair piled on top of her head, delicate lashes downcast. I bought a print immediately, and only after realized it had made me think of Delilah, who appeared in the girl's gentle carriage, and the dreamy aspect of her soft features.

By the night of the party, I was baked by the sun, salted by the sea and ready for a lifetime of nothing. With some effort I managed to put on a suit, and Susan emerged from the bathroom soon after, wearing an emerald gown with a silver stole around her shoulders, her mocha-rimmed eyes colorful behind her lashes' cartoon curls. I pulled her close to kiss her jaw. "Do we really have to go to the party?"

"We do, my darling."

"But you look so good right here, mother, dear."

She moaned, and sighed, and pushed me away with a brusque little slap. "Later. This will be good for you."

Cursing her resolve, I helped her into her gloves, enthralled as the silver silk swallowed whole the flesh of her arms. Then I watched as, before the mirror, she consulted her reflection and swiftly pinned her hair in what, to me, seemed too intricate an up-do to be accomplished in so little time. A few strands fell free at the nape of her neck. I swept them away to kiss the flesh beneath, then clasped a necklace there at her behest. It matched the diamonds in her earrings, glittering and cold. I knelt to help her into mercury shoes and kissed the sides of her feet as I did, tongue darting against the skin-tone hosiery which begged to be touched.

And I, with my silver tie, felt nothing in a three-piece suit beside her. All eyes would be, and indeed were on her as we arrived. A graying pageant judge honed in on us from the left with a gleeful cry of, "Susie!"

"Patricia, my love, how have you been?" She vanished from my side to embrace the woman, who kissed her cheek and said, "I'm so happy you made it," and all the other horrible clichés spewed by wealthy people at parties. I stood behind, surreptitiously looking for a bar until I heard the old woman ask, "And who is this handsome young thing?"

"This is my son, Richard," Susan said with a gay smile, turning a hand towards me. "But he's not on the market for your filthy hands, dear."

"You can hardly bring a man like this to one of my parties and expect me not to admire him, at least."

I smiled and took her bony hand, which I kissed, briefly. The skin was losing its opacity. "There's no harm in admiring, ma'am, but I'm afraid my mother is right. I'm spoken for."

"So am I," said the woman with a wink, "but at my age that doesn't stop me."

Laughter was the only reaction I managed, and I said amid it, "I'm going to need a drink to keep up with you."

"You already sound like my husband. The bar is over there," she said with a vague wave, turning back to Susan. "Susie, come with me, you're not going to believe who's here ..."

As I evaporated into the crowd, I swept the small of Susan's back and her head tilted a degree perceptible only to me. Then I surged through, coming out the other side to find there was, indeed, a bar, and a bar-tender. "Am I glad to see you," I told him, and a vodka tonic later I was on the edge of the room, surveying the scene. We were in a very large apartment with towering windows and almost no furniture. Most of the attendants were over the age of sixty, though a good third of the demographic seemed my age to Susan's. It startled me to remember I was the same age as people in a room like this, that I was nearly forty and still felt so often like a child. All this time, I waited for her—was that because I knew I was nothing without her?

I remembered when she found me: young, uncultured. Still no future to run to. She showed me what I was—but how much of that was what she had wanted me to be? How much of the man I was now had grown simply because Susan had sown the seeds? Had there been no Susan, I might never have been an artist. I might never have been a killer. I have told you this already, my friend, but it was then I began to realize it, and suddenly felt empty.

So I was a fantasy for her. A projection, a creation. Had I no worth on my own?

As if to answer that question, a man around my age stepped up to the bar. He had graying hair, and was dressed as if he were hoping to escape to the lecture hall aboard his yacht. When he noticed my vacant stare, he grinned at me. "I've been there, buddy."

"I'm not sure how much of this is my scene," I said, absorbing all the old smiling white people preserved by money and leisure. Just standing there was exhausting, and all the snippets of conversation—gossip, politics, children, grandchildren—could only have been less interesting if held at a church luncheon. "I don't know if all artists are cut out for the networking aspect of the business."

"Yeah? What do you paint?"

"My work is a throwback to romanticism. An exploration of mortality, primarily."

"You don't say." There was an interested twinkle in his iron eyes, and he asked, "You have your work on your phone?"

I did, actually, thanks to Delilah, who was the reason I had a smartphone in the first place. I slid it from my jacket and showed him a few paintings, including Susan's botched *Madame X* attempt.

"Hey! That's Susan," he said, then, "This stuff is great—really rich. I wish I could see it in person."

"I don't know how often you're in Columbus, but my work shows there all the time."

"No kidding? My brother lives in Columbus—say, what's your name?"

I introduced myself with a handshake, and he said, "Your name is familiar. I may have seen you a couple years back in one of those places on High Street." He was probably blowing smoke up my ass with that, but he wasn't when he asked, "Do you have a card? My niece loves stuff like yours. Do you do commissions?"

"I just finished one for Susan, in fact."

The man whistled from the corner of his mouth. "She doesn't buy cheap."

"I'm open to negotiation."

He grinned. "Glad to hear it. A portrait might be a great birthday present."

Somewhat startled, I handed a card from my wallet. He read it, then, nodding, slid it into his billfold. "Are you based in Columbus?"

"I am, but I'm always willing to travel for work."

There was a crooked slant to his grin. "I like your attitude, because I'm in Arizona," he said with a pat on my shoulder. "I'll call in a few weeks."

"Always happy to hear from a client," I said, nodding from behind my drink. Knowing better than to extend such an interaction too long, I glanced to the empty balcony. "Excuse me, ah—"

"Cassius Wagner," he said, and I knew his name vaguely from someplace but only later placed him as an author from one of Delilah's many shelves. I shook his hand again, and excused myself to the open air, where I could smoke in peace and consider what had just happened.

This was the start of something. Something I had built myself. Sure, Susan had made possible the coincidence of meeting this man, and he may have been lying or mistaken when he said he had seen my work, but even so, if I had not begun to expose my name, I would not have felt the still-heavy pat on my shoulder. It seemed a stroke of luck, a nudge from reality in the midst of a room so artificial. There was no question the food and drink was amazing, the younger women and men beautiful, the money and beach enticing. But it was small wonder Susan knew only loneliness in her world. Later, in the back of the cab headed for the hotel, I discovered she had known these people for years, since her first husband. They were his friends, really, but had adopted her after his death.

"You seem to have friends everywhere you go," I said, and she smiled.

"I try to keep a set stowed away here or there. Never know when you might need one. The trick is using them before their expiration date."

"When is that?"

"When they start to see what I am." She stroked my thigh. "Did you have a nice night, darling?"

"It was interesting. Not quite my people."

"We have no people. Only each other. But these people have their uses."

"So it seems." I kissed her cheek, then draped my arm around her shoulders. "Thank you for bringing me out. You're right. This was good for me."

Chapter

11

On the trip back to Ohio, we decided to give her a month, but in the end it took Delilah two weeks in total to reclaim me. Saturday afternoon, as I nursed the remains of my sunburn in the bathroom, Susan answered the ringing phone and her tone drifted from pleasant to frosty. A few seconds later, she leaned against the doorway of the bathroom.

"You might consider getting dressed. We're having company."

I struggled to gather the reason behind her steely look and, when I did, was rewarded with a boyish flutter of delight. Susan kept watching, and I kept wearing my mask, though surely it did little to hide my racing mind from her omniscient perception. But suddenly, I didn't care about Susan, or what she thought. Delilah was coming up the elevator. For all I knew, this would be my only chance—to do what? Apologize? Win her back? Grovel? I dawdled in the bedroom as I dressed to put off for a moment the reality of seeing her, as if setting eyes upon my wife might seal something indelible. I might be forced to face all the ways we had changed, she and I. I might not cling to the past. And, worst, I might have no choice but to acknowledge her autonomy.

The living room overflowed with the silence of a courtroom bearing witness to obvious perjury. In the armchair sat Susan; upon the settee was Delilah, settled with all the care a child might take in arranging a doll. Having been separated from her longer than ever since the start of our relationship, she seemed luminescent. A new woman. Still so much my Woman, now crystallized. Though she still wore a glistening black raincoat, it parted to hint at the macaw-red fabric of her dress. The air around her was still. She regarded the space behind Susan's head with the impassive stare of a bus commuter avoiding conversation. But her pale hands were all the paler near her knuckles, so tightly she'd folded them together. The left was still adorned by our wedding ring, just as mine.

As she noticed me, her head lifted. Her expression did not change, but I saw her eyes light, and something warm blossomed in my chest.

"Delilah." I exhaled her name as Susan looked on, even her malignant gaze fading into the background.

"I just came to say you should come home."

That my homecoming should involve a great deal of terse conversation was implicit, but a terse conversation at Delilah's mercy seemed somehow preferable to a lifetime lazing about with Susan and peeling sunburned flesh. Punishment meted by Delilah's tender hands might straighten me out. I had faith in her strength, and found bizarrely that I wanted her to help me. I felt weak, and tired, and wondered if, after all this time of pretending to be Susan's victim, I truly was just that.

"I'd love to come home," I said as she rose. "I'll follow you in my car. Only give me a moment, please."

"I understand."

She was nearly to the door when Susan, smirking, piped up with, "Good to see you, too, darling."

While I shot her a dagger stare, Delilah faced her with a smile and widened eyes, and she looked beautifully, wildly insane just then, and I wanted to kiss her feet as she asked, "Do you really want me to say something to you?"

"I'm curious what you might come up with."

"I don't waste my time thinking about you. But I guess I'm sorry for you. At least Richard loves, or tries to. At least he's intrigued by the concept of love. You're so busy seeking control for its own sake that you don't know or can't admit that you're lonely as you are. You've lived such a terrible life that you think cruelty is the only way to earn someone's respect. That's why you need Richard: you think money will make him stand you, and blood will make him stand you, and all he missed from you the first time around will make him stand you. But you could live to be a hundred, and surrounded by people, and you'd still die alone, because your heart is full of poison and everybody knows it. I'm glad you had Richard for a while."

Still with a venomous smile, Susan answered, "Oh?"

"Mm-hmm," said Delilah, digging through her purse, removing her keys like the sword from the stone. "When that loneliest hour comes, you can remember what it was like to be with someone you loved, and then lose him. Honey," she said in the same breath, "I'll be in the lobby."

I nodded, got the door for Delilah, and then, with it closed, said to Susan, "I need to talk with her."

"You do." Her words were tarnished echoes of themselves, distant, as if from a tape player. "Don't think of me. Go to her and settle your business, however you must."

I nodded as I bent to kiss her. She turned her head so I might only have her cheek; then, at the touch of my hand, she relinquished her mouth, the satin of her tongue, the breath of her lungs. As I stood, we shared a long and silent look. She smiled—more smirked, really—and I did not, because I knew this was the last moment we would have together as friends.

Eventually, I found myself downstairs, where my woman in red stared out the window through the rain, through the world from which she seemed so far apart.

"What are you, nuts?" whispered the doorman as I passed, "Leaving a girl like that to hang out with your mom."

"Mind your business," I barked, but he was right, and as Delilah turned to the sound of my voice, I wrapped her in my arms.

After a long stare, it was she who kissed me. In our desperation our teeth clattered, our noses bumped, and we laughed, the heat of her forehead pressing against mine. Like kitten's paws, her hands worked the lapels of my jacket until she exited, her smile so faint it was hardly there. Outside, rivulets of rain rolled down the curve of her nose, into the corners of her lips. She did not look at me as I helped her into the car, followed her home, and found, as the gray tom greeted me by throwing himself against my legs, that she had managed just fine without me. Better, even, than I had without her. A hint of my reflection in the mirror over the key-holder revealed a degree of strung-out exhaustion typically only observed in junkies, but Delilah seemed possessed by a new spirit which turned her sunshine smile to somber moonlight, still light all the same.

"I see you wasted no time replacing me," I said playfully, the cat taking my attempt to tickle his ears as invitation to gnaw on my fingers.

Her wince—small, unnoticeable to all but me, localized around her eyes—made me regret my joke. She didn't respond, too busy arranging multiple courses upon the dining room table. I had the strange and terrible fancy that I was a guest in someone else's home, watching the exquisite hostess arrange her meal. Even the house seemed vaguely foreign, an effect I attributed to a fern missing from beside the couch.

"What happened to your plant?"

"I was very upset when you left." A thump echoed over the wooden floor as she jerked my seat from the head of the table. It squeaked as I sat. It never had before.

She had lain out a stew, a salad rich with staring eyes of tomatoes and feta and sprinkles of black olives, two plates of baked chicken carbonara with balsamic glaze, two bottles of wine, and all the finest silverware. She sat to my left and neither took nor served none of it. Her distant expression reminded me of the one she often wore at the height of her benzodiazepine dependence, and I wondered if she hadn't squirreled some away for a rainy day.

"I've quit working," she said. Her matte eyes lifted to mine. "I gave them my two weeks' the Monday after you left."

"You keep saying I left. You threw me out."

She thumbed the edge of her plate. "But you didn't try to stay."

"Wasn't it better I left with no fuss?"

"I think it was," she said with a furtive glance towards the void once marked by a plant. "I hated you for a while. As a matter of fact, I still do. But I love you more than I hate you and everything you've—brought out in me. Somehow, my hate makes me that much more desperate to love you. To prove to that angry, empty part of me that it doesn't matter."

"It doesn't."

"It does. Everything we do and feel matters, Richard." She held her head high, her shoulders back, her gaze welded to mine. "You sneer and dismiss. I know you think you're superior to the rest of humanity, but evolved or not, you're a human. Just like every other human being—a sperm and an egg with a spirit, whatever it consists of. You've convinced yourself that you and I and that awful woman are the only ones with any substance, but the world is infinite. Everybody, a different story, a unique experience. Have you ever imagined what it would be like to be one of the women you murder?"

"It's not just murder. It's a channel of creativity."

"Just answer my question."

I shook my head. "Once, I tried to imagine it, but I do not think I could ever imagine what it's like for a woman in any circumstance. There's too much difference in the way people interact with women and men." I didn't bother mentioning it would be difficult enough to imagine myself in the place of another man: defending myself now would just irritate her.

"What about me?"

"I have trouble sometimes, but you're not just a woman."

"But I am." She placed her hand flat upon her heart. "So is Susan. So is every woman on the street. So are our victims."

I leaned back, Susan flashing through my mind to sympathize on the tedium of the lecture. "What are you trying to do, Delilah? Save me? Convert me?"

"No!" As she spoke, she swatted the table, the plates rattling under their cooling loads. "I just need to make you understand—understand—"

"Why you hate me?"

"Yes." Softening now, she slipped one dainty hand into my palm. "I refuse to be sorry for it," she added.

"So long as you love me just as much."

"Of course. I love you so much I can't bear the idea of being parted. I told you once that I could understand the things you did, because I knew I was capable of murder, too. That when someone came between us, I would kill them, because that's how desperately I want to be with you." Her grip tightened, and from behind wild eyes, she said, "That's why I'm asking you to bring me Susan's heart."

Though her hate had thrilled me as a sign of her burgeoning strength, the back of my skull now opened so dread might slither in. "I agree," I said, measuring each word. "When the time is right, we'll kill her and leave."

"When will the time be right?"

"When the painting is finished."

"Didn't you work on the portrait at all when you stayed with her?"

"Yes, but I mean to say your painting. The Piece."

"Uh-huh." She licked her lips, then covered our clasped hands with her free one. "But you did finish your work for her."

"Yes."

"So you have the money."

"Yes, but leaving isn't about money. It's about the Piece."

"Why? Why does it have to be finished here?"

My face was so hot I felt as if I were coming down with a fever. "Because we hunt here. You want us to stop when we leave."

"I do. But why do you have to paint in human blood?"

"It's the meaning in the medium. My sacrifice to you."

"I don't want the blood of women who have never hurt me," she said darkly, regarding the empty seat across from her, eyes narrowed at an apparition we shared. "And shouldn't the blood of one woman be enough? There's been so many."

"I'm hardly Ted Bundy. I'm only taking what I need until I finish the painting. It's so close, but it's still missing something."

"What are you waiting for?"

"It must be perfect."

She was gnashing her teeth now, or baring them when she spoke at any rate. "It's never going to be anything if you never do it. When was the last time you actually finished a fucking painting that wasn't for Susan?"

I had never heard her use that word outside of sex: my ears rang like I'd been slapped. When next I opened my mouth, I actually was.

"No! I don't want to hear it. Justify, justify, that's all you ever do. Well, you listen to me, mister. You've justified yourself into another reality. Don't you talk."

Delilah inhaled sharply, her hands quivering as the reddened one lowered again upon mine. "You keep saying you want immortality, not just some flash-in-the-pan murder attention. That you want fulfillment. You could've had that already. You could have finished a painting, a tremendous painting, if you'd stop caring about everybody's opinion. Even mine—and especially hers. You think so lowly of yourself that you feel you have to be an artist or a killer or whatever to be a complete person, but you already are one. What does it matter if nobody remembers you? Doesn't it feel good to paint, just to paint? To be here, alive, with me? Susan can fast-track you to being famous, but I can make you happy. You can make yourself famous and rich because you're so talented, and stay with me while you do." Tears welled in her eyes. "Wouldn't that be nice?"

The nausea that overcame me was but one symptom of a sudden clarity. What was this fulfillment I sought: fulfillment of what? An ego—my ego, towering, hungry, growing ever-larger, seeking to grow as large as possible, a tumorous bubble to be burst by death. But even if it began to grow, when would it be satisfied? There could be no fulfillment if I swallowed money and fame and sex and murder. The need would grow as it had from the start. This temporary, fragile thing I couldn't even prove existed demanded I nurse it like a parasite. There was fulfillment every time someone nodded at my painting for a few moments, every time Delilah paused to smile over my shoulder before resuming her path. All this beauty had been met with scorn. There was beauty in the simplicity of being with Delilah, of savoring the process of growth rather than seeking to be grown. I had wasted so much in the name of comforting a dead man about his death. Why should I long to echo in others when it was no literal continuity? This moment, that moment, all the past and future moments and the sheer odds against any of them happening at all—this was all I could have, and even then, the moments slipping ever-away were no more mine than was Delilah, or my art, or my self. I had only that moment in painting or lovemaking or murder where the self dissolved and I grazed against the satin curtain to feel the air of Nirvana whisper at my feet. Goya, painting black murals across the walls of his home; Dickinson, stuffing her drawers with scraps of poetry; Vasko, slaving his Piece to perfection. Unseen by any but the artist, still a part of the artist, meant to be slivered off and become art upon the death of the self, where it became work with no other purpose but art's sake, with the creator dead to praise.

Suddenly, I was free. Free from slavery to Susan's money. Before me, sat someone who appreciated my work with the same intensity I put into creating it. A girl who sent me a letter, because she had been so moved by my work that she needed to become a part of my life whatever the cost. I slipped free my hands to grip Delilah's face, my whole body relaxing. I wanted to create. I kissed her hard on the mouth, into her mouth, her cheeks, her tears. I said, "I need your help. Pose for me, then help me take care of her, and when the painting is finished, we'll leave."

"But you'll never—"

"I will. I understand now. You've made me see something beautiful, Delilah. And when you're holding Susan's heart in your hands, I'll have returned the favor."

She exhaled, clutching my shirt. "Do you mean it?"

"Of course I mean it. I know I've lied, but I'm naked now. And even naked, you still want me, want to be with me. I understand what it needs, now." Again, I kissed her, and against her mouth murmured, "What you need."

She gasped, and tugged us from the table, me upon the floor, on my back to gasp as she leaped upon me. I inhaled her breath, her tongue, her very soul if I could have. We became savage as she clawed and bit, and I responded with teeth which sank what seemed centimeters into her soft white flesh to make her shriek and moan. The cat watched with an amused, knowing eye, then wandered down the hallway to make himself scarce in a bedroom. We tumbled into the living room and scrambled briefly for positions before, eventually, I got a grip on her, and pushed her towards the pair of stairs, where she was forced to catch herself and lay grinning as I held one arm behind her back.

Right there, still half in our clothes, I took her and felt her, saw her, not just the Woman, but her: just Delilah. Happy and sad. Patient, demanding. Separate, distant, yet so entwined with me we might as well have been two branches of one tree. Our disparate ages and upbringings faded. The things I did, the things she'd permitted, all of it trickled back and it seemed we were twins, yes, marked by death rather than life. We died in each other again and again, like there on the stairwell, Delilah's brow furrowed with her clutching spasms which killed me, too, and I grasped her, buried myself in her, in her neck, in her body, in her soul. She seemed to shrink against me, turning to nuzzle and kiss the sweat from my brow. Then, she laughed, and so did I. After, we fixed our clothes, sat down to eat, and I explained my sunburn while she listened with a smile.

Chapter

12

Though we agreed the matter was better handled sooner than later, I managed to negotiate two more weeks. As she had disposed of the head, our necessary arrangements were limited to domestic ones—what to do with furniture, books and clothes, for instance, and the finer details of our destination. Nogales, Arizona seemed the best choice: half in the States and half in Mexico, we could skip the border as tourists and fade into the southern country, from where we could easily reach and settle in South America. As I saw it, we would have a three-day grace period following Susan's murder; though the doorman was likely to report her missing, he was no doubt familiar enough with her comings and goings that he wouldn't rush to make a call were she to vanish for a few days. Indeed, we had stayed at the beach a week with no note, light baggage, and no fuss, so it was possible we had as many as seven days before an investigation began. Still, ever-bracing for the worst case, I planned for three: one day and night to produce the painting that tickled the tip of my brain, and just under the two and a half days required for a train to Tucson, which seemed the most sensible and least-monitored mode of transport in a post-Patriot Act America. In the interim, we had two weeks to pack our things, obtain our tickets, and find hotels south of the border. Two weeks to kill Susan. Our future was finally set—so what sent apprehension to wake me at four, three, two in the morning and hold me back from a night of rich unconsciousness? Each of the three days following my return I suffered in the early mornings until Delilah once awoke at three to find me staring at the ceiling. She had been quiet since our reconciliation, but in her quiet was a warmth—the intimacy of a mausoleum. She, like I, felt our destiny, and seemed calmer now than in four years, since I first bloodied her with my secrets.

"Are you thinking about her?" There was no judgment in the question, so I told her the truth. Delilah placed her hand over my heart, her cheek on my shoulder. "Do you want to see her?"

"I don't know if I should."

"You'll have to at some point between now and then. It's going to be odd if we go two weeks with no communication, then suddenly invite her to dinner. Especially after all this."

"I'm not sure I'll be able to help myself—if something happens."

Mouth twisting, Delilah kissed my cheekbone. "It doesn't matter now what happens. You chose me. You choose me every day, every night, and you'll still choose me when she's dead. She's dying. Maybe it wouldn't be so bad if you made her last days happy. And we'll lull her into a false sense of security if she thinks nothing's wrong."

I nodded, then buried my face in her hair and fell finally to sleep, where I dreamed black dreams only to awake to a different one. As if drugged, I drove downtown to see the woman who kept me up nights, to feel the air around her as much as I could before I did what needed to happen.

In Susan's apartment, her portrait filled the wall-space once occupied by a set of shelves and a hanging scroll. Her tigerish likeness surveyed our meeting with the insolent stare of a predator. She settled beneath it. "I'm surprised to see you. I was certain she'd snapped, and that any day now I'd read in the papers about a murder-suicide."

I chuckled. "I'm as shocked as you. She's even made a serious change of heart—so much so I almost think she's planning something."

"Sweetness is the finest veil."

"I think I've begun to turn her around. She understands I need both of you, so long as both are near to me."

Cheek artfully upon her fist, Susan smiled. "How did you manage such an evolution in her thinking?"

"You're no threat to her as far as I'm concerned, so long as the two of you are mostly kept apart. She is my wife; you are my mother; and I adore you both."

"A more malleable woman than I knew."

"Anyone will agree to anything with a bit of persuasion."

"But you know," she said, one leg crossing to push her skirt an inch higher, "you'll have to pick one of us eventually. Tolerant though she may be, I cannot imagine the three of us could long be a happy family."

"I know." The wind trickled between the tassels of stained-glass chimes in the window. "I need some time to think about it. This can't last—but I can't decide."

"Take a little time," she urged. "Consider what you want for your future."

"I know what I want."

"Then consider not desire, but prudence."

Dimly, I nodded, my eyes trained on the window. The room, warm and silent but for the hum of electricity. Her presence, disdained and beloved.

All of this would be gone. No matter how I waited, there would be no third coming. That alone tempted me to choose Susan, even if briefly. But I was sure that as soon as I had her, the weight of my sacrifice would crush me.

The cushion beside me depressed, and I turned to find her settling by my side. One arm draped my shoulders while the other caressed my face, which she drew to her breast. As I lost myself in her heartbeat, my mother's heartbeat, I realized it was true: she did love me. Had never done anything but love me. If she didn't, she wouldn't have stopped herself from smothering me all those decades ago. She wouldn't have tracked me down that day in the butcher's shop. She wouldn't be holding me, as the sounds of an argument wove up from the street to melt with the tick of the clock and the beat of her heart. Of course, she was cruel and selfish, but that didn't falsify her love. I should have seen it, known it better than anyone. My dread, I realized, was not because her death needed to be perfect, but because I was not sure she would die still loving me.

"Will you sing for me," I asked against her breast.

"What shall I sing?"

"Anything you want."

A vibration built first in her sternum, then her breast, reverberating through her throat to burst as song. Like an airborne virus, it rattled through the air and into me, where I peeled apart gossamer notes and found beneath the rich tones of gentle age. After a fashion, I recognized the '50s tune of romantic obsession and transcontinental possession, and in my own stumbling voice, joined her. Her smile brightened the sound, warmed it, and I embossed the moment in my memory so I might never forget what I could never have. As we crooned (and cawed), her fingers worked each button on my shirt. When it was over, we made love in the still-humming silence.

At times it seemed Susan knew our plan and was trying in her gentle way to change my mind. Together we visited galleries all over the state, saw *La Traviata* in Columbus. As a lover, she grew more tender. Perhaps she sensed not my plan, but my pain. No matter what we did, what she did, she could not help that I went home, where the taste of my mother's kisses were washed away by the rain of my wife's. Though she never mentioned my activities with Susan, she, too, did all she could to distract me from both my mistress and the task at hand. Her methods were less extravagant. In fact, but for food and gas, we spent hardly a thing. One day she sat up in bed. "I want to take you somewhere."

A ninety-minute drive over golden highways, and we stood beneath a mountain arranged from stones of every size and shape, limestone nestled against keystones and urns, no logic but for a beauty that was organic, as if the stones had always been, would always be, just there, rising out of an ocean of rich green grass stretching the middle of the city block.

"The Temple of Tolerance," said Delilah, and though I chuckled at the name, I knew it at once, as if I had my whole life. Not a mountain, but a temple, and as we stepped through the gate, I felt a lightness in the air. We explored every inch, all the coves and altars, and as tranquility's other worshippers drifted away, we filled the seats at the top of the temple steps and watched the setting sun. We did not speak. In those last few weeks of our lives, in fact, we said precious little. Words were mere symbols of the things we felt together. As the sky's ember cooled to the soft bruise of night, Delilah held my hand. When I looked at her, she smiled her real smile, wide and natural, and I realized that was the first she'd worn it since our fight.

Our fight. It seemed so small now. Had it even happened? It seemed we had always been there, united, hands clasped under the awakening stars. Upon our temple, we were all that was, aside from the lightning bugs beginning to glow, the crickets fiddling in the trees. When we left, we would choose to emerge again into a world—no, create with our perception a world of people. As God perceives the world and it exists, so we in our perception would bring to existence the harmony of life, because our perception was God as much as we were, and eternity disguised itself in seconds through which we saw, in which we could create a world with just the two of us. For just the two of us, and the glowing fireflies, and the crickets with their violin orchestra.

Chapter

13

The day Susan died was longer than the years I'd dreamed of it. Now her death possessed true meaning. This was my sacrifice not just of Susan, but of murder. After her, its meaning would be lost. Things would change. I might change.

We invited her to dinner under the pretense of, as Susan once put it, "rebuilding bridges." Delilah's scheme was of artful simplicity: ply everyone, not just Susan; behave as the most intimate of friends; and, when the time was right, we would shoot her with heroin I procured through Gavin, who was thin as a Halloween prop when we embraced outside his Marion trailer.

"Rick! Can't say I'm glad to see you. You're not on this shit again, are you?"

"No, no," I said as I slapped a roll of twenties into his palm, "most of it is for a friend."

He cast me a skeptical look while pocketing the money and ushering me inside. "That's a lot of dope. Sorry it's hot, the a/c's broken."

"It's all right." The trailer seemed much smaller inside, partially carpeted in a gray-orange rug and smelling of cat piss, though I saw no cat during my abbreviated visit. "What's new?"

"Mark died last year."

"I'm sorry to hear that." More, I was sorry the concept of Mark I remembered wasn't around, though I doubted he had been alive as I remembered him for quite some time preceding his death. "Overdose?"

"Needle still in his arm."

"Drano?"

"Bleach, the moron. He started to clean and got distracted, thought he'd sterilized it," he said, reaching deep into the cushions of his couch and producing a lock-box. "He was manic."

"You always pick the worst stash spots," I said, laughing.

His grin revealed a missing molar. I remembered the first whore. They'd both had teeth there, once. "Nobody thinks to look in the obvious places. Only a moron would hide his junk in a sofa."

As he measured out the envelopes, I smiled. "You remember that woman? Susan?"

"That cougar you crashed with? Sure."

"It's for her."

"No shit? What about Delilah?"

"We're just as married as we were before. But I still see Susan. I won't much longer." A particular track mark on his arm seemed inflamed beyond the norm, and it shouted at me from the crook of his elbow. "The hell did you use to shoot up? A rusty screw?"

"It's itchy, that's all." He tugged the threadbare OSU sweatshirt from the back of his chair and pulled it on. I slipped the offered packets into the breast pocket of my jacket, shielding them from contact with lingering moisture clinging to the leather. The dark brown wainscoting behind the gray couch depressed me, and I wanted to go. No wonder he was still a junkie, living here.

"Is this your only job?"

"Right now, yeah." He inclined his chin to scratch his neck, scarred from years of opiate itching. "Keeps the lights on, keeps me in dope. Somebody I know can get me a position with the sanitation department, though."

An immense, almost unreal sense of pity—no, more than that, something else, perhaps compassion—swept me. The boy I had known was not bad, just clever and bored, and eager to try everything once. We had never been so different, just people trying to get by—but here he was, and here I was, and the gulf between our lives seemed vast, unknowable. I stared a time at the stuffing leaking from the arm of the couch before I asked, "If I give you some money, will you spend it on dope? Or will you take yourself to the doctor and have them take a look at your arm? Think of how much dope you can shoot in a lifetime if you don't die or lose your arm to an infection."

He grinned a little. "You make a compelling argument."

From my coat, I withdrew my checkbook. "It's money you wouldn't have otherwise, so please don't spend it on heroin."

And I wrote him a check then, but for some reason it came out as ten-thousand instead of one-thousand. The thought of giving him such a small sum if he really needed medical care seemed almost cruel; and if he had some left over, so be it.

As he read the figure, his pupils bloomed. "Christ, Rick, I can't take that."

"Just do it. Cash it soon, before the ink is dried, if you can."

"What the hell."

"I sold a painting recently."

"No shit!" He looked up, eyes aglow. "You in any galleries?"

"Not lately, but keep an eye out. Never know when I'll be in the paper."

We embraced again, and before releasing, I urged him, "Go to the doctor."

"I will," he said, and I don't know why, but I believed him. Stepping into the rain with the heroin in my pocket, I felt lighter. I breathed the fresh, white air and returned to a house warmed with Delilah's preparations. As she cooked a feast comparable to Christmas, I cooked heroin, though I set some aside for myself. No point in wasting it all on Susan. Soon, after all, she would be dead. By this time tomorrow, in fact. I stretched on the couch and Delilah curled next to me. "How are you?"

"I'm ready," I said.

"Me, too."

But now I wonder what we were ready for.

Susan was prompt at six o'clock, kissing cheeks (mine so long that Delilah glanced away) and crying out with delight at the tom against her ankles.

"You never told me about a cat."

"He's not ours," Delilah said, smiling as she watched him. "He just visits us awhile."

"I like his style." Shifting her bottle of wine into my hands, Susan tickled the creature's jaw until it loped away. Her hair fell from her shoulder in dark streams, a lewd backdrop for the curve of her neck and the first few notches of her spine.

If either woman considered the dinner tense, they didn't show it. I myself was disconcerted by Delilah's ability to hide the loathing which glinted from her eyes every time Susan turned away. The conversation was kept comfortable (books, films, etc.) until the meal was over, at which point Susan said, "I'm very impressed by you, Delilah."

"Well, as you said yourself when last we had lunch together, I'm nothing if not discrete." She refilled Susan's glass, smiling all the while. "I'm not silly enough to think you're a threat to our marriage."

"Of course not. I'm only his mother."

A spell of laughter burst from Delilah as she cleared the table. So that was where her hate went—to her laughter. She poured her pain into joy. Not joyful in spite of it, but because of it; because every laugh she emitted in Susan's presence was a scream, a slap in the face. Every act of kindness, every liberty she had allowed, these were all knives slipping into Susan's ribs, her lungs, her heart. We settled in the living room, Susan in the couch, Delilah near her. I took the chair across as if an audience watching a two-woman play.

"I'm sorry for what I said to you the other week," Delilah offered then.

Susan smiled and took her hand. "No harm, darling. If I let words get to me I wouldn't be worth much. Crueler things have been said to me."

"I'm sorry."

"I deserved every bit of it, really."

This made Delilah laugh into her glass. "You don't care at all."

"I never have. Some say it's bad, but it's a survival skill as much as anything." Then, settling back, my mother said, "You're a very forgiving spirit."

"I try to be."

"Why? Does forgiveness bring you anything but heartache?"

"Yes. It also brings me joy, and warmth, and compassion. It makes me feel happy and strong. When I forgive, I'm making the decision to forgive. I'd be a lot weaker if I dwelt endlessly on all the times I've been wronged. There are so many more times when I've been happy, fulfilled. You're just like Richard."

Susan laughed. "You don't say."

"Yes. You both see ugliness, first and only. I try to see beauty."

My mother and I shared a look of mutual fondness for Delilah, the same adults share in the presence of a precocious child. This was meant more deeply, though, and Susan said, "Then it is a good thing you are married to this artist, because he could use beauty pointed out to him from time to time."

After Delilah refilled her empty glass, she snuggled one cushion nearer to Susan to top her off, too. "Do you mean that?"

"Mean what?"

"That it's good I'm married to Richard."

I saw every tooth in Susan's Stepford mouth. "Of course. It's not as if I want to marry him. I just want his company, Delilah."

I sank back in my seat, hand drifting over my mouth. No, she didn't want to marry me: but she did want complete control over me. She wanted to have me for herself, the way I had Delilah. And my little wife knew that, and smiled with narrowed eyes which almost passed for the crescents that accompanied her true smiles. "I'm sure you do. I've tried to be understanding. It's—an unusual situation."

Susan's hand landed on Delilah's leg, technically upon her knee but nearing her thigh. My wife blushed while my mother said, "That's why I appreciate your patience. I don't think it's worth explaining how all of it happened—there is no justification for the manner in which we established our relationship. But now he knows I am his mother, and he has made a choice about how to express that relationship. I'm glad you understand it has nothing to do with your marriage."

But Delilah didn't hear this curt reassurance, caught instead on the sentence before, intoning, "You didn't tell him who you were beforehand?"

"Oh my. He didn't mention it?" Susan's expression of annoyance was a tight moue of narrowed eyes and pursed lips. "Yes, well. Things slipped from my control. I was young, and it was such a strange subject to broach with a young man so obviously attracted to me."

Though she listened, Delilah stared at me with furrowed brow. "You never told me that part. My poor Richard—oh, Richard."

I glanced into my glass. "It can't be any different now. So let's not."

"Indeed," said Susan, a hint of relief in her heavy-jawed word. "There are no secrets in this room. How about we're all honest with one another?"

"I think we're being genuine," said Delilah, "aren't you?"

"Well, yes, but I mean, I'm curious. How many girls have you two killed?" I cleared my throat. "Five. Delilah has been in on four."

Susan turned her gaze upon me, bright and fascinated. "Do you kill them all by strangling?"

"No. The last one right before Julius died, I slaughtered her as one does a pig, upside-down to harvest the blood."

She crossed her legs and leaned forward. "May I see the paintings?"

I chuckled as I rose. "You cut right to the chase."

"What else would you be doing with it," she asked, laughing as I led the way to the studio, Delilah heading up the rear. There, I slid open the closet and removed several canvases, leaning them against stacks of sketchbooks to reveal the true treasures behind them: old incarnations of the Piece, from *Echo*, on. I presented them to Susan, who revered them in silence, her fingertips pressed to her lips. Delilah stood in the doorway, still drinking, almost to the end of her glass.

Susan's mask soon erupted into the slowest of smiles, pouring forth with the steady ooze of lava. "These are beautiful," she said.

"Thank you."

"This is not just a Piece, but a series of them."

"No." I shook my head. "They're not right. If I could I'd destroy them, but I can't find it in my heart." I glanced at Hypna and Thanatos lounging upon their bed and ran my fingers along the edge of the canvas. "There's one for you, as well."

Susan glanced in the direction of my gesture, to the sheet-covered painting in the corner. "A surprise! How lovely. You're spoiling me, sweetheart. One and a half portraits, and something else entirely ..."

Having passed the wine into my hands, Susan drew the sheet from the painting, then grew very still as she regarded this second image of Clytemnestra's death, her hair and Electra's dress and Orestes' sword colored with the blood of Ms. Daniels. Each detail had been carefully considered, the fabrics bouncing in the midst of the motion, Electra's eyes touched by the shimmer of pre-remorse. I was proud—like a photograph in some ways, that painting. If Susan had been silent while observing Delilah's blood Pieces, she absorbed sound while admiring hers. Without looking, she reached back, grasping at the air, and I pushed the drink into her searching hand because she surely needed it.

"Your work has truly blossomed, my boy," she murmured, leaning close to the painting, examining every detail, her lips parted in wonder. I looked away as Delilah shut the door, locked it, and drained her glass. My mother continued, "It's a shame."

"What is?"

"You're wasting it all, this talent. What are you going to do when you've killed me?"

"We're going away," Delilah said from behind her. "We'll have a new life, in a new country. Things will be different."

"They'll be the same wherever you go, Delilah." She smiled over her shoulder, condescending even in peril. "You will never love him into being a good man. You will never make him less a killer. You can make him repress it, and smother it, and then one day it's going to come bursting out, and it will be directed at you, and he will be in jail, and you will be dead. You want to run away—why don't you? Leave him behind, to me. Someone who knows how to deal with him."

"You, who just got done telling me you're no threat to us!" Delilah's sneer was learned from me, it seemed.

"I'm not, because your concept of being a couple is illusory, at best. It's sad. You're a clever girl, Delilah. Too clever to let him fool you like this."

"Shut up. Nobody's fooling anybody."

"We're all fooling each other. All of us, acting. Everyone in this room is as bad as the next person, as much a sinner, a liar. Act superior as you please, but I've never had to kill a person my entire adult life."

I laughed a little at the qualifiers she slipped in, and Susan went on, "I've come to Richard because I'm ready for the inevitability of being with Richard. You're a little girl with no idea. You still carry the fear of death in your eyes, your body. Yet you know by now there are consequences to being with Richard."

"It's not me he wants to kill," Delilah said, baring her teeth. "It's you."

Susan chuckled behind her glass, draining it fully, now, then passing it back to me. "Indeed he does. He wants to throw his life away, just for the satisfaction. Just to prove something to you. You're a very lucky girl."

Gently, I grasped Susan's arm, and bent to kiss her shoulder. "It's more than that. It needs to happen. It's always needed to happen."

"It always does happen. Richard," she looked up at me, smiling, her eyes near-glimmering, "are you happy?"

"This is the happiest I could hope to be right now."

"Are you going to torture me?"

"I've thought about it awhile," I said, holding her close, swaying with her body to mine as lovers in the middle of their bedroom. "I've done a lot of torturing. Torture makes ugly corpses. That's not why I'm doing this. Normally I carve them up, beautiful work like stained glass in their skin, but I don't know if I can do that to you."

"I want to do it," Delilah said, taking a step towards her. "It's going to be me."

Susan laughed as if expecting a joke. I looked at the painting instead of her, and heard her laugh even harder. "But surely—"

"This isn't about what you want," Delilah said, "or what Richard wants. This is about what I want." She was centimeters from Susan's face, so close their eyelashes might have touched.

"Fine," Susan said. "At least grant me the courtesy of a kiss from my killer."

"What?"

But Susan had already leaned forward, and her mouth clamped upon Delilah's, and my brain lit up like a dopamine slot machine, the sight so beautiful that for a few seconds I considered calling the whole thing off. Delilah even seemed to enjoy it, taking swift control by pushing Susan back against me, her kiss a punch in the face. But there was passion in it—real desire, fostered for months in total silence. Here at last was the break in the tension, and it was exquisite for all.

As Susan clutched Delilah's body to hers, I drew the syringe from my pocket and stuck the needle in her arm. Susan gasped away from the kiss, stared down at the sting and said, breezily, "You could have asked me to come along, darling."

"Fewer risks this way," I said as the heroin started to hit her. Her body slumped against mine in a cartoon swoon. Delilah swayed a few seconds, still stunned, her face flushed as if shocked at herself.

I grinned at my wife. "See what I mean about the effect she has?"

Her mouth twisted, and she looked deeply sorrowful as she stared down at Susan. She bent and stroked her hair, while my mother's head lolled up for her to say, "Goodness, you may have given me enough for an overdose."

I patted her as we hauled her through the hall to the garage. "Just hang in there. You'll make it to the show."

As I opened the back door of Delilah's Nissan, Susan's body tensed, even in the middle of a rush which relaxed her lids to beatific hoods and had forced us to drag her down the hall. "No," mewled my mother, tilting her head against my chest. "Passenger's, please. Don't want to fall asleep."

Roses bloomed in my lungs. I opened instead the passenger door and eased her in, then taped and bound her wrists, which, secured between her knees, would not be in much danger of some other driver's line of sight. Delilah followed us in Susan's Cobra, which we intended to leave in the garage of the house.

As we mounted the highway, a weight pressed upon my shoulder: her lolling head, which in a hickory purr said, "There's still time. Just keep going at the exit, and we can visit Prague. I know a lovely bakery, though I don't know what to call the things they make. Scrumptious stuff."

"Another time," I suggested, and she smiled.

"Another stream?"

"Sure."

"All the possibilities." Her head rocked now against the window, whose cool glass made her sigh as she splayed down her seat. "Who would I have been if things were different? Who would you have been?"

"There are certain possibilities I don't care to entertain," I said, thinking of Julius.

She laughed. "Why not? We might have been almost normal if I'd known you when you were little."

"That's why I don't care to entertain them. I can't do anything to see them, feel them."

"But you can. That's the secret of reality, my darling, my Dick, the secret of the Universe and all these streams of consciousness. They're endless, infinite. Whatever one imagines is real, whatever choices one can imagine making, somewhere there is a time and space where molecules have aligned and made that choice. Somewhere, my darling," her voice tightened and I glanced over once, twice, shocked to see her eyes glistening in the highway lights we swept past every few seconds, "somewhere I did suffocate you. Somewhere I didn't and kept you, and abused you in one way or another for one reason or another. But somewhere, my darling—somewhere in the infinity of the cosmos, somewhere we are happy. Somewhere, we struggle for awhile, but never seriously, and live together a happy, wholesome life of success, and maybe, my darling, even Delilah is in that life, too, and no one is crippled, and we may even have that white picket fence you want to get yourself. And if I could select my next stream to see, I would pick that one, to see what it's like being happy."

I looked at the side mirror, adjusted the rear-view. I shot fluid over the windshield to wipe it clean while I blinked a few times and read the reversed license plate of the Cobra behind us and focused on the reflection of Delilah's resolute face. "I'm happy," I decided at last. "Aren't you?"

Still weeping silent tears in manner more stigmata than sob, she giggled. "I'm on heroin. But I believe I am happy, yes, and happy to be here with you, my love. A little anxious, perhaps. I wonder if I'll even know it's happening. Maybe it will be like falling asleep. That's what they say but I'm not sure I believe it. And then what, after the stream of consciousness? Will I spend time in a lake of it? Or will it all begin immediately over again?"

"What makes you so sure this will all happen again?"

"Goodness, darling, what else could happen? Heaven?" She laughed, her toes wiggling free of her heels to curl and uncurl and stretch. "Think of it this way. The Universe expands, and so too contracts. The Big Bang, then, has happened more than once, assuming it happened at all. The Universe has happened more than once. Our lives, small as they are, are eternity, are beautiful, and happen more than once. That's what people mean by the idea of Heaven and Hell as self-created circumstances. Living a miserable existence means you are always, for eternity, choosing to live a miserable existence. We never learn our lessons. These things happen just the same, every time, and when the play is finished, the only place for the characters to go is back to the very beginning. We are creatures limited by an incomplete view of the fourth dimension. Otherwise we would know this is forever, and nobody would fear death. Everybody would realize we're a brain in a jar in a universe in a brain in a jar; the brain creating reality by being within it to observe it."

There were no tears coming from her anymore. She lifted her chin, and shared a smile with her side mirror reflection. "There, see? We're not afraid anymore, are we?"

Silent, I placed my hand on hers and held it the rest of the way there. At the house, Delilah and I set up shop in the motions of our routine. Susan slumped in a nodding pile upon an armchair, and while she did, I turned to Delilah.

"Are you sure you want to do this?"

"Yes." She lifted her chin. "I asked for this. I'm responsible for it."

I nodded. "How shall we do it?"

"Like you do it. I want to strangle her."

"Take me to the water," sang Susan from the middle of her heroin-dreams, and I laughed. The whole thing had the surreal quality of a family reunion as filmed by David Lynch. We were happy, or at least I was, as we prepared to kill my mother. Even my little wife had her share of smiles. As beautiful as Delilah was, she seemed freshest and most beautiful then.

As I arranged her hands and ankles, Susan made a better effort to rouse herself from her doze. "Do you think you can do it," she asked Delilah. "You've watched him kill, but can you do it yourself? That's what's sad about you. You still want to be a good person."

"No," said Delilah through snapping jaws. "No, I don't care about being a good person anymore."

"You do, and it keeps you up at night."

"What keeps me up at night is thoughts of killing you."

"No, darling, that's what keeps Richard up at night. You're getting what you want and what he wants all mixed up again."

Straddling Susan's chest, Delilah hissed, "I know what I want."

"So do I." Smiling, divine, sensuous, Susan leaned her upper half from the floor and whispered something. Delilah scooted down the length of her body and bent over her to listen, hair tumbling over Susan's face, tickling her cheek, the two of them like the lovers I wished they were. But as she listened, Delilah's breathing stopped, and soon she yelped, "Shut up!"

"You must," laughed my mother. "It would be so perfect."

But her words lurched into a rasping gurgle as Delilah's hands squeezed around her throat. I was heartbroken. I had envisioned for Susan something beautiful and romantic, but instead it was quick, quiet, with her last words barbs aimed to mock. Her mouth flew into a silent 'o' for seeking air, which she seemed to be getting, and Delilah squeezed harder, letting out a cry of frustration.

I did not speak. I knelt by her side, and covered her hands in mine, and showed her how to really squeeze, to cut off the arteries and dry the brain of oxygen. As I kissed the temple of her forehead, I stared down at my mother, whose gaping mouth amid her reddened face transformed into a wide-open smile upon seeing me, a smile that was soon purple, then blue, and then so was the rest of her face, and her limbs flapped, and Delilah's hands squeezed tighter beneath mine, and I kissed her neck, and bent, then, to kiss my mother's mouth, and when I lifted my head, she was dead, and Delilah was gasping, her breast heaving beneath her dandelion dress, and even when I fell back she didn't let go.

I stroked her shoulder, and said, "That's enough."

Just once, Delilah shook the corpse, then fell away. She scooted beside me, and burst into tears, hot and angry, the kind she shed during our fight. I didn't know what she shed them for now, but I held her, and stared at Susan's body, and felt freer than I'd ever hoped to feel. Here I was, with Delilah, the limitless future before us, my work exploding, money in our pocket, South America so close. We were going to make it. And then what? Well, we'd figure it out. But until then, there was this, us, on the floor, clutching each other before the corpse of my mother.

Alone in the upstairs bathroom where once I had dismembered Evangeline, now I did the same for Susan: again, this process was slow. Reverent, rather than rushed. First I cut off her dress, her underwear, all of it slit down the back as in a mortuary. For the first time, she was nude and powerless, and full of tremendous silence. As I washed her, I kissed her lips, gray and chilled, still soft. Still her. I clutched her to my breast as if she were a little girl, stroking her hair and murmuring her name. Gradually my hand slipped between her legs. Then, I was in the tub with her, my face buried for the last time in her hair, myself a part of her body one final time, this claiming of her, this marking of her. She was mine, now, forever mine, and although I had won, the love I made to her body was bittersweet. A celebration, and a goodbye.

After a few moments of final peace with her, I made an incision in her abdomen and stroked the tissue of her uterus, the lining of her stomach. I reached into her chest cavity and felt my mother's lungs. All this was what I'd come from. These sinuous vocal cords, this blood running red in the tub, up my arm. I kissed her cold lips and they were not hers, but once they had been hers, and perhaps if she was right, they would be hers again, and I would kiss them again, but here and now, this could never happen. If I did kiss them again, I doubted I would know it. As she had said, the next 'again' would be the first time.

I will say this: she may not have been drowned, but even in death, she was a beautiful corpse. Even in death, I smelled only frankincense and femininity. In the end, but for her heart, blood, and the exploratory incisions, I left her intact, carried her to the dusty bed, placed in her arms mildewed books from her old library—*Philosophy in the Bedroom*, *The Epic of Gilgamesh*, and *The Myth of Sisyphus*—and draped her in the moth-eaten blanket with a last kiss on her chilling forehead.

Delilah cleaned downstairs while I toiled, and, understanding the intimacy of my work, remained until I returned with a small wooden box purchased for the occasion. She smiled and, without opening it, cradled it to her breast. "Thank you, Richard."

I gripped her, kissed her, and at home, I locked myself in my studio and brought to life the Piece begun a few weeks before. I had let go. There were no grand designs here. No Woman. No story but the one told by Delilah's smiling face, told in the raw blood of my mother. As I drew my brush across the canvas, I lost myself. There existed a singularity of creation marked by the tingle of limbs, the opening of the head, the loss of time. Vibrant honesty poured out and I kept the gates open so not a single drop would be missed. Alone in the studio I remembered Delilah at the gallery, Delilah at the picnic, Delilah crying and smiling and screaming and moaning. Her sweets and her meals, and her way of moving across the room to turn off the light before bed.

This was God. This was pure. Death made me feel closer to God, to the Universe; so did painting. Creation and destruction were the same for me as for the Universe. They swelled in me and nothing mattered. There was no question of what we would do next, because in the creative instant, like the sexual instant, there was no next. No us. Just the act. That's all we have, isn't it, you and I? This act. This expression of me to you. This moment, here. I do not know what you are, or how I perceive you, but I know I have lived in you and you in me and all this just by hearing me, viewing me, reading or watching me, if Susan was completely right. Whether you perceive me as a viewer perceives a work of art or as a God perceives an ant, some distant part of you understands me, and that is why I repel you, and maybe even attract you, even if only a little. Mirror neurons shimmer between us and we are closer than telepathic. We are the same, dissolved without identity into a gaping maw of inky sound.

I finished the painting thirty hours after Susan's death, nine hours before our train was scheduled. Elated, I dragged Delilah out of bed, saying, "Come and see."

And as she stumbled into the studio, morning bleariness cleared completely. She gasped, covered her mouth, and released a dry sob when confronted by her rufescent likeness, who, smiling, cradled the gray tom against the bosom of her sunshine yellow dress, her face glowing. Her soul was in it. That was the Piece: Delilah, herself.

The hand upon her mouth curled into a fist, and her eyes watered, and she hid her face in my chest. "What is it called?"

"*Delilah, My Woman.*"

"I love it," she said, "I love it."

"We can leave now."

"Why don't you take a shower and make sure we're packed," she murmured, pawing at my chest. "I'll make breakfast."

Smiling, I kissed her, and obeyed. As I left my studio, where Delilah remained a time to ponder the Piece, I almost tripped over our feline visitor. He meowed conversationally, then threw himself against the glass door to the back yard. I chuckled and, stroking his head, got the door for him. The tom gamboled across the grass, climbed up our fence, and disappeared down the other side.

By the time I was finished packing, I discovered a plate spilling over with biscuits and sausage gravy, steak, eggs, grits, hollandaise, and hash-browns. Famished, I devoured, and noticed a strange, at times almost minty tang, which I attribute to frozen potatoes and washed away with orange juice.

"We'll have a transfer in Chicago. Would you like to visit Julius?"

She shook her head, barely picking at her food, the circles under her eyes calling into question how much sleep she managed to get. "No. I don't think we should. He wouldn't want to see us if he had a choice, anyway."

I chuckled. "I suppose that's true."

Halfway through the plate, the nausea set in, but I kept going, convinced I was filling up and needed to be plenty full for the long haul ahead. Delilah watched as if staring through me, her eyes dim. I smiled at her.

"Don't look so sad, daisy. We're almost done."

And she smiled—tiny, muted. I was about to remark on it when my mouth began to hypersalivate. My hand froze with the fork in mid-air. Calmly, I placed it aside and realized the urgency of the situation. The bathroom was too far away, so I settled for the kitchen sink, and, doubled over, purged what was easily three-fourths of the rich meal. As I expelled the first wave and lifted my gasping head, I heard a sob.

"Oh God, Richard, I'm so sorry."

She stood, and I was about to ask her why she was sorry, but there came a second wave, and I was incapacitated again. I turned on the water to wash it down the sink. My gut spasmed. Delilah grasped my arm, crying out, "We need to call the ambulance."

"No," I snarled, straightening up. "Delilah, what did you do?"

With trembling fingers pressed to her mouth, she began looking for a phone. "I poisoned you," she gasped between her sobs.

As I stood, nauseous and shocked to breathless silence, she whispered, "Everything I could find to put in it, I put in it. Old Klonopin, some heroin, even Comet—I can't stand it. Couldn't stand it." Her hands vanished into her hair, where they tangled. "Susan made me realize—this isn't going to stop. This is never going to stop, not unless I stop it, but oh, God, I can't stand to see you die." Tears poured down her cheeks and she gasped, "It hurts too much."

Wonder. Sheer wonder. I felt like the first man atop Everest, surveying the world real and true for the first time in human history. My heart ached, now, not my stomach, and I gripped it. The progressing overdose was likewise not responsible for my watering eyes and constricted throat. "You killed me."

"And I'm so sorry!" The phrase burst from Delilah as she gripped me, her face contorted by anguish. "Please, Richard, we need to get you to a hospital."

That face! That red-speckled, sobbing face, exquisite, vibrant! Everything was alive. Even the objects breathed. I smiled at my wife; my wife who had brought me here, who had inspired my greatest glory and moved me with this greatest gift. I touched her face, and said, "I think there's a phone in the living room."

She nodded, planted a kiss on my mouth, and turned to go fetch it. Relying on momentum, I grabbed a knife from the butcher block with one hand, grabbed her robe with the other, jerked her to me, and buried the blade in her stomach. She gasped, the gasp crescendoing into a soft, mournful cry as I gripped her to me.

"Don't you see?" I smiled down at her, cradling her face as I slid the knife out and buried it in her again, and again, saying, "This is just it. This is perfect, what we need. Just you and me, together." I laughed, dropped the knife, held the bloodied stomach her hands frantically clutched. "This thing you've done for me—this is the greatest gift you could have given me. A beautiful life, an exquisite death."

Indeed, what else was there? No white picket fence. No life with Susan. Certainly no jail cell. This was all there could be—our happiness, our only happiness. The only way to assure we would be together was to be together like this. A rabbit, nibbling on a blade of grass.

Sobbing, retching, Delilah fell against me, and the both of us slammed into the counter. We laughed, half-cried, and she gripped my shirt, saying, "All I want is to be with you."

"You are. We're together now. We'll always be together." I smiled and kissed her tearful eyes, then hauled her up and fought the nausea that dizzied me so, urging us on to the studio. She seemed heavier, but it was because my muscles were nothing. I was nothing, fading from my muscles, fading from life. Sleep seemed appealing. I had to get Delilah to the studio. It was the only place for us to go, to be surrounded by my art, my life.

As I dropped her into the couch, she moaned. I fell next to her a moment, then stumbled up and, swaying with vertigo, claimed a brush. As I dipped mink fur in the pooling red of Delilah's stomach, she winced only slightly. I was gentle as possible in collecting the medium, and quick in using it to sign the Piece before I lost the energy to stand. Already it was difficult, and when the Piece was signed and titled, I fell at her feet, then drew myself up the couch beside her. She smiled at it, then at me.

"I love it," she said, trembling. "Thank you."

"It never would have been anything without you."

She smiled, stroking my hot face with her bloodied hand. "Richard? Will you please—please kill me first. I don't want to see you die."

I borrowed one of her smiles. My forehead rocked against hers and I kissed her once, twice, cherishing the metal of her mouth. "Thank you for what you've done for me."

"What have I done for you?"

"You've made me feel God," I said as I wrapped my hands around her throat.

And she smiled, and gagged, and Delilah's beautiful eyes locked on mine as her face glowed from amber red to plum purple, until, mouthing the word 'love', she faded to the blue-gray of a headstone in the rain. Tears of my own welled as she slumped. Everything was still. I held her to my chest, crying her name, burying my face in her hair and happy, happy as I've ever been. Or, if not happy, peaceful. Blissful.

Comforted, I lay her back on the couch and looked around, my vision blurred. What if she hadn't given me enough? Say I only fell asleep a time and woke up puking, or died choking on vomit, needlessly vulgar. I needed to make sure. A box knife found its way into my hands, and I didn't feel the pain as I gouged up my arms. The blood mingled with Delilah's. Our hands clasped, I rested my head upon her breast and focused on the beauty of the

Piece, the beauty of being there with Delilah, soon with Delilah, forever with Delilah. The beauty of finishing something true. My vision faded, faded into black, the black of sleep, the black beyond sleep, and I jolted awake as Delilah nudged me on the train to Tucson.

"We're almost there," she said. I opened my eyes to find my head on her shoulder, our hands entwined, our bodies intact. Intact from what? I was baffled by my own thought process and sat back, seeing dark mountains from my window. As the scenery whipped by, I had the sense that Susan had been on this very same train, and had gotten off just ahead of us, at Prague, but it couldn't be Prague, how silly.

Beside me, my smiling wife smoothed her sanguinary dress over her knees. "Are you excited?"

"I am," I said, and wondered if this really was the train to Tucson. It had to be, right? When did we get here? Had we always been here?

Her legs kicked. "What do you think it will be like?"

"Like being born again." The mountains began to slow, and the land, and the cacti and rocks. Hopping from her seat, Delilah pulled me to my feet.

"Come on," she said, dragging me into the aisle and then, at last, letting go of me to run ahead. "Let's see what it's like!"

And I laughed, and chased her, and only half-realized there were no other people on the train, but row after row of closed cars not so different from the one we'd been in. Had we been in a car? I could have sworn at the time I was in a seat—but it didn't matter, because I was at the door to the train, and Delilah was getting off, and I had to catch her, and I stepped off of the train, and everything splintered into a beautiful black womb where the chime of her voice said, "Richard!" before it disintegrated into a fractal of vibrations which rattled until there was nothing but the exploding cosmos, unfurling beyond the bounds of space and readying itself for the whole thing over again, where I met you, my friend, and now I remember what I am, this fantasy I am, all of this a fabulous dream, your dream or my dream or God's dream, and now Delilah, and Susan, and Richard wake up, and a woman walks into a butcher's shop.

About the Author

Though at the time of this writing she resided in Tucson, M.F. Sullivan is a playwright and novelist currently living in the scenic town of Ashland, Oregon. There, the author is hard at work on a new trilogy for which two books are already written, and a slew of plays not yet produced. Sullivan's interests include consciousness, language, and how the literary arts can be used to expand them both. Be sure to follow the blog at www. delilahmywoman.com for news, updates and the occasional free essay.

Also by the Author

The Lightning Stenography Device